YOU Again

BOOK 1

DIANNA ROMAN

WILD ONE
PRESS

Published by Wild One Press
Edited by The Fiction Fix
Cover design by Wild One Press

Front cover images:
363856871 by Anetta / Shutterstock.com
1153635637 by Nigel Stripe / Shutterstock.com
1838077009 by ZinetroN / Shutterstock.com
Old red brick wall damaged by Boris Rabtsevich from Getty Images Pro / Canva.com
Luke Matthews by Angel Kolbe Photography / angelkolbephotography.com

Interior spread images:
361708277 by Anetta / Shutterstock.com
1153635637 by Nigel Stripe / Shutterstock.com
Luke Matthews by Angel Kolbe Photography / angelkolbephotography.com

Chapter artwork by Stephanie Henigin

ISBN: 979-8-9853313-5-6 (eBook)
ISBN: 979-8-9853313-6-3 (Trade Paperback)
ISBN: 979-8-9853313-7-0 (Special Edition Cover Paperback)

Also available in Audiobook

Visit the author at www.diannaroman.com

Content Advisory

This work contains the following topics that some readers may find sensitive:

- Self-image-shaming
- Discussions about and assumed biphobic attitudes
- Adult language
- Consensual sexual content

YOU
Again

He's met his match,
if only he could
convince him.

DEDICATION

To Bob—for the pep talk and the faith.

CHAPTER 1

Johnny

The worst thing about being left by the one you love is that they don't take the happy memories with them. You're stuck with those things forever, left questioning what purpose they served while you try to figure out how to get back to being a half instead of a whole.

Things you once did holding someone's hand, nights you spent pressed against a body that felt like an extension of your own, cafes you sat in drinking coffee over the exchange of your secrets and dreams— you get to learn to do all that shit by yourself again—a complete reprogramming. But how do you learn how to be you again when being you is what got your heart ripped out? People who want to be in relationships should have their heads examined.

As for me, solitude is now my life partner—solitude with a side of distraction. Unfortunately, most days it seems distraction greatly outweighs solitude.

The only thing worse than my family being proud of being Greek is how proud they are to be American. They like to show it by attending every ridiculous festivity in our area code. Under no other circumstances would I have allowed myself to be persuaded to attend the public revelry of questionable fried food scents, screaming children, and precariously constructed amusement rides that is a carnival. No one who is miserable can tolerate that much merriment. It is sensory overload.

The irony? Where is my family after they brought me here to socialize against my wishes? Nowhere in sight of one "Johnny Andro".

"Are you nearly finished, Bits? Pretty sure I just saw the guy who used to use my head as target practice in dodge ball during high school. And…oh! It looks like he procreated. Isn't that wonderful?"

Bitsy, my beloved best friend, feigns ignorance of my tale of woe. Turning away from the food vendor, arms loaded with her pillage, she chomps off a bite of a loaded hot dog. The hundred- and thirty-pound woman just ate two funnel cakes and a taco. How is there any room left in her stomach?

Extending one of her pale, freckled arms, her flaming red hair glowing under the setting sun, she tries to hand me one of the mechanically processed faux meat in a bun.

"*Yer vant vun?*" she calls around a mouthful, cheeks stuffed like a squirrel.

I shake my head at what's become of her. This is so undignified, even for Bitsy. My idea of relaxation does not include dripping in my own sweat while constant reminders of my youthful outcast status lurk at every turn.

"I'll pass. Can we please go?" I grab onto her wrist, but only make it two feet before she's snatching her arm back, smearing… Is that mustard she just got on my shirt?

"No! I just bought a beer. Let's go grab a seat at one of those picnic tables."

My huffing as I grab a handful of napkins from the food truck is useless in dissuading her. There is no reasoning with Elizabeth Fitzgerald when there's food within a mile radius.

Her short legs make quick purchase of the trampled fairground grass toward a cluster of picnic tables I doubt have been sanitized in the last decade, where she drops her tiny backside down on one of the benches with her armful of pirate's booty. In short, we are never leaving this damn carnival.

Fuck my life.

"Tell me again why I moved back to Olympus," I grumble, another napkin disintegrating in my useless attempt to de-mustard my favorite, spearmint green, *Jerry Rennoux* polo shirt.

"Because your mother guilted you into it," Bitsy supplies matter-of-factly, draft beer foam framing her upper lip.

Her words to my rhetorical question catch me off-guard. That's not entirely the truth as to why I left my life on the West coast in favor of returning to Olympus, Wisconsin, but it is the fragment of the truth I told dear Bits.

"Right. Thank you for reminding me what a good son I am. Prodigal and all."

"You've got me," she adds enthusiastically. "Your invitation saved me from a life of marketing livestock, so…win, win. Right?"

"Bits, you could have put your marketing degree to use anywhere, literally anywhere, other than Kill-Me-Now, Idaho, and we both know it. Mm-kay? You just have to get over your fear of spreading your wings."

That place between her brows puckers ever so slightly. "First off, you've never been to Idaho. It's beautiful. Second, I'd call moving halfway across the country to start a business with my best friend spreading my wings."

"Mm. Yes. Well, grateful as I am to have your skills solely at my disposal, I am obligated as your friend to tell you there were probably wiser career choices."

Bitsy is rarely ever swayed by the sulking attitude I hauled back to Olympus with me. Maybe that's why I asked her to move here—I knew I'd need a good angel on my shoulder to help keep my surliness at bay. She beams around another bite of we're-never-leaving-here, which means I will probably see at least a dozen more former classmates that will serve as a reminder that high-end polo shirts and hair products cannot erase the awkward Greek nerd memories of my teen years. As if I don't question myself enough already.

"Hey! We're doing great. You have more clients than you did when…" She cuts herself off at my dubious look about the one thing she knows I won't discuss. Or rather, the one someone. "Anyway," she segues, "business is booming, and I've gotten you featured in more magazines than any other photographers our age."

"*Booming*. Yes. Cuisine magazines and *Blushing Bride* have always been my life's dream."

"There was that youth adventure spread in Colorado," she adds.

"Thirty teenagers complaining they had no cell service the entire photo shoot—what was not to love? And do you remember how long it took me to edit out all the acne?"

"Well, they can't all be swimsuit and underwear models or destination weddings. You've built a great client-base here. If you didn't insist on traveling every few weeks, I could book you more local shoots or…maybe even scout local models." Bitsy shrugs and laps one of her sauced-up fingertips like it's a popsicle.

"More local obligations doesn't coincide with the spreading of wings, Bitsy! *Wings!* Do you ever listen to a word I say? And fuck no to models. Could you please stop that? They make baby wipes for a reason, you know."

Rather than heeding my etiquette advice, she looks at me defiantly with her big blue eyes and continues to suckle her digits. I thrust my remaining napkins at her. "Here. Take these. I'll just go bathe myself in that hand sanitizing station over there. Do you not feel how sticky this table is? You just had those fingers on it, and now they're in your mouth. Who knows what you could be ingesting!"

"Johnny, this isn't about wings. You avoid your family."

"Ha!" I snort, unsticking my sweaty cargo shorts from the junctures of my thighs as I stand. "Either the beer or the sun has gotten to you because now you're not making any sense. Avoiding the Andropolis family is like trying to out-dazzle a figure skater. It cannot be done."

Her shoulders slump. A sobering look in her eyes makes me hold my breath for what looks to be a scolding. The woman has been the only one close enough to peek into my emotional diary since we roomed together in college.

"Johnny, do you know how lucky you are to have such a big family? They could be gone one day."

Fuck.

She went there.

I practically set the GPS and guided her right to it. Me and my big, unfiltered mouth.

My stomach churns as I stare at my best friend—a woman who lost her mother at thirteen and has had no one but her father ever since. Well, no one but her father and me. When he decided to get remarried, she returned to Idaho after college, wasting away her brilliance to be near the man who raised her.

Bitsy's loyal like that. It's what I love about her. It's what I counted on when I dried my tears two years ago and called her up with faux enthusiasm, spinning some bullshit about starting our own business in my hometown because as much as I didn't want to move back here, she's right.

I had avoided my family, but two years ago their relentless zeal seemed like the distraction I needed after my breakup from my one and only serious relationship. It did not mean I was prepared to fully re-immerse myself in their daily shenanigans.

I was twenty-five at the time, an age when a person should not be buffaloed by the guilt that comes with being part of a Greek family where one is expected to attend family meals seventy-three times a week with a smile on their face. My smile was last seen going out to tide in the Pacific. Bitsy has a dazzling smile, so big I hoped it would camouflage the absence of my own. Therefore, I selfishly and wisely enlisted her as my buffer for my grand return.

In my defense for using my best friend as a shield from my family's concern, Bitsy had lost her purpose for being in Idaho once her father found happiness again. She wasn't content at the time either. You *could say* I was her knight in shining armor. So, she jumped on a plane to the city where my family makes up one-eighth of the population and helped me find a suitable building for a studio and living space a tolerable enough distance from my mother. She is my person. The world needs more *Bitsys*.

"I'm sorry. I just…" My hand flaps pathetically in the air. "Sunstroke and…a mustard attack and whatnot. Don't mind me. I'll just go rinse my wings in the bird bath over there to cool off. You…enjoy your meal, Typhoid Mary."

"With pleasure." She beams, and I know I'm still in her good graces. *Way to go, drama king.*

Fanning myself with the front of my disheveled polo, I try to imagine what animal shapes my ex would say the sweat stains on my back have formed because even that unpleasant memory is less discomfiting than admitting I have sometimes envied Bitsy's lack of family since moving home. She doesn't have an army of people to ask her what's wrong on a daily basis.

Across the makeshift wagon circle of food trucks, I spot my sister, Sofia, yelling at her children who are beating the shit out of each other with giant foam fingers. Sofia thwaps my brother-in-law, Makis on the chest as though she expects him to wield some type of authority over their three hyenas…er…cherubs. I mean sweet little cherubs.

Makis ignores her as usual, going back to watching my brother Andreas wallop the strong man hammer down on a scale. Andreas lets loose a curse and throws a hand up. His wife, Thespina, is oblivious to his loss, speaking animatedly with three of my cousins to two middle-aged local women who have that deer in the headlights look. It's a look that says, oh-fuck-we've-been-cornered-by-the-Andropolis-family-again—a look no one in my family but me seems to ever recognize.

I spot my mother's fire-red, bottle-dyed hair amongst the gaggle of women. And oh, no. *What* is she doing?

My breath catches as she takes a funnel cake from Mary Peterson and hands it to my cousin.

Dear Lord, no.

Now she's reaching into her over-sized purse. I shudder, knowing what's coming next. She retrieves a giant freezer bag of her handmade cookies, *biscotia*, and thrusts them at a bewildered Mrs. Peterson.

"Oh, Mamá. No."

My whispered plea is solely to feed false hope to my mortification, as I watch my mother likely telling Mrs. Peterson that her cookies are far better and healthier than this deep-fried carnival food because nothing beats a *purse-cookie*, right? Mamá's probably correct, but must she insist on being the spokesperson for my parents' restaurant at every public gathering? There are vendor tents and permits and other legalities for that.

Sighing, I pinch my eyes closed to ward off the treacherous-son thoughts as I reach the hand wash station at the edge of the makeshift food court. A young boy is depressing the soap dispenser, so I inspect my shirt once more.

Bitsy's mustard attack left a half-dollar sized glob, and thanks to my feeble attempts at removal, inflation struck. The stain increased two-fold. I am not a neat freak, I swear. It's just the little things that get me, particularly since moving back home, where I have little say over the order in my life and little fortitude to endure the helplessness.

Another bead of sweat rolls down my back between my shoulder blades. I am melting in this humid June heat, watching the world's slowest hand washer as I await my turn, so I can *de-sticky* myself of the picnic table residue on my hands and return to Bitsy with a smile.

My word. What is this child doing? He just pumped his third helping of soap into his hands.

"Are we about finished there, little fella?"

Cold gray eyes pin me as he depresses the foot pedal with more force than is necessary and...*gasp*! He did not! The little shit just reloaded his palm with what better not be the last of that soap.

I pin him back with a look of my own, nudging my glasses up the perspiration slickened bridge of my nose. I'm an adult. Damn it, and I'm bigger. I will not be intimidated by a rogue child.

Folding my arms, I give him the stern but patient "Uncle Johnny voice" I use with my niece and nephews. "I think you've got it there, buddy. Those hands look as clean as a whistle."

By all that is holy, he just stone-faced me and....

Oh, fuck no.

He just took three more pumps of soap and depressed the water spigot pedal in unison. What is wrong with this antagonizing little *humanoid?*

"Um. Turnsies over, little man. Mm-kay? Now run along. Let someone else have a chance."

His eyes narrow. "You talk funny."

I narrow my eyes back because I am not above scrapping with a precocious child today. "Oh, it speaks."

"Why are you dressed like an apple?" he asks, eyeing my once unsullied polo shirt as though it were a ridiculous costume.

Gasping, I drop my arms. This is beyond childhood curiosity and has chartered into *Rude-ville.*

"I'll have you know there are many colors of apples, my friend. Red, for example. Perhaps you've seen one down there during your travels through Hater Land."

He...*snickers at me*. Snickers!

"Then why didn't you wear it, *friend?*"

Sucking in a gulp of generator oil and fried food saturated air, I prepare myself to ask him the location of Satan, so I can return him to where he came from when a large hand grasps my shoulder. I let out a squeak and jump, nearly slipping out of my flip-flops.

"Bradley, is that anyway to speak to adults?" a deep voice rumbles at my side as I right myself under the weight of its owner's heavy grip.

"Bradley" scoffs, but I care not at this point, squinting into the sunlight to identify who jostled me. Forcing my gaze up a dark green t-shirt that's stretched tight over an impressively sculpted chest, I swallow at the sudden dryness in my throat.

Sweet mother of mercy, I have no words—I, Johnny Andro, who always has words. I see smiles every day from behind the lens of my camera, but I've never witnessed one as breathtaking as his. Not even my ex's, and I once thought his was the smile to top all smiles.

My savior is a tanned mountain of sunshine and muscles from the sun-streaked tips of his close-cut sandy brown hair to his lopsided, boyish grin that makes poor decisions worthwhile. A pair of jade green eyes sparkle down at me, framed by crinkles alluding to a frequent smiler or man who works outdoors. My fingers itch to run through the stubble on his square cut jaw as my knees consider buckling underneath me.

My cock twitches in my shorts like we're at the pound and it has just spied the companion of our dreams. *This one, Johnny*, it says. *Can we please get this one?*

The spawn of Satan obliterates the unexplainable siren spell that has overtaken me. "He doesn't look like an adult with mustard stains on his cotton candy shirt."

Nostrils flaring, I shoot a glare at the tiny deviant, one I hope conveys the most powerful Liam Neeson sentiments. *I will find you!*

"Hey. That's enough! Apologize," Mount Sunshine demands in a commanding tone that makes my neglected dick jolt like it's just jumped the train to *Submissive Town*. What is that about?

Bradley surprisingly withers, the smirk melting from his face. "Sorry," he grumps, letting me know it is only the golden Adonis that is the forcing him to utter that half-assed apology.

I can't say I blame his forced obedience. I nearly apologized myself at the effect of that deep timbre. It's…unsettling. Folding my arms, I shrug to remove Mount Sunshine's hand and give dear Bradley one last taste of my haughtiness that he can't seem to stand.

"You are forgiven."

"Whatever," he grumbles and skulks away.

I sigh in relief but then realize my error. I just required rescuing from a child. How sexy is that?

Wait. Why do I care? There is no way this Midwestern linebacker in his bro-looking ensemble of a ratty Green Bay Packers t-shirt, work boots, and worn, faded jeans gutters his bowling balls in the same lane as I do.

"Friend of yours?" I query, canting my head in the direction my nemesis fled.

"No," he chuckles, the sound more wholesome than any sound should be, sending a tingle down my spine. "He lives down the street from my parents. Let's just say they've had a few run-ins with him before."

"Hm. What a surprise." I step up to the sanitizing station, finally scrubbing the ick from my hands. "Well, thank you, but I can assure you I had it handled."

My words bring heat to my ears, and I let out an awkward laugh. "I mean, of course I had it handled. He's just a child."

Lord, why the hell do I care about justifying myself to this stranger? Why is that charming stubble-lined smirk making another appearance? I'm not that damn funny. Yet, I don't think I'm being mocked either.

My stomach takes a flip. There's something in his stormy eyes. They haven't left me, like I'm a shiny new object he can't tear them away from. It's nonsensical and…exhilarating. Maybe I really am succumbing to heat stroke because I like it, and I sure as hell shouldn't.

"You from around here?"

"Born and raised," I enthuse with as much enthusiasm as I can muster for this hellhole.

"Really? Me too."

Wetting a wad of paper towels from the dispenser, I ignore the mystery-magnetism eyes and focus on my "apple costume." Just as I'm about to de-mustard, a calloused grip catches my wrist.

"No. Don't do that," he cautions.

"I beg your pardon?" This is twice in two minutes he's had his hands on me.

"You'll just make it worse." He takes the paper towels from my hand and tosses them in the station's trash receptacle. Dropping to a knee beside me, he takes a hold of the hem of my shirt. "Here. Let me show you a trick. The fabric's dry, so it should work."

Floundering carnival air into my pie hole, I have become a Greek statue—Johnny the Flummoxed—as I watch Mount Sunshine's bulky biceps flex. He folds the hem of my shirt up, exposing the damp flesh above my hip bone as though he doesn't share my ex's uncanny distaste for perspiration. He goes to work, rubbing the surface side of my shirt together between his fingers. His knuckles graze my side, sending an electric pulse across my abdomen.

"What…what are you doing?"

He releases my shirt and smoothes it back to my side with his palm, as if I deserve to be handled with care, dusting away flecks of dried mustard. That should not feel like a caress, but when his pleased smile beams up at me, my insides translate the innocent gesture as intimacy and beg for more. It has been far too long, and I do not need the reminder.

Standing, he once again tops my nearly six-foot stature by a good three inches. "Quickest way to get a stain out. You just rub the same type of fabric against each other," he gestures to my waist.

Several things need to be noted. One—I am slack-jawed because, *holy shit*. The baby-poo looking stain is practically gone. Two—how does this body building specimen know swatch secrets? Three—it is simply cruel to look at a man's midriff while speaking of rubbing things together. Four—this feels like chivalry.

It feels like chivalry from a beautiful man who steps through the sunlight, coming to your rescue on a beach after you stepped on a jelly fish, and then spends the evening laughing with you at a beachside tavern while you slowly fall stupidly in love with his smile.

So, yeah. Chivalry can kiss my ass. I'm not falling for that again, but I can, at the very least dole out the appropriate pleasantries.

"Huh. Well, I'll be. Um. Thank you."

Tearing my eyes away from Mr. Magic Knuckles, I search for Bitsy like she's my lifeline from this apparition of my past. Judging by the way her auburn eyebrows have climbed her forehead, I have dallied too long and made a spectacle of myself. The corner of her mouth is ticked up. Great. No doubt there will be questions.

"No problem," my beefcake in shining *Packers* garb says.

"Okay then!" I blurt with a nod and spin on my heel.

Retreat is urgent at this point. I nearly lost my wits to a man who likely has no idea about the filthy thoughts crawling around in my sex-starved brain.

"I'll see you around?"

I do a half-twist, looking back at the question I doubt I heard, nearly tripping on my own two feet. What is my response when I see the beautiful golden skinned man with thighs like a carnival ride I'd actually buy tickets for, in fact staring after me? I fucking giggle like a nervous school girl and throw an awkward finger wave.

Holy shit. What is wrong with me?

"Looks like you got more than a bird bath," Bitsy quips when I reclaim my seat at the picnic table.

Fuck me! I just stuck my hand to this nasty thing again.

"There are devil children amuck here, Bitsy. You have been warned."

Chuckling, she flips her hair and nods in Mount Sunshine's direction. "No. I was talking about the hunk. What was that about?"

My eyes search the direction of Bitsy's nod. The beefcake appears to be reclaiming his place amongst his herd, a gaggle of only slightly less fit men and a few fair females, corralling under a beer garden tent some two hundred feet from us. A just born piece of hope dies in my chest as a pretty blonde slinks her arm around his waist and hands him a beer.

There, I silently tell my misguided dick. *See? He's not for us.*

"Just a good Samaritan," I inform Bitsy with a careless shrug.

Why does my disappointment smart so much? I have a type. I'm not sure what it is yet, as I'm still recalibrating from my last relationship, but it's not chivalrous, six-foot-three, hetero hot stuffs like *Packers Man.*

Been there. Done that. Got the broken heart to prove it. Not sailing that ship again, thank you.

"Well, your good Samaritan is looking over here like you two have unfinished business," Bitsy murmurs over the rim of her beer.

Huffing at her irrational assumption, I feign a stretch and cast my gaze toward the location of Bitsy's delusion. What the hell? He *is* looking right at us. His luscious mouth with that bowed upper lip ticks up at the corner, and he waves. I whip my head back around so fast a muscle in my neck spasms.

"Aren't you going to wave back?" Bitsy asks.

"No! Why on Earth would I do that? He's waving at you."

Which just makes my hormonal outburst all the more embarrassing. I have been bewitched by an unfaithful heterosexual man.

"No, he's not. You should see how crushed he looks."

"Clearly, the sun and trans fats have gotten to you."

"Seriously. He looks so sad," she whines and sets her beer down. "Fine. I'll save him from your rudeness."

She lifts her arm, and with her million-dollar smile, waves. Wonderful. Nothing like the man who made me forget my sanity getting the full effect of Bitsy's beauty. Not that there was a snowball's chance in hell he was into me or that I even want him to be.

"Well?" I prompt when she turns a smug expression on me. "Did he give you *fuck-me* eyes, gesture for you to call him? Do tell. You know how much I love to hear you prove me right."

She snorts. "No, actually. I got a prune smile."

"A *prune smile?*"

"You know when people don't want to smile, but make themselves, and it gives them all these *pruney* lines around their mouth?" She demonstrates.

"I know what a prune smile is. I'm a photographer, for God's sake. He did not give you a prune smile, and if he did, it wasn't because of me. Clearly, he has no taste if he can't appreciate your beauty."

"Why thank you, but it was totally pruney because you cold-shouldered him."

"Bitsy," I heave, leveling her with the look of a hard truth, flicking my thumb over my shoulder. One of us has to live outside of *La La Land.* "Exhibit number one—blonde goddess wrapped around said beefiness. There is no way he's into guys."

"*His* arm isn't wrapped around her."

"Don't interrupt. Exhibit two—beefcake has the audacity to gawk and wave at my friend whilst blonde goddess is wrapped around him, denoting the characteristics of a perfidious lecher. Neither of us want what he's selling. Can we agree on that?"

"Again. *Wasn't* gawking or waving at *me*."

I let out all my air and cast my eyes heavenward, begging for divine intervention to get her to see reason. When I refocus on Bitsy, her gaze is locked on the beer tent, eyes crinkled at the corners like a spy.

"I think that's the crew that redid Uncle Dimitris' patio wall last summer," she intones as though she's solved some riddle. "I knew I'd seen them before!"

While it warms my heart that she claims my relatives as her own, it is yet another craw in my side. My family freaking adores her, and rightly so. She eats everything they throw at her and never complains, whereas I am considered the King of Protests. On that note, I scan the carnival for any one of my three hundred relatives.

"Fine. So, the beefcake has skills. This changes nothing." I wave a dismissive hand as I spot my mother.

Her eyes are scanning the crowd with my sister, who has her cell phone in her hand. My phone vibrates in my pocket.

Crap. They're looking for me. No doubt my mother wants us to parade as a family through the masses where she will introduce me to every child-bearing-aged female like I'm an overflowing sperm bank. She somehow still does not understand just how gay I am, and I must perform my duties to supply her with twelve Greek grandchildren. Reaching over, I snatch Bitsy's beer and bolt from my seat.

"Okay. Time to go!"

"What? Wait! Don't you want to walk around a while? We've hardly seen anything."

"Nope. Seen enough! You look a little green. Is that food getting to you? We should get you home and curl up on the couch."

Sofia spots me and waves her arms. She nudges my mother, whose gaze lands on me and lightens with surprise. Mamá makes a beckoning gesture that I pretend I didn't see by looking in the opposite direction.

My gaze lands on the beefcake who…looks to be excusing himself from his pack after locking eyes with me.

Oh, fuck. He's coming this way.

I can't do this right now. Nope. I am *not* watching him flirt with Bitsy while my family descends upon me.

Grabbing ahold of Bitsy's shoulders, I plead with her. "Bitsy, if you love me, if you ever loved me, please, run like our lives depend upon it, and get me away from this place of horrors. No questions."

"But…" she trails off, her cute little freckle-smattered face constricted in confusion as she glances at each of my approaching dilemmas.

"Please!" I whine, uncaring that my dignity has died as I give her shoulders a shake.

She sighs and reaches for my hand. "Oh, alright, but you owe me."

"Don't I always?"

My flip flops have never *flip-flopped* so fast as we scurry through the maze of food trucks. Behind me the cacophony of the carnival snuffs out my mother's calls. We have successfully fled, but I am now surely going to a special hell for bad Greek sons, all quite aptly, because I was tempted by the devil reincarnate in a Packers t-shirt.

CHAPTER 2

Johnny,

Thanks for letting me crash on your couch. I guess we drank a little too much.

You weren't kidding—you really can't hold your liquor!

Glad I ran into you on the beach. Watch out for those jelly fish.

Call me. We need to hang out again!

555-6843

Lance

CHAPTER 3
Aiden

Sipping my coffee, I watch the soft glow of the rising sun through the trees. The cool morning air splits the humidity seeping into my truck as I wait for my little sister, Maxine, to emerge. I don't mind foregoing the joy of riding my motorcycle on occasion, picking her up when her fiancé is home from her trips as a flight attendant and needs their car. However, after all these years, it would be nice if she'd figure out that I'm here at five o'clock sharp, but no. I'm forced to wait every time I pick her up, plus the extra ten minutes she takes on Mondays.

I don't know why people complain about Mondays. I've always thought of them as a symbol of promise. You get to start over and reset from the week prior. I'm off to a better start than usual after this weekend, having seen all my family and friends at the carnival for my birthday. You can't beat ringing in another year surrounded by those who care about you, claiming an entire beer tent like they own it. Plus, there was that *other* pleasant surprise.

I chuckle, recalling the ruffled man at the handwash station who got a taste of Bradley Reeves and about made me piss myself the way he gave it back to him. It's embarrassing that I can't remember what any of my friends or family were wearing, but I can still picture his close-shaved stubble, his meticulously combed thick brown hair, and those big, black-framed glasses that made his dark chestnut eyes go soul deep.

Phew. Not usually my type, but there was something about him. A lot of somethings. A lot more somethings than I've ever sensed from anyone. He was like a flame that lit a fuse inside me. Too bad he ran off so quick.

Too bad he was holding a woman's hand as he did. I thought for sure he experienced what I did—a bolt of invisible lightning zapping down between us.

Better luck next time, Aiden. Story of my life.

The door to Maxine and Véronique's single-story brick home swings open, and Maxie emerges in all her blue jean and green bandana glory, long brown braids hanging over her shoulders. I wave to Véronique, who gives me an apologetic smile and tugs her flowery red robe tighter against the morning breeze. Maxie stops short, turning around to pull my future sister-in-law in for a kiss.

I'm still over the moon for them, but seeing this ritual every day for the last two-and-a-half years is a sad reminder of my singledom. When their love fest exceeds the ninety-second mark, I tap my horn. Maxie ignores me as usual, but her oblivious, sated smile when she finally turns toward my truck is the worst part, worse than the countless morning kisses I've witnessed. She deserves the happiness she found, but seeing these exchanges reminds me of everything I'm missing out on.

Bounding up into the truck, Maxie grins out the window and throws a very un-Maxie-like finger-wave to Véronique that makes me chuckle.

"What?" She narrows her eyes at me.

"You two aren't going to have anything left for the honeymoon."

"Pfft. Whatever. I plan on living one very long and healthy honeymoon for the rest of my life. Drive, brother."

"Yes, ma'am." I salute her, earning me the customary punch in the arm.

When we pull up to our warehouse ten minutes later, our perpetually disgruntled brother Graham throws us a nod as he walks through the main door. Maxie scoffs over her travel mug.

"How the hell did he beat us here? Is there an apocalypse? Are all the strippers taking shelter in the loading bay, and he's going to wow them with his *hermit-y* woodsman act?"

Shaking my head, I pull the keys out of the ignition. The faded logo on the side of the building my grandfather built, reads *Brandt and Sons,* feeling like an extension of home. My father planned to change the name after Maxie started working for the family masonry business, but she wouldn't let him. She said she wanted neither special treatment nor labels because she "can do anything you three idiots can do."

I'm pretty sure she only includes me in the *idiot category* to make our two brothers feel like she doesn't have a favorite. Secret: I am totally her favorite.

"Dad," I greet, nodding at my father when we enter the warehouse floor.

"Son," he returns. "Sweetie," he says to Maxie when she gives him a peck on the cheek.

Moving on, she kicks Graham's feet off her favorite chair with her leather work boots. Graham clutches his lower back like the force injured him.

"Jack ass!" he spats, kicking the chair out of her reach when she makes to sit down.

Skyler, our older brother is still sleeping through the entire ruckus. A string of drool is running down the side of his jaw where his head is leaning back against one of the old ratty office chairs that have been demoted to our makeshift warehouse break room. Maxie tiptoes toward him with a shit-eating grin on her face, her hands out to her sides like she's either about to pounce or clap.

"Maxine!" Our father warns without taking his eyes from his clipboard. "Leave him be."

"He's sleeping on the job again. Is that the company image we want to project?"

"The twins were up in the middle of the night. He's no good to us if he's tired later."

I can't remember the last time Skyler wasn't "tired later" as I take in his exhausted form. At thirty-three with a pregnant wife, two sets of twins, and three dogs I honestly don't know how he gets any sleep unless he gets here early so that he can catch a nap.

Dad gives us our marching orders that we already knew, but we humor him as we do every morning. I think it makes him feel like he's still contributing to operations since Mom swore him to office duty five years ago.

Graham, Maxie, and I get to work, fluidly loading pallets of bricks and the forklift we need for to haul to the worksite on a trailer. I tie the pallet and forklift down, only half-listening to Maxie's latest updates on her wedding plans. It's all she's talked about since her engagement.

"Graham, are you bringing Jen or a date? I want to get a good count so we can figure out the seating chart."

"Why would I bring Jen?" he heaves in exasperation, flinging one of the tie-downs in my direction with more force than needed.

"Uh. 'Cause you always invite Jen to everything."

Here we go.

Twins are supposed to have a special bond, thick as thieves. Nope. Not these two.

"She's dating someone, Max. You know this!" Graham snaps.

"You invited them to Aiden's birthday party. How am I supposed to understand your weird dynamic with your ex-wife?" Maxie gestures wildly.

"She's known our family since we were in high school. I didn't want to be rude."

"Look. I love Jen. I always have, but I don't get it. You guys don't have kids. You didn't have any pets. There's no reason to feel tied to her and torture yourself by seeing her with another man. At the very least, Mom or I could do the inviting, so you don't have to look like you're pining over her still."

Graham chucks his lunch box in the cab of the truck. "I'm not pining!"

"Hey, wait a minute," I interrupt to stop the bickering. "How come you didn't ask me if I'm bringing someone?"

I'm answered by twin snorts that leave me blinking. Maxie shrugs. "I figured a plus-one for you was a given."

Seriously? I'm in the wedding. It wouldn't be convenient to have a date, not with best man duties.

"Why did you think it was a given? I was going to go stag."

"Sure," Maxie scoffs.

Graham snickers, pushing his floppy, sandy hair off his forehead, exchanging a smirk with Maxie as though they're concurring that I'm a dumb ass. "Bro, you'll find someone in the parking lot of the church."

"Or at the reception hall," Maxie chimes in.

"At the tux rental place," Graham adds optimistically.

"At the florist's," Maxie quips.

"At a gas station, a restaurant," Graham rattles on. "Maybe even a hitch hiker!"

They both chuckle, shaking their heads, morphing into a rare moment of solidarity. It's their evil twin dynamic. Maybe they have a weird twin language—it's called *Asshole.*

Straightening up, I rest my hands on my hips. They've got my attention now. "What the hell's that supposed to mean?"

"Wow. It's like you forgot about the harem that magically appears when you walk out the door. Man, that birthday really caught up with you this year," Graham grimaces.

"Oh, not this again. I don't have a harem."

Maxie shoots Graham an apologetic look as she locks the tailgate in place. "He can't help that his face is prettier than yours, Graham Cracker."

"Um, fraternal twin here." Graham gestures between them with a finger. "We're *both* his siblings. If I'm sub-standard, so are you."

"No. Our genes look better as a woman."

Skyler ambles over, drawing his palm down his mouth with a yawn. He leans his tall lanky frame against the trailer and runs his fingers through his sandy crew cut.

"When did you guys get here?" he croaks.

Maxie smiles serenely. "Three hours ago."

"Bullshit." He turns his bleary, green-eyed gaze to mine. "What are they arguing about today?"

"My apparent promiscuity."

Skyler snorts. "You haven't dated in like…what? Years?"

The validation stings more than I expect, but I throw up a palm. "Thank you!"

"We weren't talking about dating," Graham scoffs. "We were just pointing out the endless supply of *onesies* at his beck and call for Max's wedding."

I jump down from the trailer, my work boots hitting the concrete floor with a shock wave I feel in my knees. "*Onesies?*"

"You know, your one and done routine," Graham elaborates.

"*Routine?* What the hell are you talking about?"

Grabbing his toolbox off the workbench, he scoffs. "Aiden, when's the last time you went on more than one date with a woman?"

"Or *man!*" Maxie volunteers, giving me a supportive smile that I can't quite appreciate at the moment.

Graham's face goes beet red, and he sputters. "Well, it's historically been more women, but…whatever, you know what I mean."

"No. I *don't* know." I shrug, feeling suddenly cornered as my siblings stare at me as if they actually want to know the answer. "I don't remember. Okay? And why would I go on a second date if I'm not into the person on the first one?"

Graham slams his toolbox down on the trailer bed but doesn't meet my eyes. "How does that work anyway?"

"How does what work?"

He peers up two inches to meet my gaze, his broad shoulders slumping in a rare display of hesitation as he folds his tawny, tatted forearms over the tire well. "I mean, I get that Maxie likes women." It's odd how he straightens up and sputters. "Well, and *I* like women. Of course. Clearly. And I get that you like both men and women, but how…how do you decide when you prefer a man and when you prefer a woman?"

Maxie lets out a snort. "Oh, you don't know about his color-coded calendar?"

Graham's head jerks back. "What?"

"Yeah. Mondays, Wednesdays, and Fridays are for vagina. Tuesdays, Thursdays, and Saturdays are for penis."

"Oh. Fuck off! You know that's not what I think."

I smear my hand down my face, heaving a breath at the spectacle my sex life has become. Graham glances back over at me like he's still anticipating an answer to his idiotic question. I'm glad he's always been accepting of my preferences and know he's trying to understand me further in his typical unfiltered way, but I don't feel like being anyone's encyclopedia.

"It just works," I tell him. "I spend time with whoever I feel like spending time with."

"It doesn't seem like it's working," Skyler mutters behind me.

Wheeling around, I feel my jaw gape open. The guy never has an opinion. He's asleep half the time.

"What the hell is that supposed to mean?"

It's not Skyler who answers me. Graham grabs his ball cap off the workbench, sweeping his hair back before tugging it on his head. "*He means* you're *thirty-one*, and you've never had a relationship that lasted longer than six months with either a man or a woman. Whatever you're doing in your dating life ain't working."

"Like you're one to talk." Maxie shoves his shoulder as she heads toward her coffee tumbler.

"I've been married. *Twice!*" Graham huffs.

"To the same person!"

Graham's tanned complexion goes a shade redder. "More to the point!"

All the air leaves my lungs, a dull ache forming behind my eyes from an impending headache named *the Brandt siblings*. Monday has officially lost its appeal.

Following Graham and Skyler to the worksite in my pickup, I can't shake the accusations made back at the warehouse.

Is that what they really think I am? Some promiscuous, wandering soul who can't commit?

"What crawled up your ass?" Maxie cuts through my thoughts.

"What? Nothing."

"You're Hulk-gripping the steering wheel. I mean, I know Graham Cracker's driving sucks," she gestures ahead of us, "but you should be used to it by now."

Unclenching my fingers, I take a calming breath. "I don't…sleep with all the people I go out with."

"Well, I would hope not. There wouldn't be any room left to put notches on your bedpost."

"Thanks."

She snorts. "Aiden, I don't give a shit if you bed the entire county. You do you. Whatever makes you happy."

You do you.

If she only knew.

I shift in my seat, my secret bursting inside me under the pressure of keeping it contained for so long. I can't keep living like this. I need to tell someone.

"That's…actually all I do. All I've been doing…for a while. *Me.*"

"Wait. What?" She blinks and angles her body to face me. "You mean…jerking off?"

I throw up a hand because who in the hell wants to answer that question for their sister? Except it's my jerking off hand, so I quickly return it to the wheel like a lonely, guilty man and shift my gaze out the driver's window.

"How long have you and your hand been in this monogamous relationship?"

"Oh, forget it."

Monday, I hate you.

"I'm not making fun of you. I'm just confused. Heather Barlow was hanging on you at your party yesterday. I don't get it?"

"She asked to come. I didn't see any reason to say *no*."

"Clearly you said *no* to *something*."

Shaking my head, I let out a puff of air. I'm the levelheaded sibling. I don't…do or feel whatever this vice around my lungs is, this frustration simmering under the surface that's threatening to boil over.

"Look, forget it. Alright. I just can't believe you guys think I'm playing the field or something."

It's quiet for too long. When I look over, Maxie's staring at me like I'm one of our mother's crochet books.

"How long Aiden?"

My breath splits the breeze wafting through the open windows. "Two years," I mumble, feeling the weight of every pathetic, lonely month of it.

"*How* long?"

I nod confirmation so I don't have to repeat the embarrassing admission as I hit the brakes at a stop light. I've never had many secrets, but the few I keep, I trusted only to Maxie.

"Holy shit!" Her eyes go wide. "You haven't had sex in *two* years?" she practically yells, making me flinch at the volume of what's lived inside me in silence until this moment.

Over her shoulder, Mrs. McMann, the eighty-year-old organist at my parents' church, gapes at us through the open window of her *Buick LeSabre* in the next lane. Although her glasses are as thick as a *Mason* jar, her hearing is apparently crystal clear. Pinching my eyes closed, my finger finds the window button. I transmit my level of mortification in a glare to Maxie as the whining sound of the glass rising shuts out the sound of the city.

She glances out her. "Oh. Shit," she whispers and waves at Mrs. McMann before turning on me with a nervous laugh. "Sorry about that."

I stare ahead, grateful when the light turns green. "It'd be nice if you don't broadcast that any further."

Maxie pleads the fifth by forging on. "So, are you…asexual now?"

"What? No!" When I realize how harsh that sounded, I try again. "No. It'd be a hell of a lot easier if I was, but no. I'm still bi."

If she only knew how many times I wished I was asexual, how many times I wished I could snuff out the phantom need to meet someone who could satisfy my craving for connection.

But no. Lucky me. I'm attracted to both men and women, which makes the haystack twice the size to conceal the proverbial needle I'm looking for.

"Oh," Maxie says, sounding surprised. "Then why has it been so long? Did you get hung up on somebody?"

If only.

"No. Just the opposite. That's the problem."

"I don't understand. What does that have to do with getting laid?"

"Do you remember how Mom and Dad said they fell in love the first time they met at that community dance?"

"Uh, yeah. Mom's only told us that story about a hundred times."

"And Skyler," I press on. "He and Fiona knew after their first date."

"O-kay." Her cluelessness only fuels the frustration in my chest.

"Even Graham and Jen were inseparable in high school. We all knew they'd end up together. I remember the weekend you met Véronique, all stupid-grinning like you were drunk as a loon. You still look like that every morning when I pick you up."

"What's wrong with that?"

"Nothing! Don't you get it? *I* want to feel that." I toss my sad hand in desperation and take a breath. "I've never felt *that*."

"With anyone?" The pucker of Maxie's lower lip is a solid reminder of why I've kept this to myself. Shit. Maybe it was better to let them think I was a revolving door of one-night-stands and loving every minute of it.

"No," I force out. "Not like that."

"Wait. What about Meg? You guys went out for months and you always looked happy together."

Meg Parrish, a woman I dated about five years ago, was probably the best and longest relationship I ever had. We went to games and worked out together. She took me rock climbing for the first time, and we'd hop on my bike on weekends, exploring restaurants we'd stumble upon.

"When she stopped us in front of a wedding boutique one day in some little town we stopped in, I felt instantly sick with panic. I knew then I'd never want to marry her, and our relationship was nothing more than friendship for me, so…I ended it a few days later. I didn't want to lead her on."

"But…I mean, clearly you guys had been having sex for a long time, so there was chemistry there. Are you just afraid of commitment?"

"No. I want commitment. I'm attracted to people, but…but that's it. There's nothing…*more*. Ever since that day with Meg, it's like it activated some kind of radar. There's been nothing longer than initial curiosity or a night of sex that lets me know they're not the person I want to have sex with for the rest of my life. That's why I…why I quit. I mean, what was the point? I knew before I slept with them our connection didn't feel like…like…"

How do you describe something you've only seen others experience? The closest I've ever come to the feelings I'm trying to convey is…

"Lightning," I blurt out, remembering that entertaining, flustered man with the severe brow and kissable lips from the carnival.

My face burns, and it's like someone tied a weight to my heart when Maxie looks speechless. "Am I too picky?" I ask in desperation. "Am I emotionally unable to connect with someone like that? I mean, I'm thirty-one! How have I never had a serious relationship? There's got to be something wrong with me."

Maxie reaches over and squeezes my shoulder. "Okay. First off, calm down. You're freaking me out." She sucks in a gulp of air and releases it. "Geez. You're supposed to be the calm one."

"I'm sorry. I don't know why I went off."

"No." She waves dismissively. "You're entitled to go off once in your life, I suppose. Shit, Aiden. I wish I'd known you were having a crisis all this time."

"It's not a crisis. I think you guys must have just hit a nerve."

"I blame Graham." She nods solemnly and then inhales like an athlete going in for a big play. "Okay. Well, I don't really know how you judge your dates, so I can't tell you if you're being too picky. If you don't like the brand of shampoo someone uses or the way they put on *ChapStick* then, yeah, I'd say that's picky. Otherwise, you can't force yourself to like interests and beliefs you know you'd never like."

"*ChapStick?*"

"Yeah. Haven't you ever noticed how some people put *ChapStick* on by moving it across their lips, but some people hold it still and move their head around the *ChapStick?*"

I stare at the strange person who is supposedly related to me. "No, but I will now for the rest of my life!"

"Well, the *head-movers?*" she says, her mouth forming an *O* as she rotates her neck, eyes wide. "It's creepy."

"Now who's picky?"

She smacks my arm and laughs. "I know! I have issues, but see? You're not picky." She sighs and rests back against the seat, folding her arms. "No. I get it. You want *forever*—the fairy tale. Everybody wants that. You're…a romantic." She flashes me an appreciative smile like she's just uncovered a label written on my forehead. "You have to be capable of emotional connection to want that, so…don't go all heavy on the psychoanalysis. Okay?"

Her reassurance kindles a flutter of hope in my stomach, but it doesn't alleviate the self-doubt I've stacked up like a brick wall over the years. "How can I be a romantic if I've never had a real romance?"

"Well, you want one, don't you? I mean if I understand what you're telling me. Why else would you deprive yourself of intimacy for so long? You're holding out for that emotional connection that only exists when we're in love."

When we're in love.

A pang resounds in my heart at the *we* in that sentence. There is no *we*. Only Maxie and every other member of my family have lived the definition of *we're in love*. Yeah, I want it. God, I want those smitten expressions I've seen on their faces. I want to know the secrets of that phenomenon, have it fill the empty places inside me until they solidify like mortar.

"Yeah," I concede, "but do you know how many dates I've been on? If they were lottery tickets, I'd have won the jackpot by now."

She scoffs. "Aiden, I'm only a year younger than you. I was starting to feel like you do before I met Véronique."

I hadn't realized that. A swell of empathy for my little sister washes through me. We're a block away from our worksite for the day, so I need to be selfish and nip this in the butt before we're stuck with Graham and Skyler all day.

"Yeah, but you had relationships before you met Véronique. Sarah, Elise, Alissa," I rattle off the three serious girlfriends she's had. "I know it didn't work out with any of them, but you were happy and in love for a while. You got farther than I ever have."

"Aiden," she snorts. "If you're serious about this, how do you ever expect to meet this forever person if you don't date?"

Pulling into the new strip mall we're working on, I give her the side-eye. "Uh, I think you guys already established that I date."

"No, moron." She sighs. "I don't mean sitting back like a lazy spider waiting for a fly to run into your web. You can't just rely on your pretty face to make people flock to you."

I scoff and jam the truck into park. "I'm *not* the pretty one. That's Graham's title. Let's just set that straight." I ignore her chuckle and rest my forearm on the steering wheel, flexing for effect. "I think of all your brothers, I'm the least lazy."

"I meant lazy in love. I'm talking about putting yourself out there, making a concerted effort. I've never actually seen you try. Decide what you want and go look for it."

Every muscle in my face goes slack as I recall how I met my last handful of dates, or…shit, all of them. Karen—brushing into my shoulder at the coffee shop. Mark who asked for the next game of pool when

I was out with Graham one night. Tara—who asked me which ready-mix pasta I preferred at the grocery store. The list went on.

"I'm an idiot," I murmur.

I don't realize I've actually said it aloud until Maxie laughs and opens the door of the truck. "No." She grins. "You're just too damned pretty."

I roll my eyes at her, even though I'm starting to believe it. I can't remember any of my *onesies* who didn't start or center our conversations around what they thought of my looks or my body. I never minded until now. It was how I knew someone was interested in me—they spelled it out. Maybe that's why all I've got to show after a decade of dating are evenings that never went deeper than sex and a few laughs. In the light of morning, there was nothing left.

"Hey!" Maxie slaps my shoulder, and I realize I'm scowling. "Geez, if you're that worried about it, put a bag over your head on your dating profile."

Her words stop me in my tracks. All the pressure of this morning's epiphanies dissipates. I've never used a dating app. Maxie's right. I have been a lazy spider.

"What?" She halts her trek and looks back at me.

It feels good to laugh again after the last hour pummeled my life choices like ground beef. Shaking my head, I slink an arm around her neck in a playful headlock. "Nothing."

As the gravel of the lot crunches under our boots, a newfound sense of control comforts me. I can take charge of my destiny. I don't have to force myself to go out anymore and wait for someone who's snared by my appearance to approach me. Dating apps have profiles. You put your business out there ahead of time for everyone to see. I'm not naïve to think a profile will signal I've met the love of my life, but it's a road map at least. Something to point me in the right direction. Something that puts me behind the wheel.

"Dude," Graham says, dropping the tailgate of the trailer. "You drive like Mom. I swear."

His face contorts in confusion when I grin at him, bounding with a spring in my step onto the decking to unload the forklift. If someone could fall in love with and marry Graham twice, there's hope for me. If I'm lucky, maybe even lightning. Monday is still my favorite day.

CHAPTER 4

Johnny

"At ten o'clock, we have the Horvats coming in," Bitsy says through a bite of my mother's *biscotia.*

A crumb tumbles off her lip and lands on the white linen tablecloth at our favorite table on the back patio of Oikos. My father hums a Markos Vamvakaris song, setting out salt and pepper shakers on the tables, the silver at his temples glinting in the morning light.

I roll my neck, trying to reclaim the limber sensation of the run I took hours ago, before I shuffled a groggy Bitsy out of our apartment for our Monday espresso ritual.

"Some people shouldn't take family photos," I reply, inhaling the vibrant burst of my *café daki.* "Can we put a limit on how many sessions one family can have in a single year?"

"They're regular paying customers," Bitsy emphasizes as her fingers fly over the screen of her tablet, orchestrating whatever secret magic she does to get me clients. "Regular and paying is good."

"Children under the age of ten in matching outfits—cute. An entire family in matching outfits six times a year—not cute. I am not cleaning up after that damn dog again."

She yawns and picks up her cup for another dainty sip. "It was only four times last year, and…um, Mrs. Horvat said Sheera needed a companion, so…"

My attention snaps away from my father trimming the bougainvillea back to Bitsy's guilty eyes. "What?"

"*Limu,*" Bitsy declares. "She's a six-month-old Lhasa Apso."

"Oh, fuck me." I drop my head in my hands, rubbing my temples. "They named it after an insurance-selling emu?"

"I think it's cute."

"Of course, you do." I glare at her.

The bells over the restaurant door chime behind us. I hear my mother call out to Sofia, sending my heart rate into a frenzy.

"Hurry up! Let's go," I tell Bits and scramble out of my seat.

She gives me that open-mouthed pout she does, like I just outlawed fried food. I am not doing this right now.

"But we didn't finish our coffee yet."

"You're Scottish! You don't get the customary three-hour Greek coffee break, and even if you were Greek, you'd have to get out the door before eight a.m. to be productive enough to earn a *siesta*, baby! So, move it!"

She folds her arms over the cookie crumbs on her t-shirt, her lips pressing into a thin line. I need a new best friend.

"*Giannaki! Kali mera!*" Mamá greets me *good morning*, breezing through the door onto the patio.

Her sturdy heels clip over the stone pavers as she descends upon us, the sleeves of her cotton dress pulling tight over her outstretched arms. Before I can fumble back into my chair, her calloused hands clamp around my jaw. Her waxy lips smack kisses on my cheeks, leaving the familiar greasy residue of lipstick on my skin.

"*Elizavet!*" She chirps Bitsy's Greek moniker, carelessly releasing my head in a near thrusting motion. Why must Greek greetings be so violent? "*Kali mera!* You're not leaving already, are you? I can make you an *omelletta*."

Bitsy's eyes light up with joy. Her mouth opens and my usual panic rages. I've sat through more than my share of my mother's interventions thanks to Bitsy's stomach. This shit is getting squashed, right now.

"No! No. No!" I hold out a hand. "We've got a busy day. I've got lots of props to haul out before the clients start showing up."

My mother clucks her tongue. "But how can you work if you don't eat first? You need energy. And besides, I haven't seen you in days."

"Not true." I raise an index finger. "We had dinner Saturday night."

"Yes, but I didn't see you at the carnival. You left so early."

"Bitsy wasn't feeling well. She ate some bad food. I had to get her home," I rush.

"Oh! *Elizavet?* You had a stomachache?" Mamá presses the back of her hand gently to Bitsy's cheek.

Bitsy's cookie-wielding hand stops halfway to her mouth. She glances from it to me and back again to that damn tempestuous cookie before lowering it and nodding at my mother with a flicker of dejection. "Yes, but I'm fine now."

"Oh, I bet you're hungry. You need good food. You want an *omelletta* with French fries in it like I make for you?" Mamá asks. My molars grind, knowing the battlefield has turned in Bitsy's favor, and she is about to abandon the flag of friendship for a meal.

Bitsy turns big, depraved eyes up at Mamá like a starving kitten begging for milk. "With tomatoes and feta?"

I gasp at the betrayal, but they steam roll me, my opinions an insignificant background noise to Bitsy's stomach and my mother's need to mother.

"Of course, *koukla!*" Mamá preens and cups Bitsy's chin.

Little doll, my ass.

Bitsy reclaims her cookie with a sated smile that's impervious to the daggers I am sending her with my eyes. She chews around a grin like an addict who knows they just confirmed their next fix.

"Giannis." Mamá fixes her hands on her sturdy hips, making her a looming barrier so I'm trapped back in my seat. "We bought our tickets to fly home next month. Did you get yours yet?"

Home will always be a little island in the Aegean for Mamá. My throat closes up at the thought of taking their annual trip to the Greek island where my parents were born. They go for three weeks every year. That's three long weeks of being trapped in the confines of my *yiayiá's* home with my parents, brother, sister, and their families, all while being force fed as they play a game called who-can-talk-the-loudest. No, thank you.

"Mamá, I told you. I can't go. I have too much work to do."

Lies. All lies.

Not to brag, but I was somewhat of a photographer prodigy back in California and amassed a little nest egg. As much as it sucks the life out of my soul, my Wisconsin studio pays the bills and then some.

Mamá scoffs. "It's not until the middle of July! How do you know how much work you will have in July?"

"Scheduling?" I venture.

"You haven't been to see your *yiayiá* in three years! Don't you want to see her before she dies?"

Okay. My *yiayiá* has been "dying" for twenty years, according to my mother. Wiry old *Yiayiá* Evagalina, with her knobby knuckles, who used to bust my ass with an olive wood spoon. She'll outlive us all, mark my words.

"She's not dying. Please, don't say that. I'll try next year."

"That's what you said *last* year and the year before that."

We heave twin sighs. It is the only thing we seem to agree on these days. She rallies quickly though, diving into her next order of business.

"I wanted you to talk to Grace Meyers at the carnival. Her mother said she just graduated from college and is moving back to Olympus. They run a florist shop on Parson Lane."

"Hm. Sorry. Never heard of her," I hum around the lip of my cup.

"That's okay. I told them my son is a talented photographer and can help them take pictures of their arrangements for their computer page."

"You mean their website?" I venture.

"Yes. *This*. See! You are already helping." Mamá flaps a hand, nearly smacking my glasses off my face.

I know where this is going. It's a one-way ticket to matchmaking hell and takes everything inside me to hold back the aggression I have yearned to explode over the subject since I moved home. Ten bucks says the look of concentration Bitsy is directing at her tablet as I cast her a thank-you-for-this-bullshit look is a veil for her cowardly guilt.

Are you shitting me? That's the *Candy Crush* theme music I hear from her tablet. Ugh. She's officially dead to me.

"Mamá, if she graduated college, guaranteed she knows how to load pictures onto a website."

When she blinks at me, I see the old-country confusion in her eyes and take a breath. While my father emigrated here when he was seven, Mamá wasn't plucked from her small island village until the age of twenty, when my father went back to visit family and they fell in love. It's like I was raised in two countries and two different eras all at once.

"*Computer page*," I elaborate. "Besides, there are all types of services and free tutorials online explaining how to do it. I doubt they want to pay my rates just for a bunch of floral arrangement pictures. Anybody with a digital camera can tackle that. Flowers speak for themselves. No need to hire a professional."

And there it is.

The look.

The one that I always imagine says, *how is this uncooperative person my son?* Her espresso-colored eyes bore into me, studying, judging, lamenting.

Fabulous. Now…here come the pleading hands, because the state of my life is equivalent to something worth praying in earnest over.

"Giannis, she is a nice young woman. She lives *here*. She works with *artistic* things. She needs pictures taken. She would be perfect for you. What will it hurt for you to go meet her?"

Rubbing my eyelids with my thumb and index finger, I sit in the murky waters of her logic, served up with a side of guilt and a mother's understanding. She lives *here—not* in California far away from her family like I did. She's artistic—just like me. Mamá is a master of presenting both the yin and the yang, a slap with a kiss.

"Mamá, in case you forgot…*again*, I prefer looking for a nice young *man*."

"Are you sure?"

Her expression is filled with such genuine curiosity, my brain stops working. We have never discussed my sexual preference at length, but she knows I've dated men. She spoke with Lance numerous times over video chat.

When I moved home though, it's like she developed amnesia about my dating life. Most gay people come out once in their life. In the past two years, I've come out to my mother no less than ten times.

Who's still gay? Yup. This guy. Right here.

Greek children are taught to respect their elders. Family is everything. Family is everywhere. Family matters more than anything else. Expand the family. Protect the family. Love the family. Be part of the family.

No one tells the spare tire how to be a productive part of a car that's efficiently barreling down a highway on four durable tires. Biting my tongue to hold onto the tenements of parental respect, I purse my lips at her question.

Am I sure I'm gay?

"Um, let me think." I let a breath flood out my nose and catch a look of sympathy flash across Bitsy's face. "Yup. Pretty sure." Maybe it's time to ensure this conversation never happens again. "Mamá, how many more times are you going to ask me that?"

"How am I supposed to know? I've never actually seen you with a man."

My head rears back and a burst of concern unfolds in my belly. Is this the first stages of senility?

"You know I was living with my…with a man in California. You saw…" My throat squeezes so hard I taste the bitter aftertaste of my espresso. How can I not even verbalize his name? It's just a name. "You saw…Lance before."

"I saw pictures. I saw him on the computer when Sofia did the computer camera thing for you to call, but I never saw him in-person. You never brought him when you came to visit. For years you are telling me you like men, but I've never seen you with one. What am I supposed to think? You've been home for two years now, and the only person I've seen you with is *Elizavet*."

Well. Is that all? Anymore scars left to slice open? A sour chuckle hops out of my lips as I flick one of Bitsy's crumbs off the table, sending it sailing away from this spot where I have been reduced to faults that I had no ability to prevent.

How do you materialize a boyfriend when he had prior obligations each time you visited home? How do you introduce him to your family when they fly to California if he's in New York for a photo shoot he couldn't reschedule?

You don't. You play the supportive loving sap who believed his disappointment at missing them and say, *It's a wonderful opportunity. You should go. I'm happy for you. Don't worry. You'll meet them another time.*

Another time. Right.

He probably knew that there'd never be *another time.* One more Lance-secret I wasn't wise to. Now my brain has become a pout palace after a flogging from my mother. I'm not bitter, just smarter.

There's a vast difference between bitter and wise. We're given instincts for a reason. Right?

Mine know that beautiful promises are just a fog, concealing inevitable reality. Heart-stopping smiles can change course on a passing wind, fixing on a more attractive waypoint. The hands of a lover's caress that mapped every inch of your body for two years are heartless thieves when they go, taking a piece of you forever, a piece they neither want nor can ever give back. Mamá's accusations renew the aching void of that missing piece.

I don't know what's more depressing—seeing Bitsy set her cookie down like my life has killed her appetite or hearing the emotional exhaustion in my own voice as I tell my mother. "There's…just not a lot of fish in the sea here, Mamá."

She holds none of her boisterous vocal power back. "*How* do you know if you don't go fishing?" Her sigh of frustration fans over the table. "Listen. I will invite Grace to dinner this week with the family. Okay? You two can sit at the end of the table where no one will bother you and have a nice visit. Get to know each other a little bit…"

My pulse kicks up in my jugular. No! No. No. She's escalated to Defcon-four? Seriously?

How am I a twenty-seven year old gay man and in a predicament where my mother is arranging candle-lit meals between me and a woman? When will this madness end? What's next? An arranged marriage?

"I…I can't! I have a date!"

Bitsy's brow furrows in confusion. Mamá looks like I've splashed cold water in her face with my pathetic lie.

"Really? When?" Mamá asks, not concealing her shock.

Running my hand over my hair, I'm suddenly reduced to teenage Johnny before he discovered de-frizzing products—a Greek Pinocchio whose hair curls with every lie he tells.

That's stupid. Get a grip. It's a little white lie.

Except she's waiting, watching, probably planning my wedding as the seconds tick by.

"This week." I shrug carelessly.

Bitsy lifts her cookie to her mouth in slow-motion very Sherlock Holmes-like, looking all sorts of oh-my-dear-dumbass-Watson. She's been around my family long enough to know there is no such thing as lying to Greek mothers. There are only truths—dirty truths that always reveal themselves.

Fuck my life. Now I have to find a date.

CHAPTER 5

Johnny

Sometimes, I miss the sound of the ocean, the balmy scent of salt in the air, the cool mist on my skin. I miss the sand pressing against my feet, like a cool memory foam rug.

When I block out the memories of a warm hand holding mine, laughing at my jokes, I can recollect the peace those beach walks brought me. These days the closest sensation of that bliss is only achieved by the padding of my ivory sectional hugging my ass while Bitsy's hand burrows deeper into her bag of popcorn, sounding like a giant cockroach. We take what we can get.

Exhaling the trials of the day, I lean my head back, resting my feet on the coffee table. This is my safe place, my safe hours—a few evenings a week I worked hard to impress as my new norm upon my family—*Johnny time*. No one should dine together seven nights a week, not even married couples. Absence makes the heart grow fonder, after all.

On the T.V. Jennifer Grey's character, "Baby", is stuck dancing with "old Mrs. Lipman" on the film, *Dirty Dancing*, her miserable face aggrieved.

Poor Baby. I can relate.

"Here's one," Bitsy enthuses, still holding my phone hostage. "*Ramrod—men to rev every piston in your engine*."

I shudder and roll my head to the side, hoping to find sarcasm on her face. How is she enjoying this?

"Does getting rammed by a rod sound like a respectable dating app to you?"

Shrugging, she mutters, "Depends on the size of the rod."

"No. Just give it up. Maybe she'll forget about it."

Her snort makes me flinch. She could be a decent friend and humor my delusions.

"I'd rather hold out for Panos Kiamos and Mykonos, thank you. My mother can try to hetero me all she wants."

"Mm," Bitsy hums skeptically, "I'm starting to think Mykonos isn't all it's cracked up to be if you've never been there."

"*Gasp!* I was in college and then…I was with you know who and working my ass off. How am I supposed to go to Greece and literally fly over my parents' native island without them finding out I skipped a visit to see my *yiayiá* for an all-you-can-eat cock buffet?"

"If I really wanted to…*eat at a buffet*, I'd find a way to do it," she yawns over the ticking sound of her search through my phone.

"And Panos is huge in Greece. Mm-kay? It's not like the islands have venues to hold the size of crowds he'd draw. I've never been in Athens at the same time he was playing. Are you even listening to me?"

"How about *Men About Town?*" She smiles, flashing me a view of yet another dating app.

"That sounds like an STD waiting to happen. Pass."

"Well, what do you expect? They're all going to try to sound fun and flirty. It's advertising. That's how they get you—by making you think there's *plenty of fish in the sea,*" she emphasizes and jabs her big toe into the side of my ass cheek.

I jerk away like a petulant child and shove her foot back. She buries her hand into her popcorn bag again, withdrawing her leg as though it were her choice.

"I know, but they could at least make a more concerted effort to not sound like fancy phrases for *Desperately Seeking Screwing.*"

"Johnny, you created some of this mess. I'm just trying to help. You could be a little enthusiastic. It's not an actual date would be a bad thing. I mean, come on. It's been two years since—"

"Can we *please* just watch Patrick?" I cut her off. "Look! Here he comes." I motion to the T.V., but Bitsy doesn't even glance at the screen which is a heinous Swayze-crime. This is one of our go-to movies. She's stone-walling me.

Her silence wraps around me like a spandex choker. She knows I was happy, and then I wasn't. It's not like I'm fooling anyone. All my stupid, head-over-heels mouth did when I was with Lance was blab to her about it every time we talked.

Bits! He got me flowers again.

He brought me coffee in bed.

Did you know he calls me Curly?

He loves to drive and get lost in off-the-beaten path towns just like we used to do in college.

He asked if we ever got married, if I'd take his name. Married! Ah, Bits! Can you believe this is my life?

Ugh. It's disgusting how easily I became one of those yuppy, sappy, love-sick fools who smoked the hookah pipe of happily-ever-after and forgot to exhale.

It's fine though. I've forgiven myself, dusted off, and buried that crap sandwich in the backyard of my brain with the help of new life-rules.

Except…I have a mother…with a very sturdy shovel. Now, I have my trusty friend, determined to ruin one of our precious movie nights with her misguided goodness.

I don't want to talk or think about dating. The only thing I want to talk or think about less than dating is fake dating because that's what this would be—a farce. I single-handedly ensnared myself in this big fat farce because I, Johnny the Coward, cannot win a verbal battle with my mother. I don't even deserve to watch "Dirty Dancing".

An hour later after picking fourteen Limu hairs off my shirt, I have crushed some of the hateful Johnny demons inside of me. Bitsy has been facing *Patrickward* for at least a good fifteen minutes, so I suspect we're golden again. Being my friend comes with the requirement to forgive easily and quickly. Fortunately for me, Bitsy is an expert at both.

She clutches one hand to her chest and another on my arm, making me smile. *Baby* has just left *Penny's* cabin after being ignored by *Johnny*, looking ever so heartbroken after being cold-shouldered no less than twelve hours after their love making.

"Johnny!" Bitsy cries out along with Jennifer Grey.

Cue my scene. We only do this every single time we watch it. I turn my most dashing and reassuring smile on her, and she beams from ear to ear with a giggle.

My phone pings between us where she abandoned it on the couch. Bitsy beats me to it, snatching it up like free samples in the deli aisle.

She gasps and lets loose a squeal. "Ooh! You got one! You got one already!"

"Got what?"

"A match!" She grins, flashing me that hideous *Man About Town* app again with a profile picture lit up in a frame of Las Vegas-esque lights. And…is that…

"Bitsy? Are those my feet?"

"You said no pictures of your face. I was trying to accommodate your demands!"

"So, you took a picture of my feet?"

"You have nice feet," she reasons with a shrug.

Really? Hm. They aren't bad, I guess. Wait a damn minute. "Someone actually responded to that?"

"Yeah! Look!" She angles my phone again, showing me the profile image of some poor desperate soul with the handle *Looking4U*.

"Let me see that," I huff, snatching the phone from her hand. "*Looking4U*," I emphasize the ridiculously spelled moniker. "Yeah, that's not creepy at all. You can't even see his face. It's just a close-up of his sunglasses, like some *stalkerish* peeping Tom."

"*You* didn't want to show *your* face. Maybe he's shy! Look at the bridge of his nose though."

"What about it?"

"It looks sturdy. It's nice. I bet he has a great facial structure."

Sparing only a split second for her asinine comment, I can clearly see the makings of a facial structure that would put John Hamm's to shame, but a nose does not a man make. I scroll the meager details he's listed in his profile and read them aloud.

"*Athletic, loves the outdoors but not as much as I love the idea of staying in with the right someone.*"

"Aw!" Bitsy coos, cupping her hands over her mouth.

"Elizabeth Fitzgerald, this has serial killer written all over it."

Her response is a backhand to my shoulder. "It does not! It's romantic."

"I guarantee you, there is nothing romantic about a man who swipes a profile picture of another man's feet. This reeks of a foot fetish, and I don't want romance." I heave off the couch, cringing at the popcorn flecks I know she isn't going to clean up, and make my way to my bedroom. "Romance is an ideology for silly hearts. Relationships are like a contract. They're about trust, guidelines, rules about who takes out the trash and how many sips of coffee are required before speaking is allowed in the morning." She's followed me into my room, so I don't relent. "I'm not in the market for a contract. I've been a free agent for… well, you know for how long, and it's worked out just fine."

Leaning on my doorway, she crosses her arms. "So that's why you told your mother you have a date? Because everything's working out just fine?"

"Fuck." I tug my glasses off and rub my tired eyes.

Vaginas, Johnny. Vaginas!

I need a date, even a fake date, or my mother will sniff my deception out like a dog to an asshole. "Fine. I'll go for coffee."

"Yay!" She claps her hands together, transforming her into a crazed cheerleader.

This is her fault. If she hadn't sat there looking like a starved waif at breakfast the other morning instead of remembering her allegiance to me, I wouldn't have found myself in this predicament.

"One date, Bitsy! That's all this is going to be. Just to get Mamá off my back until they go to Greece, and you better talk it up for me if you want my family to keep feeding you!"

"What's that supposed to mean?"

"Greek people take great offense when someone doesn't like their cooking," I say sagely, inspecting my nails.

"I love your family's food!"

Tossing my head, I know it's low, but it must be done. She could make or break this ruse for me. "So, you say, but what would they think if I told them the truth…about how you were just trying to be polite?"

Her sharp intake of breath almost makes me feel guilty, but I'm not the one taking pictures of feet and sending their best friend off to be slaughtered. There must be consequences for treachery, damn it.

"You wouldn't! That's food blackmail!"

Ha! I've finally discovered something she won't eat. Bitsy doesn't like them apples! "Oh, I don't know. Keep snapping foot shots without my consent and see what happens."

Her posture straightens as she folds her arms. Bitsy's a good five inches shorter than me, but I whither. She has somehow managed to grow with that crazed food fanatic look in her eyes. "Then *I'll* just have to tell your mother you're not really dating."

Gasp. "You wouldn't! That's pure evil!"

Eyes narrowed, nostrils flaring, she looks like she's mentally prepared for a cage match. Holy shit! Over *food!*

I toss my hands at her, wishing they'll ward off her conniving energy. "I said I'd message the foot collector, didn't I? Look! I'll do it right now!"

My fingers scramble to open the dreaded app, but Bitsy's on me like the ants that'll be on my couch if she doesn't clean up her crumbs again. She wrestles the phone out of my hands by delivering a Vulcan death pinch to the tendon behind my elbow.

"Ouch! What the fuck, Bits?"

"No way! *You're* not messaging him. You'll screw it up!"

"How can one screw up a coffee invitation?"

"You can! By being…*you*—all grumpy and disgruntled!"

"I am neither, thank you very much! This is me under duress. I've been threatened *twice* in one day. First by my mother with a vagina, and second by you, with your lascivious plans to tattle on me to satisfy your abnormal taste buds. I'm operating on survival instincts at this point. There's no way I can botch a coffee request."

Her steely gaze flies over her shoulder as she stomps out of the room with my phone captive. "I'm your assistant. Let me assist. How's eight o'clock?"

"Wait! He answered you already?" I hurry after her as her nimble fingers fly over the screen. "Jesus, he must really be into feet."

She nods, flopping back down on the couch. "He said he wants you to wear sandals."

"For reals?" I squeak, my stomach flipping at the mental image of a creeper sucking on my toes.

Her Montana-sky-blue eyes peer up for a fraction. "You're really an idiot sometimes, you know that?"

Well, I walked right into that one. Fine. I'm letting my imagination run wild, but she could withhold the teasing. I am the baby of my siblings. I put up with enough of that when I was a gangly curly-headed freak who hadn't grown into his glasses yet and got wedgies from my brother every time he caught me declining one-on-one basketball in favor of ogling Sofia's popstar posters. Excuse me, if George Michael spoke to me louder than sports.

"I told him your name is Johnny and that you wear glasses," Bitsy drones.

"Wow. I sound so sexy."

Her brow goes all contemplative. "You *want* to come across as sexy? I thought you didn't want to go?"

Of course, I don't. Floundering, I wave away her psychoanalysis. "I'd just like to have a little more game than my future murderer. Don't read into it."

"His name is Aiden. He says he's looking forward to meeting you at Beans on Banner." She smiles.

"And how will I know who Aiden the Foot Felon is?"

Her shoulders rise and fall carelessly. "He said he'll find you."

"He'll *find* me." I hold her gaze, waiting for signs of rationale. Nope. Nothing but fantastical Bitsy optimism. "He'll find me and then murder me. Fabulous."

I jerk my phone out of her hand and spin on my heel toward my room. This time, the enemy doesn't follow. Good. Maybe she realizes she's gone too far. Maybe…

"You know…" a coy voice cuts through my walk of shame. "I think your mother would be more at ease after say…hm…three dates. Might be more convincing that way."

My soon-to-be-amputated feet stop in their tracks, my spine rigid in straight-up terror. I don't dare turn around to witness the redheaded demon possessing my living room.

"Yee-ah…three," Bitsy purrs. "Such a nice penitent number for someone who threatens their best friend after she uprooted her *entire life* to move across the country."

Breathe in. Breathe out. Breathe in.

Wisconsin is hell. I am in hell, and my roommate is the devil's handmaiden.

CHAPTER 6

45

Johnny,

I'm meeting some people for a pickup game down the beach later. You should drop by.

We can grab something after as long as I can get a quick shower—I hate sweat!

Lance

P.S. – I really need to get a cell phone!

CHAPTER 7
Aiden

I am a man about town—a calm, cool, collected man about town. I've been on plenty of dates in my life. I can do this.

So, why is my pulse fluttering? Maybe because I never had to try before, and now that I want to, I don't have a damn clue how to.

Man About Town.

Shit. That's a stupid name for a dating app. Isn't it? This guy will probably think I'm as pathetic as I feel. At least Maxie is covering for me at work—both physically and verbally.

If I told Graham or Skyler I bugged out for a date, I have no doubt Graham would be running off to spy on Jen and her new boyfriend, and Skyler would declare he's allowed equivalent nap time for every minute I'm gone. We really need to hire more help, preferably people without the last name *Brandt.*

The café's bells chime again, but this time it's not coming from the front door of Beans on Banner, which I've been staring at for the last ten minutes. My eyes locate another door at the far end of the coffee shop near the restrooms that opens to the back parking lot.

Shit. I was so anxious I forgot there was an entrance back there. My date could have come and gone already without knowing who I was. I realize now I didn't tell him anyway to identify me. I know it's only five minutes past the hour, but maybe he…

No way.

My heart catapults into my throat and lodges there, blocked by my suddenly restricted airway. A zip of electricity runs from my belly all the way down to my toes.

Breathe, Aiden. Breathe.

It's *him.*

It's apple-polo-shirt-guy from the carnival—*my*-apple-polo-shirt guy.

Mine—the thought realigns the focus of every cell in my body. All my pre-date nervousness shifts into an entirely different sensation—one that feels a lot like possibility. Possibility, and the fear of it slipping through my fingers again. It's an odd mix of joy and despair.

He gets his coffee and makes his way to a table on the other side of the café. Something lightens in my chest, seeing that he's staying. He's staying, and that redheaded woman doesn't appear to be with him this time.

Resting my chin in my hand, a smile forms on my lips, witnessing that comical look of severe displeasure on his face—the same one he had at the carnival. He frowns at the table as though the cleanliness or color of it is offensive, before finally taking a seat.

His snug, blue jeans are impeccable compared to my worn, relaxed style. That distressed, chalky blue t-shirt looks like one of those fancy "well-loved" looking ones people pay extra for. I have to admit, the look on him is well-loved by me.

The thin fabric lays just right against his tan almost olive skin, showing off the extent of the muscular definition in his slender body. He's like a grumpy ray of sunshine, with his perturbed expression paired with a physique and skin tone that scream health and vitality.

His gaze meets mine from behind those sexy glasses. There go my lungs, seizing up again, but it's not from being caught gawking. I can't remember having such a strong reaction to someone. Not only has my blood gone up ten degrees, I'm…intrigued. I want to know everything about him and figure out how to turn that frown upside down. It's the stuff of teenage crush lore, feelings I've only heard about but never experienced.

I can see the surprise on his face. *Yes!* He remembers me. The thought makes me smile, and I wave.

His brow furrows, and he glances around, like I've just asked him to do something illegal. Not the reaction I was hoping for. Now he's scowling at his phone.

Huh. I've been forgotten. Just like that. Maybe he's waiting for someone.

Shit. *I'm* waiting for someone, but there's not a lone man in here other than the two of us. It's ten past eight. My date seems to have stood me up, got lost, or isn't punctual. I should really send him a message. It'd be the polite thing to do, but all I can see when I look at the sexy grump across the room is a window of opportunity that's about to close.

To hell with it. With my luck, if my date shows up, it wouldn't work out anyway. It was a little odd he used his feet as his profile picture, but I was trying to be open-minded. I mean, they were nice feet.

I'm up and moving. It could be my only chance to learn this hot nerd's name and find out if he's even into guys. I can't explain it, but I need to know more about the man behind those glasses.

"Hi, there," I stop at the edge of his table.

His mouth, lined by that thin layer of neatly trimmed dark stubble falls open as he gazes up at me. My confidence takes a dip, and I shift my weight.

Crap. Maybe he doesn't remember me. I want to jog his memory, but words are difficult when your breath has been stolen.

"You again," I declare like a chump.

His brows dip toward the bridge of his nose, his lips flattening into an unimpressed line. Geez. He's practically scowling at me.

"Um. Maybe you don't remember me," I try again. "We met at the carnival the other day."

I extend my hand. He eyeballs it, hesitating for a moment before slipping his palm into mine. There it is again, that heated charge. This isn't normal, but whatever it is, I want it to keep happening. I don't want to let go. I've never given much thought to the way someone's hand fits in mine, but his feels like it was meant to be there—a perfect match.

He casts a dubious look at our grip then quickly lets go, curling his fingers in against his palm. I cringe, remembering the state of my cracked and calloused hands from all the times I've forgone gloves on the job.

"Sorry about that. I'm a brick mason. I work with my hands all day. My name's Aiden. Aiden Brandt."

"Johnny," he says cautiously.

Wait a minute. *Johnny?* As in my-name's-Johnny-and-I-wear-glasses? He must take my silence as curiosity because he clarifies, "Johnny Andro."

"Your name's Johnny Andro?"

"What's it to you?" He folds his arms.

I bite back a chuckle at his annoyance. Man, he's touchy today. "Nothing. It's just…different. It sounds like a superhero name."

"No." He shoves his glasses up the bridge of his nose, which totally does it for me. Who knew that was a kink of mine? "I promise you, I'm completely ordinary."

"I doubt that." I guarantee there is nothing ordinary about this spitfire.

He blinks like he thinks I'm making fun of him or something. Interesting. I press on. "So…I'm going to venture you're *Hard-to-Handle?*"

"I beg your pardon?"

Beg your pardon—who says that anymore? I love it.

I flash him my phone. "Uh. I'm meeting a guy from a dating app named *Johnny* who wears glasses and has a screen name called *Hard-to-Handle.* So…just a lucky guess."

Apparently, I'm not as funny as I think. He pinches the bridge of his nose and mutters under his breath, "Hilarious, Bitsy."

"Are you…alright?"

"You're…*Looking4U*, I presume?"

Geez, it sounds worse when someone says it aloud. I smile to put him at ease. "My friends call me Aiden. Mind if I sit down?"

He waves a hand at the other chair, but his tone lacks any hope of enthusiasm. "Suit yourself."

Wow. This is new.

Usually, I'm painfully uncomfortable while my date goes over-the-top trying to impress me. I have to say, there's something about Johnny's complete lack of excitement makes me want to do the impressing for once.

Teasing, I take the seat across from him. "Do you always pull out this much charm on a first date?"

"I didn't know there were prerequisites. Is charm a requirement?"

That salty reply actually brings me relief, remembering all those over-the-top dates I've had in the past. "No. It's overrated and always feels kind of insincere, if you ask me."

Blinking, the corners of his mouth turn down again. Crap. I thought that was a window to common ground.

Inhaling, he leans forward, clasping his hands together on the table as though we're at a business meeting. "Listen, let's level with each other. This isn't going to work."

"I beg your pardon?" Apparently, that phrase *is* still relevant.

Sighing, he leans back against his chair somehow looking careless but with perfect posture. "I'm a gay man."

"Um. Y-yeah. I…kind of figured that part out."

"Mm. Well, you should know that means I like cock."

Damn. Can you say blunt? I never knew the word *cock* could sound so sexy when wielded ase a threat. He just *cock-wielded* me. "Okay. Well, we already have something in common," I joke.

Frowning, he raises an index finger over his coffee cup. "Excuse me for having doubts, but if you lost some kind of bet where you had to go on a gay dating app, now's your chance to fess up. Because I clearly recall seeing you hanging on a woman at the carnival the other day, where you then proceeded to make eyes and wave at my roommate."

I have to bite my cheek to keep from laughing at the irony. This explains the attitude. The poor guy thinks I'm a big flirt or worse, some asshole trying to prank him.

"First off, I'm bisexual. Thanks for making assumptions though, and *Heather Barlow*…" I pause to bait him and smirk, "invited *herself* to my birthday party at the carnival the other day after which, I went home alone…alone and *still* thinking about the flustered guy in the apple-green shirt who ignored me when I tried to *make eyes* and wave at *him*."

The fight goes out of his face. His focus switches to picking at the lid of his coffee. "It was spearmint," he mutters. "And…um, happy birthday."

"Thank you. Anything else you need cleared up?"

Chewing his lip, I can tell he's battling with whatever's going through that head of his. I make a sweep of my hand over the table. "Go ahead. Ask me anything."

"You're really bisexual?"

"Yes."

"Is this…a recent thing for you?"

"I didn't know there were prerequisites," I tease.

Folding his arms, he looks across the café. "Of course not, but there's a prerequisite if you're just looking to experiment."

That sounds like there's a story there, but now doesn't seem like the time to push for it. "I can assure you I passed that test years ago."

Thank you, Mom, for making me go to that gay bar to keep an eye on Maxie for her twenty-first. I left all my high school repression behind when I left there that night, but Johnny doesn't seem like he's too interested in small talk or an Aiden-history lesson. I'm not giving up hope yet. I mean, that app matched us for reason.

At a loss of how to segue, I'm grateful for the waitress who breezes up to our table with a platter of appetizers and a caffeinated smile.

"Would either of you like to try a sample of our new garlic brioche bites?"

"Pass. Thank you," Johnny says with a tight smile.

"No, thanks. I'm allergic," I tell the young woman who excuses herself to barrage the next table.

"You're allergic to garlic?" Johnny asks. "I can't imagine."

Nine times out of ten when people find out my food allergy, I get the obligatory, *what are you—a vampire?* After the way I've been striking out since our introduction, it's nice to see he doesn't fall into that cliché.

"Well, if you're used to not eating something because it makes you ill, you really don't miss it.'

"No, I totally get it." He raises a hand, and I'm wondering if I'm finally hearing his unguarded sincerity. "I'm allergic to alcohol. I just meant, it's like…everywhere, so trying to find something to eat or wonder if somebody's about to poison you must get tiresome."

Wow. Someone who actually understands. That's a relief. Maybe we're done playing defensive. "Alcohol, huh? I'd have to say the same."

"You have no idea." He scoffs, hooking his arm over the back of his chair all casual. "My family tries to kill me on a daily basis. Allergies are just a suggestion to them," he says with a cynical laugh, but cuts it off suddenly. He goes rigid again like he realized he might actually be enjoying my company.

What is the deal with this guy?

Turning his wrist, he glances at his watch and clears his throat. "Well, it was nice meeting you," he says and gets up. "A-again."

Shit. Is he really leaving already?

"Hey. Wait up. I'll walk you out."

Brushing a nonexistent something off his jeans, he gives me a prune smile and keeps walking. "No need. I'm a big boy, I think I can find my way. Plus, daylight and all." He gestures to the glass door to the back parking lot with a nervous laugh.

"It's fine. My parents taught me to use my manners."

"How sweet."

I don't know much about him, but I think it's safe to assume at this point that anything that *should* sound like a compliment from Johnny Andro's mouth is not intended as one. Lucky for me, I'm not easily offended.

Thanks for that, Graham, Maxie, and Skyler.

I reach around him and hold the door open. I'd give anything to know why he looks at me like a kid looks at a doctor holding a syringe.

"Oh, look. We made it outside. Safe and sound." Johnny praises skyward, but when his gaze returns to mine, he seems to flounder for a second like he isn't as curt as he lets on. Damn it, if I'm not doing the same. I don't want this to end with him all pissy, especially when it barely started.

He sucks in a breath and quips, "Well, this was fun."

Four words have never sounded less like fun.

"You sound like you don't mean that."

"Hm. You are handsome *and* perceptive."

Is he for real? What the hell did I do?

"Do I get a chance to return *half* that compliment?"

He snorts and folds his arms over his chest. "Smooth talker too. I bet the ladies eat that up."

Oh, hell no. This again?

He turns, presumably to abandon me, but I rest my hand on his bicep.

"Hold up a minute. Will you? Is me being bisexual a problem for you or something?"

"What?" His eyes widen in shock. "No! I get enough shit from my family to not judge anybody's love life. That's not what I meant."

I store that depressing factoid away for later…if there is a later.

"Well, then can you explain that little dig to me?"

"I…I'm sorry. That was rude. I've only seen you with a woman, so it just came out."

Raising my index finger, I counter, "Not true. I'm with

you right now."

"Noted," he grumbles. Man, even his grimace is sexy. He does that glasses-nudging thing again, looking all sorts of insecure and sophisticated. "I apologize."

"No worries," I reassure him. Man, this guy needs a handler. Great. Now I'm thinking about handling him. Get ahold of yourself, Aiden. "So…do you want to go back inside and try this again?"

Why is he looking at me like I suggested we shave our heads? What the hell am I doing wrong?

"Wouldn't you just rather spare ourselves the pleasantries and say goodbye now instead?"

"What? Why? Did I offend you?"

"No, but we both know *this*," he waggles his finger between us, "just won't work."

"Why is that?" I at least need some notes about why I'm getting tossed off without a thought.

Folding his arms, he does the impossible and looks even angrier. "Really? You're going to make me say it?"

I am speechless at this point. This guy's mind is a labyrinth. All I can do is shrug, holding my palms out.

He lets out a breath to show me how exasperating this is for him. "There is no way someone like *you*," he gestures as though indicating my physique, "can be into someone like *me*, so why waste each other's time?"

And then…he's quiet. Hand on his hip, he looks off to the parking lot as though he's bracing himself for me to concur. The tense lines of his profile indicate how much his belief in that declaration wounded him.

His defeated posture is absolutely heartbreaking, amping up the powerful need to touch him I've had since locking eyes on him the other day. It's ironic we've been bickering about other issues only for me to find out it was a deflection tactic, because he thinks I'm not really into him due to our differences in appearance.

I know more about self-doubt than people think. The last few years of soul-searching have given me a painful education.

I take a step closer to avoid the door in case anyone comes outside. The tension in Johnny's face turns into apprehension like he thinks I'm going to clobber him.

Wow. The guy really has no clue. He moves back, bumping into the exterior wall of the building as I lean into his space, reaching out and touching his jaw. He gapes up at me, perplexed.

"We can easily clear that up," I murmur.

"W-we can?"

When he swallows, my eyes are snared by the undulation of his throat. The well the movement creates under his Adam's Apple leaves my lips begging to kiss it. All the bravado in his eyes is gone, and, my God, he's even more handsome when his claws are retracted.

I can see it all in those big brown eyes blinking up at me. He's just a man, putting on a show. I don't know what brought on the show, but there's a different guy behind the mask than the one who tried to chew me up and spit me out. The desire to reassure the version hiding behind the veil draws me in.

Half-daring, half-unable to resist, I run the pad of my thumb across his jawline. When I make it to the edge of his lower lip, he sucks in a breath. It's barely audible, but I hear it—a needy little whimper that goes straight to my balls.

"Yeah," I breathe at his lips, feeling the heat of his breath mix with mine. "Like this."

Brushing a slant across his soft lips, his mouth remains immobile against mine. I was sure if what I was feeling was so powerful, it meant he'd be experiencing a modicum of the same. His lack of reaction makes it clear I'm an intruder, a guy who got his feelings hurt and is trying to recoup his pride by way of an unwanted kiss.

Shit. I must look like a pushy creep.

Pulling away, I run my hand over my offending lips, my cheeks burning at the confusion on his face. I'm never going to figure out this dating thing. How could there be nothing when I was so sure this felt like something?

His shocked eyes are asking for an explanation, but all I can manage to get out is a dumbstruck, "Oh."

"*Oh?* Oh, *what?* What is *oh?*" he demands, the heat in his voice returning.

"Just…uh. Nothing." All I can do is shake my head as I take a step back to give him space from my idiocy.

Pursing his lips, he makes a halting gesture with his hand. "Wait. Forgive me for not understanding, but please explain why you initiated what was, I presume, an effort to prove you're attracted to me, and yet you look disappointed. My assessment was correct, wasn't it?"

Another blast of mortification pummels me from head to toe. I realize I've never been turned down, having never really been the pursuer in my illustrious love life. Shit. Now, I'm wondering if my skills are lacking.

"No. It's not that. I just…Sorry. Some people aren't good kissers."

He sucks in a sharp gasp. "Ex-cuuuse me?"

"Oh! No! I didn't mean—" Before I can clarify that I was taking the blame for the lackluster kiss, he grabs two handfuls of my shirt and jerks me forward with a surprising amount of strength. My palm slaps the wall to keep my balance as he crushes his mouth against mine.

Damn. Offended Johnny is a man of action.

He's demanding, prying my lips open with urgent nudges. Holy hell—his taste. That first taste pulls me from my shock. When his tongue crests my lips, I welcome it with my own, clutching his arm when he wraps a hand around the back of my neck. It's ten-fold what I hoped for.

Drowning. Tugging. Giving. Taking.

Something inside me is waking up, ravenous for whatever is in this fiery kiss as we slant and devour, slant and devour. Johnny Andro can freaking kiss.

I'm eating his little moan-y puffs of breath, exchanging them with my own, decimating the word *stranger* between us. My fingers are in his hair, his in mine, our bodies pressed against each other like it's a battle to crawl inside the other person.

The gritty texture of mortar crumbling against my elbow reminds me we're pressed up against a building in broad daylight, but I don't care. I've waited my entire life to feel this level of want, *need*, for someone. When he bucks his hips into mine, and I feel the outline of arousal press into my own, I groan, clutching his jean-covered ass to keep the connection. I will never have an errant thought about dating apps again.

The problem with this much delirium is that you eventually have to breathe. When we break and our foreheads rest against each other's, I'm panting right along with him.

"That…that was better. Right?" he gasps.

"Yeah." I nod against him, my eyes memorizing every inch of shocked pleasure on his face, imagining mine must look the same. "A lot better," I add, brushing a soft peck against his lower lip.

His grip slackens on my shirt. I'm forced to relinquish my hold when he straightens up and smooths down his mussed hair.

"Okay!" he chirps, startling me. "Fantastic. Bye now!" He spins on his heel and takes off across the parking lot.

"Wait! Where are you—"

"Nice to meet you. Have a nice life," he calls, flapping a hand over his shoulder without giving me a second glance.

"What? Johnny! Wait. I—" My calls are futile as he does a perfect impersonation of a man whose ass is on fire and slides into the driver's seat of a black Saab, turning the engine over the second he's inside.

Shielding my face from the spray of gravel when he peels out, all I can do is stare. Who on God's green earth can walk away from a kiss like that, and how the hell am I supposed to forget it?

CHAPTER 8

Johnny,

Why are you always gone when I stop by?

Last night was...amazing.
I don't know now why I've only been kissing girls
my whole life.

See you tonight.

Lance

(Can't wait!)

CHAPTER 9

Johnny

You know what's worse for your metabolism than being force fed at every turn? Eating dinner at nine at night. When your family owns restaurants, that's when it's most convenient for them to have supper.

Tonight's binge is courtesy of Uncle Dimitris and Aunt Donetta's restaurant, Tapas, rather than Oikos, because everyone must contribute to the weekly gluttony, lest someone feel slighted. There's a reason I didn't lose the baby fat in my cheeks until I was fifteen and discovered the school's track team. Size doesn't matter, but there are these things called arteries and cholesterol. I just so happen to give a damn about mine.

My little cousin Damiano unceremoniously takes the seat next to me, bashing me in the shoulder as he squeezes into the tight space around the packed banquet table. Yes. Fuck elbow room. That shit doesn't live here. Nothing says family like rubbing someone else's sweat on your arm.

"Let me guess. You just came from the gym?" I ask, eyeing Dami's glistening arms.

"Yeah." He beams, loading up his plate with pastitsio.
"It was arm day."

"Mm. Lovely."

It is an injustice that he can shovel that many carbs into his pie hole and not suffer the consequences. The boy hasn't done a lick of cardio in his life, while I'd feel like a lead weight if I had his appetite. It's also not fair that he got a cool, sexy name like *Damiano*, who we affectionately call *Dami*. I got stuck with *Giannis*, which may sound wholesome in Greek but screams *weird-foreigner* to Americans.

If only my father had married an Italian like Uncle Dimitris did, then maybe I'd be a foot taller like Dami with his bronze skin and stupidly straight ebony hair that sweeps over his brow like a damn underwear model. Four years younger than me, the guy makes me look like I still haven't gone through puberty.

"You need any help with setting up props again?" he asks.

"No." My answer is quick and bitter, indicative of my foul mood since yesterday's fiasco.

Dami will do anything to get out of washing dishes at Tapas since returning from college, so I'm aware it's rather salty of me to crush his dreams. It's just because I'm in a funk, but it's not my job to help him find himself. Sighing, I slice off a sliver of *saganaki* and set it on my plate before my mother can see it's empty.

There. Deep fried cheese. That should be unhealthy enough to appease her. "Maybe," I concede, but his hopeful look weighs on my stupid conscience. "Yeah. Whatever. I'll call you."

"Great! I'll do anything you need."

"Mm."

My brother strides through the door with his brood in tow, and my gaze zeros in at the bane of my existence. I know it is neither normal nor acceptable to stare at your brother's penis, but I blame his penchant for wearing sweatpants and the way he walks like it would be a burden to his nuts to maintain a normal stride. He is the reason I am scarred for life by a conundrum no man should have to ponder.

Just in case anyone doubted that my family came *straight off the boat*, as they say, my darling parents decided to stick to tradition and forgo the American custom of "snipping" the foreskin of their male children. I had no problem with this until a place called the high school locker room, where Ignorant Johnny was given an education on what penises in America are supposed to look like.

Andreas rebelled after his wedding, removing my parents' cultural preference from the end of his manhood. He did not however give me the hope that I too could one day have a coveted American-looking penis.

Instead, he related a very detailed complaint about how "the snip" procedure greatly reduced his sensitivity, therefore infringing on his love life. Alas, I am still carting the dreaded flap of skin around the tip of my dick, and every time my brother struts into a room, I am reminded of the what the outcome would be should I allow some doctor to maim *Flapper*.

Yes, *Flapper*—because all men name their penises and naming mine for the flap of skin sheathed around its head sounded much swanker than *Sheather*.

My dick dilemma is interrupted when Uncle Dimitris lets loose a cloud of smoke from his cigarette into my face, leaving me sputtering for air. He thwaps me on the back, surely dislocating a rib.

"*Daksi*, Giannis?"

Fuck no! I'm not okay, but I nod as my eyes water.

Mamá hands me her wine. "Here. Drink something. Are you

getting sick?"

Yes. Of course. My complete intolerance to alcohol will cure a sec-ondhand smoke cough, which must really be a cold since I am the weak-ling of this posse.

"I'm good." I wave her off and force down a sip of my tea.

"Dami, how is Angelica?" my mother prods Dami about his local girlfriend.

"Good. She got a job in Chicago."

"So far away? How are you going to make it work?"

Dami lets loose the painful laugh of Greek children being forcibly paired. "*Thia* we're just friends."

"It's okay. You are young and handsome. You have plenty of time." She turns to me next, however. "Giannis, Grace and her mother are com-ing to Oikos Friday night. Can you wear something nice to dinner?"

I spray a mist of *Lipton* across Dami's face at her words. Now the woman's mother is involved? That's two mothers to contend with or worse—two terrified women my mother brow beat into meeting my mother's disappointingly less than average, very un-straight, fore-skin-sporting son.

"I can't!" I wheeze and toss Dami my napkin. "I…I'm dating already. Remember?"

"You're dating?" Dami asks.

"Uh…yes. Yeah. Yup."

"Who?" Mamá asks.

"His name?" I blink, my throat suddenly dry. I was not told I'd have to provide a name. What's next, a hair sample?

"Aiden Brandt," Bitsy supplies from across the table. I'd kick her but there's too many legs under the table to trust my accuracy.

"Brandt," Dami hums, "Brandt and Sons redid our patio wall last summer. Those Brandts? The brick masons?"

Uncle Dimitris grunts. "It's beautiful. Look at it!"

"Yes, but it was just one date."

Mamá gasps excitedly. "You had a date? That is such good news! How did it go?"

"I…it…" Just lie. It'll be fine. Damn it, I have no backbone. "I think it was a mix-up."

"What is a mix-up? What does that mean? Did you go on a date or not?" Mamá asks.

Bitsy arches an amused brow as she licks tzatziki off her fingers. I send her a glare still remembering the sound of her triumphant laugh-ter when I told her the Foot Collector ended up being none other than Carnival Man.

Waving a hand, I whack off more saganaki. Maybe if I consume enough grease, Mamá will leave me be.

Fuck it. Be bold. Lie!

I decide to stick with the stupid accusation I tried to convince myself of yesterday to protect me from Aiden's potent magnetism. What the fuck will my family care anyway? "It means, I don't even think he's gay."

"Wait," Andreas pipes in. "Did you say Aiden Brandt?"

How the hell does Andreas know him? "Yes. Why?"

"He played for Olympus West."

Rolling my eyes, I jab a hunk of heart-attack cheese and shove it into my mouth. Football. Of course, the brick-handed, foot-profile-swiper played football in high school. Just like Lance. One more reason it would never work. I am not even coordinated enough to clean a football.

"And this useless knowledge concerns me because?"

Andreas snorts, dropping ice cubes into his ouzo. "Because if that's the guy I'm thinking of, then I heard he was bisexual." He teeters his hand back and forth, which makes me wish Aiden were here to snap his wrist. Christ, where did that come from—the Aiden part, not Andreas being an ignorant asshole?

"*Heard*?" I ask, mocking his rude caveman gestures with a hand to my ear. "Wow. You should become a spy."

"No." He laughs. "I saw him at a bar a few years ago, kissing a guy."

Why the fuck am I still putting cheese in my mouth? Andreas' intel stops my hand's trajectory. The thought of Aiden kissing another man makes me want to toss my tea in my brother's face for putting that image in my head.

Go with the lie. Be the salty crab ass they think you are, I console myself.

"Kissing *and?*" I challenge, which has nothing to do with an odd bit of jealousy over some man I don't even know kissing Aiden before I knew him.

It must be this fucking cheese. It's making me nonsensical.

Andreas scoffs and pops an olive into his mouth. "It was in public. What do you mean, what else? Isn't kissing in public enough proof?"

"Mm. Yeah, he's good for that," I mutter.

A peculiar sound takes over the patio, a sound I rarely hear around my family—silence. When I look up, all eyes are on me.

"You kissed him," Bitsy stage-whispers accusingly, as though I betrayed her yesterday by omitting that detail of the coffee date fiasco.

The cheese in my stomach swirls. Yes, the fucking cheese. Not butterflies or whatever other insects romantics use to describe attraction. Plus, it's hot out here with Dami's arm shoved up against mine.

That! That is the only reason why a heat wave is running through my body thinking about that kiss.

And…okay. He was attractive. I wear glasses. I'm not fucking blind.

Judging by the *trouser tower* in his pants that tried to do battle with mine, maybe he was attracted to me for those sixty seconds. He's definitely not straight. It wasn't a confused kiss or a curious kiss, it was a full-on exploration of my aura. The man went in hot and left me in ashes.

Well, technically, my pride went in hot. It's my damn crutch. I'm not proud of it, but my bark is usually loud enough to be a trusted defense. The sexy *"swiper"* clearly is not intimidated by the bark, which makes him dangerous.

I can still feel his hand on my ass. He *handfulled* me! I can't even remember the last time I got *handfulled*. He swiped more than my profile for damn sure, *Swiper* indeed. I didn't take him for a man of action, especially action with…well, someone like me. Lance thought I was interesting for about the first year until he learned everything about me. Then I got real boring, real fast, which is why I shut off the part of my brain that sought companionship.

It's cruel actually, what *Swiper* did. He woke the Kraken—that nautical beast of arousal that has been asleep in my bloodstream for six months, when I last scratched an itch on a shoot I did in Chicago.

My cheese addled brain is whispering lurid suggestions that he might be able to scratch better than that blow-job from that DJ at that Chicago modeling expo. Well, I've got one message for that noise.

Zip it!

The overwhelming helplessness of desire I felt for him is too much like the initial reaction I had to the biggest mistake of my life. Not to mention he's built like Adonis, has a lethal smile, easy laugh, and was initially chivalrous. People like him can't be satisfied with people like me long-term. All signs point to a catastrophe of epic proportions.

Kraken, stand down.

The scariest thing I've ever seen stares back at me. My mother's face softens, a slight tilt of her head moving the way I move my clients to get the light to splash their face. It is the face of someone saturated with ideas of love. On her at this moment, it is absolutely terrifying.

Damn it.

"Giannis, when can I meet him?" she practically pleads.

"Oh, no. Not him." My panicked laugh probably betrays the dismissive wave of my hand. "Definitely not a repeat."

"I don't know. You looked a little flustered when you got back to the studio yesterday," Bitsy volunteers, smugness in her eyes. "That must have been some kiss."

Oh, hilarious, Bits. *Hill-arious.* I am putting this noise to bed right now. Slapping my palm to the table for emphasis, I declare, "I was *not* flustered. I do *not* fluster. He's simply not my type, stolen kisses or not. Mm-kay? That's all. End of story."

Mamá's forehead creases, as though she's trying to program computer pages as she studies me. I hate being Mamá-studied.

Cheese. Eat more cheese and you will live.

"What is your type then?" she finally asks.

"Oh, you know…employed, single."

No one at all. Not gorgeous or helpful or polite or a mouth that could incinerate fire-retardant jock straps.

"He's unemployed? I thought Andreas said he is a brick layer?"

"Mamá, he's allergic to garlic. Okay? It would never work."

"Allergic?" she snaps as though giving away *biscotia* on the street is a violation of an enforced law. "What do you mean he doesn't like garlic?"

Sure. Let's stick with that translation.

I throw my hands up in solidarity. "See? Exactly!"

"Sardines?" my father asks, holding a plate in front of my mother with his perpetually innocent smile. I don't miss the wink he throws me. The man's *Columbo* act is brilliant. I return a semblance of a smile to thank him for trying as my mother waves off his offer with a grunt.

"But if you are not dating him," she continues, "then why did you say you are dating? Is there someone else?"

Damn you, solidarity! You have the stamina of a bubble.

"No. Yes!" Cheese poisoning is real. Someone help me. Why are they all staring, like my life is suddenly of the utmost importance? "I am… dating or, well, I *plan* to date again. Soon."

Mamá makes a *tisking* noise, her hands clasped together in prayer pose. "Giannis, you need to meet a good Greek boy like you."

Have I consumed too much dairy? Am I in a lactose-induced hallucinogenic state? My mother just said I need to meet a *boy*—as in a human with a twig and berries.

"Mamá," Andreas chimes in, "we're related to every Greek in the area and none of them are gay."

"So," my sister pipes up, "Stavros, our coffee supplier, met his girl-friend on a Greek dating app. She's from Milwaukee, I think."

Oh, no.

"They have Greek dating apps?" Bitsy brightens.

No, no, no!

Mamá gestures urgently for Bitsy's phone. "Oh, *Eliza-vet*, you show me."

Fuck! The only thing worse than my mother trying to find me a woman is her and Bitsy combined trying to find me a Greek man.

CHAPTER 10

Aiden

It still counts as a dress shirt if you roll up the cuffs, right? Why do people dress up for dates anyway? It's false advertising if you ask me. You're presenting a better version of yourself than what someone would see every day. This was so much easier before I started analyzing everything and…got old.

Stay optimistic, Maxie said.

Right. Okay.

There were some nice women on this new app. None of them jumped out at me, but that could be because I purposely scrolled for feet pics for two hours before I gave up and plugged in all my details. By that point, however, it was futile to think of women. Not with feet and that kiss on my brain. Okay, not feet in general. Just…a certain pair of feet.

Johnny didn't waste any time deleting his profile on *Men About Town*. Great for my ego. I still don't get it. I nearly came apart against a building at eight thirty in the morning, and I swore he did too, then *poof!* Vanished.

Maybe I'll get lucky and lightning will strike twice in one year. Yet, I have the foreboding feeling that skittish, bossy man just set the bar higher.

Damn. I'm totally screwed, aren't I?

Okay, Aiden. Stop thinking about him when you're here to meet another man. It's called dating, so date.

"Oh, sweet baby Jesus! Please tell me this is not what I think it is?"

I know that aggravated voice. Whipping my head to the side, my vision has manifested in a light blue polo shirt and a scowl under the dim glow of the restaurant's patio twinkle lights.

"Johnny?"

"What are you doing here?"

The instinct to greet the man I shared the most passionate kiss of my life with mere days ago overrides my ability to react to his clear displeasure at the sight of me.

"I…it's good to see you."

He thrusts his hand out, palm up, and wriggles his fingers impatiently. "Answer the question, please."

"I…I'm here for dinner."

"*And*…you're wearing *white*," he adds accusingly.

"Y-yeah…" I glance at my white dress shirt and then take him in again. Oh, no way. You've got to be shitting me. "And you're wearing…blue."

He makes an exasperated sound at my declaration and pulls his phone from the back pocket of his jeans. His fingers fly over the screen before he thrusts a screenshot of my new profile on *Adelphi* in my face.

Maxie was right. This shot of my forearms does make them look pretty buff.

"Please tell me you're not *AmericanMade*."

Covering my grin does nothing to suppress my laugh. "*Giannis?*" I venture, remembering the way his backside looked in that speedo he wore for his profile.

"It's pronounced *Yannis*. Mm-kay, but you're not even Greek. So, how…why…." He rubs the bridge of his nose on a long sigh before holding his hand up. "You know what? Don't even tell me. I have officially lost all faith in technology. You have a good evening. The *souvlaki* is delicious."

He drops his hand and starts to turn, sending a shot of panic through me. I remember how fast he can walk, so I shove out of my chair.

"Wait. Wait." I hold out a hand. "I told my family I went on a date with a Greek guy, and my dad mentioned his grandmother was half Greek. I know. It was a reach."

"You told your family about our date?"

"Just that I went on a date with a Greek man." I'm not sure why he looks conflicted, but at least I've got his attention. "You're not going to make me eat alone, are you?"

"Look. You seem like…like a…"

"*Like?*" I prompt.

"*Likable*," he huffs as though the word means *murderer*, "but this is never going to work."

Yeah. I've heard that line already. Not buying it.

"You think I'm likable?" I smirk, although I know that was like pulling a splinter from his palm.

"I said *seemed* likable."

"Is this about the whole attraction thing because…I thought we cleared that up."

The way his face blooms is the best reward. He gives an airy laugh and tugs at his collar. "No!"

"Do I make you nervous or something?"

"Pfft. Nervous? I don't get nervous."

I might not know shit about dating, but I can tell when someone is nervous. Folding my arms across my chest, I don't hold back my smile this time.

"Ah ha! There!" He points at my face. "You see? *Smug!* I knew you had to have a flaw."

Wow. Could he be more entertaining? The fact that he thought I had no flaws goes off in me like champagne bubbles. I also recall him slipping *handsome* into that deflection tirade the other day.

I think he's bothered by me—hot and bothered. I've got news for him: I'm happy to be a bother. It's freaking cute, the way he doesn't seem to want to yield, as though he's being true to some decision he's already made about us being incompatible. As backward as it sounds, I dig it. It's a genuine reaction, a welcome change from the dates I've had who tried too hard to impress me or had no other intention than wanting to get laid.

"It's just dinner," I concede.

He huffs and glances over his shoulder. "Yeah, but my uncle owns the place. I eat here twenty times a week."

"Dimitris Andropolis is your uncle?"

Johnny arches a brow, his gaze unimpressed.

"*Andropolis*," I murmur. "*Andro*. Ah. I see."

"Congratulations. You solved the mystery. I shortened it. Okay? It was a business decision to not be the fifty-seventh Andropolis business in this city. Is there a problem with that?"

So angry. So much passion. Just like that kiss. Since when am I attracted to hostile rejection?

Stop staring at his mouth, dumbass.

"No." I hold up my hands. "That makes sense."

His shoulders settle like maybe I've won one battle and taken some of the fight out of him. His gaze darts around, never landing on me for more than a split second. I need to say something before he rushes off to delete another profile.

"Well, seeing that you've got connections here, why don't you stay and be my cultural advisor?" I gesture to the chair across from mine.

"Wow. Such a tempting offer—pretending to be Greek for thirty more minutes of my day."

"You're not?"

Scoffing, he yanks out the seat from under the table. "Don't be cute. Look. My uncle will report to my mother if I skip out. Her insistence that I date is the only reason I'm staying. And...I may actually be hungry."

Thank God.

Casually, I sit back down, lest any sudden movements frighten him off. "What do you recommend?" I ask, reaching for the dip the waiter brought earlier, thankful I can finally put something in my empty stomach.

Johnny's hand clamps over top of mine. Is he some kind of stingy bastard with food?

"Do you have a death wish?" he demands.

I'm too distracted by the fact he touched me to figure out what he means. His smooth skin is warm over the top of mine like two people holding hands at a romantic dinner. He glances down and pulls his hand back, then shakes out his napkin.

"That's hummus." He gestures to the dip. "*Loaded* with garlic."

He remembered my allergy? Secondly, he took it seriously? Nine out of ten people assume I'm joking.

"It's a Greek restaurant." He shrugs, thrusting his jaw to indicate Tapas. "Just assume everything has garlic. And eat fast. If we stay a minute longer than when our plate is clear, out comes the ouzo, and it'll get ugly."

"That's liquor. Right?"

He does that grunting huff noise he does, like an entire word would be too exhausting for him to form. "Mm."

"I thought you couldn't drink liquor."

His gaze flickers to mine, blinking. The surprise in his expression tugs at my heart, knowing it suggests people disregard his allergy as well. I gaze back, giving him a sympathetic smile.

His eyes dash to the menu. "I can't."

"Have you ever had it?"

"Oh, yeah." He lets loose a sour chuckle.

"Did you like the taste?"

"Not particularly, which is just one of my many crimes against being Greek."

We're almost on our way to an entire conversation and he's still sitting here, so I stick with the chit chat. It seems safe so far. "Is it bad? I've never had it."

And…he frowns. Aside from Graham, I don't know anyone who's ever looked so annoyed by my presence. It is now my life's goal to get this man to smile.

"How have you never managed to drink ouzo while living in Olympus all your life?"

"I work a lot. When I go out for drinks it's usually to a bar with my siblings after we're done working for the day."

"There's more of you?"

His widened eyes are amusing. "Two brothers and Maxie."

"What's a *Maxie?* Your cocker spaniel?"

Does he know how funny he is? "No," I chuckle. "Maxine. She's my sister."

"Oof. Treacherous nickname for a girl."

"More like treacherous for anyone who messes with her," I warn.

Johnny's entire demeanor changes before my eyes. "Oh. Um. Sorry, I…"

"No. It's alright. I just meant, she can handle her own."

"Well," he makes a cursory scan of my torso, "if she has the same genes as you, I can imagine."

Hm. Someone just checked me out. Now his face is a shade pink, and he won't take his eyes off the menu I assume he knows by heart. Hot and bothered indeed.

Johnny wears a smoke screen, and I think I have a chance of blasting through it. Maybe I don't suck at dating as much as I thought. I just had to meet someone as wary about it as me.

"Aiden! *Kali spera.* Welcome. How are you?" Dimitris calls, bustling over to our table from behind Johnny. "How you like, huh?" He extends his arms in a sweep toward the patio wall we put in last summer. "Still looking good."

"It sure does." I smile, giving him a nod. "It's good to see you again, Dimitris."

His face lights in surprise when he sees Johnny who's resting his forehead in his hand like he's either trying to be invisible or has a migraine.

"Ah! You know our Giannis?"

I have no idea what Johnny tells his family about his love life, but his wary look sets off a protective instinct inside me. "We…just met, actually."

"Giannis, I thought your mother said you have a date tonight," Dimitris exclaims.

"I…" Johnny stammers and then swallows. Damn. It's surreal to see him speechless.

Dimitris' furry eyebrows twitch as he looks from Johnny to me and back again. His hands smack together with a *crack* noise, and his face brightens. "Oh! Of course! Okay. Is good. Is perfect! Yes. *Aiden* is your date." He beams, clearly pleased with his intuition. "This is wonderful. Aiden, such a good boy!" He gestures to me, but then slaps a hand on Johnny's shoulder a little harder than comfortable, by the way Johnny flinches. "And our Giannis is…is such…" The dimming of Dimitris' gusto wouldn't be as comical without that pout on Johnny's mug. "He is…uh, heh heh…*Giannis,*" Dimitris finally amends as though that says it all about the man I'm trying to figure out.

As Johnny's expression darkens from that pitiful shout out, the recipe for some of his grumpiness becomes clear. It makes me wonder what's earned him the unspoken title of sourpuss. Yet, there's a part of me that understands how our families can embarrass the crap out of us.

"Um, Thios?" Johnny straightens and clears his throat. "Can we order, please?

"*Lipon*. Of course!" Dimitris says something in Greek.

Johnny replies by rattling off his response in Greek too, placing his order, I assume. The sounds roll effortlessly off his tongue, strange yet intoxicating. He's clearly in his element in his family's mother tongue, confident, natural...calm. There are so many layers to this guy, each one more intriguing than the last. I'm transfixed by his entire sexy package.

Now they're both staring at me. Shit. Did Johnny say something to me?

"Sorry, what?"

"Do you know what you want?" he asks slowly like I'm a five-year-old.

You, echoes in my head, but I rein in my brain which is becoming so besotted with the enigma of him and this compounding attraction, it's alarming. "Uh, why don't you surprise me?"

That was a mistake. Another stream of Greek flows from his lips, this time more commanding, his gestures more pronounced. Why do I find that so erotic?

I don't know a word of the language, but by the way he holds Dimitris' gaze as he motions to me, I'm pretty sure he's warning his eccentric uncle not to feed me any garlic. This feisty, nerdy looking guy, who thus far has acted like my existence is a nuisance, looking out for my best interests—that's hot as hell.

Yeah. I never saw this coming, but I'd like an endless order of it.

Dimitris nods and chuckles, ruffling Johnny's hair as he collects the menus. Johnny's gasp goes unnoticed by his uncle, but I can't ignore it. He strokes his hair back, continually running his palms over the top of his head, scowling all the while.

"I think you got it."

Exhaling, his serious cocoa eyes find me. "He *fluffed* me," he huffs. "One more reason you really don't want me. These sleek locks?" He points at his head. "That's all product, baby, but in the morning, you wake up next to a *McDonalds fry guy*. It's not pretty."

Baby. The word makes me shift in my seat at the mental picture of waking up next to him looking like that. That would be a first for me—waking up next to a man, not bed head.

All of my evenings with men have been just that—*evenings*. Does Johnny have evenings that turn into mornings or is it just me he wants to exclude from that possibility?

"Can you explain to me why you keep going on dating apps if you're not interested in dating?" I inquire.

"Do you have a mother?"

"Yes."

"What's she like?"

"Um, well, she was a homemaker, raising me and my brothers and sister. She used to mend our clothes, which needed mending a lot. We were kind of rambunctious."

The corner of his mouth ticks up, so I continue. "After we got older, she kind of made a business out of it, being a seamstress."

"That explains your abilities with swatches," he mumbles into his tea.

"Oh, the shirt thing?"

He shrugs, his gaze scanning the restaurant as though it's paining him to give me his attention. Damn it. Maybe there's no cracking Johnny Andro.

"Well, Mom's sweet and caring. Funny, easy going, I guess."

Johnny's lithe fingers toss an olive in his mouth, his jaw working. "Of course, she is. Well, mine's…Greek."

That's it. That's his description.

"And?" I prompt.

"Really? You want to go there?"

If it keeps those glasses pointed my way and lets me peer inside his ironclad vault for a second? You bet, Salty.

"Yeah. So far, all I know about you is what your feet look like and how you look in a speedo."

Scoffing, his face goes red. "Ahem. That was the result of my best friend collaborating with my mother. I'm a photographer, just so you know. If I were to pick a profile picture, it would be of an appropriate body part."

Shifting in his seat, he must know the mention of "body part" could have been better worded. He sucks in a long breath and waves that dramatic hand of his. "So, I'm twenty-seven. Wait. How old are you?

"Thirty-one."

"Really?" He frowns and gives me a quick once over.

"Yeah. Why?"

His head rattles back and forth. Another bat of the hand. "Nothing. So…*mothers*. Mamá invades my apartment twice a week to make sure I have clean underwear. Because as the youngest of my siblings, I simply cannot be trusted to properly care for my own underthings—no matter that I'm pushing thirty. When it rains, I'm going to get pneumonia and die, which means I was practically wrapped in cellophane until the age of twelve. I am not gay. That is just a suggestion…well, until recently.

Maybe. I don't know, but if she introduces me to another Mary Sue, Helena, Sarah, Katie, Pamela, Leigh Ann, Alexa, Colleen, Bridget, or my favorite—Bonnie Rae—so I can fall happily in love and produce her twelve strapping Greek grandchildren, I may have to move out of the country. What else? Let's see."

He drums his fingers on the table. "Food can cure sadness, anxiety, insomnia, and probably tuberculosis. Think you're full? Nonsense. Your stomach can't think for itself. Three more helpings will solve that. Insolence, a.k.a. having your own opinion, is heartbreak of the severest kind. Oh, you moved out of state to go to school to learn how to press a camera button? *Why do you want to abandon your family?* You finally moved back home? We need you to go take pictures at Mikhalis' wedding. He's your second cousin twice removed whom you've met once!" He emphasizes with his index finger. "*Once*, so you can't very well charge him or any other relative for taking a few pictures with your *little* camera, and don't miss dinner at the restaurant tonight. We've only seen you thirty-seven times this week. It's like you're practically a stranger." He ends with a sardonic laugh.

Jesus. I can feel the weight of his crushed soul from across the table.

"That…sounds like a lot."

"Exactly. So maybe go easy on the swiping, *Swiper*."

"*Swiper?* It takes two to swipe."

"*I* didn't do the swiping. My phone was…bushwhacked. Literally. Keep up."

Oh, ho. He thinks that's how this is going to go? I lift cinder blocks for weights. I'm not afraid of his bark or his bite.

He steamrolls on, "So, why don't you lay off the app circuit for a couple weeks since the universe has affected the alignment of the satellites or whatever technological fuckery led to this…whatever this hopefully, one day, hilarious joke is. At least, until I've met my quota to satisfy *the boss*," he says with air quotes, "so you and I don't have any more mishaps."

"I'm a mishap, huh? Gee, thanks."

I've got thick skin. I was half-joking, but he ruffles, once again telling me this tough-guy act is all a routine.

"I…you're just…not my type, and I'm not yours," he adds with finality.

He's just thrown his gauntlet. I can think of a dozen arguments to his bossy plea disguised as a warning. Dimitris arrives with our food though, so I lock it up.

How does he know what my type is? I don't even know what my type is. It's insanity that I want to tip this table over and get his mouth on mine again. I don't understand it. The guy practically hates me. Maybe it's because I've never had to work for it like Graham and Maxie suggested. Maybe I feel cheated that he's not even giving a thought to giving me a chance. All I know is, I'm certainly not going to push him, and for a guy who does a lot of talking, it feels like he isn't saying something. That makes me want a chance at finding out that *something*. I've never given much consideration to fate, but there has to be a reason we keep running into each other.

CHAPTER 11

Johnny...

I know we just said goodbye, but I also know how
much you like my notes ;)

You are...perfect.
I don't know why I never thought of being with a
man until I met you, but I don't care about
trying to figure it out. That was the hottest
experience of my life. Looking forwar to more of them.

My place tonight? The 49ers are playing.
I'm counting on you to distract me.

Lance
xoxo

CHAPTER 12

Johnny

Eating is the act of shoveling food into one's mouth, which makes it a completely inopportune activity to mix with speaking. So why do I feel compelled to say something to the big hulking swiper across the table, who's gone mute since I delivered my motives?

Okay, maybe it was a bit…blunt? I mean, he should know what he's getting. Right?

Nothing. He's getting nothing. I even spelled it out. Judging by the little prune smiles I'm getting between every few bites, he can spell. He's a damned *Scrabble* champion. God, he looks so sad.

Fuck me. Why do I care?

Because we know what sad feels like, Johnny.

Yes, *Self!* I remember. Now shut it!

"My, um, brother played football at Olympus East," I say.

"Yeah?"

"Ahem, uh, yeah. He mentioned your family name sounded like someone who played for Olympus West back in the day."

He folds his tanned brick worker hands under his chin, the cords in his exposed forearms flexing. I swallow. Lord, he is simply awful—awful freaking delicious.

"My brothers and I all did."

"Mm. That's…"

That's what? That's I-hate-how-much-you-remind-me-of-Lance nice? I need some damn cheese. "Um…interesting."

"You like football?"

Why he looks like he's hoping I say no is baffling. The man screams goalie or quarterback or whatever it is they refer to them as in those little tight pants and pads.

"The pointy one or the round one?"

He…*snorts* at me and chuckles. My hair curls in anger, but the hint of that maddening smile behind his hand makes my cock buck in my jeans. Damn it.

Down, Flapper! I know it makes him look shy but he's the devil in a unicorn costume. Stick with the program.

"You like European football then, I take it?" he ventures.

"Does this body say athlete to you?"

It wasn't meant literally, but he gives me a cursory perusal that makes my heart hammer, before he looks back to his plate. "Yeah." He shrugs. "It kind of does."

Hm. Fine. *Devil Reincarnate* can have one consolation point because my ego is not a cactus.

"I…run. Everyday. I mean, it's practically a requirement in this family if you weren't born with Zeus genes."

"Zeus genes?"

"Greek god. It was a figure of speech. Some people come from the womb ready made to evolve into their natural state of physical perfection. Others? Well, let's just say some of us are cast to be the palm boys, the ones who fan the higher beings with those giant leaves."

Am I boring him? I mean, that was kind of the point—shake him off this silly interest he thinks he has in me and cut him loose, but can you say, *rude?* What the hell does he keep looking at?

The direction of Swiper's gaze takes me to three unemployed figures leaning on the sill of the pass-through window of Tapas. Thia Donetta, Thios Dimitris, and Dami are perched, looking like bobble-head dolls, as though Swiper and I are one of those nature mating programs you can't tear your eyes from.

Fuck.

How long have they been peeping on us? The nosey Cretans.

A hundred bucks and my box set of Panos Kiamos' greatest hits says they've made a phone call to my mother.

Thia Donetta flashes a cupid smile and waves her fingers. No! No, no, no.

"You about done there, big fella?"

His fork pauses halfway to his sculpted lips. I can see the tip of the tongue I tasted, but I don't care. I also don't care how attractive it is that he eats vegetables like a boss. This is code red.

"Uh, yeah. Why? You need to get going?"

"Yes. Pronto, and we need to walk out together."

He makes that amused puff of breath thing he does when he thinks I'm funny that gives me goosebumps, and sets his fork down. "What made you think I was going to up and leave you?"

"No time for flirting. There are spies among us." I tilt my head to the interior of Tapas as I shove my phone in my pocket. "It won't look good if we go our separate ways in front of everyone."

Oh, great. Now where the fuck did Dimitris go?

Probably to go dial one-eight-hundred-Mamá. That's where.

"Hey, Johnny," Swiper's voice intrudes, his index finger landing a single tap on my knuckle. "I've got you. Relax."

Perhaps it's the result of duress, but that understanding in his eyes is…soothing. For a second or two, I'm not a naked T-bone in a piranha tank. But what does he know? These are Andropolises we're dealing with here.

Relax? What the fuck is that?

Jumping to my feet, I straighten the stupid, baby blue polo I dug out of my closet to conform with Mamá and Bitsy's Greek flag color scheme for this mis-matchmaking scheme from hell.

"Yeah, well, move it or lose it. I don't mean that as a command. It's advice, if you want to get out of here alive."

Swiper is….surprisingly agile for a mountain of bricks and surprisingly tall, looming a good three inches over me. The wingspan of his shoulders makes me feel safe, want to climb him like a jungle gym, and take lessons on submissiveness.

For the love of Telly Savalas, I didn't even eat any cheese. What is wrong with me?

Sleep, Kraken. Zip it, Flapper. Feet, move!

A quick scuttle through Tapas, a few cheeky laughs to Thia Donetta, and we're safe on the sidewalk out front. The glow from the streetlamp highlights all the right places on Swiper's face as he catches up beside me. It's one of those hold-my-breath shots, where my lungs won't expand until the aperture has clicked open. I wish I had my camera. He's so damn beautiful, I want to laugh deliriously.

And then I smell it…

Thios Dimitris is sitting in his people-watching chair under the canopy of the restaurant window. The cherry on his cigarette illuminates in the shadows like the Terminator's laser eye, a plume of smoke billowing around us. His thick mustache rises at the corners.

Yes. He's just a sweet, old, innocent man enjoying the night air with a side of lung cancer. Nice try, Dimitris. I've got your number.

I narrow my eyes at his nosey-tattling-bastardness. He sees my glare and raises it with more mustache athletics, his pleased grin widening.

Fine. Ignore him. Cue the awkward goodbye.

"Well, this was fun," I tell Swiper.

"You said that last time."

"This was…almost as much fun."

He glances at Dimitris. When he speaks next, it sounds staged, like… maybe he actually understands my predicament and realizes what a pain in the ass my uncle is. "Can I walk you to your car?"

Okay, it's…almost sweet that he's making an effort to go along with this ruse. Almost.

"Um, no. I walked actually, but…thank you."

"Oh, well, I can give you a lift." He gestures to a black and chrome Harley Davidson propped on the street. I have now lost my ever-loving mind.

Me with my legs wrapped around his hips, the motor rumbling beneath us, my arms clutching his thick frame, my face pressed to the back of his neck, inhaling a hit of that scent I got at the café—call a fucking ambulance.

"Johnny?"

"Huh?"

"You want a ride?"

Oh, I want a *ride*.

"No," I mouse-squeak like my nuts are being pinched. "No need. It's just down the street." I flip my thumb toward the studio.

"Oh. Well, I can walk you home," he suggests, darting a peek at Dimitris.

"No. Really. It's like three blocks."

Mamá's chain-smoking henchman bursts, "Ah! Is a nice night for a walk. Romantic!"

Burn in hell, mustache! Burn. In. Hell.

My nostrils flare at my now least favorite uncle. One day I will wear big boy pants and be in charge of my own life. As God as my witness, Scarlett!

Spinning toward home, I throw over my shoulder, "Sure. Let's hit it."

His long muscular legs catch up to me in two strides. I can feel Dimitris investigative reporter vibes on me like cooties.

"He's going to stare at us until we're out of sight," I warn under my breath.

Warmth envelopes my hand, rough calloused warmth. My pulse goes off like a missile. Swiper is holding my hand.

Relax.

Right.

Holding hands doesn't mean anything. He must have taken my Dimitris-warning seriously, having my back so we look…couple-y. This is good, actually. Run in and phone that to Mamá, Thios. I can handle three blocks of hand holding. Three long blocks of…did he just graze my knuckles with his thumb?

Uhn.

Don't feel, Johnny. Don't feel!

Lock that shit up.

Why would it be a problem that his chivalry checks another one of my Lance-boxes? That big, straight-but-gay-for-me, stupid, surf-er-haired, handholding, rescue-me-from-jelly-fish, football-loving, morning-snuggling, love-note-writing, dirty-cheater.

Nope. No matter.

"You moved back here after college?" Swiper glances at me, look-ing all rugged school-boy with his other hand tucked in the pock-et of his jeans.

"Two years ago. I…had a little studio in California." How sad is it that's it's still difficult for me to say the word *California?* I swallow the lump in my throat, but the fluttering in my stomach from this perfect scratchy hand in mine forces it back up. "I…did a lot of traveling for shoots, so I didn't need a big place. Mostly modeling shoots. You know, jet setting to paradise and all. It was no Mykonos or anything, but yeah. Horrible life," I say sarcastically.

"*Mykonos?*"

Stupid me and my worldly mouth. One more reason I cannot blend in with Midwesterners.

"It's like the *Gay-Sex-Island* of the Cyclades in Greece."

He lets out an airy, sexy puff of air like sex talk might embarrass him, which is *not* adorable. Not at all. *Groan.* Kill me now.

"Oh. Well, the photo thing sounded like a sweet gig. Why'd you move back?"

My hand finally remembers what's good for it and makes a break. Pounding the last few steps of pavement toward Studio Andro, I blurt over my shoulder, "Parental guilt. Okay! Here we are! Thank you, for the evening stroll."

"This is it? Huh?" he asks, glancing up at the sign—a little smile on his face, admiring my name in lights. I refuse to let it do things to me.

"Yeah. Yup. Where the magic happens. Engagements, senior pictures, family portraits, and on occasion, because people are bat-shit crazy and financially irresponsible, family pet portraits. I am a full-service house of wild and crazy dreams."

He cants his head, smirking. "I have a dog."

"Oh. Um…"

"I don't think he needs a professional portrait though."

"Heh, heh. Okay, good, because I'm booked full."

We trade glances. Awkward ones.

This is the part where you leave, Swiper, and I go upstairs to throw a pillow over Bitsy's snoring face.

"Can I take a look?" he asks, pointing to the studio door.

"Inside?"

"Well, I've seen the outside. I don't think I've ever been in a studio."

Does he know how to pull every one of my strings? That's like telling a baker you've never eaten cake. I make quick work of unlocking the door. This doesn't need to be a production.

"You're not missing much."

Waving him through, as soon as his large frame passes through the entrance, I know this is a mistake. The thought of kissing him again would be less discombobulating, and that was the most discombobulating kiss of all kisses.

There's something about sharing your work with someone outside of work hours that's so…personal. I have customers in here all day. This shouldn't be any different, but my customers don't scan every corner of the studio. Their eyes aren't stormy sea green and full of smiles and laughter. Their eyes don't pass over all my work with attentive appreciation. Swiper is not just looking at my stuff, he's peering into my soul, peeling it off like a dress shirt, one button at a time.

I can't afford to be peeled open. The last time I was peeled open, it turned me into a *grumpapotomus*, made my best friend uproot her life, and led to the genius decision of transplanting myself into the armpit of my family's hive. People don't make sound decisions when their soul has been seen. I went to college, damn it. I should be smart enough to resist a pretty face.

CHAPTER 13

Johnny

We pass by Bitsy's desk, where I begin the dollar tour. It's a studio. There's not much to show, but Swiper's turned into that eccentric child on a field trip with five hundred questions. I know because I was that kid.

What is this for? How does that work? How do you figure out which lighting to use? Do you develop your own film?

I left the main lights off to hustle this parade along, but the dim glow from the wall sconces is making everything more intimate. His proximity transfers the warmth of his skin as I lead him to the office to show him my film processor. After twenty questions about how I mix and handle the chemicals, I've inched toward the doorway enough that he seems to get the hint and follows. Except he stops in the hallway back to the studio to study some prints I have on the wall.

"These are incredible," he says almost to himself, staring at a series of candid black and white portraits of my family. "How come you don't put these out front where everyone can see them?"

"Oh, those are just sentimental. Ones I took over the years of my family when they weren't looking. The best expressions happen when people don't know there's a lens pointed at them."

He leans in and studies one of Sofia half asleep, her lips pressed to my nephew's forehead when he was just a baby. My heart stretches painfully, watching the way his eyes soften. I want to believe the goodness I suspect in him the way little girls wish for unicorns to be real.

If you wish in one hand and wait for a unicorn to shit in the other, guess which one fills up first? Neither.

There's no such thing as unicorns or wishes come true. Why am I attracted to men that are all wrong for me?

He steps back. His gaze makes a sweep of the wall. Frowning, he drops to a knee. His splayed fingers run down the length of a crack in the brick below the window. Why is he fondling my crack?

"You've got an expansion problem," he says.

I suspect he's referring to the wall, but wonder in panic how he knows about the Kraken or that, in spite of my negative reinforcement, Flapper has been bewitched since the motorcycle mini-fantasy. Okay. Maybe even before that. Maybe point five seconds after I spotted that white dress shirt stretched over his back as he sat alone at a restaurant table waiting for *me*.

"Hm? Come again?"

And again. And again.

Stop, Johnny! Stop!

"It happens a lot with brick underneath windows. It's caused by moisture, when the brick expands and retracts, you end up with a vertical crack like this that runs straight down from the windowsill." His fingertip traces the seam.

Holy fuck. I will never look at bricks the same again.

"I could fix it for you," he continues. "You can put in an expansion joint, but this isn't too bad. I think some flexible caulk would fill it just fine to get you by for a long time."

Caulk. He said *caulk.*

Something about filling something with his caulk.

I should probably say something.

"You…want to fill my crack?

His head whips around, brows pinched like I spoke in Greek. Oh, shit. What did I say?

"I meant….rub my…er…*fix* my crack." By the power of Patrick Swayze, I did not just say that! "Eh heh. Um. I meant…you, uh, want to do whatever it is that you do?"

His mouth ticks up at the corner as he stands and takes a step toward me. "I thought I made it clear already *what* I *do*," he says all coy and low under hooded lashes.

Message received. Swiper just sent an invitation.

Bad Swiper! Bad!

"Well, um. You'd better get back. Dimitris is probably counting the seconds."

"Right." He stands down, tucking his hands in his pockets. "So, what do you think if we try this again sometime?"

"Supervised meals with my family? Ha! Uh, thanks, but no thanks."

That erotic, stifled laugh of his saws through me as he takes another step into my bubble. "No. I could take you somewhere they wouldn't find you. I want you to enjoy yourself."

He wants to take me somewhere safe…safe from mothers and Dimitris and ouzo and judgement? That's…incredibly thoughtful.

Nope. Can't happen.

"Look. Let's level with each other. You're clearly looking for…something, but I'm…not. I'm just going through the motions to appease my mother. I apologize if by showing up tonight I led you on, but in my defense, I didn't even set up that profile. My family did."

"You don't date?"

"No."

"Ever?"

"Well, *ever* is quite broad. Isn't it? I go on what one might call dates when…you know."

"Know what?"

My word, do I really have to spell it out? How can a man dripping in sex appeal be so innocent? "When there are *itches* to be scratched," I clarify.

"Oh." His head rears back a fraction. "So, you…hook up?" The way he says it, you'd think I told him Mykonos sank into the Aegean.

"No! I…well, only when absolutely necessary. I mean, men have needs. Relationships are complicated. Itches must be scratched every so often, if you catch my drift."

He's blinking, his face twisted up like I stabbed a corkscrew into his side. *Lord of Dance*, I was not told a birds and bees lesson would be in tonight's program. "Don't tell me you've never had a one-nighter."

"I…have. Plenty actually. I just…it's been a while. A couple of years ago, I decided I'd rather hold out for something better."

"Better?"

"Y-yeah." He scratches the back of his neck. "Something…meaningful."

Cute. How cute. Nice try, Swiper. I almost fell for it.

"Like *carnival girl?*"

"No," he chortles at my accusation. "We never dated. I think she just wanted…"

When he doesn't finish, I cock a brow. "To scratch an itch?"

"Something like that."

The blush in his cheeks can't be real. Now I'm curious.

"So, she wasn't dating material?"

"No. Not for me anyway."

"And how have you determined who's dating material?"

"I'll, uh, have to get back to you on that," he says all quiet and embarrassed.

Holy shitake mushrooms!

"Wait. Are you saying…no one?"

"Um. Yeah."

"No…sex?"

Rocking back on his feet, I know he's not casting a glance to my ceiling to stretch his neck. I've hit his Achilles heel. "No," he admits, his face full on blooming now.

"But what… What's a couple of years?"

He can fidget and smear his hand over that sexy mouth all he wants. Johnny needs to know.

"Um, two."

"*Two* years and you haven't…."

"Not…no. Nothing. Look. I know that probably sounds old fashioned and silly given my age and…experience, but have you ever just grown tired of all the bullshit?"

Huh.

Yes. Fuck yes.

I have been reduced to Johnny the Gaping Pie Hole, only brought back to the present by his nervous laugh.

"Um. Say something. Please?"

"Ye-ah. Uh. No. I…I get it."

I get it because I am exhausted with trying to find a tolerable human being to satisfy Flapper twice a year to prevent my testicles from drying up and falling off. I'm exhausted with encouragement from my mother to wade into the cock fight that is the dating world, where I would get my eyes pecked out for the miniscule probability that a soul mate exists for me.

Why must silence carry more emotion than words? How did we go from caulking cracks to kindred spirits on the love-don't-live-here boat?

"Well, um. Dimitris," I warn, tapping my watch. "Tick tock and all."

"Right." The slow sizzle of acceptance in his eyes steals a piece of me. He finally knows I mean it, but…do I?

"I…hope you find what you're looking for," I add in consolation. I'm not the ice princess everyone thinks I am.

"You too."

Shit. He's leaning in to…kiss my cheek?

That's…intolerably adorable and…nice. Really nice. I mean, who does that on a date anymore?

Oh, my God, why does he smell so good? It's making me dizzy. I need to hold onto something.

Oh. Look at that. I already am.

His bicep is all kinds of rock-hard beneath my hand. The Kraken races through my bloodstream. I can't fight it anymore. I want to color by numbers this arm with my mouth.

He pulls back enough that we're face to face. The look on his? Roughly translated, I think it says, *what is it, baby?*

"Two years?" I croak. "Really?"

Don't tell me you're that pure. Please don't tell me you've got that much control.

His Adam's apple bobs. "Yeah."

Uhn.

"That's…a long time."

"Yeah," he says again as we play a game called, *I'm-not-looking-at-your-lips-and-you're-not-looking-at-mine.*

"You must…get itchy," I say because I am a suave man who uses suave adjectives when a sexy beast's breath is mingling with my own.

"Yeah," he pants, giving me the heady power of knowing I can take his oxygen away. "You?" he ventures.

"Six months." Those lips. That stubble and how it tickled against mine. There has never been a greater need for a public service message. His hypnotic pull demands I give him clarification. "Six…long…itchy months."

"So," he swallows, "you need…scratching?"

My nose bumps his, and I grunt because who the fuck needs words? We ain't building space shuttles here.

Cave man talk will suffice, and it does because he nods in understanding. "I could…do a little scratching for you."

I can't sedate the Kraken any longer, so I latch onto the matching bicep. "Fine. Fuck it," I beg.

His mouth obeys. This dam of innuendo blows to smithereens in a hot, wet, play of lips and tongues and archaic noises. His neck is a lever I've shoved into drive as I hold his lips to mine, swallowing and being swallowed. The machine moves forward, engines primed. My feet shuffle backward obediently without breaking the heady taste of this bulldozer, until my ass slams into Bitsy's desk.

We pause for a quick panting match of I'm-staring-at-your-face-and-you're-staring-at-mine. The reality check timeout buzzer sounds, and we dive back into a fiery kiss not giving a damn about reality— that stupid bitch.

I haven't had hands on me like this in…fuck, too long. Hesitant but needy presses and strokes to my back, little begging squeezes to my hip, bad things. All bad things, all more intimate than basic itch-scratching things.

This bad decision is probably the stupidest of all my bad decisions, but if I'm going to kiss a bad decision, I might as well touch *it.*

Slipping my hand under the hem of his shirt, my palm ascends warm, rock hard ripples of flesh-covered fantasies, and he moans. *He moans* at the touch of my mere glasses-wearing-photographer-hands.

"Jesus, what's under there?" I gasp.

"Presents," he breathes into my ear.

A snort bursts from my nose because I'm sexy like that, and, once upon a time, I used to laugh at flirty things. My hand wants more presents and tugs at the front of his jeans. Johnny the Bold is in full force. "Unwrap them," I order.

Our fingers fumble in tandem. My tongue slides around his for more tastes of whatever narcotic he's got in his mouth. Elastic brushes my fingertips as I enter his House of Blue Jeans, then soft cotton covering an impressively swollen length of I-need-that-right-fucking-now. Hugging it with my palm, he moans into my mouth. His hands make a quick detour to my fly.

I freeze as my button is undone, but not before I clamp down over where his fingers are working my zipper.

Houston, we have a problem.

"Wait! Don't touch Flapper!"

"Flap— What?" He blinks at me, and I realize I just revealed my self-induced *dickname*. Even more mortifying, he seems to have figured it out.

"But you…" he trails off, glancing down at where I'm greedily gripping him, so I relinquish my hold. "Why not?" he asks, grazing his thumb along my jaw.

"It…you don't want to see it."

That smirk. Uhn.

He nips my lower lip, pressing his hips into mine. "Actually, I do."

"Actually, you don't. It's…"

"It's what?"

"Greek. *Very* Greek."

His eyes crinkle at the corners, and he chuffs, grazing the embarrassingly detailed outline of my arousal through my jeans with his fingertip. "Does it have the flag tattooed on it or something?"

Gorgeous *and* a comedian. Just my luck.

"More like…a parachute on the top."

He glances down again, his features working out my humiliating riddle. What the hell was I thinking playing *grabsics* with someone in the same area code who could run into me again and know all my embarrassing Flapper secrets? The moment of understanding in his eyes makes me want to ostrich my curly head in the sand.

"Oh. You mean you're not cut?"

A flashback to Andreas' horror story stabs my senses. "Don't say *cut*!"

Swiper's amused noise burrows into my neck, stifled when he peppers stubble-lined kisses there. "I've never seen one," he whispers against my jugular. "I bet it's sexy."

That feels…mm…good, but I resist, even at the flick of his tongue to my collarbone. "I guarantee you, it's not."

Why am I disappointed when he pulls back and stares at me, the mask of passion wiped clean from his face? It's better this way. Truly. It would have happened anyway.

Why the hell is he cupping my face in his hands? He dusts a sweet, tender kiss on my lips, like a besotted lover. When his lips leave mine, he holds my gaze.

"I guarantee you, I don't care," he whispers, placing his palm over my bulge-in-question and squeezing.

My dying noise reverberates in my ears at the delicious pressure on the turgid flesh beneath my denim. That talented fingertip of his traces my outline again, taking its sweet time over the tip as he kisses me again. "I won't look," he breathes against my lips, *handfulling* my ass with his free hand. "I swear."

Well, now I just feel petulant like a child throwing a conniption. I trade him favors, tasting the underside of his jaw and neck, working my zipper in stealth mode. Flapper cheers in relief when I shove my jeans down over my hips.

"Wow," Swiper gasps.

Why aren't we still kissing? Come back, Swiper. What is he…

Oh, fuck me.

His gaze is locked on the tight red briefs I had to grab from the back of my underwear drawer, since Mamá has been sanctioning my laundry days for refusing to join in on the family pilgrimage to Greece next month. Why would I own a washing machine when she has kidnapped mine and Bitsy's laundry on a weekly basis since I moved home? I should have grabbed a bottle of hand sanitizer and suffered a trip to the laundry mat so I wouldn't be reduced to looking like a porny Superman.

"You said you wouldn't look!" I snap, covering the electric red cucumber tenting the tight fabric as best I can with my hands.

"At your dick!" he scoffs. "I'm looking at your underwear."

"My dick is *in* my underwear."

"Barely." He chuckles, tracing my tightly gripped fingers.

Hilarious!

Grabbing the waist of my jeans, I start to yank them back up over my ass. "I wasn't planning on *shaking hands* tonight. Mm-kay?"

Swiper gets ahold of my wrist, stopping Operation Clark Kent, sucking on my lower lip.

Why is his green light still on? Shouldn't he be turned off by my fashion failure and foreskin confession?

"They're freaking hot," he murmurs between kisses, lightly snapping the waist of the elastic above my ass. "I want to tug them off," he rasps like he's in pain, hugging his other hand over mine, making me squeeze my already too painful erection.

"Fuuuck," I moan. "Fine."

I move my hand from my superhero panties and free him from the navy cotton of his boxer briefs.

Tasting and devouring, our mouths are on loop as I run my hand up the veiny ridge of his hot silk. Roughened fingers slip under my waistband at my lower back. His palms sweep down over the globes of my ass, taking my drawers with them and pulling me to him.

Uhn. Who knew callouses could feel so erotic?

We groan in unison when Flapper presses against his equally hard length, skin to sensitive skin.

"That feels good," he whispers.

"So…observant," I pant, wrapping my hand around the both of us.

"Ah, yeah," he gasps and reaches to assist me with this naughty handshake.

His rough, scratchy palm clutches the top side of my cock. When he slides up, my dick feels every crack and crease of his work worn palm. Callouses are no longer erotic.

"Ah! Brick hands!" I yelp.

"Shit! Sorry!"

In an unspoken agreement, we become synchronized explorers, our gazes in search of lubrication. Swiper locks onto something.

Hm. *Very Berry* hand lotion.

Every twig needs some berries. Thank you, Bitsy.

I nod. He pumps, then I yelp again because damn that's cold!

"Sorry." He grimaces.

And…mm. Friction is warm. Friction is good. Friction is…I need more.

Shoving my jeans down, I manage to kick off one shoe and free a leg in record time. Ass back on the desk, Swiper takes my lead, shoving his jeans and briefs down just enough. He grips the underside of my thigh, wrapping my bare leg around the satiny flesh of his hips. I look like a horny teenager who wants to get off so bad he can't be bothered to fully disrobe, but the comparison isn't far off.

Closer contact is my reward. Warmth to warmth, more skin to more skin, his soft trimmed curls brushing my sensitized flesh. I can't remember ever kissing this ravenously for this long. There's latent Swiper kisses on every inch of my neck, my face, and the sliver of my chest exposed by the horrid date-polo. I can feel every vein, curve, and ridge of his cock against mine.

We take turns grunting, "Yeah. Uhn. Yeah."

It is our own breathy language set to the backdrop of the *schick, schick, schick* sound of berry lotion as his tight grip strokes us, while my fingers work to elicit new Swiper noises with each graze of his nipples under his shirt. It's a beautiful, dirty song that I have missed and want to set as my ring tone.

His thumb finds a sweet spot only I have ever discovered, pulling embarrassingly needy whimpers from my throat.

"Uhn. Uhn. God," I choke with each graze of his thumb over the base of my foreskin as his hot heat slides against mine.

He gapes at me, glances down at my kryptonite, and then back up at Lord knows what delirious expression is on my face as my balls tighten, and I squirm against him.

"Oh, fuck yeah," he breathes, diving back at my mouth, abandoning my thigh to weave his hand into my hair.

He picks up the pace of his slides, finishing each off with that maddening twist to the underside of my crown. I've made a good man swear with my horny mating cries, but shame has left the building as we both buck into his grip.

My legs go all *sandman-tingly* down to my toes. The pressure at the base of my cock charges the gates, relief racking my body as I spill over the top of his hand.

"Coming!" I bellow too late, but he moans like a baritone choir boy who's not sure if he's seen a ghost, slow and rising in pitch.

"Johnny!"

Instinct nearly has me asking, *what?* When someone yells your name it usually means they want your attention. Well, the baring of his teeth between his parted lips has my attention as his grip clutches the back of my neck. Watching someone else come has never been so flaming hot, his cock pulsing against mine.

"Shit," he pants, resting his forehead in the crook of my neck.

His lips press and hold to the sensitized skin there. My heart slams up into my throat. I have been sealed with a kiss so sweet I know I'm going to dream about it. *Shit* is right.

The world comes flooding back to me. I need to get my hand out from under his shirt, off his hot skin. Need to get out from under the way his heaving chest is pressed against mine. Need to put the Superman panties back from whence they came. Need to get my bare ass off Bitsy's desk. I need these hooks out of me before they shred my resistance and make me lose my common sense any further.

As I nudge for my dear life, Swiper stirs and pulls back. Cue my mad scramble off the *Formica* surface, but we're both disheveled beyond repair. I can't send him back to Dimitris like this.

Bitsy's box of tissues stands like a flag of redemption. I start tugging the soft white sheets from the box and thrusting them at Swiper, stopping only momentarily to half ass my own mess.

Swiper chuckles and clamps his hand over my next round of pass the flag. "I'm good," he says.

In his other hand is a sizable crumple of tissues. Apparently, I turned into a *come-clean-uppins* assembly line worker without realizing it as the tissue box is now empty.

Turning around, I don my horny-teenager pant leg and put myself to rights. When I face him again, he's tucked up, buttoned up, and staring at me.

"So…my sister got tickets to—" he starts.

"Shit! Dimitris," I cut him off because any sentence about tickets sounds like an invitation to somewhere.

I will not be going somewhere with Lance two-point-oh, even if Swiper is shaping up to be a major upgrade in every department. It's a matter of self-control—I will clearly have none where this man is concerned and very likely hand over my heart and soul to him to feel like I just did. Thank you, Universe, for creating two men who can make me lose my mind.

"Um. Yeah," he acknowledges but there is a clear lack of the panic I'm experiencing in his eyes.

"No. Seriously. He'll have told the whole family by now we made babies."

He lets out a puff of air like it's a laughing matter. "Um. Right. Yeah. Well, look. I know you said you don't date, but—"

"I don't."

"Right. But would you—"

"Listen, we need quit while we're ahead. Okay? No need to worry about promises and all the getting to know each other mess that leads to disappointment and expectations."

Don't fall for the puppy dog eyes. Don't do it. Be strong. "I mean, this was fun. Right?" I say airily, because I can at least deflate his silly ambitions gently. "Itches successfully scratched. You're good for another two years."

How long is he going to stare at me with that what-do-you-mean-Santa-isn't-real face? Okay. Maybe the two years joke was in poor taste.

"Or, you know," I add brightly, "hopefully, sooner. Mr. Right is out there."

"And this was…"

"Um, just a good old case of Mr.-Right-Now. Hey, I mean after two awful dates, I'd say we deserved a little reward."

"Ye-ah," he says, every muscle in his face sagging. I swear the light just went out of his eyes.

Why do I feel like a dick? This is self-defense class. I'm not in charge of his heart. I'm only responsible for mine. Mine says no way am I trusting myself to not pour every ounce of my heart into a relationship again—stick to the plan.

"Then, I guess I'd better…" he trails off with uncertainty, gesturing to the door with his thumb.

"Yeah. Um. Take care."

He nods at the speed of a dying vibrator. "You too."

At the door, he glances back, lips parted. Don't say anything. Don't do it, Swiper.

"Goodnight," I cheer, finger-waving like a cheeky one-night stand with no regrets.

"Night."

As soon as the door swings shut, I gasp for air from the breath I was holding and groan into my hands. They smell like berries and Aiden.

No. Not *Aiden—Swiper*.

Don't say his name! We don't want to keep him no matter how good that was.

Except, as good as it was, why do I feel so bad?

Speed-walking to the back door leading to my apartment stairs helps distance me from the scene of the crime. I need a shower to wash away the narcotic *Swiper scent* from my body.

At the base of the stairs, I nearly jump out of my skin when the exterior backdoor of the building opens and Bitsy steps through.

"Oh! Hey," she says, looking just as startled.

"Hey. Where were you?"

"Oh. Um. Out."

Out? Where the fuck is *out*? Bitsy is a couch potato, minus her afternoon bike rides to burn off the five thousand calories she consumes in a day.

"That's detailed," I retort, because best we focus on her than her detecting the graphic romp I just had in the studio.

"I…went to the coffee shop and met Mickey after work."

"You spent your evening with the emo barista?"

Frowning, she looks me over. "How was your date?"

"You are banned from dating apps henceforth." I make a sweep of finality with my hand. "It was *Swiper part-two*. What are the odds? If I didn't know any better, I'd think you orchestrated the whole thing."

"Who's Swiper?"

"Aiden. Aiden Brandt. Foot Collector…er…okay, he's not really into feet from what I can tell, but…"

My trap shuts when I notice she's gaping at me, studying my face the way she does when she's looking past the surface of my bullshit.

"It was Aiden again?"

"Yes! Keep up."

She giggles. "That's so funny."

"Har-dee har har."

"How was it?"

Mind-blowing. Life-altering. Messy. Hot as fuck.

"Awful. That's twice now I had to let him down."

Her lip pouts. Her blue eyes uncomfortably soul-search mine.

"What's with your hair?"

Gasp! I haven't even inspected my hair since Swiper's fingers ran through it. "I walked home. It's windy."

She extends her leg behind her, kicking the back door open, never taking her bad-cop gaze off my face. "No. It's not."

"I…I'm almost out of *Curls-Be-Damned*, okay? I need to go shopping," I huff, claiming a shortage of my favorite hair product. "Speaking of plans, I have to go to Miami for some shoots."

Anywhere far enough away from dates, Bitsy's intuition, and the dangerous sex appeal of one hunky brick mason. At least my lone high school friend, Will, can serve as a logical excuse for my escape—a former fellow nerd with a gay heart of gold who, like me, escaped the hell that is Olympus.

"When?" Bitsy frowns.

Starting up the stairs, I hold back a gasp as I feel the extent of the sex-tousled state of my hair. "Um. Tomorrow? Or…the next day at the latest. It's short notice. Will said he's got some new clients for me, but they'll only be in Miami for a few days."

Determined footsteps follow me. "You wouldn't be taking this trip to avoid date number-three, would you?"

"Really with *that?* Don't you think it's time you gave up your foray into the matchmaking world? You know I was only kidding about the whole food critic thing."

"If I didn't know better, I'd say you look like you're running away. Was Aiden that bad? Did he traumatize you or something?"

"Bitsy, I never kiss and tell. You know this," I grump, unlocking the apartment door.

"Kissing? There was kissing again?"

"It was a figure of speech! Mm-kay? Put away your fortune teller cards. And another thing…" I level my index finger at her. "Can you get up before the crack of noon tomorrow? We need to go through the Sherman photos before I leave, so don't go sneaking off to Oikos for a two-hour brunch."

"I can't work without breakfast!"

"Then get carry out. Have a muffin."

She's silent for a beat, and when she speaks again her voice has reverted to that of dear-friend-I-can't-say-no-to. "Do you want to watch *Road House?*"

Ugh. She *Patrick-ed* me. Tempting. Very tempting, but she can't be trusted right now. *I* can't be trusted right now, especially not after I've just been *Swipered*.

"No, thanks. I'm beat. I'm going to bed. Lots to do tomorrow," I call over my shoulder as I hustle toward my room.

Lots to run away from. Lots to forget about. Lots to put carefully back into perspective. A few days at the beach will be a sound reminder of no matter how good something feels it eventually bites you in the ass.

CHAPTER 14

Hey Curly,

I love seeing you in my bed when I wake up—your crazy, sexy underwear laying on my floor. Coffee's on the kitchen counter. I'll be back after my surf. Don't go anywhere! I'm kidnapping you today...and tomorrow, and probably the next day.

LOL. I'm so far gone.

Lance
XOXO

CHAPTER 15

Johnny

"Ten o'clock? Really?" I make a show of glancing at my watch as Bitsy shoves through the studio door with a stack of three Styrofoam containers in her hands. "You went to Oikos, didn't you?"

Bitsy's brows pinch together. "No. Tapas."

Gasp! She went to the scene of the crime? The nosey wench.

Clean your lenses. Ignore her. Do not engage the enemy.

"Dimitris said Aiden walked you home last night," her voice carries, but I refuse to look up.

"Mm. Swiper was gentleman enough to give Dimitris a show."

"That's so sweet."

Sweet kisses. Sweet gasps of breath. Uhn. I suppress a shiver.

"So, I take it he was nice if he walked you home?" she ventures.

Her containers of breakfast booty squeak. The sound of her desk chair rolling tells me she's finally setting up camp for the workday.

"Even dictators can be nice. What's your point?"

"I'm just curious how you got a kiss on the first date and a walk home on the second date, yet you say it was awful. Dimitris said you were holding hands. What happened that it was awful?"

I am never eating at Tapas again. Pinching the bridge of my nose does nothing to alleviate my stress.

"Nothing happened, Bits. I know a fairy god mother flew up your ass recently, but I can assure you—" Oh, sweet baby Jesus. Her desk. "No! Don't put that…there!"

Her hand freezes above the breakfast croissant sandwich she just set on her desk. Let me clarify—on the exact spot where my bare ass was sitting not more than twelve hours ago, legs wrapped around Swiper.

Suspicious brow ticked up; she scans her workspace. My teeth clench. I am paralyzed in fear.

No doubt she's seeing the knocked over bottle of lotion and…yup. There she goes, picking up the tissue box. She glances in her garbage can at the mound of little crumpled white sheets. I bite my knuckle. There is nowhere to hide, but at least I'm a good friend and warned her. My soul will surely be spared for that one day.

Her gasp sends my spine rigid as she flings the empty tissue box into the trash and spins her chair around, aiming her index finger at me.

"You dirty dog! You *lied* to me!" She spares a glance at the buffet she laid on the table before I could warn her it was a contaminated area. "*And* you wasted my food!"

"I didn't lie! I just…spared you all the…messy details."

She pops out of her chair as though it ejected her. "Did you have sex on my desk?"

"No! God, no! We…there may have been a quick exchange of *handshakes*."

Gasping again? Really? Okay, now she's just being dramatic.

"You got a *handie* on my desk?"

I am the cleanlier one of this friendship. It is humiliating that I'm being scolded for not tidying up after an act of debauchery. Excuse me, if I avoided every thought or proximity to that desk when I came in this morning.

Oh, come on! Bleach spray? Really? She's acting like I'm contagious the way she's cleaning that thing.

"It just…sort of happened," I explain. "Nothing worth putting in your diary."

She pauses her sanitizing operation to stare sadly at a muffin as though she's considering if it is truly too sullied to consume. "So," she sighs, tossing it in the trash, "were you lying when you said the date was awful? Or did you just not want me to know? Are you see-ing him again?"

"No. I…it was awkward. Alright? You can still have chemistry even if it's awkward. And no. I'm not seeing him again. My needs have been satisfied enough to hold me over until my next bad decision. Thank you very much."

Why is she frowning? "So, if you knew you weren't into him, but you ended up," she gestures to her desk, making me shrink an inch, "then what? Did you just use him?"

Ouch! Can you say harsh?

"No! That's so cruel. It was mutual and…unavoidable."

That is a better explanation than telling her I couldn't control myself.

"The guy who wrote on his profile that he wanted to stay in with a special someone was up for a meaningless desk defiling?"

Are the bleach fumes getting to me? I feel a headache coming on, and my stomach is twisting up inside. He *did* write that. Didn't he? Not his mother or best friend, just him.

No. Don't go there, Johnny.

It was probably all bullshit. Come across as a sensitive guy just to get laid…or *handied*, I guess, in this instance.

Remember morning kisses and rolling in the California sand. Remember watching pick-up games when you don't even like football. Remember going on weekend adventures and believing that person would always love being anywhere with you. Remember the ache of missing someone's face so much when they were away on travel shoots that you ceased to breathe just for yourself. Remember the nitpicking as that person slowly started taking back every compliment they ever paid you. All good things come to an end.

"Listen," I soothe. "Swiper's a big boy. We're both adults. I made it very clear where I stood. You know what we need?" I snake my arm around her shoulders, leading her away from the memories of where that magic brick hand made me lose my mind. "Why don't you come to Mykonos with me? We've been talking about it forever. Let's just do it. We can go before Mamá and Papa fly home for their summer visit and meet up with them after a week in paradise. You're long overdue for a work vacation."

Her face twists with regret. "I can't. I've got…plans."

"Plans? What plans?"

Bitsy never has plans. Being a passenger in my life has always been her plan.

"Just…some obligations I made."

"What kind of obligations?"

"There's a…a…" she stammers, returning to her desk to power up her computer, "a cycling event I was thinking of entering."

"You'd trade Mykonos for cycling?"

"Johnny, for six years I've heard you rave about how Mykonos is *the* gay travel destination. What am I going to do in Mykonos?"

Eat. Keep me company while I ogle suitable men to help me erase the Swiper mistake from my mind…and my body.

"Besides," she shrugs, "I honestly don't think you want to go. It's just something you've built up in your mind. If you really wanted to go, you would have gone by now."

"Are you finished psychoanalyzing me, Debbie Downer?"

She sighs and shakes her head. "Sure."

"Good. Because if you didn't want to take a vacation with your best friend all you had to do was say so."

Why do I feel like a twat? Of course, I want to go to Mykonos. There was no need to go when I was with Lance. We made it paradise wherever we were, or so I thought. Plus, there's a cooling off period after a breakup.

Sigh. Until we meet, dear Mykonos. Miami will have to do for now.

"I…need to go pack. You good here?"

"Are there any *Hot Pockets* left in the freezer?" she asks, hopefully.

I suppress a gag. "I'll check."

"Thanks."

There is no lightness to my steps as I ascend the stairs to the apartment. My mother is on a mission. Bitsy is moody as all get out lately, and she's acting suspicious. What's that about? Despite the life-altering release I experienced last night, my shoulders are tense, remembering that sad puppy look on Swiper's face like he actually thinks he wants me.

I moved home to lick my wounds and realign, to surround myself with the understanding only one's family and best friend can provide. In the past few weeks, I've been sabotaged by my family, analyzed by my best friend, and orgasmed by a man for whom I could easily be stupider for than the last man for whom I was stupid. It is time to refocus and get the hell out of Dodge.

Just as soon as I get these damn *Hot Pockets*.

CHAPTER 16

Aiden

"Seriously? Like you don't know what time I'm out here every morning," I snap at Maxie when she finally climbs into my truck.

"Easy, *Killer*. We get there five minutes early every day. Maybe I'm trying to tell you that you're too punctual. Besides, I don't think the boss will fire us."

"Yeah, well, it's bike weather, and instead of riding my bike, I'm waiting for you. Why don't you just borrow my truck when Véronique's not flying so I can take the Harley to work?" I end with a belch and throw back another sip of *Pepto Bismol*, my stomach gurgling in protest.

Maxie squints at me. "Are you hungover? Is that what the cat's ass face is about?"

"No. I ate garlic last night, and now I'm trying not to die."

"Ooh. Food poisoning?"

Pinching my eyes shut, I cap the bottle and throw the truck into drive. "No. I'm allergic. Remember?"

"Huh. That's so weird."

Pulling onto the street, I swallow against the aftertaste of mint and garlic, shaking my head. You'd think we never had this conversation before.

"If you don't like garlic, why did you eat it?" she asks.

If I don't *like* garlic. Typical. I'm too exhausted from hanging over the toilet last night puking my guts out to correct her.

"It wasn't self-induced."

Actually, that's not true. If I hadn't let it bother me that Johnny basically shoved me out the door after that bout of epic fisting last week or that he deleted another dating app profile, I wouldn't have ventured back to Tapas yesterday in the hopes of running into him.

Genius. Look where it got me.

Despite my stomach revolting against me, it wasn't a total loss. As Dimitris was poisoning me, he mentioned how I must be missing Johnny while he's down in Miami for work.

Miami. Is that where he scratches his itches?

"Did someone force-feed you?" Maxie laughs, popping her gum.

Basically. Man, Greek people are all about feeding other people. No wonder Johnny said he runs every day.

"Remember that Greek restaurant I said I went to on my date last week? The one where we redid the patio wall last year?"

"Oh, yeah. They've got great food."

I shudder. "Well, I ate there last night."

"With that same guy? I thought you said it didn't work out?"

"It didn't." I shrug. "I just…went by myself."

When I realize it's been quiet for a while, I find her smirking at me. "You went spying on him. Didn't you?"

"What? I did not. I have to eat, don't I?"

"Aiden, no one does that. No one goes back to the same restaurant where they were turned down days before, except people who are infatuated."

"I'm not infatuated."

Except now, not only my stomach is burning, but also my face. If I have ever been infatuated with someone in my life, this is the closest it would be. Maxie's laughing her ass off at me, which is basically the white flag of defeat. I'm too miserable both mentally and physically to play proud.

"He just…" I begin. "I don't get it. We had…. I mean, he was like all surly and pissy both times we went out, but it wasn't exactly directed at me, but rather dating in general. And then," I pause for a breath, "we did some stuff, which just makes it all the more confusing."

"Stuff? Uh, do tell."

"Gross. No."

"What? Because I'm not a guy or because I'm a lesbian?"

Great. She chooses today to be offended? "How about because you're my sister?"

"Yeah. I'm the same sister who knows you've been saving yourself for two years for true love. Now suddenly, you drop this bomb on me that you did *stuff*," she says, making air quotes, "and you're not going to give me any *deets* on how this all came about?"

"We kissed on the first date. Okay?"

Her lower lip bulging out is not sympathetic in the least. I know when I'm being mocked.

"Aiden," she practically weeps, "kissing is not *stuff*."

"He… That time I met him for coffee, he basically didn't believe that I was into him, so I kissed him to prove him wrong and it got heated… like…really heated."

Shit. Now I'm heated, remembering it.

"Wait. This was a couple weeks ago when you ducked out to the coffee shop. Right?"

"Yeah." What's her point?

She laughs and fans herself. "Whoa! How do you have a heated kiss at a coffee shop?"

Outside the coffee shop, up against a wall with a hard dick pressed to yours. Nope. Not going there.

"Um, just like every heated kiss you and Véronique have *everywhere*," I counter.

"Mm. Fine. Point taken." She shrugs. "But you went out again? I thought you said something about trying another dating app."

"I did and got matched to him again. His name's Johnny. He's the same guy I had coffee with. We met at Tapas last week. Same guy, two different dating apps."

"Holy serendipity, Batman!"

"Right? That's what I thought, but he was like *no, not happening.*"

"Did you kiss again?"

Chewing my lip, I spot a convenience store and pull over. Electrolytes are a must today.

"Oh, ho ho!" Maxie evil laughs, rubbing her hands together. "That's what you meant by *stuff.* Now we're getting to it. You got dinner *and* dessert. I see!"

"Really?" I pin her with look.

"What? How do you expect me to not have questions? First, you're all like *I'm becoming a virgin again*, then you *heated-kiss* some guy who you say wants nothing to do with you. How do you go from that to a second date and *stuff*? Did you anger bang him for turning you down the first time or something?"

Pressing my fingers to my eye sockets, I know I will never unhear that. "No! What is wrong with you? I don't anger bang. We just…. I walked him home and…"

"And?"

Christ. "And we…" I toss my hand, fist closed, in the air. How is this conversation even happening?

Maxie erupts in laughter. I officially hate her. "You are now my least favorite *brother*, just so you know."

"I'm sorry," she gasps, wiping tears from her eyes. "You just look so uncomfortable."

I spare her a glower as she holds her side in amusement. She comes up for air when I pop the truck into park. "No, seriously. It's good you finally had someone else's hand on your dick besides your own. That's progress."

You're the calm one of the family, I chant in my head as she chuckles. "Are you done?"

"Yeah, I think so," she sighs. Smacking me in the arm, she chirps, "But no. That's great! You're off the celibacy wagon! You were getting all broody and depressed. So, are you going to see him again?"

"No. He looked like I couldn't leave fast enough after…."

"Maybe he's seeing someone else," she ventures, sounding more sincere.

"No. No way." I shake my head. "He said he doesn't date. His family basically forced him to use the dating apps."

"Ouch. Invasive much?"

I shrug, not one to judge someone else's family. Maybe they just want him to find happiness. Maybe it's just not with me.

"Is he a player? That could just be a line he's giving you."

Rubbing the sleep from my eyes, I shake my head. "I don't think so. I feel like he's into me but just refuses to give me a chance. I don't know what I'm doing wrong."

"Aiden, maybe you're not doing anything wrong. If it's meant to be, it's meant to be. The other person will make the effort too."

Will they, I want to ask. The thought of Johnny making an effort makes my heart skip a beat, but common sense tells me that's not going to happen. Life was a lot less complicated when I was the only person touching my dick.

CHAPTER 17

Johnny,

Get your sexy butt out to OUR patio. I've got a surprise for you, and I need my man.

Leave the boxes. We'll unpack later!

Love Lance,
xoxo

CHAPTER 18

Johnny

It is a universal truth that if your mother visits you, she will clean something, touch everything, bring food, and/or take something. While I am grateful my kitchen has been *de-Bitsy-ed* and that Mamá dropped off so much food last night that neither Bitsy nor I will have to partake in family meals for a week, did the woman really have to take my suitcases? That's what I get for fleeing to take a shower, thus leaving her unattended in my apartment upon my arrival home from Miami last night.

Silence greets me after the hearty knock I give Bitsy's bedroom door. Why the hell did I even think that would wake her? Bursting through the door, I find a Bitsy-sized lump covered by her baby blue comforter.

"Bits!" I call, clapping my hands for the extra volume required to rouse her.

The lump shifts under the covers and grunts.

"Mamá took my suitcases, which had all my running shorts in them. Do you have anything with an elastic waist I can borrow?"

"Go away," she croak-whispers.

"Oh, come on! I spent four hours in a pressurized can of farts and bad breath yesterday. I am not missing my run. I need to detox pronto!"

"Sleeping," she growls.

"This is your fault. If you'd been here last night when I got home, you could have run defense with Mamá and protected my luggage. She prodded me the entire time about my dating life and going to Greece with the family. I nearly had a panic attack. Where the heck did you go? You were out somewhere every night I called this week."

"Bottom drawer!" she snarls, the blanket pinching tighter around the area near her head.

"*Thank* you!"

I have seldom rummaged through Bitsy's things during the tenure of our friendship. Her room is a scary place of stacks of home living magazines, a nightstand full of scented lotions, bags of candy stuffed into the cushion of her easy chair, and forty-seven pairs of running shoes that have only felt the pedals of her bicycle rather than pavement.

My ankle bends at an awkward angle, nearly making me face plant as I trip on a rogue shoe. Kicking it in retribution, it sails across the room. "Son of a bitch!"

Her treasure map to clothing turns out to be disappointing. All I see is spandex. Spandex. Spandex. Spandex.

"Bitsy! These are all cycling shorts. Don't you have anything cotton or polyester? Basketball shorts? Baggie loungers to wear after one of your food binges?"

A pillow flies at my head, accompanied by a growl. She has good aim for someone in a coma.

"Oof! Geesh! No need to get violent!"

Damn it. I'm out of options.

It is too hot to wear my flannel sleep pants. I really need a washing machine. I'm down to old jock straps in the underwear department, from my relationship days when I tried to be sexy. At least a jock and spandex will hold everything in my southern region in place on my jog. My junk will be more secure than Fort Knox.

Ten minutes later, I'm hitting the pavement, feeling like I'm in that dream where you show up at school naked. This is indecent.

The only time I have gone out in public with fabric that nearly outlines every vein in my penis, so tight that it separates my ass cheeks, was when I dressed as Freddy Mercury for Halloween.

That was at a gay club in California.

At night.

In the dark.

This is early morning light near downtown in the heartland of America. At least the shops aren't open yet, and it's early enough people haven't started their commute.

Where the hell is my Panos Kiamos on this blasted playlist? Wait. What is this bubble gum nonsense? Are you shitting me?

"Damn it, Bitsy!"

Apparently, we need to have that keep-your-mitts-off-my-music discussion again. Rounding the corner leading to the north side of town toward my favorite park, I give up and hit *Bitsy's Badass Biking* playlist. Who creates their own playlists on someone else's mp3 player? Women—the same creatures who steal your underwear. That's who. Seriously, and people wonder why I'm gay.

Carly Rae Jepson's "Call Me Maybe" pumps out of my earbuds. Kill me now.

I roll my neck, the last of the tolerable morning air breezing against my bare arms in my white Hugo Maddox muscle shirt—the only one I could find long enough to conceal part of what these ridiculous cycling shorts are doing to my junk.

Sigh.

So much discomfort. Running is my one solace, and it's been ruined by spandex and candy sweet pop music. It's a terrible song.

Really.

I mean, it's a total ear worm. Right? One of those that gets stuck in your head all day long.

Oddly enough, my feet have found a good rhythm, hitting the sidewalk in time with the beat.

Okay. So, the chorus is a bit catchy.

Hm. Hm. Hm. Hm. Hm.

Humming never hurt anyone.

Fuck it.

Arm work adds a boost to cardio. Right? I'm naturally musical. It is a curse, actually. My body can't resist dancing. I'm Greek. I was genetically engineered to feel rhythm. Summary—I am now full-on bopping, probably looking like Carly's biggest fan.

What is that high-pitched noise? Did that woman in the bandana with the toned arms just cat call me?

There's one, two, three men in the park with her that… Oh, dear God. They have pallets of bricks…and construction equipment.
And…it's Swiper!

"Ah! Fuck!"

The *conk* sound of my skull colliding with metal is all I hear before my teeth click together and the flash of the word STOP on a red sign mocks me. The force of my impact sends me flying backward. In the split second I lose my balance, I remember there is nothing protecting my ass, but spandex, so I twist my body on instinct to take the fall on my hands and knees. Except, my clumsiness makes an appearance by way of rolling my ankle, a sharp pain exploding inside it.

My momentum skids my knee and palms down the sidewalk. I land with a bounce, my cheek hitting the pavement. My glasses skitter down the concrete.

Sharp pain blasts through my face. My knee is on fire and my ankle is throbbing in time to Carly Rae because my earbuds somehow managed to stay in.

"Shut it, Carly," I groan, ripping them out of my ears. I wince when I remember my palms are scuffed to hell.

"Johnny! Jesus! Are you alright?"

The familiar sound of Swiper's voice invades my verbal storm of groans and curses. There's a strong hand on my hip, rolling me over.

Fuck. He's all sexy panting like he just had a good dicking, and the cut off sleeves of his t-shirt expose every inch of his chiseled arms while I look like a sausage casing. This is his fault.

"Do you always gawk at unsuspecting runners who are trying to mind their own business?"

"I thought you were trying to tell me to call you…maybe?" He smirks.

Oh, fuck my life. Was I singing out loud? This is so not an appropriate time for him to show off his sense of humor.

No. I don't need his help up or those brick hands on my body. I bat that shit away, not caring about the surprise in his expression. And, oh, George Michael, my ankle! I let out an embarrassing yelp.

"What is it? Your ankle?" Swiper asks.

"So observant," I grit, swatting his hand again, which is not welcome on this thin fabric on my hips. "I'm fine. Just give me a minute."

"Why don't you let me give you a ride home?"

"No. I can walk. It's just a flesh wound," I assure him, squinting from behind the hand that I have pressed to my face.

"It looks like several flesh wounds."

When did he grab my glasses? That was…thoughtful. I take a step to retrieve them from him but wobble like a newborn giraffe.

Bare arms enclose me and…

"Swiper! What the hell are you doing?" I squawk as I'm lifted underneath my knees and cradled against his chest.

"There's no way you can walk all the way home on that. I'll give you a ride."

We're moving across the street in purposeful strides already. I squirm in a pathetic effort to free myself from looking like a damsel in distress, but it cracks open the hamburger meat on my knee, making me wince, so I give up and look for witnesses instead.

The two men I spied earlier appear to be confused by Swiper's chivalry. One, tall and lanky, turns back to work as though we're not that interesting. The other, a slightly smaller version of Swiper looks as though he's sorting out complex math problems in his head. And the woman… brow raised, hands on hips. I can't tell if she's amused or pissed off. Being that she's locked on us, I'm going with pissed off. It figures. A jealous co-worker. I knew there were skeletons in Swiper's closet.

"This is cute and all, but I don't think your girlfriend appreciates you manhandling me."

He snorts. "Not my girlfriend. Nice try though."

"Well, future girlfriend, perhaps. We're getting the stink eye. I think she's worried I'm cutting in on her turf, so you can let me down."

He glances over and makes a perturbed face at the woman, who then grins at us and shakes her head. Swiper sighs as though the exchange were a novel's worth of dialogue.

"Why is she grinning?"

"Because she knows it's you."

"Me?"

"Yeah. She figured out you're the one I went on a couple dates with lately."

"I don't get it. How is that funny? I mean, yes. It's hilarious in a cosmic, dating-apps-can-go-to-hell-way, but why does she think it's funny?"

"Because she's my sister, and she loves to give me shit," he says, cocking a brow as he looks down at me.

"Oh. Your…sister."

"Mm hm."

"Right. Honest mistake."

At this he looks to be fighting a smile as he sets me down next to a black pickup truck. "They don't get any more honest than you, Johnny."

I don't have time to discern if that was an insult or a compliment because as soon as my foot touches the ground, the pain radiates again. Groaning, I latch onto the bed of his truck. Could I be any less dignified?

Swiper frowns and opens the door. Before I can even try to hop inside, he hoists me up onto the seat, where I land with a *squeak,* just another way in which I am sexy.

I take the brief moment of Swiper's absence as he shuts my door to inspect myself. The side mirror is a horror show. Staring back at me is the result of the July humidity. I don't use hair product for my morning run, but my morning run has never included a collision with a stop sign where I am saved by a man who has held Flapper in his hands. Making quick work to smooth my growing curliness with my hands, I glance down at my lower half.

Fuck me sideways! You can see my entire penis in these shorts!

Did Swiper see it? Smoothing my hair with one hand, I tug my shirt over *the goods* with my other just as he hops in behind the driver's seat. The cab of his truck smells like him. It's like a box of Swiper goodness. A giant Swiper oil diffuser, and despite my pain, my mouth begins to salivate.

Eyes straight ahead, Johnny. Focus on the pain. Focus on the pain.

We pull out of the park parking lot and head down the road in silence. I make busy casually smoothing my frizz and holding a death grip on my shirt. Is he…watching me?

"Did you…" he trails off.

"What?"

His face scrunches up and he whispers with a sympathetic wince, "Piss yourself?"

His gaze darts to where I'm pulling my shirt over my junk.

Gasp! How could he think such a thing?

"No! I'm just trying to cover up! These are Bitsy's shorts. My mother absconded with mine in the night like a panty burglar."

His shoulders relax, and he covers his chuckle with his hand. I was starting to think his chivalry had exceeded Lance's, but I got news for Swiper. He just lost ten points for that remark.

His scent strengthens, and I can feel his breath near my ear. He's leaned over, and whispers, "Johnny, I've touched it. Does it really matter if I see it?"

I know he's touched it. I know he knows he's touched it, but do we have to talk about how we both know he's touched it? I think not.

This is going to be the longest five blocks in history.

CHAPTER 19

Aiden

He's in my truck. In my life again. Every time I try to accept the fact I won't see him again, there he is.

He looks so damn cute all miserable like a man in desperate need of comfort. And those shorts. Johnny may be smaller than me, but he is toned and tan and…

Eyes on the road, Aiden. The guy's in pain. Don't ogle him.

I clear my throat of the lustful thoughts. "So, how was Miami?"

"How do you know I went to Miami?"

Crap. Busted.

"Um, I ate at Tapas last night. Dimitris told me."

He frowns and for a moment I wonder if he's going to ask me if I went to spy on him.

"And what prey tell did you eat at Tapas?"

"I'm not sure what it was called." And I really don't want to think about it.

"Describe it. I'll know. I'm a cultural advisor, remember?"

Him and that smart mouth. I wonder if he got picked on in school. The thought of someone giving him a hard time makes me grip the wheel harder as I turn into the parking lot of his studio.

"It was some kind of meat on a stick with this white sauce he said to put on it."

"Souvlaki? He fed you *souvlaki* and *tzatziki?*"

"Maybe? Like I said. I'm not really sure what it was."

"It was an assassin's dream of garlic poisoning, that's what!" He mutters something under his breath about mustaches and burning. "Is that why you look on the pale side today?"

"I'm fine." I run my hand down my face as though it will bring my color back, but it's futile. Since when did he start paying attention to my coloring?

He picks up the bottle of *Pepto Bismol* and waggles it at me "Fine, huh? This is just your morning drink of choice then, is it?"

I grimace, my throat closing up just looking at it. "I'd rather not talk about it."

Sighing, he sets the bottle back in the console. "Promise me you will never go there again unless I'm with you. Unless you have a death wish, of course."

That sounded a lot like protectiveness, and I have to say, it does nice things inside me that I wouldn't mind living there. I've never needed anyone to take care of me, but the idea of Johnny out in the world somewhere, worrying about me, feels like a missing piece of me has snapped into place. Except, he's gone all rigid, probably realizing it's the nicest thing he ever said to me thus far.

I'd love to go back there with him. He'd make sure I wasn't poisoned, and I could learn more about what it's like being a part of a Greek family, but I let him off the hook. "I like your uncle, but it's probably better if I eat somewhere my allergy won't be at risk."

That seems to appease his nerves. He gives a single nod and one of his little affirmative noises as he pops open the door to the truck. I can hear his muffled whimper before I'm even around the other side of the truck.

He protests at first but lets me get an arm around his waist to help him to the back door of his studio. As soon as we're inside, he hops up on the first step to what, I assume, leads to his apartment. No way. It's time for Johnny's pride to go *bye bye*.

"Really?" he squeaks when I heft him into my arms. "Warn a guy!"

"Easy, Little Prince. I won't drop you."

I can feel those perceptive brown eyes of his on the side of my face. "You…read *The Little Prince?*"

"Who hasn't?" I haven't, but my mother read it to me when I was young. That counts. Right?

His baffled noise makes me wonder if he thinks I'm just some big oaf who can't read. I've met plenty of those in my life, but something tells me the book meant something to him too.

His apartment has a spacious living room with a cushy-looking beige sectional and limited furnishings, other than a coffee table and big screen television. There's a closed door to the left, and beyond that, an open entryway into a sizable modern kitchen. At the end of the living room the neutral carpeting looks to head down a hallway to another room.

"Okay. Here's good. I can get it from here." He squirms.

I tighten my hold a bit and nod to the door to the left. "Bathroom?"

"No! God, no. Don't go in there," he says, looking like he's seen a ghost. "Um. My roommate, Bitsy. She needs her beauty sleep. I've got a bathroom in my bedroom. Just put me down and I can make… Hey!" he squawks when I keep moving. "You sure don't follow instructions very well. You know that?"

"That depends on what kind of instructions they are," I challenge, which does what I hoped and shuts him up.

Feeling like I won a small battle, my steps are surprisingly light for having a grown man in my arms. I stop in the doorway of his bedroom though and…

I have no words.

"What?" he fidgets as I gape at the mattress floating suspended in the air from the ceiling by four ropes.

"Your bed is a swing?"

He huffs and winces as he squirms out of my arms. "It's called a hanging platform bed actually. I brought it with me from California when I… It was a gift. It used to hang on my old patio overlooking the beach. It…soothes me."

The challenge in his expression dares me to make some mocking retort, but I've got none, so I nod. He needs all the calm he can get. "Yeah. That makes sense."

It takes him a minute to hobble over to his swing bed. Yeah, I can't not call it a swing bed. It's a freaking bed that's a swing. Keep dreaming, Johnny.

"Swiper, thank you for the ride and the carry, but you can go."

"Sit," I command, pointing at the swing bed. He does, but frowns up at me, so I add, "Stay."

"Woof," he huffs.

Patting his head, I can't help myself. "Good boy." I'm quicker and pull my hand back before he can smack it.

Returning from the kitchen with a plastic bag full of ice, I find him with his shoes removed, leaning back on an elbow, trying to prop his injured ankle up on a pillow. When he sees me, he yanks a corner of his bedsheet over his junk like I'm some peeping Tom. I've never met anyone with so many penis image issues. What the hell happened to him?

"You sure don't follow instructions very well, either," I tease, lifting his calf to place his ankle on a pillow.

"I stayed, didn't I?"

"Do you have a first aid kit?"

"I'm fine. You don't need to…"

"Okay, I'll go find something."

When I return from the bathroom full of the most extensive collection of de-curling hair products on the planet, he's lying back on the pillow, arms folded across his chest, staring at the ceiling like it offended him. I guess I can add control issues to his list as well. He shifts over or, rather, scrambles as best he can with his banged-up knees when I make to sit on the not-a-bed.

It is a bizarre sensation to feel the platform shift underneath me. I have to shove images of what it would look like if someone was having sex on it. Has Johnny had sex on his swing? Does that make it a sex swing? Christ.

Dampening a swab with peroxide, I hesitantly reach for his cheek. This feels intimate. I need to stop thinking about intimate possibilities with a man who doesn't want me.

"You know, you don't actually have to tend to me," he says, holding his hand up as though warning me to stop.

"I know, but I want to."

He blinks and his mouth turns down. "Why?"

"That's what people do. They help each other out. Or they should, at least."

His silence is so loud, I can practically hear his suspicion screaming. I have to shake my head. I must have looked like a persistent pain in the ass so far, encouraging him to stay longer on our dates. Cringing, I remember that happening to me in the past. It was never a comfortable feeling when all I wanted to do was to get as far away from the person as possible.

"Look," I begin, dabbing the scrape below his cheek with the cotton. "Just because you didn't want to go on another date with me doesn't mean we have to give each other the cold shoulder. I…think of you as a friend. I mean, you have to admit, the way we keep meeting. It's…"

"Bizarre?"

"Yeah. Something like that."

Johnny sighs and rests his head back on the pillow, seemingly giving up the fight as I gesture for him to bend his knee closest to me. He grits his teeth as the wound opens, making my heart squeeze for him. All it does is reinforce the thought of growing old without someone.

"Have you…been on any more dates?" he asks.

"No."

"Really? Not going to find *the one* like that."

"Probably not."

"Well, how come? What's the hold up?"

He flinches as I dab his wound, and I give him a second before answering. "Hadn't really given it much thought after…you know. *The itch.*"

My heated face wants to know why I always have to be so honest. Johnny's eyes shift behind his scratched lenses off to a corner of the room.

"Seriously," I clear my throat to change the subject, gesturing to his bed. "Where does somebody even find something like this?"

"Island living dot com."

"You like the beach?"

"I used to."

"What changed?"

His nose twitches, and he laces his fingers together over his chest, drumming them against each other in thought. "Me, I guess."

There's a story there, I'm sure. As much as I'd like to know all his stories, I know enough about him to know he's not the type to tell them freely.

Rubbing away a bit of grime from the worst part of his scrape, his leg jolts. My hand freezes, and I cringe on his behalf. I soak a new swab and press it to the injury, watching as he bites his lower lip. I'm sure it stings like a bitch. He basically scraped the entire top of his knee cap off. Leaning in, I blow on the fizzing peroxide to help ease the burn as it does its magic and rub my thumb gently around the unaffected skin surrounding the scrape to take his mind from the discomfort.

Except, now I realize, my lips are an inch away from his body heat. My view downward is of his form fitting shorts and all they display since he moved his hands up to rest on his chest. Too intimate.

"There. That should do it."

"Thanks," he says a little less reluctantly.

Crap. I just looked at his damned shorts again. I can't help it. You can almost see every vein in his penis in those things.

"I don't always look ridiculous. You know?" he says, tugging the bottom of his shirt lower as he lists off his past ensembles, "Mustard attacks at carnivals. Superhero underwear. Girls' shorts. Running into stop signs."

Freaking Johnny. "I don't think you're ridiculous."

His mouth pouts. "Why not?"

"You're…honest. Not everybody's that honest."

He sits up slowly, holding my gaze with this sadness in his eyes I don't understand and want to dissipate. Swimming in the wake of his little vulnerable moments brings me both lightness and heaviness. Part of me wants those moments, but the realistic part of me knows I should head back, having already overstayed my welcome with a man who wants nothing to do with me. We've said goodbye several times already, but just like all those times, this one feels final too, filling me with loss.

"Well, feel better."

I stand and hold my hand to the bed to keep it from swinging. Leaning in, I dust a kiss to the side of his banged-up knee, suspecting no one's been or had a chance to be tender with him in a long time if ever. Leaving him with the knowledge that there's people out there who would be good to him is the least I can do.

When his hand touches the side of my face, my pulse hitches. His thumb drags across my skin there ever so slightly, and I close my eyes at the baffling sense of belonging that simple touch brings me.

"Thank you. That…felt good," he says, his voice all low like someone who just woke up.

It wakes me up as our eyes lock.

Maxie said the other person would make the effort. I honestly can't say it's effort, this physical thing between us. It's more like two storm clouds crashing together. It feels like we're about to crash again.

"This?" I venture, brushing my lips to the side of his knee again. I'm holding my breath, so this moment doesn't pop like a balloon. When his fingers slowly thread into my hair, I run my hand down his calf at a snail's pace because I can't help myself whenever I'm around him and he looks at me like that.

His throat undulates. That vein in the side of his neck, pulsing as he shrugs. "It's…a little bit itchy."

How has the word itchy become sexy? Only Johnny could do that.

"Where?" I breathe against his skin, slowly taking a knee.

"Everywhere."

"I'm a slow kisser. I don't know if I have time to kiss everywhere."

"Right." He nods.

He lowers his foot to the floor, dropping his hand. Maybe he changed his mind, or maybe my sexy talk needs work. Maybe he's right, and this is a bad idea. I'm ready to accept defeat, but don't dare move when his hand comes back up and goes to the back of my neck.

"But…maybe you have enough time for me to thank you properly."

He doesn't have to tug too hard. I go willingly to his mouth. Unlike our last few encounters, this is softer, sweeter. The careful press of lips has more consideration behind it. It's purposeful.

It…means something. It's what I've been looking for and from the person I've been looking to give it.

When Johnny's legs widen and our tender brushing of lips turns to stealing deeper tastes, I lean in. There's no debate this is more than a thank-you-kiss. I want to live in this thank-you.

Why is he pulling back? I can tell he wants this just as much as I do. Oh, shit.

My weight on my hands rocks the bed frame along with Johnny away from me. I topple forward just as he swings back toward me, my face bashing off his chest while I try to stop him from swinging.

"This stupid fucking bed!" He grumbles and winces, digging his toes into the carpet.

When we get him and the swing bed still, he waggles his fingers urgently.

"Stand up, Swiper."

Swiper.

We're going to have to have a talk soon about me having a real name even though I like that there's a cell in his brain dedicated just to giving me a ridiculous nickname.

And, *hello!* There goes my zipper. Did not see that coming.

Oh.

Oh, God.

Yes, please—more of those skilled fingers on me. Head bent, concentration focused on freeing me, he's a man on a mission. I'm not even embarrassed I'm half hard just from that kiss.

Holy….

He's not…

He's…

"Oh, fuuuck, Johnny," I slur as his lips wrap around my tip and don't stop until they reach my base, taking me to the back of his throat.

If this is thanking me, he can thank me all he wants. I know he's weird about his hair, but I need to touch him, need to ground myself in confusing, unpredictable, irresistible Johnny.

Diving my fingers through his locks, I grip and knead, grip and knead—the same way he's doing to my ass.

This bed is starting to serve a purpose as he rocks to and fro, working me with his mouth and tongue. Swirling, sucking, stroking. I'm out of S-words, but he's using all the good ones.

"Johnny. Johnny," I pant, probably sounding like I'm reminding him of his own name in case he forgot.

Need coils around the base of my spine. My legs are quivering. I want to give back, to take, and give back some more, but as I squeeze his shoulder to tag myself in, he grunts, sending the vibration around my cock.

"Lay…down," I gasp. "Wanna touch you too."

He moans his disapproval at my plan and maybe his desire at the thought of it, cupping my balls. My hand slips into his shirt and smoothes over his pec muscle. His whimper when I circle his nipple shoots a tremor from my balls to my toes. He likes that. Noted. I cheer inside over now knowing a part of his body that is a whimper-button.

My stupid heart takes in the rising sunlight splashing off his crisp white sheets, his hard erection tenting his silly little shorts, and all the lines of his body. I can't remember the last time I messed around with someone in the daylight hours.

Standing here in his bedroom with his mouth and hands wrapped around me while the world is just waking up outside threads an intimate tone to the experience. Like we're morning lovers saying goodbye for the workday. Like he's mine, and I'm his, and we could do this again tomorrow or tonight. No promises or plans made. No expectations, just understanding and belonging and spontaneity.

And damn it. I'm coming.

I warn him with a cry, but he's a pro at this apparently. His hot mouth never leaves me. His muffled sounds of delight draw out the aftershocks of my release.

When he finally lets me slide free, he gasps and plants a quick kiss to the juncture of my thigh. Perfect.

He's perfect.

This is perfect.

Even in spite of all his snarkiness, this was the man I suspected was in there, and now I'm a goner.

Falling to my knees, his breath hits mine, and I capture his mouth. Whiskers brushing whiskers. Noses brushing noses.

"Oh," he chuckles in surprise.

What did he think—that I'd just zip up and pat him on the back?

My head collapses into his lap, still spinning. I wrap my arms around his waist—a silent *thank you* for my *thank you*. His hand pats my shoulder.

"Heh. Heh. You alive there?"

I open my eyes to the light again. I can feel his arousal, pressed against my jaw. Shifting my head, I rub my cheek gently against it, and chuff, "Barely."

My lips find the outline of his hip and leave kisses as he pats my arm again. "Well, heh. Now you can never tell anyone I'm not appreciative."

He just can't help himself. Can he? Even awkward and snippy, I'm still a Johnny fan.

I move my mouth to the outline in his shorts that's been driving me mad since he ran into that stop sign. He jerks in my arms. Apparently, he's not the only one who can shock somebody with their antics.

"Whoa! Heh. Um. You don't…don't have to…do…*resturnsies*," he breaks off with a stifled moan as I cover and hug his bulge with my mouth. "Uhn. Un-unless…you really want to."

"Want to," I rasp, holding his gaze as I slip my fingertips into his waistband. *Returnsies* will be mandatory if it makes him unable to finish a sentence in one breath. I tug at the constricting black shorts, remembering his tight red underwear last time. "Wanna tug these off too."

"Flapper!" he gasps, bashing me in the mouth with his knuckles as he sneaks a hand in between us to cup himself. "Just…just use your brick hands!"

The battle between his panic and arousal is too adorable. Flustered Johnny is my favorite Johnny. I draw the tip of my tongue up his length and over his knuckles. Breathing against the ridge of his crown where I know he's extra sensitive, my voice has gone all throaty, "I'd rather kiss it."

His chest stops rising, and his mouth hangs open. "Fine," he says on a new breath. "Fuck it."

He's lifting his hips a millisecond later, and I'm tugging the cycling shorts over his...bare ass?

What do we have here? Lord, have mercy.

"What?" he asks, glancing down at me.

"You're...wearing a jockstrap."

"Fuck!" His palms slap his bare ass cheeks so hard, I flinch on his behalf. "It's...I...I need to do laundry! Okay?"

Now I have an uninhibited view of what's straining inside the front of that jock. Slanted to the right, the olive fabric is stretched over the intrusion, his tip snug against the elastic waistband. "Leave it on," I practically choke. "It's hot."

Mouthing his tip with hugs of my mouth, he relaxes under my touch. The smooth skin on his thighs is like velvet. The need in him displayed in the way he squeezes my shoulder and grips my hair only fuels my desire to satisfy him. Sliding the front of his jock aside reveals his engorged head, shrouded by a tight casing of foreskin—his tip peeking out and glistening for me. I track a vein down his long thick length to a close shaved patch of dark hair near his base, his sac plump and tight. The sight of him like *this* for *me*, I don't think anything has ever been more flattering.

He's fucking beautiful, but I realize he's holding his breath, his grip slackening on my hair. Glancing up into a palpable humility in his eyes that I can't for the life of me comprehend, I draw the tip of my tongue up from the rim of his crown to his head and whisper my worship, "Yes."

The flash of disbelief in his expression snares the mix of gratitude and awe in my chest. If he won't believe words, maybe he'll believe actions. His taste on my tongue, like the scent of him is a siren song.

He's smooth and sleek and turgid all the way into my mouth. Those gasps encourage my inexperienced tongue to do its best. I haven't done this much, and now I regret my lack of finesse.

I must be doing something right though, because he kneads my hair, urging me on with little nudges all the while, mumbling, "Yeah. Yeah. Oh, shit. Yeah."

I've heard lovers say those nonsensical words before, but they've never made me feel like a champion. I groan around him, his praise getting me hard again. The way his hips buck at my own sounds makes me a mad man. My mission—devour and pleasure, devour and pleasure. I don't know what's come over me, but I snap the band of his jock on the curve of his ass.

His cock twitches in my mouth. He cries out, and I know it's not from pain.

"Aw, fuck," he practically whines.

Releasing him, because I'm only an amateur and need air, I shift to his sack, licking and sucking and lapping. I'm going to dream tonight about the way his thighs are quivering around my face. Licking back up his shaft, I take him slowly this time, holding, savoring.

That sound—that slow keening sound as he runs both hands through my hair, silently begging, is enough that I have to give my own erection a squeeze. This is his show, not mine.

"Shit, Swiper. You…trying to outdo me?"

His ass deserves a swat for that remark, and I deserve the result. He yelps in ecstasy and bucks into my mouth as I reclaim a rhythm.

Tighter, faster, deeper, and I nearly forgot… I draw up to his crown and work his ridge with my tongue, clenching his thigh to hold back my own need.

"Uhn. Uhn," he whimpers, but it turns into rambling. "I didn't mean it…when I said you were straight."

Freaking Johnny. I nearly choke on a laugh, so I give him another little swat, and he comes.

"Fuh-huck!" he cries.

I hold my mouth locked around him. I can feel every pulse against my lips, on my tongue—his release, a living conduit between us.

I always preferred the receiving end of this act over the giving end. Now I know this is what it's supposed to be like. *This*—all my empty spaces being filled with completeness by witnessing someone else's pleasure. I swear, it's even better seeing him come undone than it was letting him undo me.

Releasing him slowly, I press a kiss to a bare patch of smooth skin where his shirt rode up. *Mine. This will all be mine now*, I think. I want to laugh at how possessive and unlike me that is. Shit. I sound like Graham when he talks about Jen, his ex.

But it's true. I can feel it. He *is* mine now. There's no way there's any question about it; we're both on the same page.

CHAPTER 20
Aiden

Tucking myself away, I can't believe it's already six thirty. I'm definitely going to get shit for being gone this long. I don't care though. It was worth it.

Johnny's scrambling, adjusting his shorts back into place. Maybe he's got places to be too. I hadn't even considered that. He looks so out of sorts.

"Well, that was fun," he says with a nervous laugh, but doesn't meet my gaze.

Nausea sweeps through me. I've heard that line from him before.

"You…sounded like you had fun."

That laugh—that airy laugh. It kills a piece of me.

"Still so observant, but um…shouldn't you be getting back to work? You know, to look out for more clumsy runners and all."

"No. I think most people know stop signs mean *stop…before* you get to the stop sign," I try to joke.

"Heh. Heh. Right. Sure. But um, Bitsy, my roommate, doesn't, and if she wakes up while you're still here, there will be a full-on interrogation. No stop sign in the world can prevent that woman from barging into my personal life."

Oh, shit. His roommate. I forgot all about her, and here we were with his bedroom door wide open.

"Crap. Sorry. I didn't even think."

"No worries. It takes two to swipe, as you once said."

My paranoia evaporates at his joke. The guy just needs some privacy. I can respect that, but my eagerness wins over. I need to find out when he wants to see me again.

Stepping forward, I cup his arms and give him a peck on the cheek. Man, he must be really afraid of what his roommate will think if he's flinching from that innocent contact.

"So, can I get your number to call you later? I get off

work around three."

"Oh. Um. I have to work till at least four."

"Yeah? Well, I could stop by and watch you in action, or…maybe you want to do a brick mason calendar?" I wink and flex my bicep, laughing at my own terrible flirting.

"That's…that's…" He pulls away, hobbling toward his dresser like he wants some distance. "That's incredibly thoughtful but sounds a lot like the makings of dating." As I gape at him, he adds, "Which I don't do, if you'll recall."

The air in my lungs gets stuck. Is he for real? "So….what…what do you call this?" I gesture between me and the swing bed.

"Insanity?"

That's one way of putting our chemistry. "Okay. Agreed. Good insanity. Great insanity, if you ask me. And…you have no interest in seeing if it could pan out? I'm not high-maintenance or anything. I promise."

"I can see that, but I'm not a panner. Haven't been in a long time."

I'm speechless. It feels like a slap in the face. I mean, I'm an adult. I've had casual sex and meaningless make out sessions, but never where it felt like we set the roof on fire, multiple times. How can he not want to explore this incomparable spark I've never felt for anyone else?

He makes me laugh. I know I make him *want to* laugh. We both have families that try our patience. He's thoughtful when he decides to stop pretending he's a crab ass. Sure, we're different in some ways, but I like that we're different.

How many dates have I been on that involved alcohol and talking about or watching football and local gossip? How many dates told me about their perfect family? How many placated me by agreeing with everything I said? How many looked bored when I talked about my job, while Johnny got tongue-tied over me talking about his wall.

Every time I've seen his face, I think, y*es! The party's starting*.

But he wants the party to be over. Hell, he won't even let it start.

I'm standing here, feeling like a lovesick idiot. I'll regret it. I know I will, but I have to ask.

"How can you…after we just…you felt something. Right?"

"It's not about what you feel now. It's about what you don't want to feel next Tuesday, or next month, or at Christmas, or after a long day at work two years from now when someone comes home and says *they* don't feel it anymore. Understand?"

"Somebody hurt you."

His features tighten when he shifts his weight, and I somehow doubt it's from his ankle. I've hit the nail on the head.

"What did he do?" I press.

If I could wipe that dejected look off his face, I would. He tugs his glasses off and rubs his eyes. Blinking at me when he looks up, it's so unfair that this is the moment I learn he's even more handsome without them on.

"He promised me everything, and I believed him. There's not much more to it."

This feels like a losing battle, but I have to at least try. "I didn't promise you anything, but I keep my word when I do. Are you really going to deny yourself a chance at happiness because of something one person did?"

Glasses back on, hand on his hip, I see the moment the defenses go back up. "You have to want that kind of happiness to feel like you're being denied it. I don't. I have enough happiness on my own to suit me."

That's the saddest thing I've ever heard. I don't know who to feel sorrier for—him for being content with less or me for not being content without more.

"It's not about you, if that helps," he adds. "You're…a great guy. Heck, you'll probably thank me someday when you meet somebody who doesn't run into stop signs and wear lurid underwear. Right?" He lets out a sour laugh.

Naming two of the things I like about him don't help convince me, but now I remember a woman, Tracy, who cried when she couldn't understand why I was turning her down. I'm the Tracy here.

Fuck. I don't want to be a Tracy.

"Right." I nod.

Wrong. Nothing could ever be more wrong.

My feet move to the door. It reminds me of that moment you hop off a merry-go-round and try to get your bearings.

"Thanks again for the ride," he calls.

My face heats and when I glance back, I can see he may regret his choice of words as well by the blush in his cheekbones. He lets out a nervous laugh and gives me an awkward wave.

"Yeah. Thanks for…" I don't even know how to finish that sentence, so I just leave.

I'm not sure how I even made it back to my truck. Turning over the engine, the chilly air cranks out of the a/c vent, cooling my flushed skin. A humorless laugh bubbles out of my chest.

I wanted romance, wanted to feel something. Why did I not consider that part of romance could be getting rejected?

CHAPTER 21

Hey Curly,

I know you said you weren't mad, but it didn't seem like it. I'm sorry I told you about not wanting to do oral
anymore. The whole uncircumcised thing just feels strange to me when I try it, but I'd rather be honest. If you don't want to do something to me, I wouldn't expect you to. Sorry, maybe oral just isn't my thing. Everybody's different, you know? _You're_ still great at it though ;) Promise me you won't be mad. We can still do plenty of other things.

Anyway, a shoot with Chelsea Reeves – can you believe it? I'll get her autograph for you for your studio. Who'd have thought a carpenter's son from Pismo Beach would be a cover model? Nobody'd know who I am if you hadn't gotten my photo in that swimsuit calendar. I owe it all to you.

Let's take a trip when I get back.

Love,
Lance

 CHAPTER 22

Johnny

Americans have this classy expression—*like a one-legged man in an ass kicking contest.*

With my ass going numb on this sparsely padded booth surrounded by thin cubicle-walling, I am fairly certain I would be a champion at that sport as of late.

The wall behind me shifts, bumping into the back of my head. The muffled tones of men putting forth their most convincing efforts ooze through the itchy fabric-covered panels.

It is the most disgusting background noise my ears have ever processed. I may be sick. To make matters worse, the makeshift dating booth I have been assigned to connects to an exterior wall of the building…with a fucking full-length window for any passerby to see in. Whoever designed this fiasco has clearly seen and enjoyed that "shame" scene from *Game of Thrones* a bit too much. Still, I did this to myself.

The highlight of my week was the purchase of a washer and dryer. My mother ceased any more laundry duties after my last refusal to visit the family homeland and finding out that I still do not have the makings of a life partner.

Bitsy has been increasingly AWOL the last two weeks, going out at night without me. She's *working on something*, apparently—something to which I am not privy. When she is home, the usual mood of our friendly banter has been replaced with what feels like the feigned courtesies of passing strangers. The only exception? Her continued alliance with my mother to force me to find a suitable mate.

As I sit here in this gulag of speed-dating at the old Barton Hotel, I chide myself for not being more aggressive with the people I love. Confidence might help too—the kind my brother and Dami have when they walk into a room. Maybe I should practice walking with a pillow between my thighs. Hm, so tempting.

It's Saturday, date number-three, and Mamá and Papa leave for

Greece on Tuesday. I should be relieved. This torture is almost over. No more forced dates, and I'll get a vacation from the can't-say-no-buffet for three weeks. The thought of food is nauseating.

I haven't eaten anything since breakfast. I have no appetite lately. It's the least Greek I've been in my entire life. It should annoy me that it happens mostly every time I think about that big brick layer and the way he wanted things to *pan out* after the world's best blow job two weeks ago. It doesn't annoy me, it just…well, fuck. It depresses me.

He looked so shiny and hopeful, just like Lance did in the beginning. Okay, so Swiper never promised me anything, but he would…eventually, and I'd eat it up like the Greek appetite I should have.

I mean, he doesn't really want me anyway. He can't. It's laughable and cute that he thinks he does, but let's be real here. Swiper and a guy with a voice like Paul Lind, a penis that leaves much to be desired, an unhealthy Patrick Swayze obsession, a penchant for accidents, a mother like a helicopter, and a family with the vocal ability of a stock exchange trading floor? He dodged a bullet.

Yes, I know he's not Lance. I can admit I was wrong about that, but the urge to find him and tell him needs to sit the fuck down because I was right about one thing. One of us *is* dangerous. It just isn't Swiper. It's me. I am a danger to myself. Case in point, it's been two weeks since he made me come my brains out, and I'm still thinking about it.

I can still feel his mouth on me, still hear all those sexy Swiper sounds. I still remember his scent, his taste, his gasps. His infectious smile, witty humor, and calm mannerisms are a charged mating call to my soul.

Oh, for fuck's sakes! What the hell are they doing over there?

Slamming my fist against the partition, the soft thud doesn't bring me enough satisfaction, so I yell, "It's a cubicle not a freaking bouncy house, people!"

"Hey! Easy! Geesh!" the shifty shifter on the other side complains.

I am so done with this. Speed-dating is right. I zipped through my first two prospects faster than I run from an angry toddler shoot.

The first—a banker who did that rapid eyebrow lift thing about five times within the first minute. Not just a *no*, but a *fuck no*. I may have nightmares about those eyebrows tonight.

Second—a curvy man who had kind eyes and a bushy beard. Curves can be sexy, but why men want a disgusting cesspool of yesterday's dinner on their face, I will never understand. I still can't decide which threw me off first—his invitation to his farm outside of town to show me his horses or that he kept making that giddy-up clicking noise with his mouth after several disturbing innuendos. Yeah, we're going to add that noise to the nightmares—nightmares which better not be about horseplay.

To each his own. I'm not into kink shaming, but I was not built to either be or ride a horse. *Shudder*.

I'm so drained. Why does everything in my life feel like it's upside down? The harder I try to wrangle control, the more it slips out of my grasp.

Two more. Right? That's what the event host said—four selections. I can do this.

The shoddy door creaks open, my stomach roiling already. I'd almost beg for a dating app instead of this Jack-in-the-box type of reveal. At least Swiper was charming…and easy on the eyes…and incredibly sweet…and…

Stop, Johnny. Stop!

My eyes travel up the muscular frame of a man who couldn't be bothered not to wear gym shorts to a dating event. Shit taste in clothes, but nice build. His radiant, hopeful smile is…

"Ew! Dami? What the hell?" I squawk at my big, little cousin—my very straight, big, little cousin.

"I… Johnny," he bursts in this weird laugh I've never heard him use. "I…I thought this was for straight people."

Something stinks, and it ain't me, babe. Pinning his gaze, I lift the atrocious speed-dating flyer Bitsy slapped in my hand before she shoved me out the door—the one that has more rainbows on it than a little girl's unicorn-themed party invitations.

Dami's never been the sharpest tool in the shed, so in response to his baffled expression, I arch a brow, point at the flyer, and narrate…slowly. *"Men for Men of Olympus—the dating event of the year for gay singles"*

He blinks, his trap resembling that of a largemouth bass. Sighing, I toss down my ticket to hell and lean my forearms on the table.

"Alright. What gives?"

He jolts forward, scrambling into the seat across from me so fast, I nearly jump off the ass-killing bench. His big meat hooks clamp over top of mine in a death grip.

"Look, Johnny! You can't tell anyone! Okay? I…I'm not out. At least, not around here. Please, promise me you won't tell my parents."

What the ever-loving hell am I hearing? And why are my hands all sweaty? Ew.

I manage to wrench one away from his bizarre coming out panic grip and swat the other with a *crack*.

"Ouch! What was that for?" he yelps.

"Keep your cousin mitts to yourself, please! In case you've lost your sight along with your mind, let me spell it out for you. That's a window right there. I'm not interested in being the poster boy for Incest is Best."

"Uh. Right. Right. S-sorry."

His anxious posture and metric ton secret are too much after the last few weeks. I drop my forehead into my hand. Maybe if I breath and click my heels three times, it will all go away.

Nope. No such luck.

"So, is this a new thing? Was it a college curiosity that hasn't died yet?"

He snorts at me. *Snorts!* The little shit. Okay, so he could totally clobber me, but still. Respect your elders.

"Man, you're narrow minded for a gay guy."

Gasp! "I beg your pardon?"

"Johnny, I'm gay. I've…always been gay."

"What? Why?"

Dami snorts again. Okay, I didn't mean to say that last part out loud.

"Well, I mean," I stammer, "surely you've seen the shit fest I've gone through being gay in this family. We're Greek men, the children of Greek islanders—we're supposed to impregnate women. So…yeah. Fuck it. Why?"

"Probably the same reason you are—I like cock."

"Uh! La la la la la! I can't hear this! You're like my little brother. Don't ever *cock* me again."

"Jesus, and you wonder why I've pretended to be straight my whole life. You were always my hero. I thought you'd be the most understanding, but if this is your reaction, I've got no chance with the rest of the family." His shoulders sag. He looks so defeated—my vivacious little cousin, defeated.

"Wait. *I'm* your hero? How is that a sentence anyone would ever say?"

"Are you serious?

Considering I still have a few scabs on my knees from running into a stationary object two weeks ago….um, yeah. I have no idea where he's going with this.

Dami purses his lips and elaborates. "You're kind of a bad ass. You came out to your parents when you were a teenager. You went away for school and built a life in California for yourself in spite of your parents wanting you to come home. You got to fly all over the place, meeting famous models and making nobody models famous. Then when you moved back, you put your foot down and got your own place and started your own business, doing what you love. That's…inspiring. You gave me hope it was possible to come out to them someday, that I could do more than wash dishes at Tapas."

Oh. Well…fuck. I'm someone's inspiration? That's…that's… I don't even know.

"I…had no idea," I manage.

"Yeah." He lets out a long breath and sits back in his chair as though a weight has been lifted from him.

Shit. The secrets we keep. Maybe my family isn't as close and up in each other's business as I thought.

"Well, listen. If…you ever want to talk about this sometime, I'm game. Okay? You know where to find me, but…considering that we're at a dating event at the moment and contestant number-four could walk through that door at any moment, why don't we table this for another day? Mm-kay?"

"Yeah." Dami chuckles. "Yeah, absolutely. Alright. I'll just get out of here." He stands and looks at me thoughtfully for a moment. Why is it so uncomfortable now that I can see the admiration in his eyes? I'm no monument of great decisions. He leans in, arms outstretched.

"Oh, fuck no! We don't need to hug," I warn. "We're good."

"Oh, uh. Yeah." He glances over his shoulder at the window. "Sorry. I forgot. Um. Well, thanks, Johnny. I appreciate it."

"Mm." I grunt and nod. Is this the part where I'm supposed to give sage advice to the little grasshopper? With a sweep of my hand to the exit door, I add, "No problem. Um, go forth and cock it up."

Dami laughs, his exuberant grin splitting his face. "Sure. Thanks."

Look at me. I'm Johnny the Inspirational. Huh. Who'd have thought. Why does it feel like he's somehow more in my charge than he was a moment ago when he was just my little cousin?

"Dami, wait!"

His hand stills on the doorknob as he turns back to face me. "What is it?"

"If you meet a man here named Bob who likes to talk about his horses, run."

"Uh, okay."

"No. Seriously. Like sprint like you've never sprinted before. Mm-kay?"

"S-sure. Thanks for the tip."

"Mm. See you at dinner tomorrow."

"See you."

When the door clicks shut behind him, my fingers dig into my eyes and rub, shifting my glasses up my forehead. I may die alone and single, but until then I sure as shit will have plenty of stories to tell anyone who wants to listen. My shoulders shake on an exhausted laugh.

A hinge squeaks. It's sad that I've been sitting here long enough I know it's the sound of the entry door to this closet of emotional torture.

"Listen," I warn the next contestant on *The Price is Wrong*, face still in my hands, "just keep on walking, pal. Tonight's not the night."

A deep, happy sound like a stifled chuckle splits the stuffy silence of the cubicle. My heart flips at the familiarity.

"Funny," the voice beyond the table says, "Every time you tell me that, it is the night."

Dropping my hands, Swiper is revealed before me in all his beautiful brick-handling glory, a chalky, navy-colored button-up hugging the phenomenon of his biceps. With his hands shoved in his pockets, he looks like he's lost something since the last time I saw him. The corner of his mouth is ticked up just a fraction from his little quip, but it's sadder… less *Swipery*, and fizzles out a second later.

I don't want to go through this again—the sweet, sweet taste of undeniable attraction, the bitter taste of denial for both of us, the strength to fight either. Who is doing this to us?

"What the… Wh-why? Just…just why?" I babble.

He shrugs and throws his palms heavenward, looking just as baffled. A puff of breath leaves his lips, and he shakes his head. Something inside me twists like jagged metal. I miss that twinkle of excitement in his eyes he had the last few times he saw me. It is nowhere to be found in those once lively green eyes.

"What did we do?" I ask. "Why does this keep happening to us?"

The corner of his mouth twitches, and it's like Christmas. "I don't know. Do you have a curse on you or something? Do Greeks believe in curses?"

I snort because that was close enough to some Swiper-humor. My spirits have been restored, knowing he's not so upset he can't tell me jokes.

"I'm sure I have a few," I concede.

His hands dig back into his pockets. Glancing out the window, he shifts his feet as though he's in a waiting line. The thought of him walking into three other cubicles makes my molars grind.

"Didn't meet Mr. Right from the glorious pool they have here?" I venture.

"No. You?"

"A serial brow-wiggler, a burly bearded Bob who might have wanted to make me his horse, and believe it or not, my cousin. Not telling my mother about that last one."

Swiper's teeth bare when he grimaces. "Ooh. Ouch."

More silence. I need small talk. I hate small talk.

"Rest assured; I'll be noting that in the survey at the end of this glorious event."

"Ah, crap. I forgot about that," he mutters, smearing his hand over his mouth…that mouth I shouldn't look at. "Maybe we can sneak out."

Why in the hell didn't I think of that in the first place? I took a photo of the damn hotel to prove to Bitsy that I arrived. Goodbye, ass-killing bench.

"Now you're talking," I concur, trying not to catch that delicious scent of him as he holds the door open for me, like the gentleman I don't want him to be.

Out on the sidewalk, we come to a halt in front of the hotel entrance. It occurs to me we're both taking turns glancing up and down the street at the steady stream of evening traffic. This is goodbye. Again. Time to go home and curl up on the couch with a movie marathon all by my lonesome…

"Oh, shit," I curse, checking my watch. It's only six-thirty.

"What's wrong?"

"Mm. Nothing. Just…Bitsy asked to have the apartment to herself for the night. Something stinks with that woman. I don't know what she's up to."

"Maybe she just needed some privacy."

For what, I want to ask, but fold my arms and frown through another bout of traffic watching. I am now homeless for the next few hours—homeless from a home that I bought and paid for. Once again, I did this to myself.

Swiper is shifting his feet again. Either he has to use the restroom or is that thrilled with my glorious company, trying to find the appropriate form of farewell for our most recent cosmic aligning. I still don't like how things were left between us the last time.

I'm defensive, okay? I know that much. I've got cause to be. I made a life choice two years ago, and I stuck with it, but it's not Swiper's fault we can't keep our hands off each other and keep getting thrown together.

"So…do you have anywhere you need to be?" I ask.

"Uh. No. Not really."

"Well, um. There's a bar just down the street. You look like you could use a drink after that," I suggest, nodding my head toward the hotel.

His brow wrinkles. "But you don't drink."

Can he stop remembering everything I say? It's annoying. And…attractive. I hate it.

"I'm sure they have *other* things."

One of his sandy brows rises, along with what I swear is a flicker of joy in his eyes that makes my stomach settle. "You're inviting me for a non-drink?"

"I mean, I have time to kill. You have…time, and…well, you said you think of me as a friend." I shrug. "I mean, you probably have plenty, and maybe that was just polite lip service since I was just maimed by a stop sign, and I'll warn you, I'm kind of a shit friend. Just ask Bitsy, but…" Holy fuck! Could I shut up, please? "Um, you know. Maybe we can be….friendly."

Has he always taken this long to answer simple questions? Simple, run-on, rambling questions? This ain't an after-school special. He can spare me the suspense.

"It wasn't lip service." Nodding his chin in the direction I pointed, he adds, "Lead the way."

CHAPTER 23

Hey babe,

You looked dead to the world, so I didn't wake you. I'll call you when I get to New York. Tell your family I'm sorry I couldn't meet them this time.

I'll miss you.
Lance

P.S. Could you take my grey suit to the dry cleaners? I want to take it to the Fiago shoot when I get back.

CHAPTER 24

Aiden

Friends?

Yeah. I don't know how simple a task that will be. How do you go from speech-altering orgasms with a person to friends? But my Johnny-crush overruled my common sense so I'm walking the two blocks to Ale Mary's because the thought of him sitting anywhere alone to kill time before he can go home just doesn't sit right with me. He's a light and I'm a moth.

The soft blue glow of the evening sky matches his faded denim jacket—his sleeves, perfectly cuffed like he fell out of a fashion magazine. I want to ask him how many pairs of those dark blue jeans he owns, and where he buys those one-cut-above t-shirts he's always sporting. This one's a navy blue to match his pants, retro in length with a v-cut neckline that shows me a hint of his flawless chest, one I definitely don't need to be thinking about.

Friends.

Why shouldn't we be friends? I've had two weeks to decide that not only do I not want to be *a Tracy*, I don't want to be *a Graham* either. Listening to Graham disparage Jen's life choices the last two weeks gave me a good example of how unattractive bitterness looks. I'm too old to be bitter. Plus, if I had to have another friend, I sure as hell would want it to be Johnny. He may be prickly on the outside, but he's all soft candy center.

I take over holding the door to the bar open as Johnny steps inside the darkened atmosphere. The thump of music cocoons my ears as I blink to adjust to the change in lighting. Figures of people dancing and milling around slowly coming into focus.

Is that…Madonna?

"What in the name of Elton John's closet is going on here?" Johnny blurts at my side.

"Um, I think it's a costume party? An eighties costume party?"

"Nuh-uh. That is clearly Sandy and Rizzo from *Grease* over there." He indicates with a thrust of his chin, hands on hips. "Nineteen seventy-eight."

He knows what year *Grease* was released? That's…impressively nerdy and cute.

"What?" He shrugs when he catches my surprise. "I saw a documentary on it…*recently.*"

When he doesn't move, his posture rigid still, I nudge his elbow. "This too much for you?"

Scoffing, he rolls his eyes. "I've survived seven Greek weddings. These people don't know the meaning of the word *party.*"

Somehow, I get the impression he either really hates the George Michael song that's playing, or he's putting up a front and can't handle the chaos in here.

"Look," he blurts. "There's an open table."

I follow him as he weaves through the pub tables, jolting to a stop some three feet from every person who gets near him, like he's worried he'll be mowed over or catch their germs. I missed his eccentricities more than I should admit. Man, it's good to find humor in something again.

"You want a soda or something?" I ask when I make it to the table. "I think it's bar service only right now."

"Oh! Right. Sorry. I'll get it. I invited you. What do you want?" he hops up.

"No. It's fine. I'm good."

"Really, order a drink. You'll probably need it," he says, grimacing at a group of people our age by the shuffleboard table dressed as all the characters from *The Breakfast Club*.

"Alright. I'll have a beer."

When he returns, carrying a draft pint like it's an artifact he doesn't want to drop, I take it from his nervous grasp. My stupid pulse kicks when our fingers touch.

He takes his seat and scrunches his nose up after a sip of his iced tea, but then turns a polite smile on me. "So. Um. How are things in the world of masonry? No big bad wolves trying to blow your houses down, I hope?"

"Maxie's getting married this Fall, so I have to listen to her wedding plans all day, while my brother Graham has been married twice and complains about her talking about the wedding the entire time. That keeps the day entertaining, if you think gauging your eardrums out is fun, but the weather will be changing in a couple months, so I won't have to hear them bicker for much longer."

"You don't work during the winter?"

"I do, but mostly indoor jobs, which are fewer. Mortar only sets up within a certain temperature range, so there's a limited window to do outdoor and exterior brick masonry during the year."

He proceeds to ask me question after question about the process, the equipment we use, jobs I've done. The worry that I'm boring him like every other date who regretted diving deep into my career fades as he rests his chin in his hand and stares at me with rapt attention. He looks fascinated, which is…fascinating. I still can't believe he gives a damn about bricks or what I can do with them.

"So…what do you do all winter when you're not laying bricks and trolling dating apps for me?"

I snort in front of the lip of my beer at his little smirk. "You're full of yourself. You know that?"

"Couldn't be helped." He shrugs, squinting at the Madonna look alike gyrating on the dance floor, but that hint of a smirk is like a medical breakthrough.

"I worked on my house the last few years, but I kind of ran out of things to do, so I'm not sure what I'll do this winter. Hang out with some friends and family. Go for runs with Dalton."

"*Dalton?*" he asks, whipping his attention back to me. "Who, um, who is Dalton?"

"My dog. He's a Golden Retriever."

"Oh." His posture relaxes. Was Johnny jealous, or am I seeing what I want to see again?

"That's not a common name for a dog."

"It's from one of my favorite movies."

He frowns, nudging his glasses up the bridge of his nose. Damn, I love it when he does that. "You don't mean…*Road House* with Patrick Swayze, do you?"

"Yeah! Did you like it?"

This is too funny. He's the first person to ever guess it right.

Straightening up, he swallows. "It, uh,…it was alright."

"It was epic is what it was! Probably his best film."

He takes a breath like he's gearing up to share an opinion on it, but then snaps his mouth closed. All I get is one of his little grunts of approval.

Hm. Maybe he's not a Swayze fan. That's disappointing.

There's probably little appeal in a stay-at-home movie night for him when he can jet off to places like Miami for the weekend. Speaking of that, I probably shouldn't want to know what he does to entertain himself when he's away.

"Do you do a lot of photography shoots out of the area?"

He shrugs as though there's no appeal in what he once dubbed *para-*

dise destinations. "When I need to get away."

"Don't you enjoy it? Travelling? I've never travelled much."

"Mm. You're missing out, but it's better if you have someone to travel with, otherwise at the end of the day you're sitting in a hotel room in your underwear looking at the room service menu when you're not even hungry."

That doesn't sound like *itch-scratching* activities, which brings me relief I shouldn't need, but the curious part of my brain wonders what kind of other crazy underwear he owns and sits in when he's at these hotels.

"That sounds depressing. Why don't you stay around here and take photos like those ones you have outside your office? Those were great. I bet people would like that candid kind of look you had going in them."

He studies me for a second before answering, "Thank you, but I hate to break it to you—sentiment doesn't pay the bills, honey."

Honey. Is that what he calls friends?

A very buff and bearded Boy George walks by our table, headed to the dance floor as "Karma Chameleon" plays. Johnny gives him a critical once over.

"Wow. This makes me wish I could drink."

"What? Everybody loves this song."

"Excuse me, but *red, gold, and green dreams?* What does that even mean? Is it referring to a flag? Lithuania? Bolivia? The Congo? Does he dream of being there?"

"I think maybe you just don't know how to have fun," I challenge.

That glare. I have to bite my cheek to not crack up.

"I beg your pardon? I am barrel-of-monkeys-fun."

My smirk only seems to make his deep brown eyes stormier. He reaches for my pint and throws back a healthy gulp.

"Whoa! Hey, what about your allergy? Should you be doing that?"

"Probably not, but this just happens to be one of those glass-eating situations that requires substances or a head injury to fully lose one's grasp on common sense in order to enjoy it."

"Well, are you going to die on me now or what? Because that doesn't sound like fun to me."

"I don't get apoplectic or anything. It's more like I'm highly sensitive. Imagine my liver is the size of a peanut, and what probably takes you to get inebriated takes me a tenth of the amount. I'm doing this for you, since I invited you here. At this point, I think it's the only way I can stand it."

That is the most asinine logic I've ever heard, but this is Johnny I'm dealing with here. "Johnny, we can leave or go somewhere else. No need to poison yourself."

He waves dismissively. "It was just one drink. We're here. Our asses have already indented the stool cushions. It's fine."

Why does it feel like something has shifted between us? Is it the friend thing?

I wouldn't say he's relaxed. I don't think I've ever seen him relaxed, except for about a minute after he comes. Okay, not thinking about that again, but this is definitely the first time he's not rushing out the door or rushing me out. It feels like he's letting me in a little bit, so I take my chances.

"Hey, I told myself I wouldn't ask because I know you won't answer, but…I always think every time I see you will be the last time, so…" I preface, watching that curious little wrinkle between his brows form. "How come you don't date? Or was it just me who was the problem?"

Shit. Judging by how quick he looked away, I didn't word that carefully enough, so I jest, "I'm not looking for closure or any-thing. I promise."

"No." He lets out an airy sound. "You're a big boy. I'm sure you can handle yourself. I…if you must know, I guess I have very high expecta-tions, limitless actually, and I've accepted there's no one who can meet them, so it really has no appeal to me."

I don't know if he's uncomfortable with the topic or uncomfortable that I'm the one who's asking, the way his eyes map my face, but he adds, "Like I said, it had nothing to do with you. You were…you were… well, worth forgetting about my decision…several times, obviously," he stammers, going red in the face as he swipes my beer and finishes it off.

I think that was more difficult for him than that time Maxie, Skyler, and my dad had to hold Graham down while I pulled a nail out of his foot. If I got to be the one guy who could almost make Johnny Andro forget about his dating rule, I can live with that.

Smiling, I stand with my empty pint and grip the back of his neck with a friendly squeeze. He looks at me like I'm about to pick him up by the scruff as I lean in and plant a quick kiss at his temple. I can feel him relax the instant my lips touch his skin. "Thanks."

When I get my pint refilled and start back toward the table, I nearly trip over my own feet. Johnny's bobbing his head and tapping one of his feet in time to "Man In Motion". There's a little smirk on his face as he watches two Molly Ringwald look-alikes engage in a heated debate by the dart board.

Holy shit. I think he's actually enjoying himself.

"Something catch your eye there?" I tease when I reclaim my stool.

He stops bopping and straightens up. "Mm," he hums, angling his chin toward the two Mollys. "I think the Mollys are about to throw down. My money's on *Pretty in Pink* Molly."

"Hungry Eyes" by Eric Carmen kicks out of the bar speakers.

It's official. Tonight might be the best night I've had in a long time. Best song ever!

It's subtle, but I catch Johnny shifting a shoulder in time with the beat. I nudge his elbow.

"Do you want to dance?"

There's that startled lamb look again. "Are you for real?"

"Yeah," I laugh, getting up. "Best eighties song ever."

I don't know why he's gaping at me, but if he talks shit about this song, this friendship is officially over. Now he's biting his bottom lip.

Ha! He's thinking about it.

"Swiper, why don't we leave the reenactments to the cosplayers?" he finally says in that perpetually unenthused tone of his.

I think I'm onto his weakness. He's a sucker for a dare, and every time I stumble across one of his rules, he throws out that Swiper nickname. Thank you, Johnny for showing me your instruction booklet.

"Oh. You can't dance, huh?"

"Pfft. I'm Greek. I was born dancing."

I mimic his signature hum, which is actually quite satisfying. "Mm, I somehow doubt that. Hey, it's okay if you're embarrassed."

He pops off his stool, sending the legs scraping against the hardwood floor. Did he just sway?

"You'll be the one who's embarrassed, my friend. Give me a code word for when you change your mind about this fuckery."

He takes off toward the dance floor, his stance wide like someone bracing the deck of a ship at high tide. Is he…drunk?

"Hey! Are you okay?" I ask when I catch up to him.

Nose in the air, he blinks but his eyes don't reopen very quickly. "I am barrel-of-monkeys okay. Now, get this dance-off started before the *Mollys* mow us down."

Wow. Meet Drunk Johnny. He only had like half my beer.

"It'll be fine," I reassure him, making a sweep with my arms. "I'll just tell them this is our dance space and that's their dance space."

I grab his hand and place my other on his waist. He might need the support. When I start to do the famous cha cha style steps from *Dirty Dancing*, Johnny gapes at me and doesn't even move.

"What?" Shit. Does he get paralyzed from alcohol? "Johnny, are you okay? Is it the alcohol?"

"Did you really just *dirty dance* me?" he asks, giving me a once over.

Laughing, I grab him again, but this time when I move, he moves with me. "I tried, but you stopped me. Don't tell me I need to add that movie to the long list of things you don't like."

His haughty scoff is more emphasized than usual. Yeah. Johnny is buzzed.

"*Johnny* wasn't that insulting to *Baby!*"

Oh, my word. He's priceless. I spin him and catch his waist when his back is to me, leaning in so I can speak at his ear. "Ha! You *do* like that movie. I knew it! It was in the background of your first profile picture."

"Everyone likes that movie!" he seethes kind of slurry. "It was choreographic genius!"

I let out a low whistle and wrap my arms around the front of his waist to satisfy the protective instincts his off-kilter state is stirring inside me. "Touchy," I tease.

He doesn't respond, at least not with words. No. His response is worse than words. He settles back against me, his hips in tune with the slow shift of mine.

I've spent the last two weeks trying to forget about how I feel. Seeing him even more defensive about silly things just makes me want to crack his shell even more.

The reward?

Shiny little vulnerable moments he gives just to me like admitting he likes Patrick Swayze, doesn't think someone would want to be his friend, and apparently has a thing for dancing.

He does need another friend. Lots of them, actually. It's extremely difficult to think like a friend when he feels so right in my arms, but damn it. He's having fun, so I'll fight whatever I have to in order for him to continue to do so.

CHAPTER 25

Johnny,

I hate fighting with you. It seems like all we've been doing lately. If I'd known it was make or break with your family, I'd have cancelled my trip for their visit. I just always got the impression they didn't like me when we'd video chat. Maybe it's the whole cultural difference thing.

Anyway, hope you like the flowers. See you at dinner.

Lance

CHAPTER 26

drunk Johnny

There is a brick wall with a penis attached to it pressed against my back. The man's definition of fun is apparently sexual torture.

Aiden Brandt is an agitator…*agitant*…whatever. I am his allergic reaction—the thing that is agitated by the alligator…the agilator…agi-tit-or?

Fuck me.

I can't even think without slurring. Why did I drink that beer?

Soft stubble and warm breath tickles my ear. "Hey. Do you want to do the lift?" he whispers like a kid eager for a Christmas present.

Every fiber in my body doesn't want to disappoint him and wants to *Baby* it up to see if he can hoist me in the air like Patrick Swayze did to Jennifer Grey in the movie, but, hello! This is fucking reality, and the few non-foggy brain cells in my head have a firm grasp on the reins of maturity.

I snort, in a super sexy way, wiping a fleck of spit off my lip that he fortunately didn't see fly out of my mouth.

"Hilarious, Swiper. *Hill-arious.*"

Shit.

Am I actually drunk talking out loud now? Why couldn't I be allergic to mushrooms or bananas?

If Breakfast-Club-Molly flails her arms any wider, she's going to take my eye out. Can't they just scrap and get it over with already?

"You don't think I can do it, do you?" Swiper's breath warms my ear again as our pelvises slowly grind in ways our pelvises should not be grinding.

Yet, I am leaning back into him like a magnet, a horny, want-all-the-Swiper-presents magnet. I have no control over this traitorous body of mine right now.

"I'm *suuure* your super *brickoid* strength allows you to toss humans into other galaxies, but I'm like lead weight. Little but heavy, and I think one facial injury is enough for you to witness."

The husky laugh in my ear sends a zip of static electricity up my spine. "Chicken, huh?"

The fuck he…

He did not!

Tearing out of his Hulk grip, I spin around slowly because these damn lights and that eighty-proof beer of his have gone to my curly head. I focus my death glare on the grinning fool and wait for my heavy eyelids to lift all the way. "You did not just throw down below the belt!"

He seems amused by my hostility. The stupid, stupid man.

I am not a coward, and I will not be mocked by a man who has had my penis in his hand…and his mouth. Uhn.

Fuck.

Stay angry. Stay angry, Johnny. Friends can get angry.

Laughing, he shrugs. "I don't know. I think I just did."

My nostrils flare. Angry accomplished. Turning my head to the two squabbling redheads, I hitch my thumb toward the corner of the dance floor. "Beat it, Mollys. Shit's about to get real," I warn, backing up several paces, as I refocus on Swiper.

Yeah. He should look scared. I level my index finger at him for added effect.

"Hurt a hair on my body and authorities will be called, and then my mother. You have never known fear until a Greek mother hunts you down for harming her offspring."

Gasp! He's *laughing* at me again?

There are three things you do not do.

One—ruin the best eighties song ever with fuckery.

Two—Oh, dear God. Why did I drink that beer? This floor looks really slippery.

And three—never question my dancing skills.

CHAPTER 27

Aiden

Holy shit.

Arms pumping, he is seriously charging right toward me, making a noise that can only be described as squeal-growling like an angry piglet. Bending my knees, I reach for his waist and shout over the music, "Jump!"

He does, but instead of launching himself upward to help me give him the height we need to pull off this lift, he thrusts all his momentum forward. I can feel the strain of his weight in my arms and back as I arch and try to lift him to compensate for his poor trajectory.

I grunt, my lower back twinging in pain. It's all I can do. My face is smothered by Johnny's stomach as he yelps, likely realizing this has all gone to shit.

Moving my feet to balance the extra weight, I can't see a damn thing, but can feel his arms clamp onto my head and shoulder. What the hell is he doing now? Is that his leg, trying to hook over my shoulder?

"Shit!" I croak, staggering back. It's not like I took lessons on how to extract a hundred- and eighty-pound spider monkey from my face. I only did this move a few times when I turned twenty-one, and some girls at a bar asked if I could lift them.

He must fear gravity because he wraps his other leg around the side of my chest. It helps to stop his flailing, and I manage to get one of my arms braced underneath his ass.

"What the fuck, Swiper!" he squawks like this is all my fault.

"Why did you lunge at my face?" I grunt into his side; grateful I can't see how many people are watching us.

His leg finally slides off my shoulder. I help lower him down my front. We're both panting, pressed chest to chest.

He adjusts his askew glasses and huffs, "I didn't lunge! I vaulted!"

Damn. He looks so mad I might piss myself.

"Okay. Why did you *vault?*" I ask through my laughter. "You're supposed to just jump straight up."

"I didn't know this was *Dancing with the Stars*!" He shoves away from my chest and spins to abandon me.

I catch his bicep, ruining his angry exit. Sidling up behind him, he stays still when I capture his hip with my other hand.

"Hey," I soothe at his ear, trying not to chuckle. "Never leave a man behind."

I can feel him relax against me after a second, so I start dancing against him again. He unwinds a little more with each passing moment as we sway to the beat.

I probably should move my face out of the crook of his neck, but I want him to know you can recover from fumbled dance tricks and that I was laughing at *us*, not him.

He moves like liquid with me. I don't even know where my body ends and his starts at this point as I wrap my arms around him, and he draws them in tighter.

He's tracing my forearm with his fingertips. I feel like I've tamed a porcupine, but it's always been like that between us. This is the part I love most—when he puts his quills away. If he ever decides to stow them for good, whoever snares him will be a lucky man, and I'll be jealous as all hell.

Returning his comforting gesture, I lower my hand from his arm, palming his hard stomach, tracing faint circles with my fingers. A vibration rumbles underneath my touch. The growl from his stomach is so loud I can hear it over the music.

"Did you eat dinner yet?"

"No. There's a squatter barring me from my apartment."

Shit.

This place doesn't look like it serves food. I sure as hell am not letting him wander the streets on foot until his buzz is gone. He needs to sit down and chill out.

"I…have steaks thawed out for a cookout tomorrow with my family. I could cook us up some and pull two more out for tomorrow."

He stops dancing and stands still without looking back at me. His hands are still wrapped over my forearms, so I don't think this is the moment where he runs off like he always does.

Finally, he turns his head to look at me. "You want to cook for me?"

"Either that or we let your stomach eat itself."

I don't think I'll ever forget that look or know what it means, but the way he's staring at me, like I just told him he was cured of a disease, wraps around my heart and squeezes.

He turns all the way around to face me, taking my hand in his. "Fine. Fuck it," he says, tugging me off the dance floor, pausing only to signal to the two redheads, blocking our path. "Move it or lose it, Mollys!"

CHAPTER 28

Johnny,

Chelsea's in town again. She invited me to meet her and her agent later for drinks. I'll be home late. Sorry. I know it was my turn to pick up take-out. Eat without me. Maybe you can binge on those eighties movies you like so much.

Lance

CHAPTER 29

Johnny

The walk back to Swiper's truck and a fortunately cool, summer breeze help burn off some of the beer haze. Thank God it was only beer. If it had been hard liquor, I'd be half naked and getting a piggyback ride from Boy George by now.

The cab of Swiper's truck smells all sorts of Swiper-y again. The soft yellow glow from the dashboard functions casts an intimate illumination into this bubble of charged silence as he drives us out of town.

I have no idea where we're going other than it's called *Swiper Land*, and I am a special invitation guest.

I have become Johnny the Rigid, every one of my muscles locked in place, my eyes fixed straight ahead. It is a posture of preparation for the momentous occasion that I think is about to occur.

We're going to have sex. My brain is flashing the message over and over in both warning and anticipation.

We're going to have sex.

Because that's what a man you've messed around with three times means when he invites you over to cook you dinner in the middle of the night. Resistant Johnny is saying, *no, we can't do this.*

The choir of every other Johnny in my head, however, is belting out a chorus to remind me I'm only a man, Swiper isn't Lance, and, gee golly, we sure do miss sex.

I have rarely done casual since my break-up. Each time I did, the moment of satisfaction was quickly replaced by a feeling of emptiness and disappointment, leaving me to realize I am a relationship person. It is so unfair to be saddled with a desire your very fiber fears.

Maybe Swiper finally accepted that I am not datable and decided to give into our explosive chemistry one more time. I mean, why else would a guy like him want to be friends with someone like me? I knew that was code for something.

I'll give him credit though—he's probably the sweetest most patient man I've ever met. For all I know, he initially did have the best intentions, but one thing post-Lance-Johnny has taught me is to not be delusional. It would never work because I am still me.

My loud, eccentric, Greek family who make me want Quaaludes to come back most of the time is still mine and mean the world to me despite all my protests, but that doesn't change the fact that an outsider would be faced with discovering how loud, eccentric, and Greek they are. I couldn't bear another passive rejection of them. Nor does it change the fact that I am clumsy, don't know shit about football, am a bit of a hothead, and have a penis that may seem interesting only during the first showing or two of heated passion.

I can feel his eyes on me. To make matters worse, Peter Gabriel's "Solsbury Hill" is wafting out of his speakers.

Oh, Peter. I can relate. My heart *is* going *boom, boom, boom*.

"You doing alright?" Swiper finally breaks the silence.

"Mmhm," I hum all casual, but it comes out in an octave closer to Bitsy's.

Clearly, he thinks I'm still buzzed and acting awkward, because he chuckles. "You'll probably feel better after you get some food in your stomach."

I know he said *food*, but my mind latches onto the most interesting words of that sentence. I might feel better after *something* gets in me.

Why, yes. Yes, I will.

Stop, Johnny! Stop!

Passing a windrow of cedar trees, he turns into a gravel driveway of a white two-story farmhouse, complete with a screened in front porch. Is that an old windmill? Swiper lives *here*? Can you say wholesome?

Fuck me. It's so cute, I can't stand it.

There's enough moonlight that I can see how well his yard is maintained. If he tells me he did the landscaping himself, I might tackle him before we even get to the steps.

He waits for me to close the door of the truck, spinning his key ring on his finger. Is he nervous too? Turning, he starts up the stairs, and now my gaze has become a tractor beam, locked onto that firm ass of his.

"Oof!" Shit. I just ran into his back.

"Sorry. You okay?" he asks, unlocking the door.

"Mmhm."

Can I only speak in two syllable noises? Get your shit together, Johnny!

The flick of a switch illuminates several stained-glass lamps on rustic oak end tables on either side of a long brown leather couch. The floor is a unique paver stone pattern that reminds me of an English garden. There's a fireplace below a big screen television. On the mantle are several floral vases and tea pots of various sizes and patterns.

The walls look to have been refinished in repurposed barnwood and are adorned with what I would call old-lady picture frames that haven't been sold in three decades. I am gawking as he watches me, so I move toward a side table with another grouping of photos above it on the wall in an attempt to appear to be a normal perusing guest.

A clicking noise precedes a cold wet touch against the back of my hand. I let out a squeak and jump an inch.

"It's just Dalton. Hey, buddy. How you doing? Did you miss Daddy?" Swiper asks, taking a knee to pet the rusty brown mutt by my side.

Daddy?

I can't. I just cannot. I mean, he talks to animals and now he's hugging the thing, while it groans the same sound I am holding back.

Fuck. I have never wanted to be a dog so badly in my life.

He's getting to his feet, so I continue my exploration of *la casa de Swiper*. The photos above the side table appear to be nearly as dated as the frames.

And, hello. There is little Swiper—maybe sixteen or seventeen. On either side of him are who I can only imagine must be his siblings, two boys and a girl. They're at a work site, standing in front of what looks to be a nearly finished brick building. Each of them is a bit dusty and dirty, but the focal point is the ear to ear smile on his face. Happy looked good on him then, and it still suits him tonight.

"How long have you been here?" I ask when it's apparent he's waiting for some type of reaction from me.

"About eight years."

"And you did…all of this?" I gesture to the impeccably clean, but cozy room—a throw blanket over the couch, lace curtains around the front window.

"Yeah. What do you think?"

"It's very…Grandma meets *Outdoor Man*."

He runs his palm down his blushing face and glances at some pottery on a nearby shelf. "Uh. Yeah. It was my grandmother's house, actually. I kept some of her things up because it reminds me how her house always felt like a home away from home, and also so my family can still *feel* her when they come to visit. You know?"

My God. That may be the sweetest thing I've ever heard.

Shit. He's gnawing on his lip, looking all sorts of sexy and insecure like I offended him, and he actually gives a shit about my approval. "I like it!" I blurt. "That was a compliment."

"Thanks for clarifying." He chuckles.

I don't really know what I'm supposed to do as I haven't been in a home alone with someone other than my family in…well, maybe ever?

Stuffing my hands in my pockets, I turn back to the pictures on the wall and try to ignore the Swiper scent permeating this house. Someone needs to make a candle out of that shit and sell it as an aphrodisiac.

"Can I take your jacket?" he says behind me, grasping either side of my collar.

"Yeah. Sure."

His knuckles brush over my shoulders as he helps me slip off my denim. My brain sends critical messages in short wave bursts, announcing the significance.

He's taking off my jacket for me. We are so having sex tonight.

Turning around to face him, I refuse to be Awkward Johnny for this. I'm going to enjoy myself. He's going to enjoy me. We're going to enjoy each other. Damn it. We're adults and it doesn't matter that we're not right for each other or that I once dated a dickhead who crushed my soul.

"How do you like your steak?" he asks.

Is that how we're doing this? Through innuendos or by seeing which one makes the first move? I have no problem being the mover. I've made my decision.

Closing the distance, I rest my palms on his chest. He glances down at them and then back at me, his breath hitching under my touch. I don't blame him. I already feel like melted jelly under that green gaze of his.

"I like it…*after*."

"*After*?" he asks, swallowing.

Nodding, I run my hands down to his stomach, inching forward until our chests are touching. Surely, that is proof enough to let him know he can dispense with the dinner ruse.

His scratchy hand covers mine. He runs his thumb back and forth over my knuckles. "You, um, realize you can't kick me out this time."

I blink at him. Is he serious? This is not a hand job or swing bed blow job. There will be nudity and time-consuming activities, if I have my sex-starved way.

He must think I'm confused because he adds, "Because I live here," but it's all breathy as hell, and he's rubbing my arm now.

Oh, hells yeah. Swiper is all in. I forgive him for the bait via dinner invitation.

"So observant," I whisper, cupping the back of his neck, bringing his mouth to mine.

It's a miraculous act of nature really—the wild hot mutual attraction between us that always happens when we touch. Lips caressing lips, tongues sliding over tongues. We are freaking artists of kissing. Why does he always taste so good?

His little groan stretches every muscle across my abdomen taut like my body knows what's coming and is prepping for an impending release. Shifting, I feel his arm extend to our side. The whoosh of fabric follows—my jacket hitting the floor.

That's right, Swiper. Don't be a gentleman right now. That jacket can die there.

I'm clutching his side, discovering new ripples and ribs. His fingers dive into my hair, fucking it up for sure, but I don't give a shit because it deepens our kiss. He slinks his other arm around me, running his hand up the back of my shirt. Every inch of my skin turns to gooseflesh under his warm, roughened palms.

"Yeah," I moan, "Put those dirty hands on me."

"They're not dirty," he complains.

"Don't ruin the fantasy," I scold, tugging his mouth back to mine.

He lets out a puff of breath into our kiss. I'm glad he gets me enough that he can take my humor. Maybe that's the appeal.

"I like *dinner*," I gasp between kisses and then dive back into his laughter.

I don't know when we started undulating against each other, but he's bigger, so we're backing up. Going where? I don't give a damn.

With one hand on his back and another in his hair, I have the perfect leverage for this dance of bump and grind…almost. Sliding my hand down, I find a new home for it in his back pocket. Swiper takes my lead and *handfuls* me just the way I like it. Our groans intertwine as his arousal presses hard against mine.

Fuck. This man makes me want to do *all* the bad things.

My hip slams into something hard that gives way a smidge. There's a hollow *thunk* sound on the floor and then the bursting of something breaking into a million pieces.

Oh, sweet child of mine. My ass knocked one of the Grandma-vases off the side table!

"Shit! Was that old?"

Swiper's lips sweep across my cheek on a direct line for my mouth. "Very," he murmurs and then devours my lips.

Hm. I rate higher than an heirloom. My ego says *thank you* with a laugh and a squeeze to each side of his ass as I arch into him again.

I just broke something. I don't think I have the right to make any demands, but I do anyway, hoping he'll like this one. "Presents," I request, tugging at the front of his jeans.

He dips. Why is he squatting down, and clutching the underside of my ass, and…lifting?

"Vault," he whispers.

Oh, shit. We're doing this. I press on his shoulders as I vault. The next thing, I'm airborne and wrap my legs around his waist with an embarrassing *yelp*.

But the Swiper train is already moving, and I'm aboard so I enjoy the ride, kissing the side of his neck. "You like to carry me."

There's a soft nip to my shoulder as we pass through a doorway. "Less injuries that way."

Hm. Swiper's got jokes.

I catch glimpses of more repurposed barnwood wall paneling, another grandma-lamp. We dip, and my ass has landed on a firm mattress. Swiper's knee rests next to my hip, never breaking our kiss.

Catching the hem of my shirt, I whip it off, and then start on his. He takes over, tearing it over his head and…sweet mother of mercy!

I gasp so harsh, I cough. Really? He's looking at me like he doesn't understand, so I wave my hand at his ridiculously sculpted torso.

"What the hell is all that?" I fold my arms over my much less impressive chest, one I was proud of until this moment. "Jesus! Warn a guy, would you?"

He glances down at himself, as though he still doesn't understand human beings aren't supposed to be that chiseled in that many places. "I lift bricks all day."

"Shit," I mutter, glancing down at myself for another depressing comparison.

His hot breath hits my neck, the warmth of his arms, caging mine. "Johnny, you're in great shape.'

"Uh. Ye-ah, but fun-sized."

My head bobs to the side with another of his playful kisses. "I knew you could be fun," he murmurs, making me snort when I can feel his smile against my jugular.

"Mm. More of the smooth talking."

He hits my *shut-up button* then, which is a combination of the place below my ear and a tug at the button of my jeans. Noted. Shutting up.

We concur on a silent break to de-shoe and de-pants ourselves, then reassess for public relations. Thank God, I am wearing normal underwear for once   black boxer briefs.

And Swiper is…

Uhn. He…him…*himina*…fuuuck.

We were supposed to get fully naked already, huh?

"What?" he asks, shifting nervously, his hand idly rubbing above his close-shaved sandy hair at the base of a very ready-for-me root.

Sigh. Hello, Swiper's cock. I remember you.

My head rattles back and forth to ease his self-consciousness. "Um. Provisions?" I manage to ask, covertly slipping my briefs over my hips.

He takes a knee on the bed next to me and kisses my shoulder. "Right," he says all breathy and nods toward the wall. "Nightstand."

Sans underwear, I lean back, executing an impressive twist while also concealing Flapper with a bend of my knee as I wrench open his drawer of sexy time wares. Swiper palms the bed with one hand, planting a trail of slow kisses up my side while he glides that rough hand gently up and down my thigh. It is highly distracting.

I don't mind it at all.

"Yes. We'll take this," I announce brightly, pulling out a bottle of lube. "And we'll take these," I declare, retrieving a two-strip of condoms.

Not that my mind is on snooping, but a man's nightstand is his sex treasure chest, so I take note. Swiper's is a bit barren. Other than a bottle of over-the-counter pain pills and what I claimed, there is nothing else in here but an old phone charger cord and some cough drops.

"Tisk. Tisk," I tease, dangling the condom strip from my fingers. "A little low. Naughty Swiper."

He scoffs and sucks my nipple into his mouth. *Gasp!* Shut-up button number-two.

"Did you blow the dust off them?" he jokes, reminding me of his two-year hiatus.

Oh, my.

I am about to receive the gifts of two years of chastity unleashed. Yes, please.

Leaning over me, I have a glorious view of his flexed muscles, propping himself up as he stares down at me. I have missed running my hand up and down a warm body, smooth skin, dips and lines and angles. Never though have these hands been treated to a body like his. I'm practically drooling just looking at him. Okay, and that hard cock of his pressed against my thigh might have something to do with it too.

Except, he's shaking too, and I'm glad for it. Knowing his need is getting to him too helps a little. He reaches for the condoms from my hand, but I tug them away.

"Oh, no," I warn, setting my glasses on the nightstand and tearing one of the packets open with my teeth. "You may have…all this," I gesture to his physique, "but I have tricks."

"Tricks?" he arches a brow skeptically.

Pushing him back, I snort as I rise up on my knees, taking care to cover Flapper with one hand. "Yes. Let a man up his game, please," I sass, motioning for him to join me on his knees.

Bending down, I take his moan-lever into my mouth—his long, thick, silky moan-lever. I could live off that sound, a mix of sweet anguish and relief from deep in his chest as he cards his fingers through my hair.

See? I can be just as sexy, damn it. It just takes a little more work. Releasing him torturously slow, I tug the condom from the packet. Carefully placing it in my mouth, waggling my eyebrows at the shocked expression on his face.

That's right, Swiper. Johnny's got tricks.

I saw this at a house party in college once when I went in search of a bathroom. Thirty seconds of staring through the wrong doorway gave me an education. How hard can it be?

CHAPTER 30

Aiden

Holy crap.

Is he doing what I think he's doing?

I didn't think my cock could get any harder. I've never even seen this in a movie. I assumed it was a sexual urban legend.

Johnny dips down to my cock, the muscles in his back going taut. I can feel the heat of his breath contrasting with the sheen of his saliva still on my dick, sending a new chill of arousal up my spine, helping to ease my nerves.

He grabs my base in his grip, pulling another needy moan from my throat. I run my fingertips down his back and up the sleek line of his spine to his hair.

I can feel his mouth on me and… Ooh, yeah.

There's the condom going on—the rim of the latex, peeking out just beyond his lips. It's the slippery restriction I remember, but hugged by the hot heat of his mouth and little nudges of his tongue. This is now officially the only way I want condoms put on me.

His mouth tightens inching down my shaft. I can't take it much longer. Gripping his hair, my hips twitch forward, needing more Johnny.

His lips slide further down, soft and wet.

Wait.

It's wet.

Why do I feel his mouth more than the condom?

Shit. I don't even see it anymore.

"Oh, fuck," I whisper as his eyes go wide, and a gagging sound chuffs around my cock, making his back lurch.

He grips my thigh and pops off my hard on, which is…completely bare. Where the hell is the…

Oh, no.

Double fuck.

"Did you—"

Johnny's violent sputtering and gagging answers my question. His hand goes to his throat, and he leans over the bed, his naked body racked by coughing.

Oh, my God. I killed him with a condom!

"Shit! Did you swallow it?"

I slap hard between his shoulder blades, the force thrusting him forward. He turns his head, his watery eyes narrowed as a crow-like caw emits from his throat.

Okay. Maybe that was a little hard, but I'm freaking out here. If he's pissed off, it means he's still breathing.

"Pull it out!" I yell, reaching for his mouth.

He slaps my hand as his back lurches from another painful retching noise.

The condom tumbles out, hanging off his lip. The air finally floods back into my lungs when I hear him suck in a healthy breath.

I'm clutching his shoulder, probably making bruises, but holy shit! I did not expect to go from aroused to terrified in two-point-five seconds.

Rubbing his back helplessly while he pants, I hear him spit. The droopy latex falls from his lip to the floor along with a bead of slobber.

"Are you okay?" I ask, running my hand down the back of his head.

He comes up red-faced, waving a hand before collapsing down on my pillow. "Yeah. Good," he wheezes. "All good."

His chest still rising and falling heavily, he closes his eyes and lets out a sigh of relief. Freaking Johnny. I don't think I want to know any more of his tricks.

Laying down beside him, I rest on my elbow and run my hand over his smooth chest while he catches his breath.

"That was…impressive."

"Save it," he grumbles, digging his hand into his hair. "I know—I look like an ass. There's a precision to certain things, you know?"

Kissing his collarbone, I run my hand down to his stomach. "It was hot for the first few seconds, but then I was worried."

"Yeah," he drones, turning his head toward my lamp and covering his cock with his hand. "So…maybe dinner *was* a better idea."

I make a slow path with my lips down his chest. Ignoring his humility seems like the best strategy. Now that the panic is over, I'm in complete awe that he tried to do that for me. It was sexy and playful and…open— an act that required trust.

"I don't think I can eat right now," I murmur at his stomach, tracing imaginary lines on his thigh.

"Yeah. That was enough to make anyone lose their appetite."

"No. Not at all." I place my hand over his, drawing it away from his cock, but he resists when his palm gets to his tip, looking down at me.

I hold his gaze, remembering how he thanked me for the stop sign incident. Peppering the shaved skin around his base with kisses, I shift my hips, pressing my renewed erection into his leg. He must notice because he arches a brow and glances at my hips.

"You don't have to cheer me up. I'm a big boy," he says all salty, but the way he licks his lips betrays his show of indifference.

"I know." I smirk, drawing the tip of my tongue up his shaft.

I wait patiently when I reach where his fingers are still covering the head of his cock. He swallows and slowly moves his hand away, clearing a path for me to take his plumped tip into my mouth. I give it a slow circling lap, savoring the taste of him again after two weeks of hopeless confusion. I'm pretty sure he's in this time. Why else would he have spent the entire evening with me and then made the first move?

I sure as hell know I'm in. I gave up fighting it the second I saw that horrified look on his face when he broke one of Grandma Nelly's vases. It was that soft-candy center of his I can't resist, but now I want to give him mine. I just…fuck. I'm nervous again now that he's not choking on a prophylactic.

I take him deep, gently palming his sac. He's smooth and shaved and heavy for me—*for me*. Why has no one else ever felt like such a gift?

I can do this. I'm ready. I'd started to think maybe it would never happen, and I'd just keep sleeping with women or messing around with men at the PG-13 level for the rest of my life.

My sex life started out with women. I learned how to do it and kept doing it. Then I kissed a man and kept kissing men, adding experiences to my repertoire with them. I never went all the way. Looking back, I think that's how my quest for something meaningful began. I always wanted to know what it was like to sleep with a man. My embarrassment at be a virgin with men at such a late age fueled some of my apprehension, but something bigger held me back. I know what that was now.

It was never the right time because it was never the right person. It was never quirky, insecure, sassy, sexy, blunt as hell Johnny.

His moan renews the gnawing need in my abdomen as he pulls me off him. "Okay," he pants, thrusting the other condom at me. "Can I get a mulligan?"

I stare at it for a beat, swallowing a lump of nerves in my throat. Right.

I mean, we were putting one on before. Well, *he* was putting one on me. I knew what we were about to do. It's just…finally real.

Focus, Aiden.

Okay.

He was putting it on *me*. That means he wants to *bottom*. At least I don't have to ask or worry that there's some code for finding out his preference that I don't know about.

I take the packet from him and rest on my haunches to suit up. Johnny joins me on his knees. The kisses and caresses he's treating my body to are only making my trembling worse.

I should tell him.

I should.

I…I will.

I just don't want to make it awkward. He'll probably think that, because I haven't slept with a guy, it means I lied about doing all the other stuff I've done with men and was only experimenting with him. This is a fragile conversation that could ruin the most intimate moment we've shared so far.

"How…how do you want to do this?" I stammer once I get the condom on.

Chuckling, he runs his hands up my arms and kisses the underside of my jaw, his cock, brushing against mine. "Oh, you know. The usual way. Something goes in. Something backs out then goes back in. Set to loop, please," he coos, nearly giggling as he lays back down.

"Right. Yeah. I remember that part." I chuckle, happy to see that at least he's relaxed for once.

Leaning over him, I stick with what we're good at—kissing. I could kiss him for hours with his hands cupping my face like that. The smooth skin of his inner thighs slides over my hips as he raises his knees, letting me know how he wants me. I don't know if my gooseflesh is from all this first-time skin to skin between us or knowing that so much more is coming.

His scent—sweet and salty just like his personality—and his presence are so overwhelming I can barely breathe. I knew something was missing with all those other partners.

His nimble hands move to my ass, pressing my hips into his, aligning our cocks between our stomachs. I have to close my eyes for a second, burying my face in his neck, the sensation of that added connection too powerful. When I look up, his expression is nothing short of mesmerizing—lips parted with a shadow of anguish from his level of want as he wriggles beneath me. Responsive and eager—two things I never imagined I'd see in him after he stormed off that day at the coffee shop a little over a month ago.

His hips undulate against mine, frotting us together. I move in tune with him, eager to contribute. When he tilts his hips, my cock slips into his crease. I have to hold back a gasp, being that much closer to where I'll soon be. With a shaky hand, I retrieve the lube from the nightstand and coat myself.

"Do you…need me to get you ready?" I ask, tracing my finger along the curve of his ass.

"Mm. Such a gentleman," he purrs, kissing my shoulder. "Go for it, but we don't need to make it a marathon. I want to remember this for a while."

He wants a certain amount of pain so he can think of me after he's left my bed? I press a soft kiss to his lips, my heart expanding in my chest. I'm going to remember every moment of this forever.

"I do, too," I whisper, circling his entrance with my fingertip.

I can't tear my gaze away from his face as I tease and stroke. His little hums and gasps, the way his hands anxiously trace my back and arms—I want him undone and to be undone right along with him. Pressing the tip of my finger inside, he lets out a stifled moan and grips my arms, rocking his ass into the contact. Sucking on his lip, so I can be a part of all those reactions, I start working inside him.

Fingers kneading the back of my shoulders, little groans passing over his lips to mine, I'm experiencing every sense of our chemistry at once—touch, sight, sound, smell, taste. When I add another finger, Johnny's mouth breaks away from mine, his hot breath on my cheek as he keens.

God, I want to drown in him like this.

Reaching for his cock, I just catch it in my grasp to drive him even crazier, when he clamps his hand over my wrist. "No! Don't touch Flapper!"

Is he seriously still hung up on being uncircumcised?

"Um." He chuckles. "I swear I've got will power, but you know… just a man here."

Ah. So that's the problem. Mission accomplished, but still his nicknames bother me. Sucking on the soft skin below his ear, I work my way across his jaw.

"Don't call it that."

"What?"

"Your cock. Don't call it that," I repeat, capturing his gaze. "You're sexy as hell, Johnny."

He blinks at me, his laughter gone. His Adam's Apple bobs, making him look so exposed. I brush my thumb across his crown for emphasis. "*Every* part of you."

A soft whimper puffs past his lips. "Oh, well. Um. Prep complete." He pats my arm.

"Are you sure? Because I can—"

"Nope. We're good. All runways clear for traffic."

Him and his little nuances. Rising up, I lean back on my feet, taking in the view. He's fucking perfect all olive-skinned and solid, looking drunk on us.

This is it. This is really it.

I wouldn't want it any other way. Okay. Well, maybe not the choking on the condom part.

Running my hand from his chest down to his stomach, I let out a slow breath and meet his eyes. "I hope it's good for you."

"Well, that makes two of us," he purrs, grasping my hips and shifting his lower. "Come on, Swiper. Show me what you've got."

Playful Johnny—I knew he was in there. Swallowing, I line myself up with that tight pucker he's offering me. Am I going to hurt him? Am I going to be terrible at it?

Shit. I haven't even told him yet.

"Johnny, I—"

His heel digs into my ass as he thrusts, his body swallowing the tip of my cock. He's tight and hot, clamping around me so hard, I suck in a breath. Johnny groans, long and feral.

Was not…expecting…that, but it's…it's done. I'm inside him.

Trembling, I scramble for the lube and drizzle more, gritting my teeth just to function. Johnny's not waiting though, writhing in little thrusts, using his foot on my ass as leverage.

Palming the underside of his thighs, I lean in, nudging slowly deeper into his firm, hot grasp around me. His face looking completely blissed out, he lets out encouraging little *yeah, yeahs.*

"Johnny," I pant, needing to let a piece of him go like a pot boiling over, because this much of him is just too damn much, and I'm not even all the way home.

"Yeah! Fill me up."

This man. Fuck.

Pinching my eyes closed, I groan and plunge until his ass slaps my pelvic bone. Our cries come out as twin tortured souls.

"Yes! Thank fuck," he gasps.

Glancing down, I can't see a single centimeter of my manhood. He owns it. All of it. My heartbeat is in my ears, while his is around my cock.

It's all-consuming and beautiful. It's…just, holy hell.

Easing off is torture and relief at the same time—less restriction yet reducing that sense of connection. I thrust back steadily, shards of current bursting through my balls, my legs, my cock.

Johnny lets out a cry of relief. "Oh! That will do! *That. Will. Do.*"

Palming the mattress by his head, I swoop down, capturing his mouth. He needed this as much as I did. I can see it in his face, hear it in his sounds.

It's taking everything in me to not move, holding myself still deep inside of him as I feast slowly on his mouth for this tender kiss. Tracing his side down to the svelte skin on the curve of his ass, I never knew sex could foster such a reaction in me or another person. I had hoped for something more than what I've felt in the past, something more than thrusting and a sense of satisfaction, but *this*…this unparalleled intimacy far exceeds any expectation I could have imagined.

Johnny is starting to squirm impatiently beneath me. I can't imagine what the pressure of me inside him feels like, but I want to give him what he needs. Brushing his jaw with my thumb, I draw back to deliver for him.

My man.

I never cry, but I can't deny the mist in my eyes. My heart wants to burst. The last two years of thinking I was emotionally faulty. Hell, even longer than that. It is such an epiphany and moment of vindication on top of all the other delights.

He's it for me. He's the one. I found him, and now he's actually mine.

CHAPTER 31

Johnny,

We need to talk. See you after work.

Lance

CHAPTER 32

Johnny

I'm not sure what I was expecting, since I wasn't exactly expecting anything, but this…this is…different. Swiper is all slow and tender, treating me like I'm some delicate spectacle of worship. Which is… uniquely erotic.

And arousing.

And totally doing it for me, although it seems like this behavior should violate some friend code, sub-section B, paragraph A, titled: *rules of benefits*.

I mean, the gentle heart eyes thing is nice, but for the love of my Aunt Donetta's bougatsa, I need an orgasm like yesterday. A man can only be chalk full of Swiper cock at this Barry-White's-greatest-hits pace for so long. What has abstinence done to the poor man?

Patting his side, I signal that it is time to enter into negotiations.

"Okay. I know slow and steady wins the race, but can we try something else?"

"Sure," he says, looking all concerned.

Adorable, but if he's worried this snail's pace will break me, he's in for a surprise. Planting a foot on the mattress, the thrust I give serves two purposes. One—damn, that feels good. Two—roll over, big fella. Let Johnny show you what we need.

He catches on, rolling us until he's on his back. Don't worry prostate. I'll get you what you want.

Flap—

I mean *my cock* slaps against his stomach.

Shit.

The man's got me calling…my cock…*my cock*. Why do I feel more naked than naked?   He's going to have to get rid of that innocent schoolboy look on his face soon, or I'll melt into a puddle of Harlequin-style lovemaking instead of the good old romping we both need.

Since California, I am one hundred percent a power-bottom. Non-negotiable. He'd better not fuck up my mojo.

Straddling this big hunk of man, restores my sense of control. Sliding down onto his moan lever, the way he grips my hip and thigh and gasps is indicative that he approves of my methods. I purr happily, welcoming the stretch that I missed. There is a whole lot of Swiper to take in, and I am up for the challenge.

"Fuck yeah," I moan, settling all the way down his length, because good friends moan, and, holy shit, he feels fucking incredible.

I can't help but take a heap of pride in his puffs of breath and throaty moans as I rock and slide, rock and slide. We're doing a duet to the world's simplest song.

"Johnny."

"Yes."

"Johnny."

"Yes."

"Johnny."

I nearly miss my line, tempted to cry out, *I love bricks! I love bricks*, as his chest flexes under my palm. Reaching for *my cock*, it is time to get to the first chorus.

"Let me?" he asks, wrapping his hand around mine.

Oh.

Hm.

Okay. That's…generous of him.

Swiper takes over, his gaze never leaving mine. The remnants of the lube on his hand slide his thumb over that place under my crown.

Uhn.

Buttons. He knows all my buttons.

I might die of ecstasy right here on his cock with this warm sensation of tenderness wrapping so tightly around me, I can hardly breathe. Maybe if I close my eyes…

Yeah.

I don't even want to know what my face looks like, but judging by the noises I'm making; it would be a blackmail-worthy-photo. The tidal wave is approaching. I can feel it with every twist and glide of his talented hand, every undulation of my hips.

"Yeah. Oh, yeah. That's it," I babble like a sex life coach.

I clench around him, no longer having any control of my sphincter. It's coming, that storm of tension in my lower half that's about to explode like a ton of dynamite. My eyes fly open. Swiper's are as wide as saucers.

He glances from my face to our connection and back again, whispering, "Holy shit."

A laugh bubble pops in my throat at his expression. It almost looks

like he's never felt someone's ass clench around him. How cute. He gets
an A for flattering expressiveness.

What…what is he doing?

Why is he sitting up?

I'm about to snarl, *don't you dare ruin my orgasm*, when he wraps
an arm around me, keeping me in place. It actually shifts him inside me
just right, hitting my prostate. I let out an embarrassing cross between a
bellow and a whine.

"Jesus, Johnny," he breathes at my mouth, silencing me with a
soul-eating kiss. "So sexy," he rasps, rocking into me. "So incredible."

I am a hundred and eighty pounds of naked man, being bounded up
and down on this Swiper see saw. How does he keep doing that, tagging
that perfect spot inside of me? I have struck gold tonight. Does the man
have the stamina of a pack mule? All I can do is hang onto his neck and
warble the song of my people—my people being those who are fans of
Swiper-lap-dances.

"Look at you, Swiper," I joke with precious air I should save
for breathing.

What the fuck?

Why did he stop?

He's cupping my jaw, our gazes locked. His voice is all sex-wrecked
and low. "No more nicknames. Okay?"

And then…he presses his lips softly to mine and holds them
there for a beat.

What…

Um. What…the hell was that?

Why is my throat closing up? The adoration in those green eyes slays
every locking mechanism on my tear ducts.

Holy shit. He's making love to me. We're…making love.

Friend code, subsection B, paragraph A disintegrates into a puff of
ashes. This is not a friendly scratching of itches.

Fuck me. I can't…I can't….

This wasn't supposed to….

But it is, isn't it?

And part of me wants it to be and mean what that look in his
eyes means. I can feel every defense in my body tumble down like
a damn *Jenga* tower as he brushes my cheek. I am a broken man.
He just broke me.

My forehead collapses against his. This wasn't supposed to happen.
It's not safe. It's terrifying and hazardous. It's all-consuming and wonderful, which is why it's terrifying and hazardous.

"Fuck," I garble when I can't hold my breath any longer.

He must sense my dilemma the way he always senses everything. Kissing my neck, working his way to my collarbone, he starts to rock into me again, whispering, "We are what we are, Johnny. I like what we are."

"Fuck," I practically weep, undulating on him like a damned addict, holding onto his neck for dear life. "Are you going to come?" I gasp in desperation, a last-ditch effort to end all this sugar sweet talk that is sure to kill me.

Both his hands cup my head, weaving into my hair. His teeth bared in restraint. "Want you to come…first, baby."

There are over one hundred thousand four-letter words in the English language, but apparently the word *baby* is the only one that can make me come on command and lose my ever-loving-mind. "Shit. Aiden! Aiden!"

My head arches back, my release hammering out of me with helpless melodramatic cries as I scream a man's name for the first time in two years. I can't stop it.

"Oh! Aiden! Aiden!"

He's jerking into me erratically, probably breaking my hip with that grip of his, but it's my life light. Each pulse of his cock inside me, each one of his deep cries makes something in my chest shine and consume me with all its light.

"Johnny! Oh!"

The echo of my name cried from his lips tumbles around inside my brain. Clinging to him like a security blanket, I am paralyzed by this new sky that cracked open and rained down on me. The dead weight of my emotions is too heavy to move my face out of the crook of his neck as we pant against each other.

What the hell was that? I never want it to happen again because I want it to happen again and again.

Aiden's arms wrap around me. *Aiden's* arms…

Listen to me.

I'm totally broken. He fucking broke me.

He sweeps us around, laying me back on the bed. More kisses. More soft, soft kisses.

Uhn.

Why?

Why is he doing this to me?

Fuck. Now he's smiling a smile of a man who's on top of the world.

I know that smile. I used to see it in the mirror.

My lips stretch into what I hope is a complimentary semblance of that for him. I'm not heartless. It was wonderful. He was wonderful. It just shouldn't have been so wonderful.

Maybe I've got it all wrong. Maybe he's just a big softy in bed.

Okay. Bad analogy. There was nothing soft about him a minute ago as evidenced by my very sated ass.

When he disposes of the condom, he returns with a hand towel and…

Oh.

Really?

He's…cleaning me up.

Lance used to toss a t-shirt at my face with a laugh, if I was lucky. Now he's climbing back into bed. Shit. I should… I don't know. What should I do?

I should…be pulled tight against his warm, bare chest and like it a little too much. He's nuzzling me. I have just been nuzzled. Little kisses to my jugular that send delicious shivers across my skin. I should say something.

I nervous laugh because all sexy men nervous laugh. "Wow. That was…that was…"

"What?" he asks, kissing my temple.

Too romantic. Too intimate for friends with benefits. Too fucking perfect for me to ever forget so you have now ruined sex for me for the rest of my life?

"Um. Like how precious any boy's first time should be," I jest.

He burrows his face into my neck and groans. Great. I embarrassed him for his technique.

"Sorry. Too far with the sarcasm? In case you haven't noticed, I'm good for that."

"No. I…I'm sorry. It... You're right. I was nervous."

"Big strong Swi— Er…um. You? Nervous? Whatever for?"

"It *was*…my first time, and it…it *was* precious. Thank you."

He kisses me. It's like a bird running into its reflection in a window for how unresponsive I am.

Jesus, Mary, and *Joseph's Technicolor Dream Coat*, I did not just hear that!

CHAPTER 33

gobsmacked

Johnny

"You…you're kidding me. Right?"

"No." He grimaces. "I tried to tell you, but things escalated so fast, I…does it bother you?"

I blink at his ceiling. Gobsmacked is not even an adequate word for what I'm experiencing right now. Have I just deflowered a thirty-one-year-old virgin?

"When you say…*first*. What exactly…"

"I've slept with women."

Oh, thank fuck. I can breathe again.

Almost.

"And I've been intimate with men, frotting and oral, but not… I never went *that* far with a man before."

Fuck. Fuck. Fuck!

He's watching me, waiting for my reaction. I can feel his gaze on the side of my face.

My liberal response tumbles out like a giant gumball from a dispenser. "Oh."

"You're freaking out. Shit." He sighs, drops his face into the pillow, and groans.

Superb. Now not only have I taken his man-flower, but I've felled his mighty steadfast aura of confidence.

This is why we can't have nice things, Johnny.

"No! No. I…it's…it's fine. I just… You know. Uh. Maybe warn a guy next time so he doesn't ride you like a jockey."

Chuckling, he turns his head toward me. "Well, technically there won't be a next time. There can only be one *first*. Right?"

Holy shit. I'll always be his first. *Me*. Forever me and this night.

"Right. Um. Well, was it everything you'd hoped it'd be?"

"That and then some." He bends, pressing a quick kiss on my mouth.

"Um. Good. I mean… I'm good or glad you're good. We're good."

"You *are* freaking out. Aren't you?"

"No!"

Yes. Hell yes. "It's just… I might have done things differently had I known."

Shit. That got his attention, more of his attention I can't handle right now.

He props up on his elbow, his bare leg shifting against mine. Mercy, I nearly forgot we're still naked.

"Different how?" he asks all curious, stroking my hip.

Why is *now* the moment I recognize the innocence in his face as clear as day?

"Well, that's neither here nor there, is it?" I wave the question off, but his puzzlement is so poignant, it cracks another piece of my heart. He's a grown man. This was his decision. Why do I care how he fares in the aftermath of his first man-shagging?

Ugh. It's those damned hopeful eyes and that sweet face. Also, possibly because he gave me something incredibly precious that he could only give to one person in the entire world. You don't squander a gift like that. Regardless that the glow of me will eventually wear off him later, this night should be special for him.

Damn it. I do care.

Shit. I am so going to regret this.

"Okay. Just so we're clear. I *never* spend the night, so don't get any ideas, and this is not my forte by any means, but…I hear a proper canoodling is in order for a *first*, so I'll make a concession. Just this once."

I roll onto my side toward the Grandma-lamp and scoot back, closing my eyes when I feel hot warm parts connect with my skin. A big, heavy arm wraps around me. His hand, finding my forearm.

Wow. He's wasting no time getting into it, snaking his other arm underneath my waist, which should not be comfortable but somehow is.

"*Canoodling?*" he asks.

"As in *to canoodle*." I gesture to our state of *pretzelness*. "Like two noodles in a can all…stuck together and romantic and shit."

His smirk presses into my neck, and he squeezes me tighter against him. Yes. Laugh at my pain over intimacy that wasn't supposed to happen. I'm not lying right here or anything.

"I think you mean *cuddling*."

"Cuddle—canoodle." I squirm, but it's difficult in his canoodle-hold. "Look. We don't have to. I was just trying to be thoughtful."

He tugs me back and, *hello!* His thigh just thrust between mine. We are now super canoodling.

"It's very thoughtful," he murmurs. "Canoodling sounds nice."

"Mm." I grunt.

Why am I stroking his forearm?

You see? This is how this shit starts. Canoodling, unconscious arm stroking, then morning breath kisses, and then doing laundry together.

He's so warm.

Why do all his parts fit so nicely right up against all of mine? I have sorely underestimated the joys of proximity. Is it selfish of me to rejoice in being his first man-canoodle?

"Aiden?" I tremble at the sound of his name on my lips.

"Yeah?"

"Why…me?"

Silence.

Okay. He's always Chatty Kathy. What's the deal?

His stubble scrapes my neck down to my shoulder. Another one of those little butterfly kisses.

"You do it for me, Johnny. Why anyone other than you?"

What?

I beg his pardon?

Insert frowny face. Insert erratic heart flutter. Insert why-the-fuck-am-I-thinking-in-emojis now.

The quiet is only cut by more peppered kisses across my shoulder blade. The heat in my belly spreads with each press of those lips and those words that are still floating above us like a glorious halo.

Damn it. I'm getting hard again.

Highly inconvenient. We do *not* get hard over emotions and fluffy words.

That hand he's trailing all torturously slow up and down my thigh is no help either. His hips shift. Uhn. Doesn't he know you do not shift during canoodling? Perhaps, I should have explained the rules.

Oh, Patrick Swayze, he's hard again too.

Uhn.

My hand and ass have voted my brain off the island and become dirty little *gimme-magnets*, squirming against him and stroking the curve of his hip. Well, fuck you, *body*. My brain is still functioning a little.

"Why did you never…before?"

"It just didn't feel right."

Insert frowny face part-two as a calloused hand circles my belly. This sounds like a conversation we should have had at the coffee shop.

"Did…all the other things you did with men feel *right*?"

"They felt good. I was attracted to them. This might sound silly, but a couple years ago when Maxie met her fiancé, Véronique, and I saw how happy they were, how they just had this spark together, I decided I wanted-ed to wait to have sex again until I knew the person was really worth it."

"*Worth it?*"

"Yeah. You know—special."

"*Special…*"

He thinks I'm special? "Well, eh heh. I've certainly been called worse things."

"You shouldn't be," he scolds, leaning in to kiss my cheek. My cock decides at this moment to twitch into those big, calloused fingers at my naval. The damned traitor.

"Um. Careful. You're getting dangerously close to getting your second *first time*."

"Really?" He chuckles, drawing the pad of his finger over that blasted spot on my cock.

Uhn.

Hold on. What does he mean—*really?*

"You're not the only one with stamina. I'm a runner. Remember?" I say all breathy like someone with no stamina whatsoever as he twists his wrist on an upslide of my length.

"I remember," he rumbles, his cock twitching against the seam of my ass as though it recalls our swing bed exchange.

Mm. That was the best *I remember* ever spoken in history. Now I'm moaning like a shameless hussy, *handfulling* him to get closer to those enticing twitches and rocking my hips into his talented grip.

What the hell am I doing? Danger! Danger!

"I'm glad I ran into you tonight," he whispers, sucking on my neck.

Well, no shit he is. We light buildings on fire.

"Heh. Yeah. Maybe the universe was trying to tell us something."

His hand tilts my jaw back toward him, and I realize I've said the wrong thing, but also maybe the exact right thing because the reward is fantastic. His tongue deep dives into my mouth, devouring, sucking, sweeping, swirling. We exchange the vibrations of our moans. Seriously, someone needs to donate us to science for studies on sexual chemistry.

Who the fuck could fight this?

"Do you have any more condoms?" I blurt like it's a level-five emergency.

"No. Just the one we…" he gestures to us, "and the one you ate."

"I did not eat it! It went rogue when you tried to deep-throat me!"

Fuck him and his laughing mouth on mine.

"You were too good at it. I lost control."

"Hm. Okay. Fine. Forgiven."

Sweet baby Jesus, he's teasing my balls and grinding that hot rod of beef into my crease. The last shred of my willpower is being eaten alive by the second. Decision time.

When will I have sex again?

Damned if I know.

Will it be anywhere near as good as this?

Not just *no*, but *fuck no*.

Uhn. He just drew the tip of his tongue up the curve of my ear. He doesn't fight fair. Well, that settles that. Completely rushed and careless and probably how decisions by invading dictators are made but a decision, nonetheless.

Thing number-two after canoodling that I have only done with one other person—go bare. Don't say it, Johnny. Don't say it.

"I'm clear, you know. Are you?"

"You mean, *testing?*"

"Mm," I grunt so my sanity can't blast out wise protests as I press back into him.

"Yeah. Me too."

No. Yes. No. Yes!

"Mm. Well then. First time part-two?"

I am Deviant Johnny, all sexed up on wild lovemaking emotions. It is the only explanation for the way I raise my leg to open myself in invitation and thrust the lube back at him. Taking it, he slickens up then strokes his fingers slowly up and down my crease.

"You're not sore?"

"Thank you for the concern, but I am a seasoned professional."

More silence. Now what? It's not like I'm in a precarious position here.

"Did…was it alright for you?" he asks, lightly gliding that plump head through my seam.

Oh, my. That's anxiety-talk while I'm all eager beaver again. Way to spout words like *seasoned professional* to the virgin, dickhead.

"Yeah. It…it was so fantastic I want to do it again, and I've rarely ever wanted an immediate second helping."

When his breath floods over the back of my neck, I feel his entire posture relax against me. That luscious tip finds its way and presses just inside as he whispers, "Same."

We join in our new language again, twin moans of white-hot desire, but his was-it-good-for-you question is still there like a fucking mosquito. It is suddenly apparent to me that I have the responsibility of giving him a proper first time. This needs to be good for him.

I swore I'd never be someone's first time again, never someone's launch pad into gay sex. I can't believe I'm actually going to do this.

I drop the veil—the wall that has protected me from poor decisions for the last two years. For however long this takes, I can be Johnny Sunshine, the carefree, clueless nerd who smiled taking pictures on the beach every morning. The Johnny who was open to life and new experiences so much so that he left the cradle of his family and moved halfway across the country. I feel lighter already.

I feel every inch of hot, bare flesh sliding into me, fitting and expanding me in a way that is so exponentially wowing it should be illegal to feel this wonderful. It's like hot molasses spilling through my veins, a chemical reaction bursting inside my body, oozing slowly down through all my limbs. How is it too much and not enough all at once?

Yeah, groan for me. Just like that, I want to tell him. *Let it all out. Use me for what you need. I've got it.*

Gripping his thigh and pulling him against me, I want every last centimeter of that hard body on me. When I roll to my stomach, he rolls with the teacher, never breaking our connection as he ends up pressed against my back.

"Johnny," he gasps, rutting against me, nipping my ear. "So good. It's too good."

He's pawing through the back of my hair and kneading my pelvic bone. We're animals in the basest of rituals—please and repeat. Please and repeat.

Not enough. Not enough.

With every upward motion of his hips, my greedy ass scoots back and higher, lifting and chasing. We can't get any closer or deeper, but this ravenous anomaly inside of me doesn't seem to understand that. Aiden does though. He knows. He always knows.

Gripping my hips, he rises to his knees, drawing me back into him. That angle. Oh, I love geometry. Good geometry makes me loud.

"Nai. Dosto mou, moro mou!"

"God, it's so hot when you speak Greek."

I did? Oh, shit. I did.

"What did you say?" he pants as his skin slaps against mine.

"Yeah. Give it to me, baby!" I mean it just as much in English as he groans and picks up the pace. "Sorry. I'm loud, if you…hadn't noticed."

His chest presses to my back. His arms hooking underneath mine.

"I love it," he rasps in my ear, drawing me up onto his lap.

With my ass resting on the tops of his thighs, I am now an Aiden hood ornament. Uhn. I am so down for being that part of this ride, so I cup the back of his head and reward him with more of the mother tongue.

"Nai. Étsi akrivós!"

Yeah. Just like that.

He whimpers into my mouth, stroking my cock in time with slower more sensuous little jerks of his hips. My entire body is thrumming with this charged wavelength we create. How am I ever going to forget this?

"Johnny. Fuck. You're perfect. This is perfect," he mumbles with a level of gratitude I've never heard in anyone's voice.

For the moment, I believe his words. Because it is perfect.

My limbs are heavy as lead, my body saturated with the weight of a lust I've never experienced, all these sweet words he's whispering into my skin. All this pressure inside me and around my cock—every inch of me is immersed in him.

"Aiden," I whimper, barely recognizing my own voice. "You're going to fucking ruin me."

"No," he murmurs. Then he says the magic four-letter word. "Baby."

A tidal wave of satiation slams me. I paint his hand and my stomach, making incoherent sounds.

"Baby," he cries again, prolonging this blissful torture as he pulses inside me. "Oh, baby."

Fuck. This is just a dream. It has to be a dream.

CHAPTER 34

You changed the locks? Really? That's fucking mature.

We're having a baby. What did you expect to happen next? Can't you at least be a little happy for me?

I can't find my watch in any of my moving boxes. Check my nightstand. I have to meet Chelsea to pick out rings and then meet her parents for dinner. I'll be back around 9pm.

Be here!

Lance

And don't pretend you have anywhere to go. You never go anywhere anymore. Let's just do this like adults and get it over with.

CHAPTER 35

Johnny

I have often wondered what people who wake up from a coma feel like. Do they have the same sensation of terrifying dread that is locking up every single one of my nerve endings at the moment?

I'm in Aiden's bed. In Aiden's arms. Under Aiden's sheets. Under the darkness of his bedroom with no Grandma-lamp lit.

Fuck. I fell asleep.

I remember lazy kisses, lazy wiping of skin, lazy arms snaking around lazy arms. I remember burrowing my heavy head into this pillow, mumbling *just a nap*. I remember hearing *stay* and even smiling at that plea.

But now…

The veil is back, choking my throat. I let myself fall into quicksand and now, I'm up to my neck.

One helping of Aiden's full-on affection nearly snared me tonight. I don't even want to imagine how I would fare after weeks or months of it. Lance has nothing on this man and look what that did to me.

Would I shave my head and move to Tibet? Join a traveling circus? Move to Greece to take care of *Yiayiá* where I'd never set eyes on another appropriately aged gay man in her little village as long as I live? Anything would be better than surviving the carnage of recovering from an Aiden addiction. I do not want to go through that again.

I have been nothing a but a pain in his ass. As soon as the sex pheromones fade for him, whatever appeal he thinks he sees in me would evaporate.

That is why I am very carefully extracting myself from this incredibly comfortable bed. God, his arm is heavy. His fingers just brushed my cock.

Uhn. Keep moving. Resist!

Okay. Feet successfully on the floor. Good. This is good.

Where the fuck are my—

"Hello, puppy," I whisper and crouch. "Give me the

underwear, please."

Tugging, my elastic band stretches underneath his paw, which has his head resting on it. His dark brown eyes shift up, looking at me as though to say *you think I'm fucking moving for anybody right now? You took my bed, asshole.*

"Get! Get! Shoo!" I wave, but Dalton the golden bastard is either deaf, failed obedience school, or is punishing me for what I just did to his *daddy.*

"Fine. Fuck it."

I realize the less noise I make the more likely I am to not disturb my bed partner who looks…so peaceful and…not my concern.

Sliding into my jeans, the sight of his sated figure all sprawled out under the sheets is such a temptation, I know I'm making the right decision. If it's this difficult for me to even leave the room, what would it be like when he left my life after I let him in?

I need to be smart. I am under no obligation to play boyfriend to anyone. I never asked for this. It was wonderful and toe-curling, and that's that. It is a memory I will bottle and keep with me for the rest of my life. Everyone should have one of those to warm them at night like a souvenir they sell in Monastiraki Square.

After *not* looking back at the gorgeous kryptonite in bed, I successfully rescue my denim jacket from the living room floor. I am covertly out the door, down the stairs and into the early morning darkness.

Now I realize, however, that it is three-thirty in the a.m., and I am in the middle of fucking nowhere. Standing on Aiden's lawn under the black sky, this is where my plan ended. What the hell do I do now?

Bitsy and every other person I know are likely dead to the world, just like Aiden. Just like I should and could be back in that big warm bed.

No! No. Foolish Fairytale Johnny, shut your pie hole.

We're walking—walking toward civilization and the first sign of an address other than this one, where I will phone for an *Uber* to pick me up. There. Plan B in effect.

Lots of people walk down country roads in the middle of the night. Right?

Lots.

Why do I feel dirty? I don't mean because of the remnants of sex residue still on various parts of my body that I want to wear like a badge of honor. We're grown men. Someone once told me to act like an adult. Acting like an adult isn't supposed to be fun. Is it?

I can at least check my messages while I get ravaged by mosquitos. Ouch! The little bloodsuckers!

> **Mamá:** Did you change your mind yet? Yiayiá will be so disappointed not to see you.

Sigh. Let's throw another heaping load of guilt on the fire why don't we?

Greece. Three weeks in Greece with my family. That certainly would make Mamá happy. Well, as happy as she can be with a son eternally stuck in singledom.

Actually, that sounds like a perfect idea. I mean, it has nothing to do with the fact that Aiden knows where I work and live and what kind of bed I sleep in. I won't have to worry about resisting temptation. The thousands of miles between here and Greece will solve that problem. I mean, Mamá really wants me to go. What can I do?

Oh, thank God, a farm. What's the address?

Wait.

What was that? Do I hear horses? Oh, shit. Those are horses. Suddenly, every spec of darkness around me takes on the form of a bushy beard moving out from the shadows. Is this where the Bearded Bob lives? Is Bearded Bob Aiden's neighbor? Why am I just now realizing that the word *neighbor* has the word *neigh* in it?

You know. I really can't miss my run today. I mean, if I'm going to be on a plane for nearly fifteen hours, cardio seems imperative. Just a little run. Just a little, full-on sprint past every creepy horse in this corral.

CHAPTER 36

Aiden

"Mm. Johnny?" I groan, sliding my hand across the mattress, rousing from the best sleep I can ever remember.

But there's no body to meet my grasp. There's no pool of body heat on my sheets.

I sit up, rubbing the sleep out of my eyes in the early morning light coming through the window. Dalton rests his snout on the edge of the mattress, letting out a sad little whine.

Don't ask me why I know. I just do. There's something about the sorrow in his big brown doggy eyes that tells me he isn't in misery for a bathroom break. He gives me this same look whenever my back hurts after a rough day on the job.

Dread winds up like yarn into a ball inside my stomach as I get out of bed. My clothes are on the floor where I dropped them last night, but Johnny's aren't. Slipping on my shorts, I pad into the living room. Before I even get there, I know from the eerie stillness of the house that he's gone. He's fucking gone.

My first instinct is to worry, but then I remember who I'm worrying about. Would he really up and leave without a word after last night? Once I spot the note on my kitchen table, I almost wish he had.

Aiden,

Last night was wonderful.
You are wonderful.
I hope you find everything you're looking for some day. Take care of yourself.

Johnny

I'm not the angry guy. I've never been the angry guy. I'm often the biggest one in a room, but never the one anybody needs to be afraid of losing his temper.

Crumpling up the paper with a shaky hand, my entire body trembling, I can feel something in me die. All the magic of last night makes the impact of the fall that much more painful.

He left.

He fucking left.

No. He ran just like he always has.

"Are you fucking kidding me?" I rage, whipping the wad of paper through the open doorway, but it bounces back and tumbles on the floor in between me and where Maxie is standing, wide-eyed with a giant container of potato salad, Véronique at her side.

"Whoa! Aiden, what the hell? Are you alright?"

Shaking my head, I stomp past them back to my room. "No."

I'm not alright. He freaking left without any intention of ever coming back or seeing me again. I know it. How do I know it? Because I realize I still don't even have his phone number.

And…what the hell is that in Dalton's dog bed?

Underwear?

Johnny's underwear.

He was in such a hurry to leave, he didn't even take his underwear.

I'm a fucking idiot. People who want to see you again make sure you have their phone number. What pisses me off the most is I know he felt something. I can't be wrong about that. What did I do to him to be left like a meaningless piece of ass that I've been avoiding being or doing to someone else the last two years?

I am not a Tracy, but for fuck's sake. He's at least going to tell me why he's such a damn coward.

CHAPTER 37

Aiden

It's been two days. That's as long as I could stand waiting for Johnny to show his face.

Not a word. Not a ping on any of those stupid apps on my phone. No sight of him running around town. Not a single knock on my door. Apparently, he doesn't want his one normal pair of underwear back.

The bell to his studio chimes as I walk inside the crisp air-conditioned space on my lunch break. His red-headed friend sits behind the desk where we went at it like teenagers a few weeks ago. Bitsy, I presume. The studio lights are off behind her with no trace of Johnny.

"Hello," she calls, halting a donut halfway to her mouth. Without taking her eyes off me, she palms a box of tissues and deposits it somewhere underneath her desk.

"Hi. You must be Bitsy," I say, approaching with my hand outstretched.

She nods, reaching for my hand as one does a bear trap. "Aiden. Right?"

"Yeah. Is Johnny around?"

Her mouth hangs open for a second. Has he sworn her to secrecy? What the heck is with the hesitancy?

It's not like I'm a threat. I just want him to have to see my face and say whatever he was thinking instead of writing some cop-out note.

"Um. No. No he's not."

"Do you...know when he'll be back?"

Her features sag. Am I really that scary looking? Maxie said I looked like an angry badger this morning. I watch in curiosity as the slight woman shoves the entire donut, worriedly into her mouth, her cheeks puffed out like a squirrel.

Chewing vigorously with something akin to sorrow in her eyes, she doesn't break her gaze, but holds up a finger for me to wait a moment. Dusting her hands off as her throat undulates, she licks her lips and then nibbles on the lower one.

"He…he'll be gone for three weeks."

"Three weeks?"

Why didn't he tell me? Did he have something planned? He could have easily mentioned this. He could have mentioned it to a person he wanted to start a new relationship with, but I'm not that guy. Am I? That's why I'm here.

"Where did he go?" As I say the words, my bones grow heavier. I already know.

"Greece," she says, cringing as though it's as painful for her to say as it is for me to hear it. "The whole family goes every year."

"But I…just saw Dimitris when I drove past his restaurant," I ramble, running my hand through my hair.

"Ye-ah. Um. Johnny left early."

"Was something wrong? I mean, that he needed to leave early?"

I pinch my eyes closed and hold up my hand at the sympathetic look on her face. This is stupid. I'm being stupid. He said from day-one he didn't want anything, and I didn't listen.

"Never mind."

Shoving my hands in my pockets, I make one last sweep of the studio for who knows what reason. Is this what Graham felt like when Jen left? I guess I owe him a beer or three for not being more sympathetic. I was there for him, but fuck, I never knew it hurt this much.

Bitsy's clear blue eyes are blinking at me, her bow-shaped mouth set in a sympathetic pout. Wonderful. I don't know who I'm more frustrated with at this point. Johnny for not even trying, or me, for trying too hard.

"It was nice to meet you," I say, forcing a smile.

"You too."

I head for the door, not looking forward to the building I have to finish or the lunch I didn't eat. I feel worse than I did two years ago, when I first realized I was lost. A lot of good my soul-searching did me.

"Aiden?"

"Yeah?" A stupid spring of hope bounces in my chest at the sound of my name, wondering if she'll tell me some serendipitous news.

"For what it's worth, he didn't look happy either. I don't think he wanted to go…without saying goodbye."

I chew on her words for a moment. "Yeah, but he did."

Her shoulders sag and she picks a sprinkle off a donut in the box on her desk. "He's…a complicated man. He wasn't always like this."

I know she means well, but her words only sour my wounds. If he wasn't always like this it means there was a time when he might have taken a leap of faith. Maybe it's my pain, or this new animosity in me that I can't stand, or maybe it's just everything I've gleaned from my time with him that makes me answer. "Actually, I don't think he's complicated at all. He knows exactly what he wants."

It's just not me.

CHAPTER 38

Johnny

I, the Sopping Wet, Melting-in-his-own-sweat Johnny, am officially never taking a vacation again. They are overrated. Why do Greeks like heat? And the sun? And liquor? And mixing all three of them as the dangers of UV exposure, dehydration, and heat exhaustion do not apply to us?

The fumes from the citronella incense coil burning on my *yiayiá's* patio table for the last hour to ward off the national blood-sucking bird of Greece are exacerbating my hangover after the dreaded name day celebration for my cousin last night. Your birthday wasn't enough to make you feel special this year? Be Greek, then you also get an annual name day. One more reason to party like a rock star.

Head pounding, eyes burning, I close my lids and press my glass of iced tea to my cheek. My feet are throbbing, propped up on the spare patio chair after three hours in *Yiayiá's* garden being her whipping boy as she sat in the shade, calling out orders whilst addressing me by each of my cousins' and uncles' names. My *Gucci* pants and self-esteem are destroyed, thank you very much.

They're rolled up to my calves and smattered with fig sap. I resemble what the locals call a *badzakleros*—rough translation: a redneck. To top it all off, in my mad dash out of America on an expensive red-eye flight, I forgot my *Curls Be Damned*. This bandana makes me look like a cross-dressing Rosie the Riveter with a heavy five o'clock shadow.

"Giannis!" Yiayiá barks, making me flinch. How she can sit there and stare out over the white-washed balcony wall at the blinding reflection of the sun on the Aegean, hydrated only by homemade wine at the ripe old age of eighty-four, is beyond me.

"*Ohi, Yiayiá. Parakalo,*" I beg for my life, even though I'm flattered she got my name right for the first time today.

No more, please. Sweet baby Jesus, no more.

Why am I stuck Yiayiá-sitting while the rest of the family went shopping? Clearly the woman is no threat to anyone but the liquor cabinet.

"Young people," she mutters, taking another slow sip of her undiluted wine.

They used to fuel their motorbikes with it during the war when supply lines were cut off by the Nazis. Most normal humans water the high potency stock down. Not *Yiayiá.*

Water? Who needs that shit? I don't have to taste it to know it is liquid devil fire.

"Tell me about your life," she growls.

I have been here for two and a half weeks, and that is the first personal question she has asked me. Actually, it's probably the only personal question she's ever asked me. I certainly did not expect it now that she's been going senile these past few years. The woman rarely speaks unless she is cursing under her breath or playing armchair general to grandchildren conducting forced labor in her garden.

"My life?" *Sigh.* "Well, what do you want to know?"

"Eh."

A grunt. That's all I get. Can you say *rude*? Who does that?

Wiping the sweat from my brow, I decide on the *Dear Abby* approach, as she will neither remember nor care about a word I tell her. "My life… Let's see. Well, first off, I'm gay. Gay as in I am attracted to men and will not be producing twelve Greek babies. So attracted that I once fell in love with and lived with one in California, for two years. Except, he decided at some point he didn't like the things he said he liked about me. I'm not sure if it was while he was impregnating a famous model, one he never would have met if it weren't for me, or if it was after or before." My humorless laugh doesn't seem so humorless for once. It really is an absurd story. It's good to find humor in something for a change.

"Oh. Then what happened? Well, I cried myself to sleep for weeks, until I realized everything I looked at reminded me of the nightmare of my humiliation and that he was really gone. So, I packed up my swing bed and moved back to Wisconsin. The laundry service there is impeccable, but the cheap real estate was really what sold me, so I opened my own photography studio with the best friend a guy could ask for. She may have an appetite and lotion problem, but she gets me. Then… well then, your beloved daughter decided I needed to find my soul mate, which led to me sort of dating a very big, very sexy, sweet, sweet man who, for some reason, seemed to think I was perfect for him when, in reality, nothing could be further from the truth."

I have to pause for a breath, my chest heavy with thoughts of a perfect night that is becoming one day further away in my memory with each passing morning. What is he doing right now? Was he upset when he woke up? Bitsy said he came to the studio and looked crushed. Thank God, I wasn't there. I'd have probably vaulted and affixed myself to him like a *Fanny Pack.*

It was for the best, I say my silent mantra again—the same one I've been saying every day for the last two and a half weeks. Maybe, if I say it enough times it will carry across the Aegean and the Atlantic and hit its target. Maybe the thought of it hitting that target won't make me sad anymore.

"He took me to dinner," I volunteer to my silent companion. "I complained the whole time, but he was just…Aiden. Always Aiden. He walked me home when he didn't have to and…" Fuck it. She's not even listening, and this feels therapeutic. "…and he kissed me. He always kissed me like there was no tomorrow, no today, nothing but us and precious seconds. Then…there were other things. Namely, a swing bed, and a stop sign, and dancing. And…I shouldn't have. I think I knew it would hurt him when I walked away, but we made love—beautiful, loud, perfect, hot, canoodle-worthy love. Twice." Fuck. Everything hurts worse now. I splash the tightness in my throat with tea. The red bougainvillea hanging over the garden wall looks blurrier. "Then…and then I ran away."

Clearing my throat, I glance at my ward, now aware I have just stripped my soul to my oldest relative. Knotty, weathered fingers are still wrapped around her glass. Her eyes are closed. Superb. My life is so depressing she fell asleep.

Leaning my head back on the chair, I let out a sigh in a feeble attempt to rid me of my misery. The craggy bark of her voice gives me a jolt.

"Giorgos Dramthakis."

"I beg your pardon?" I ask.

Her eyes are still closed. Maybe she's having one of her spells.

"He was a sailor on a cruise ship. He came to the island the summer I turned twenty. We used to meet every night on the beach and make love."

Excuse me? Did Yiayiá just tell me about sexy times with someone other than my *papous?* People didn't do that back in the day. They waited until their wedding night and stuck with what they got for better or worse.

"Um. Then you met *Papous?*" I venture.

"Heh. No. I already knew my Nikos. I wanted nothing to do with a farmer who had no passion. There were plenty of those already on the island."

"Oh. So…but how…what happened with this Giorgos?"

"One morning, Nikos came to see me. He was very upset. You see, he saw me and Giorgos making love on the beach the night before. He said Giorgos was no good for me and that I should be a nice girl and marry a nice man from the island. I told him, I did not want a nice man. I wanted a nice man who would make love to me on the beach whenever I wanted."

Resting my chin in my palm as I lean on the table, I smile at her profile. There's no one here to see me be a sucker for a good love story.

"So, *Papous* came to the beach that night, didn't he?"

She makes a savory sound that no old woman should make. "Mm. Yes, and I had them both to myself."

Excuse me? What the actual fuck?

"They wanted to fight for me, but I told them there was only one way to solve our problem. I needed to make love to the both of them at the same time to decide who had more passion for me." She draws a sip of her wine and smiles at the horizon as a fucking mosquito flies into my gaping mouth. Ew! Yuck!

"Well, you…you picked *Papous,* right? My name's not supposed to be Dramthakis, is it? I mean, I have business cards and a logo and everything. This could get expensive."

"Mm," she grunts again. So fucking rude. Is she going to finish this story? "My Nikos surprised me. He was a virgin, but he did not make love like a virgin."

My throat closes up at the word *virgin.* Apparently, Aiden wasn't the only gifted virgin this family has run across. Images of touching and tasting him on a moonlit beach conjure in my mind's eye.

"And…this Giorgos?"

"Hung like a mule, but a little selfish."

Oh, for fuck's sake! That was not where I was going with that.

"Watching them kiss was more beautiful than any painting, any sunrise I have ever seen in my life. When they stopped and my Nikos looked at me, I knew by the fire in his eyes that he would hang the moon for me and make me cry out to it any time I wanted."

My body is suddenly as hollow as an empty well. I know that look, that feeling. Why do I remember it from a man who was in no way intended for me, rather than the one I built my world around for a while?

"I was washing sand from places on my body for three days," *Yiayiá* purrs.

"O-kay! I think that's enough of that," I declare, reaching for her glass. "Ouch!"

She slapped me! Pulling my throbbing hand back, she seems unconcerned, her gaze still fixed to the horizon and possibly the memory of the first three-way to ever rock this island.

"Giorgos," she mutters, shaking her head. "I owe him everything."

I know in about five minutes she will probably call me my father's or uncle's name and tell me to light the candles for Christmas, even though it is the end of July, but I envy her moment of clarity. Pulling out my phone and leaning back out of her arm's reach lest I be slapped again, I snap a candid shot of the look of reverence on her face. It seems critical to capture this moment. It's…beautiful and heartbreaking all at once, and possibly how I will always remember her from now on.

After all these years, she still feels this sense of gratitude toward a man who didn't meet her expectations. I certainly could never think the same thing about Lance. What good did that catastrophe ever do me?

He was a selfish lover. Why I never considered this before and instead focused on the ways I disappointed him, I don't know. Even now, I still allow him to be selfish. He's ruined everything after our relationship for me, or rather, *I* let him ruin it by allowing him in my headspace.

Staring out at the Aegean, it seems so vast and home, so far away. The only thing I'm certain of is that, without a doubt, I will still remember Aiden when I'm *Yiayiá's* age, and maybe…maybe the right man already came to my beach.

CHAPTER 39

Aiden

If I have to see Dalton look at me with those big sad eyes one more evening, I might start making him sleep outside. There is no amount of pretending that can fool a dog into thinking you're happy when you're not. With everybody else though? I'm doing the best I can.

I need to figure something out, so I don't ruin Maxie's wedding with this perma-scowl on my face. That's three months away. How sad is it that I'm anticipating still being depressed in three months?

For the moment, I tell myself this beer is helping, but it's more so the ambiance of this sports bar. The noise of the game and the patrons is louder than my thoughts, and the occasional looks I get aren't eat-my-heart-out Golden Retriever eyes that can see through the window of my soul.

"This seat taken?"

I shift on instinct, not wanting to offend anyone with my sweaty aroma from a day's work on the job site. A striking, sandy-haired man with crystal blue eyes, who looks close to my age, smiles as he tugs off an Olympus West ballcap. Shaking my head, I gesture to the free stool next to me.

"No. Help yourself."

He slides into the stool, letting out a long sigh. I've been in enough bars to know that kind of sigh means someone wants to talk. I haven't made that sigh in three weeks since I woke up with Johnny's underwear on my floor but no Johnny. Eyes retrained on the television behind the bar, I continue to nurse my beer, waiting for a dinner I'm going to have to force myself to eat before I have to go home to let Dalton out.

"Oh! Nice pass!" the stranger cheers with a controlled fist pump as a Packers wide-receiver palms the football at a dead run off a twenty-yard throw.

It was a beautiful catch, but I could care less. How can one person make you lose interest in all the things you used to find entertaining?

I've given up on Johnny. Honestly, I have, but I'd like to know why nothing is back to normal. It's not just the sight of my own bed and every person with glasses that's depressing. It's how everything that should have nothing to do with Johnny has lost its luster.

Three times last week, I was ten minutes late picking up Maxie. It still feels like I have to drag my ass into work each morning, even though I lent her my truck so I could ride my bike. My motorcycle and my job were two of the things I used to look forward to each summer. I'm starting to worry they aren't ever going to hold the appeal they used to. Am I going to turn into Graham?

"Rough day?" the stranger asks.

"Mm," I grunt, sending a pang of longing through me at that familiar sound.

"You want to talk about it?"

That's usually a line from a bartender, not a patron, so I glance over. He's removed his ballcap and is running his fingers through the length at the front of his hair, brushing it back. With his navy workout shorts, clinging to his toned thighs, and the way his gray t-shirt hugs his biceps, which are a bit smaller than mine but still have definition, the guy looks like he could do athletic equipment commercials.

"Not really."

"Understood" he intones. "Well, whatever it is, I'm sure it'll all work out."

My humorless laugh echoes in my beer bottle. "Thanks, but I don't see that happening."

"Got your heart broken, didn't you?"

The lip of the bottle stops just before my mouth. It's probably juvenile and whimsical, but I really did give Johnny my heart, or was at least prepared to do so. With a lump in my throat, I set my drink down.

"Something like that."

"What did she do?"

My shoulders rock on a chuff of air. Maybe this is the quickest way to end this conversation.

"*He*…didn't do anything. He just wasn't looking for long-term."

My muscles relax, anticipating an awkward silence before the guy probably excuses himself to move on. Shit, or I suppose he could blather about any non-hetero person he may have met once to make himself seem unphased by my admission on preference. What I didn't anticipate is the hand that touches my forearm and squeezes.

"Hey," he says. "Then that's his loss."

Looking over, I'm met with compassion in those vivid blue eyes, a comforting smile as his thumb makes a slow stroke across my arm before he pulls away. I guess my mood has made me judgmental—one more thing I hate about myself right now.

"Thanks," I say, and now I notice the Olympus West football team mascot on his t-shirt. "Did you go to Olympus West?"

Taking his beer from the bartender, he smirks. "Yeah. Today, yesterday, and all of last school year."

When I blink at his riddle, he chuckles. "I teach physical education there, and I just came from coaching summer football camp."

"Oh. Wait. You coach the football team there now?"

"Yep. Guilty. That's how I can recognize a broken heart. I'm surrounded by teenagers eight hours a day."

There's something about the way he's able to get me to laugh at my circumstance that makes me feel lighter for the first time in weeks. "Um. I played there back in the day. Aiden Brandt." I offer him my hand to make up for my closed off demeanor earlier.

"Aiden Brandt, huh? Yeah, I think there's a few trophy cases with your name in them. I'm Sam. Sam Sorenson."

"Nice to meet you. Uh. Sorry about…" I wave a hand to indicate my mood.

"Hey. No worries. We've all been there." The telling expression he makes tilts my sympathy. I need to remember that I'm not the first guy to get turned down. Yet, in spite of his implication of past heartache, there's something about Sam that makes me think he's always this optimistic and easy going. It's admirable.

"So, I take it Coach Rutledge finally retired?"

Sam chuckles. "Grudgingly, I think, but yeah. He came back after retirement to give me a courtesy tour of the facilities and to show me how he ran his program, but I think it was just an excuse to spy on his replacement."

"He was a ballbuster for sure. Can't say I miss my football days much when I think of him."

Grinning, he nods. "Oh. I can imagine."

"Was he not impressed with his replacement?" I venture, happy for this moment of comradery.

"More like he took one look at the pride pin on my hat, and it was all downhill from there."

"Oh." My cheeks heat at my clipped response. His admission isn't what I expected.

"Ye-ah," Sam sighs, seemingly still regaling his thoughts on his meeting with Coach Rutledge, rather than my reaction to his preference. "It could have gone better. Let's just say, I don't envy you being a gay teen under his tutelage."

"Um. Well, I wasn't out then. Hell, I didn't even give it a thought at the time. I didn't work it out until later, but you could say Coach's comments might be to blame for some of that. And…and I'm bi actually."

"There's nothing wrong with that," he says in this soothing tone of an understanding mentor. His smile of complete acceptance over my dual preference is so opposite to Johnny's reaction, it restores a piece of me.

"That's really great," I say. "I mean, I'm glad there's someone like you for those kids to learn from. They're lucky to have you."

"Thanks. I like Olympus, a city with everything to offer, surrounded by nature in every direction."

When my food arrives, it seems rude to eat without him, so I wait in spite of his protests for me to start. In no time, I feel restored, commenting on the game along with him and telling him stories about my football days at Olympus West. My bill comes, and I almost don't want to leave. His company is better than the silence of my thoughts awaiting me at home.

"Well, it was nice to meet you." I extend my hand after I give the bartender my money.

"You too." He turns, giving me his full attention as though our exchange was genuine for him too, rather than idle chitchat that's already been forgotten.

"Good luck with the Rutledge coaching plan," I jest.

He lets out another of his easy laughs. "I don't know. I might need some tips from a seasoned veteran. Maybe we should do this again some time?"

"Yeah. Sure." I laugh, giving him that throw away comment.

Except, his hand stays in mine when I slacken my grip—his thumb, grazing lightly over mine as he holds my gaze. "How about Friday night?" he asks a bit softer, smoother.

Something flutters in my chest, a mix of panic and warmth at being complimented by what he's offering. I'm holding my breath as he stares at me hopefully. I need to say something, but the flicker of guilt at the thought of saying *yes* confuses me. There's nothing to feel guilty about, no one's feelings to spare.

His hand is warm and dry in mine, no light hint of nervous perspiration I used to feel on Johnny's. He's not complaining about my roughened hands. I find myself blushing at the direct eye contact. It's a change after chasing a man who avoided looking at me most of the time.

For a moment, I imagine what it would be like if Sam pulled me against the wall outside and kissed me. It actually brings me relief that the thought doesn't overwhelm me with crazed desire.

Maybe this is the way it's supposed to be. Maybe love isn't a storm you crash into, but a slow and steady breeze that stays constant. Everything about Sam says constant.

He didn't try to impress me. He was just himself. Honest. Exposed.

No holding back. He likes to cook and wants to check out the trails in the area. His dog passed away the year before he moved here, and he has an obnoxious sister. I can easily see our conversations holding my interest more so than the casual acquaintances I've spent evenings with in the past. Nothing about the idea of him makes me feel unrealistic passion, and that's…comforting. I no longer want to feel things I can't control.

"Friday night sounds nice."

CHAPTER 40

Aiden

"Ooh. Look at that," Sam enthuses, his hand sliding to the small of my back over my t-shirt, as I'm chopping up chives at my counter under his direction. "Such precision. You sure you don't want to try out for my team?"

Chuckling, I check his hip with mine. "I already play for the same team, remember?"

Laughing, he squeezes my side before moving alongside me to start on an onion. "Yeah, I remember." His coy smile gives my stomach an anxious flutter.

I'm still processing how I feel about our first time messing around last night. It's been two weeks since our first date. It seemed like it was time to do more than kissing after days of all his lingering looks and light caresses—a touch of my arm, a squeeze of my hip.

I told him a little about Johnny last week—only about the continual dating matching. Warning him I'm a bit gun-shy felt like the right thing to do. He's been so patient with me, and to be honest, it was nice to be touched again. Using our hands on each other last night on his couch before I left for home doesn't seem to have affected our easy rhythm one way or the other, with the exception of Sam's little grazes being more frequent today.

That's a good sign. Right?

I'm not dying to drag him to bed, but I also don't want to run for the hills. I only wish I had the urge to return more of those caresses, but maybe I'll get there. Maybe I won't feel that twinge of heartbreak the next time we do something intimate.

Dalton lets out a low woof, looking at the door. A knock follows. Sam and I exchange curious looks.

"Expecting someone?" He smiles, and I don't miss the hopeful look in his eyes. He's made it no secret that he's eager to meet my family.

"No, but it could be anyone of my family. They don't seem to know how to call ahead of time. I'm just shocked they didn't barge in like usual, but maybe they saw I have company." Dusting my hands off, I make my way to the door, ginning at Sam. "You ready to handle meeting another Brandt?"

"I don't know," he purrs, shooting me a wink. "I'm still recovering from meeting this one."

My face blooms with heat at the sexual innuendo. I asked for that, didn't I?

Tugging the door open, the squirmy mix of mild arousal and uncertainty screech to a halt. They're squashed by a comforting sense of belonging that warms all the dead spaces inside me and a pain so sharp in my chest, I have to take a gulp of air.

Johnny.

"Hello," he blurts. "Hi. H-hi there," he adds, all jittery, shifting his sandal clad feet.

His striped, yellow and white tank top compliment his tan. His arms and chest are an extra shade of bronze. A picture of him sunning on the beach while I was here pining like a fool helps me find words, cold bitter words.

"How was Greece?" I mutter accusingly.

His nervous smile fades. His fingers re-grip the white box in his hands.

"Hot. Mosquito-ridden. Full of alcohol and an unreasonable amount of family time. How-how are you? You look…good."

Now I'm the one shifting my feet. His skittish compliment is a cold splash of water on my annoyance. I want to grab him, pull him forward and punish him with my mouth until all the pain is gone, while another part of me wants to slam the door in his face. I do neither, because yet another part of me acknowledges this is the first time he came to me willingly, not because of some dating scheme Bitsy or his mother made him use.

Dalton slams into my leg, shoving past me. He makes a b-line right for Johnny's nuts, giving him a loud sniff.

"Whoa, boy!" Johnny shifts, deflecting the greeting with one hand.

"Dalton," I scold, but he ignores me.

"He's fine," Johnny says, patting Dalton's head awkwardly, but murmurs, "I forgive you, you rotten little underwear thief."

Dalton's tail thwaps against the floor where he plops down and rests his chin on Johnny's foot. Odd. He doesn't usually get that friendly with people.

"When did you get back?"

"Um. About a week ago." There's a flash of guilt in his expression that I don't understand. Does he feel bad for just reaching out to me now? What's one more week after disappearing for three without a goodbye?

"You've been back an entire week?"

"I-I was going to call, but realized we never exchanged numbers, so I figured I'd better stop by, but then I wasn't sure if that would be weird or…or if you'd want me to, but….well, is it weird? I hope it's not. I mean, it's clearly a little weird seeing as we haven't talked since…you know. I don't think I've ever babbled on a porch for this long. Heh. Or ever, maybe. Um. I should stop talking. I just… Do you want me to? To be here? I…*I* want to, but if you don't want me to then—"

"Aiden?" Sam's voice cuts through Johnny's increasingly adorable rambling that's slowly cracking the armor around my heart. "Everything okay?"

Sam's arm slinks around my waist. Johnny's face looks like he just got slapped as he blinks. His gaze flickers to Sam, then to Sam's arm around me, and then to my face. Hurt. Why does that look like hurt in his eyes? I force myself to swallow.

"Hi!" Sam chirps, glancing from Johnny to me as my face heats. I completely forgot about him. "Family, friend, or salesman?" he quips to Johnny.

Neither of us say a word. As Johnny's mouth hangs open, the laugh lines by Sam's eyes smooth out, as though he's just missed the punchline of a joke.

"This is…Johnny," I explain, but remember I guarded the word *Johnny* like a secret when I divulged our dating app mishaps to him. "He's…."

Poor Sam blinks, waiting for normal behavior from either of us. Luckily, Johnny finds his voice and blurts out, "*A friend.*" The word pelts me like hail. "I…I've been out of town and wanted to drop off this baklava from my family's restaurant since I didn't, um, get a chance to say goodbye before I left." Johnny hands over the box I hadn't paid much attention to before, but I still can't move.

"Oh! I love baklava," Sam coos, taking the box.

Johnny's brow furrows like his gift has just been stolen, but then clears his throat. "It, um. I was kind of in a hurry the last time we went out to eat," he explains, adjusting his glasses that don't need adjusting. "You didn't get to try dessert. That was rude of me."

I realize it's some sort of peace offering, but all I can think is that I actually did get *dessert* that night I walked him home from Tapas. He must figure it out too, because his chest rises, and his face goes even more red. Now is not the time to think about *dessert* with my new boyfriend standing at my side.

Sam pops the lid of the pastry box open and hums. "Mm. I love Mediterranean food. Lebanese, right?"

Johnny frowns so severely, I almost want to laugh. "*Greek*," he says with a hint of that saucy tone I've missed. "It's Greek, actually."

"Oh. I didn't know they made it too, but I bet they all steal stuff from each other." Sam laughs, rubbing the place between my shoulder blades.

I try to crack a supportive smile, but Johnny looks to be fuming for someone who seemed embarrassed of his culture half the time I was with him.

"Oh. I'm Sam by the way. Sam Sorenson. Sorry, so rude. Does your friend want to come in?" He asks, turning to me.

"Um," I babble, looking to Johnny.

"We were just making lunch. If you two need to catch up, I can finish." Sam hip checks me. "This one's all thumbs in the kitchen, but I have a little time to remedy that before school starts."

"School?" Johnny asks.

"Yeah. I'm the athletic director at Olympus West. I coach the football team and teach phys ed. Well," he chuckles, "more like try to get the clumsy, uncoordinated ones to not be afraid of any type of ball by the end of the year."

"Mm," Johnny hums, making me realize he hasn't directed that unenthused noise at me once. "What a challenge."

An awkward silence swells between the three of us. Sam rubs my back again. "Aiden, hon?"

"I…I should get going," Johnny rushes, pointing over his shoulder and extricating his foot from Dalton, who huffs in protest when Johnny backs up toward the porch door.

"Oh. Well, don't go on account of me," Sam says.

"No. I…I have…things to do and underwear to wash and whatnot. Um. Enjoy your lunch. Aiden it, uh, I..." Johnny stammers, his ass hitting the screen door. "Oof. Heh heh. There's a door there. Um. Well, nice to see you again. Bye!"

"Nice to meet you!" Sam calls, but Johnny's already double-timing it down my sidewalk toward his car.

When Sam turns back into the entryway, I force myself to shut the door.

Why? Why is it that the things you want come to you when you can no longer have them? What was this life lesson supposed to teach me?

Blowing out a heavy breath to ease the tension in my chest, I find Sam studying me, hand on hip, head tilted in concern.

"That was *him*, wasn't it?"

Shit. Even a blind man could have figured it out.

Running my hand down my face, hoping to erase whatever expression gave me away, I mumble, "Sorry. That was unexpected. I honestly didn't think I'd see him again."

Stepping forward, he tucks his hands in his front pockets. "Do you… need to talk to him? Because I get it. I've been there."

His overwhelming understanding is sobering. It would be rude to talk to a…a what? Johnny's not even an ex. What would I say to him or expect to hear from him anyway? More hot and then cold? I need constant. Constant is safe and reliable and standing right in front of me.

"No." I smile and shake my head. "There's nothing to talk about."

He takes a deep inhale as though I've brought him relief. Giving me a sympathetic smile, he steps forward and hugs me, wrapping me tight in his arms.

"Okay then," he murmurs into my shoulder.

I hug him back, resting my chin on his shoulder, grateful for the comfort he has no obligation to give me. I'd like to believe there was remorse behind Johnny's visit, but he made his choices, and I made mine. A box of baklava doesn't mean he had a change of heart, or that I should hurt the man in my arms who gave me a chance the second he saw me. Lightning strikes aren't reality, and for my heart's sake, I hope they don't happen twice.

CHAPTER 41

Johnny

"All thumbs in the kitchen," I mutter around a mouthful of ice cream and tug the throw blanket tighter around myself on the couch. Dr. Phil is on, scolding his guest for stealing her mother's credit cards, providing me with a much needed ego boost and reminder that my life could be worse.

"Thumbs," I snort because I've resorted to muttering to myself like *Yiayiá* as I sit in the darkness of my living room alone. "He was going to cook me a steak! You have no idea what he can do with his thumbs you…you stupid *thumb-nazi*."

I might be sick. I don't know if it's from over-thinking about how Sam-pawing-his-hands-all-over-my-Aiden implied he was going to teach Aiden things, as though he can't see how perfectly talented the man is already, or from the half a gallon of dairy I have shoveled into my mouth in the last hour.

I blew it. I freaking blew it. It shouldn't hurt this much that Aiden moved on already. It's like he said—he never promised me anything. I sure as shit never promised him anything either. But that's the problem, isn't it?

If I'd gotten my head out of my ass long enough to…to…ugh. To what? To tell him how it scared the shit out of me every time he looked at me like I was his next breath, but that maybe…very much actually, I wanted to be? I just had to go to Greece first and hear about a sixty-year-old three-way to figure it out.

Fuck. Even Dr. Phil wouldn't know how to analyze that shit.

The doorknob rattles. Bitsy steps inside, her intrigued expression pinning me as she halts in place.

I swivel my head back toward Dr. Phil casually as though I'm not cocooned in self-pity. "How was your secret rendezvous? Bring me back anything good?"

"It wasn't a secret," she says, keys jangling behind me as she makes her way to round the sectional. "I…was meeting a client."

"*A client?* Since when do you meet our clients off-site…after dark?" I take in her appearance, noting the mascara on her lashes and her favorite peasant sleeve blouse paired with what she deems her *best-butt* jeans. "Bitsy, are you engaged in illegal activities?"

Sighing, she flops down on the opposite end of the sectional on top of my feet. Yanking them out from under her thigh, she props one on her leg, then the other. "No. It was one of my clients for my marketing business."

"I beg your pardon? Come again now?"

"I started my own marketing business last year. I did some graphics for Mrs. Lyman a couple years ago. Remember her?"

I nod, suddenly no longer able to bare the sound of Dr. Phil, so I turn the volume down. This seems important. Like finding out your roommate has been living a double life important.

"Well, after I did that, she referred a friend of hers to me who wanted her website revamped, and the woman offered to pay me. It just kind of spiraled from there."

"Did you need the money? Because I can give you a raise."

"No! No," she practically snorts. "You pay me more than you should, and we both know it. I do these jobs because I enjoy it. I like being my own boss."

"Oh. I see." I try to tug my feet back, but she clamps onto my ankles.

"That's not what I meant! I love working with you, but you don't need me as much as you think you do. I got bored and this just sort of happened. Now I've gotten so many inquiries I've had to turn people away."

"Bits, you know you can say *no* to people. Just because Mrs. Lyman side-tracked you, doesn't mean you had to answer the supply and demand of everyone in Olympus who comes knocking for marketing services."

She scoffs. "Well, I kind of did…at first."

As she chews her lip, the ice cream churns in my stomach. What the hell is that look for?

"So, I like it here…in Olympus. Like a lot. I love you and your family, the trails, the business district, the people. I love the neighborhoods."

"Got it. You love everything. Where is this going?"

"I decided not long after I got here that I want to stay here…permanently."

I wait for other news, but that's it. She says it as though a weight has been lifted from her shoulders. I never stopped to consider this move might only be temporary for her. How self-absorbed of me was that? I was in such a *Lance-coma* I didn't consider more than her basic needs of food, shelter, and my miserable companionship.

"I'm glad to hear it." I reach over to squeeze her hand. "I'd hate to lose you."

"I know." She frowns. "I worry about you."

"Me?" I sputter. "What's to worry about?"

"Johnny," she scolds as I pull my hand back. Why is this couch suddenly so uncomfortable as my name lingers between us?

"What?"

I don't like how she sighs. I know I can be a pain in the ass, but if I've become a sigh-worthy friend, just ship me off to Dr. Phil right now.

"I want to buy a house…here. In Olympus. I've been saving for two years and now I have more than a substantial down payment, thanks to you not charging me room and board."

Scrambling up to draw my legs underneath me, I gasp. "You do want to leave me!"

"No. I don't."

"Is this about the food fight thing again? Because you know I would never tell my parents you didn't like their food. Mamá would somehow find a way to blame it on me, like I fed you something that counteracted with Greek cuisine somehow and—"

"Would you stop? You idiot."

Ouch. Name calling. Rude!

"It's not about the food. I just think it's time I build my own life and have my own place."

"And a giant closet for all your stinky tennis shoes?" I venture.

She clasps her hands together under her chin and grins like an imp. "Yes! Absolutely. And a huge backyard I can landscape like my mom used to do."

Oh. Double ouch. I'm not the only one with scars. Some people want to drag a ridiculous swing bed halfway across the country to remember the good times, and some people want to plant roots, literally.

"That…that sounds nice, Bits. I can picture it already." I force a smile, hating that I have to force it. This is my best friend in the entire world and I am genuinely happy that she's found something she wants out of life. It's fitting she chose an attainable dream, unlike me, longing after a man who didn't want me and then throwing away one might.

"Thanks."

"So, you…that's all? I mean, you're not harboring some secret resentment for something I may have done? Say…sullying your desk for example? Because it feels like we haven't talked in a minute or two."

Holding up her index finger, she levels a stern look at me. "I might forgive you if you get me a new desk—one with more drawers so I can keep my client files in the same workspace."

"Done! Is that all? I mean, we're still good? You were just throwing me into dating app hell and absent so you could sneak off to bank shoe palace money?”

What the fuck is with the frowny face again? That was a logical assessment of recent events.

“It was time to move on, Johnny.”

“Yeah. I get it. You’re a big kid now. You’ve got the shoes. You want the shoe closet to go with them.”

“No. I was talking about you.”

“Me? Move on from…”

Her pouty lower lip isn’t necessary for me to fill in the blank and put the pieces together. Shame and humiliation rain down on me, pummeling me deeper into the couch cushion.

“Johnny, it’s been two years since that asshole cheated and left you. Don’t give him any more of your life. Don’t waste anymore of yours being heartbroken over someone who didn’t deserve you.”

Ouch.

Hello, reality check coming out of left field.

“So, you sound like you know things,” I venture, mixing the melted ice cream into the still frozen portion.

“We knew some of the same people in San Diego. It wasn’t hard to find out when you didn’t elaborate.”

Shrugging, I scoop a dollop into my mouth, crunching a walnut with my molars. “Well, I’m not heartbroken. Just so you know. He’s not even a blip on my radar anymore.”

“Then what’s with the Monkey Butt?”

“I beg your pardon?”

Gesturing to the sweating container in my lap, she elaborates. “My ice cream. That was almost full yesterday. You’ve made love to at least half of it.”

Turning the carton, I read the label and frown at the hideously happy cartoon monkey on it. “Who names ice cream that? Or any food for that matter?”

“It’s delicious. No one cares what it’s called.”

“Well, it’s addictive and should come with a warning label.”

Glancing at the television, she purses her lips. “Did Dr. Phil tell you that?”

Gasp! Now she’s just being mean. “That man has restored more order to the world than traffic cones! Show some respect, please.”

“Oh, my gosh. I can’t listen to this. Give me the ice cream. You’re cut off.”

She reaches for the only source of comfort I’ve had this evening. I cling to it on instinct like a mother protecting her baby. “No! I’m not done eating my feelings yet.”

"Ah! Ha! And what feelings might those be?" she asks, giving the Monkey Butt another tug.

I know I'm being ridiculous and should let go. My fucking nipples are freezing with this thing clutched to my chest, but you do not waltz in and crash a man's evening alone, then try to liberate his comfort food, no matter how irrational and pathetic he is.

"*My* feelings!" I counter. "*My* personal, private, none of your I-have-a-secret-second-job business."

"*Lance-feelings?*" she spouts, tugging again.

"Fuck no! Fuck him!"

"Then why are you acting like you did after he ripped your heart out?"

"I…" Nothing else comes out as a flood of snot barrels through my sinuses. Bitsy's hold slackens, her blue eyes blinking with such concern it bursts the levee. "Aiden," I squeak. Fucking squeak.

Sinking back onto her cushion she frowns. "What happened?"

"He… I went to his house to see him today."

"Yeah?" She asks, sounding hopeful and happy and…proud like I made a good decision.

I have to swallow to get the rest out.

"Yeah, and his new boyfriend was there—Sam McSporty McPerfect."

"Oh. Shit. I'm sorry."

A sour bubble of laughter pops in my throat. I flap my hand, resting my forehead in the other one on the back of the couch. A half a gallon of ice cream can sure weigh a man down.

"What's to be sorry for? I was too late. I took too long to figure out he…" Apparently, it's possible to choke on words. "That he wasn't anything like Lance."

"Oh, Johnny." Bitsy rubs my knee.

Damn it. Do not cry. Do not cry. You didn't even date him, you idiot. The fact that he practically begged me to date him makes holding back tears near impossible.

"It's fine. Really," I rasp, rubbing my eyes. "No need to worry. I won't mope or build a shrine or anything."

"Well, at least you got back out there finally. That's why I pushed you to go on those dates. I'm proud of you."

"Proud of me? What the hell for?"

"You saw someone for more than a hook up and you developed feelings. That's huge. It means you're finally over Lance. You can start dating again. Maybe you'll meet someone who makes you laugh like you used to."

Like I used to—how depressing is it to hear your best friend refer to you as a shell of your former self? This pep talk is getting a one-star rating.

"Bitsy, I'm done with dating. I know you were trying to help, and I appreciate it, but let's just let sleeping dogs lie. I'm better off on my own."

"What? Why? You were happier each time you saw him even though you denied it. You really don't want to feel like that again?"

"No! Not just *no* but *fuck no!* What's the point? One day you're having the best sex of your life with someone who'd hang the moon for you, the next you're elbow deep in monkey ass. Who in the hell wants to ride that rollercoaster more than once?"

She's quiet, so I glance up to figure out what I spouted now that may have shocked or offended her. Me and my unfiltered mouth lately.

"You had sex with him?"

Fuck.

"Not on your desk. It was…after that stupid speed-dating event, that I'm still mad at you for, by the way."

Folding her arms over her chest, she smirks. "The *best sex of your life*, huh?"

Pinching my eyes shut, I breath out the last of my pride, handing it over to this witch woman. "Twice, actually," I cringe at the bittersweet memory. "In one night. And…and he may have been a virgin."

"What?" she shrieks, shoving my knee so hard it jars my hip socket. "Shut! Up! He was not!"

Now her hands are cupping her mouth. Wonderful. I have shocked someone into muzzling themselves.

"A *gay virgin*," I clarify. "Not a full virgin, but…you know. A monumental moment for him nonetheless."

"Oh, my gosh! Wow!"

Okay, she can really stop with the exclamations. They're not helping my guilt.

"So, what happened? I thought maybe you blew him off again. I mean, I know you left the next day, and he came here looking for you. He knew you were coming back, though. I told him. Couldn't he wait a few weeks?"

Biting my nail, I get a grave look in return, so I confess before she can make any assumptions. Unlike with Lance though, I tell her everything, from the beginning to the end. How many more nights will I have my friend all to myself? I figure I can use the practice, telling the story for when I'm *Yiayiá's* age and some great niece or nephew needs a lesson on taking a leap of faith.

"Oh, Johnny," she sighs. She's somehow ended up with the Monkey Butt in her lap, swirling the spoon around to pick out selective bits of fruits and nuts. "You really know how to kick your own ass. This is exactly why I was worried about leaving you.”

Instinct tells me to protest, to be offended at the implication that I need to be watched so I don’t run with scissors, but I clamp my mouth shut. It’s not an inaccurate assessment.

For two years, I’ve moped over a person who may have never actually loved me. Now that I’ve had a sampling of Olympian brick layer, I have to wonder if I ever really loved Lance. Maybe it was just the idea of being somebody’s someone—the special feeling that comes with being able to claim you’re part of a couple, one half of a whole.

I was alone in California after graduation when Bitsy left, and then I met Lance, and I wasn’t. Except, after a while, I felt more alone with him than without him.

Burrowed into my couch with half a gallon of ice cream in my stomach is not how I pictured a moment of clarity presenting itself. Yet, I have never felt more alone, knowing Aiden will never be mine. He made me a better person, made me see myself as a better person than I am. He saw me at my worst and still liked what he saw. I let the passion and immeasurable chemistry scare me, since it well surpassed any I had with Lance. I looked a gift horse in the mouth.

Fuck. Is there a better euphemism that doesn’t involve horses?

Folding the blanket, I rise from my cradle of self-pity. Bitsy’s sad eyes, brimming with concern, turn another screw in my heart. The amount of disgust over being blind to the loyal homage she’s paid to broken-me these past years is worse than the roiling dairy in my belly. How can I ever make it up to her?

Stepping forward, I wrap my arms around her shoulders in a tight squeeze. “Listen, babe. Ditch the sad face. Mm-kay? I promise to rally this time. No more pity parties. I’ve learned my lesson, so you don’t need to worry.”

Her scrutiny nearly makes my forced smile falter. “Are you sure? Because I haven’t even started looking for a place yet. It’s not like I’m in a rush. I can wait a while.”

“Nonsense. Go forth and find that shoe palace. Just, you know, make sure you get a big couch and T.V. for bestie movie nights.”

“Definitely.” She grins, but then bites her lip.

“What?”

“I have another surprise.”

“Oh, please no. I can’t take any more surprises right now.”

“Stop! It’s a good one.”

I wait patiently, bracing myself for more changes I’m sure I won’t like. Adulting has lost its appeal in the span of twelve hours.

“So, since I was able to save up so much money, and we won’t be living together anymore in the near future, and you’ve done so much for me—"

I open my mouth to refute that last bit, but she silences me with a stop-sign-hand. God, I hate stop signs.

"I thought it'd be nice to take a trip together. Kind of one last hurrah before we can't curl up on the couch together every night."

"What did you do?" I ask suspiciously.

Grinning, she does jazz hands. For the record, Bitsy doing jazz hands is terrifying.

"I booked us a two-week trip to Mykonos next month."

Thick dread clogs every one of my pores. I think I might actually be sick. Monkey Butt must be more potent than cheese.

I have yearned for an epic jaunt to Mykonos my entire adult life, but at the moment, I wouldn't even go there if promised a nude photo shoot of Henry Cavill. However, Bitsy's looking at me with such giddiness over this incredibly generous, sickeningly thoughtful gift, I couldn't possibly destroy this moment.

Where is a video camera when you need one? I'm about to deliver an Oscar-worthy performance.

"Shut up! You did not!"

Her giggle helps to boost my spirits. "I did! I reserved us a private villa with its own pool overlooking the beach. Two-minute walk to the best clubs and resorts. I got us tickets on the high-speed ferry from Piraeus, so you don't have to squeeze into one of those tiny seats on an island hopper flight, since I know how much you love airplanes."

"Wow. You…thought of everything." My laugh is breathy. She really did think of everything. I don't deserve her, and now I feel even worse.

"Did I do good or what? Sofia helped me plan the whole thing."

"Sofia helped? Oh, God. She's probably told Mamá by now."

She shrugs. "Your mom was happy when we told her. She thinks it's a good idea."

"Wait. My mother knows I'm going to number-one gay destination of the Cyclades, and she thinks it's a good idea? Great!" I throw my hands up. "She probably expects me to come back married to some strapping Greek pool boy."

"Well, at least that's better than her trying to get you to marry a Greek pool girl," she enthuses.

"You are hilarious. *Hill-arious.*"

"Oh, come on. She just wants you to be happy."

Everyone wants me to be happy. Mamá, Bitsy, Thio Dimitris, possibly *Yiayiá.* Even Aiden wanted me to take a chance on what he deemed *happiness.* I am suddenly more exhausted than I've ever been in my life.

I smile and give her another hug, grateful for the shadows of our darkened living room cut only by the glow of Dr. Phil.

"I know," I agree. "I'm a lucky guy. You're so sweet, I don't deserve you. Hey, let me know what I owe you for my half of the trip, and I'll—"

"No! Absolutely not. This is my treat. That's not up for debate."

The determined look on her face tells me there's no point in arguing. "Well, fine, but I'm paying for all your meals and your drinks. Tomorrow morning, find yourself the nicest desk on the market. We can't have Olympus' newest businesswoman looking shoddy."

Her pleased smile stretches from ear to ear. "Consider it done."

I start for my room, no longer able to keep up this ruse of elation, but throw some faux teasing over my shoulder. "Hey, who knows? There's a lot of Aussie tourists in the Cyclades. Maybe you'll meet the Patrick Swayze of the Outback."

"Mm. We'll see."

I force a chuckle at her coy enthusiasm. I'm going to need the practice, pretending to be happy while my heart is leaking like a damned sieve.

CHAPTER 42

Johnny

Okay. So, being happy is excruciating. I think I'd rather take a jog in Bitsy's shorts through rush hour traffic, or possibly even a stop sign factory, than try to keep up this façade much longer.

Except Bitsy's so damn bubbly, I can't. She thinks she's saved me from Lance Land, and I want to keep it that way. I refuse to let my misery surface and get in the way of her dreams. So, here I am, performing happiest bestie in the world, sweet gesture number twelve—buying high carb baked goods to surprise one optimistic foodie when she surfaces in the studio later this morning.

Yanking the door of the café open, I strain against its weight. It's been twelve sleepless nights since the Monkey Butt intervention. There is not enough coffee in the world to give me the energy I need to make it through the day with a smile plastered on my face.

Let me clarify—that is twelve sleepless nights filled with images of Sporty McSportson's hands and lips all over Aiden's beautiful body. The worst was the one of them cooking together naked, while Aiden nibbled garlic-covered strawberries from Sam's fingers, while I screamed from outside at the soundproof windows.

I am never eating strawberries again. Note to self—it may be time for therapy. These thoughts of a man I didn't even officially date cannot be normal.

Digging in my pocket for my wallet, a deep chuckle ahead of me churns the ache in my chest. I search for it in desperation, the way kittens paw at their mother's belly for sustenance.

Oh, fuck me. It's them.

I know that firm backside in those snug carpenter jeans. Those broad shoulders and sun-kissed arms. I know that big, calloused hand that's intertwined with one that's not mine. Sporty McBubble Butt turns from where they're waiting for their order, frowning as if he can read my thoughts. When he recognizes me, his face masks into a fucking prune smile.

I get a prune smile? What's that shit about?

"Oh! Hi, there! *Johnny*, wasn't it?" he calls, nudging Aiden's hip with their still interlocked hands.

"Good morning," I luckily get out before Aiden turns his head and locks gazes with mine.

My heart is in my throat. I put that damaged look on his handsome face. Me. The *abandoner*.

Fuck.

I'm the abandoner man. The bad guy. The breaker of hearts.

I've become my ex—the thing I despise.

"Aiden," I mumble, trying to convey ten thousand messages in a pathetic, remorseful little smile.

Why aren't you at work, I want to ask. Since when do you ditch out to get coffee mid-morning with slimy, hand-stealers? It'll be too hot when you get back, and you'll get sunstroke.

You should be building buildings and smiling that contented smile you get when you talk about it, not here laughing at jokes that aren't mine. You should be…*mine*, but I fucked it up more than once, and…I'm sorry.

"Johnny." He nods, then turns back to face the counter.

Sam glances from Aiden to me and frowns before ignoring me as well. Of all the coffee joints in Olympus, I had to walk into this one. Now I get to carry this encounter with me all day as I listen to Bitsy ooze about the roaring good time we're going to have at my parents' anniversary party this weekend and on our trip to Mykonos next month.

Kill me now.

The customer in front of me moves along. I step up to the counter, feeling every pound of the proverbial scarlet letter on my chest with Sam and Aiden mere feet away.

He's looking at me. I can feel it. Not Aiden. The other one—the nosey bastard.

I overhear him enthuse something about Maxie's wedding, and I have to bite my tongue to keep from snapping that Aiden doesn't want to hear about that shit. Nor do I care to hear the implication that Sam the Perfect has already wormed his way into Aiden's family circle, if he's bandying on about their lives in public as though they've been dating for months.

"Triple espresso. Black. Two sugars, and I'll take three of each of your pastries," I rush to the young barista before she can even greet me.

"Um. We have like twelve different kinds of pastries."

"Mm. Yeah. So that'll be *like* thirty-six pastries then. Perfect," I concur with her ditzy bafflement.

"Okay. Um. Do you like want them all heated up and individually wrapped?"

"Honey, you can get a snow shovel and dump them in a bucket for all I care, but chop chop with the coffee, please."

Sam snickers. I glance over, unable to resist discovering the source of his amusement only to find it's me, while Aiden gapes at me in concern as though I have pock marks on my face.

"A little hungry there today, Johnny?" Sam quips.

Fuck him and his audacity to throw my name out like we're pals.

"Mm. Famished."

They collect their order and make their way to a table, selecting chairs that put them facing me. Superb. Now I have an audience as I stand here waiting like a man who looks to be eating his feelings.

I've nearly erected the invisible gawk-proof wall at my back to block out the feel of their gazes, when someone sidles up beside me. Sam—with a creepy little smirk on his face.

As he takes his sweet time, gathering napkins and sugar packets from the condiment rack, I peruse him with a careful side eye.

He's about an inch shorter than me, but with shoulders a few inches wider. Sandy hair, raked back in the front. Sparkling blue eyes with laugh lines at the corners. Sculpted arms in his stupid Olympus West football t-shirt. He's like a grown-up version of a jock. He's perfect—perfect for Aiden.

I fucking hate him.

"You're the one who hurt him, aren't you?" His candid question catches me off-guard as he focuses on dumping sugar into his coffee.

Glancing over my shoulder to see if I'm imagining this inquiry, I catch the paint of intrigue on Aiden's brow. He has no fucking clue.

"I beg your pardon?"

Smiling like the world's perfect boyfriend, he continues. "He said he just got hurt by someone he went on a few dates with. I'd appreciate if you wouldn't drag it out by coming by again. You've already hurt him enough."

My blood rushes to my ears at the passive aggressive smile on his face. I had no intention of stopping by again. I'm not a home wrecker, but the nerve on this guy, laying claim to Aiden's cute little house like he has some authority there.

I hope my mother's baklava gave him the shits.

But what can I do? I'm just the Lance here.

"And if *you* hurt him, I will find you."

He scoffs at my warning, his smile triumphant as he brings his coffee to his lips.

"That won't happen. *I* know what I've got."

His hand slaps my shoulder in what I'm sure is meant as a friendly bro-gesture for Aiden's benefit, but it rocks me an inch forward, most definitely leaving a red handprint on my skin as he slinks off. My breaths are coming in quick succession, like I'm about to either pass out or shed real tears. I will not lose it in a coffee shop over a salty, possessive football coach who bro-slaps strangers and dispenses unwarranted advice.

Gathering up my espresso and embarrassingly large grocery bag of Bitsy bribes, I spin on my heels and bolt past patrons toward the door. I know I shouldn't, but I can't stop my head from turning.

Sam's smiling at Aiden, running his mouth like nothing lascivious just happened. His hand is firmly clamped on top of Aiden's thigh like a fucking *Lojack* device. But Aiden...

As I pant for breath in that split second plea of *please be happy*, I send to him, he looks at me. God, it stings the way his face says he knows I'm not okay, but that he's too hurt to do anything about it and can't do anything about it, because he's not mine, and all I do is push him away when he's kind. I trained him to stop caring, to stop being him. I'm a goddam monster.

The fresh air on the sidewalk hits my face, washing away the overwhelming sweetness of baked goods and bitter bouquet of gourmet coffees. Now I know what vomit feels like, jostled and ejected out of a cavern.

This was no big deal, I tell myself. You'll get over it. It was just a couple of dates. Sam's probably not the world's biggest a douche bag.

Smile.

Be happy.

Smile.

Go feed Bitsy.

Okay. I can do this.

Turning toward the studio, I start walking, but something equal parts solid and squishy slams into my lower half, nearly making me drop my thirty-six pastries. Righting myself, I hear a froggy villian-esque voice accuse, "You again?"

Gasp! No. It cannot be!

"You!" I retort to one four-foot, hot fudge sundae-wielding Bradley Reeves, my nemesis from the carnival. Except, he's only half-wielding his hot fudge sundae. The other half, mainly the hot fudge half, is now taking up residence on the front of my spearmint green polo shirt.

Bradley glowers at me. "You ruined my ice cream!"

"You ruined my shirt!"

"Then I just did you a favor. Don't you have any other shirts?"

My offense is narrowly overtaken by my grief. This was the shirt I wore the day I met Aiden.

"Of course, I have other shirts, but this was my favorite." My voice is not garbled. I will not lose it over a fudge collision.

"Are you going to cry?" Bradley asks, head rearing back in shock.

"No!"

A woman descends upon us, a woman whose features closely resemble dear Bradley's dark hair and eyes. "Oh, my word! Bradley! What did you do now?"

"Nothing! This idiot ran into me and ruined my ice cream," devil-child says as his mother takes a knee in front of us.

"Don't say *idiot*, and I told you to wait for me," she scolds, tugging napkins out of her bag from the creamery next door. "Is this how you're going to behave when school starts tomorrow? Sir, I am so so sorry about this. Here. Let me help you," the devil's mother says as I stand dumbstruck by my own horrid luck.

When the fabric of my shirt shifts against my skin, I finally snap out of it. Mrs. Reeves is holding my hem, coming at my fudge stain with her wad of napkins like a woman on a mission.

"No!" I yelp, but she's too quick, smearing the brown goo around. "You're not supposed to wipe it, you're supposed to…rub the fabric… together," I trail off, knowing what Aiden would do if he were here.

Blinking up at me in confusion, she doesn't understand the symbolism. My once beloved *Jerry Rennoux* polo is a vestige of my time with Aiden, signifying both the beginning and end.

"I…I'm sorry. I'll pay to send it to the dry cleaner for you," she says, tugging her wallet from her purse.

"No. No. It's fine. Really." I hold up my coffee cup to refute her offer, painfully aware I am nearly in tears over a damned shirt. "I'll just…burn it."

Shuffling around them, I hurry down the street, spouting my mantra.

Be happy.

Smile.

Feed Bitsy.

Forget how great you could have had it.

CHAPTER 43

Johnny

My father says God has a sense of humor. Papa clearly has communed with the man. My state of rolled up pants, sweat-drenched hair curled as all get out, dirt-covered white tank top, and blistered hands is nothing short of laughable as I crouch in Papa's garden, pulling weeds and picking vegetables.

Atonement, I tell myself. This is atonement for my careless behavior.

Papa groans, stretching his back as he straightens up. The slight paunch of his belly flattens with the pose, reminding me of his figure in my childhood days.

"Ah, *Giannaki. Edaksi*," he chuckles, motioning for me to abandon our cause for the day.

Thank fuck. Atonement is not for the faint of heart.

I join him at the patio table under the shade of the big oak, still adorned by the tire swing Andreas tied me to when I was nine and spun me until I puked. My skin is saturated with enough sweat that the faint breeze brings a modicum of relief in the August heat.

Papa pats his bald head with a handkerchief, staring contemplatively at a dried-up fig tree sapling. It's only the tenth one he's tried to grow over the years.

"I don't think it's going to make it, Papa."

"Ah." He chuffs with a smile and pats my hand. "Maybe next year. *Nai*?"

I nod, the only proper response to the world's most optimistic man. "Yeah. Maybe next year."

Bitsy has more of a chance of giving up her lotion addiction than the fig tree seeds my father smuggles home each year from Greece have of enduring Wisconsin winters. I suppress a laugh at the tiny bubble of joy that percolates through my stagnant mood.

Papa's hope is admirable. He always has hope. Since the Sam *McSmarmy* assault and fudging the other day, I have contemplated all sorts of fantastical ideas.

Girding my loins, literally, by becoming the world's oldest circumcision patient. Relocating to Miami near Will, who is more bitter than I was post-Lance, pre-Monkey Butt intervention. I barely know him these days. Plus, his high-maintenance boyfriend and the affluent company they keep are not my scene, with the exception of the pretty faces that attend their parties that I can add to my photography catalog, should I ever completely lose my mind and push model photos again with more vigor.

I even considered a photography tour of Greece. Island hopping after Mykonos. Capturing old men in the *tavernas*, flicking their prayer beads as they argue over backgammon. Shooting all the beaches, then the graffiti of Pireaus, the stray dogs that litter the Acropolis stairs. It brought me moments of hope that I may find solace in what I do again, but the problem with being at peace is that, eventually, you want to tell someone about it. You want to share it with someone.

Mamá emerges from the back of the house, carrying a tray of ice waters. She sets it down on our table, *tisking* as she snags Papa's tumbler of grapa. Glancing at the full plate of cheese, olives, and bread she set out for me earlier, she frowns and takes the empty seat.

"Giannis, you are not eating. You never eat anymore. Are you sick?"

"No, Mamá. It's just too hot to eat. I'm not hungry."

"You barely ate at dinner all week. I made *saganaki* just for you last night, and you didn't even touch it. Something is wrong."

"Mamá, I'm fine." I smile one of my newly practiced smiles. "I promise."

Jaw set, her eyes study me, but I am too exhausted to fear whatever assumptions she may be conjuring. Clasping her hands together under her chin, she narrows her eyes as though she's peering into my soul.

"*Giannaki*, I am sorry," she says sagely.

I must be succumbing to the sun, because my mother has never apologized for anything in her life.

"For what?"

"For making you date. When you moved home without your boyfriend and didn't date another man, I thought, maybe he doesn't like men anymore. So, I tried to find women you might like, but that didn't work. And then I pushed you to try these dating computer pages for men, and now you're even more miserable than before. I'm sorry. I can see it wasn't good for you."

I don't know why it occurs to me only just now that she hasn't so much as mentioned dating in the past few weeks. A puff of laughter bubbles out of my throat at her confession. She loves me so much she over-analyzed things and thought I might be into women? It's almost comically endearing. And now I know where I get my over-imaginative brain.

"No, Mamá. Actually, it was," I concede, but not just to soothe her remorse.

I am older and wiser and no longer in a festering Lance-funk. Give me a few more weeks, and maybe I'll be out of my Aiden-funk. It has to be only a few more weeks. I don't think I can tolerate any more than that.

Mamá's face brightens. "You are seeing someone?"

"No. It didn't work out, but he was good for me, so…I…I know what to look for next time."

"The Greek man or the first one from the American computer page thing on your phone?"

I pinch my eyes shut and suppress a chuckle. *Oh, Mamá.* I've actually missed personal discussions with her and will do harm to anyone who ever laughs at her for saying *computer pages.*

"They were actually the same person," I admit. "I went to a dating event downtown, and we ran into each other there too."

I choke on my water as Mamá and Papa gasp in unison and declare *fate*, signaling to the heavens.

"No. It was just coincidence. A very odd coincidence."

"And you say it will not work?" Mamá presses. "What is the problem?"

I'm the problem, but how can I convince a Greek mother her child is flawed? Granted, she can point out my flaws to me on a daily basis, but no one else is allowed to give them credence.

"We were too different, so I…I sabotaged it, and there's no going back."

"Oh, Giannis," she heaves, squeezing my forearm.

My new goal in life is to not hear that phrase when I dispense un-filtered honesty. However, as I sit here in my own sweat, I realize I've essentially just gutted myself to my parents, something I haven't done since I came out.

Andreas comes through the gate to the backyard, calling out a greet-ing. His look-at-my-dick walk annoys me less than it used to. Perhaps I *am* sick. I've just discussed my love life with my parents and don't care about the circumcision info pamphlet that's been sitting on my nightstand since I snagged it at the doctor's office during my annual checkup last week.

Papa cups my face in his hands and plants a hard kiss on my sweaty head, before patting my shoulder and walking off to direct Andreas to haul away the garden bounty to Oikos. Mamá returns her attention back to me, clasping my chin in her hand.

"Giannis, come to our anniversary party tonight. Laugh, have a good time, be around people who love you no matter what."

The lines of concern in her face couldn't speak any louder. My family really does love me *no matter what*. Even Mamá. Even if she loves me so much, she sometimes shows it in the most backward ways and gets things wrong.

Maybe that's what love really is—loving imperfections.

Maybe it's liking when a man wears obscene underwear and has an uncut penis, and knowing his prickliness is just a front. Maybe it's liking how genuinely thoughtful and attentive a big, gorgeous, burly man is to a clumsy, snippy nerd, and the way he looks at that nerd like that nerd is the thing he's been looking for all his life.

I didn't think I could feel any worse.

Chuckling at my own morose logic, I nod at Mamá. "Yeah, Mamá. I'll be there. It'll be a great party."

Her painted lips stretch into a smile that she presses to my cheek as she stands. "My sweet boy. Good. Now, don't sit out here too long. Go home and rest for tonight. I have to get these vegetables to the restaurant."

She hurries off to the house. Andreas swaggers back through the gate, this time with his wife, Thespina, in tow. Odd, how they're holding hands and laughing like young lovers. Half the time, they act like the other isn't in the room or argue over how they raise their children.

Thespina whispers something in Andreas' ear, then she laughs and races ahead of him. Goodness, he's chasing after her toward the garden, and…oh.

Oh, my.

I gape at the mating ritual before my eyes as my older brother grabs a handful of my sister-in-law's ass, pulling her against him, while they kiss like they're dying. What the actual fuck?

Glancing toward the house, Mamá and Papa seem to have retired to other things for the day. Which means, I am the lone spectator of the *Andreas and Thespina Show*. Disgusting.

Oh, sweet baby Jesus! She just grabbed his junk.

I let out a screech and cover my ears at the horrifying sound of my brother's groan.

"Oh!" Thespina gasps with a giggle. "Giannis! I'm sorry. We didn't see you there."

I make a whimper noise, as one does when asked to stick their hand into a viper pit and wave. "No problem."

She grins at Andreas and whispers something else. He answers with a rough kiss and little swat to her ass as she turns to leave. When he turns around toward a basket of tomatoes, beaming like a bank robber, I flinch at the sight of the bulge in his look-at-my-dick-shorts.

Okay. I really need to stop that. I know it's not normal, but this time it's hardly avoidable—emphasis on *hardly*.

He smirks and adjusts himself, tilting his chin at me. "What are you looking at?"

I choke on air. Is he kidding me?

"I don't get you. I thought you said getting snipped…*ruined it*." I wave my hand toward the direction Thespina fled. "What's the deal with the mini porn show and…and the ten-second wood in your shorts?"

He scoffs at me. "What? Are you serious?"

"Uh. Does Thios Dimitris have a drinking problem? Yes, I'm serious. You scarred me for life, and now you're popping a boner with your wife of ten years after twenty seconds of patty cake?"

I wish I had something to swing at his head, the way it rears back as he bursts out laughing. When he finally calms himself enough to breathe, he shakes his head and mutters, "*Malaka*."

He calls me the Greek version of *wanker* on a regular basis, but I will not have it when discussing topics such as the cock formally known as Flapper. Thrusting my hand, palm out at him, I return his slight with the Greek symbol for the big *fuck you*.

"Don't *malaka* me! *That's* what you told me after you got cut! I remember with perfect clarity."

He snickers and hoists up the basket of tomatoes. "Shit, Giannis. Don't take everything I say to heart. Of course, it was weird at first." He shrugs. "It was different because a piece of me I had my whole life was missing. I wasn't used to fucking without it yet."

I shudder at his choice of words—*a piece, missing*. But is he for real?

"So…it works though? And…and it feels…feels like…"

"Feels like it still loves pussy?"

"Ew! *Malaka!*" I seethe, hearing him infer about my sister-in-law's womanhood. She's like another sister to me. I don't want to hear about how much Andreas loves any of her *parts*.

Cackling, he hoists the basket higher in his arms. "Yes, dumbass. It works better than ever."

I'm grateful those are his parting words because that was enough brotherly bonding to last me until I'm *Yiayiá's* age. Leaning back in my chair, I press my palms to my eyes.

The predicament I fretted over for half my life has evaporated in the summer heat via the exchange of several curse words.

What has happened?

My parents are my diary. My cock is no longer in mortal danger if I choose to put it under the knife, and I'm oddly grateful to have an insane Greek family.

Who needs a drink?

CHAPTER 44
Aiden

Graham shoves the last of his steak in his mouth, chewing with the grace of a rabid animal. Grunting, he closes his eyes and exhales like he's communing with the cow that sacrificed its life for him.

Glancing around the bar and grille, I check to see if anyone else has picked up on his peculiar eating rituals. They never get old. Now I remember why I avoid dining with him in public.

"Are you going to be alright, or do you two need a minute alone?" I ask, gesturing to his plate.

"Piss off. It was good. I'm just glad somebody knows how to cook a steak right beside me. You invited me out. Did you not want me to enjoy myself?"

"Yeah, but define enjoying yourself?"

"Laugh it up. I'm a picky eater. You know this."

I smirk. Getting his goat is bringing me too much joy tonight. I needed this. To think I had to drag myself out of the house while Sam's out of town for the weekend. Who knew I actually missed quality time with my crabby little brother?

"You want to go get a beer after this?"

Graham's shifting gaze stops scanning the restaurant. He frowns and shakes his head. "Nah. I'm gonna head home."

"What? It's early. You're not still driving by Jen's house at night, are you? I'll bail you out of jail if I have to, but stalking is not cool."

"I wasn't stalking her! She had just moved out, and I was worried about her, so I took that way home a couple times to check on her."

My expression must convey my thoughts on his innocence because he throws his hands up. "Oh, forget it. Fine! Let's just talk about you. How's your new…boyfriend."

"Why do you say *boyfriend* like venereal disease?"

"I did not! It's just…different. Okay? You've never had a…never dated a guy this long before."

Fair enough.

Graham took the brunt of the shit kids slung about Maxie being the first out and proud lesbian in our high school. He has his issues for a reason. I shrug at the topic of my love life.

"Sam's…nice. It's…nice."

I'm answered with a snort. "Wow. I thought that big love you were looking for would be more than *nice*. Is the sex bad or something?"

Now I'm the one who's wowed. He can't say the word *boyfriend*, but he can ask about men having sex? To his nature though, his leg is bouncing under the table and he's scanning the crowd again, like he didn't just ask me something incredibly personal.

"We…haven't yet," I admit.

"Really? It's been like a month."

"So? It's just not time yet."

He scrutinizes me as though I'm an idiot. "Dude, if you're not into it yet after a month, you never will be. Do yourself a favor and move on."

I have to bite my tongue when the waitress stops by to drop off our check. "Are you just saying that because I'm dating a guy?"

His face goes a shade red. "No! I don't care who you date. It's just basic statistics at our age. If it doesn't feel right after all this time, what's going to make that change?"

I don't think I miss brother-time anymore. He's just cut the cords of webbing I thought had been slowly and intricately woven over the last month by Sam and me.

I'm being patient this time. I don't want to rush anything. Sam understands that or at least says he does. He's getting increasingly more hands-on though, and I think his pouty face isn't just a coy flirtation each time I've declined to spend the night or have him stay over. He certainly did look a little disappointed that I didn't take the trip to Ohio with him this weekend to meet his family but agreed when I said we should get to know each other better before we start doing joint family visits.

Graham distractedly excuses himself to go off and do whatever it is that he does at nights these days. I watch his agitated behavior as he makes his way toward the door, eyeballing a group of businessmen at the end of the bar. Shit. One of them better not be Jen's new boyfriend and he's thinking of starting something. Is that why he suggested this place?

He moves on though, and I can breathe easier until I spot the redhead at the end of the bar.

Bitsy.

Instinctively, I scan the crowd for Johnny. Nice, dickhead. Your boyfriend is out of town for one weekend, and you're looking for…for your last hook up. Except, it doesn't feel right to call Johnny that. Maybe, if I knew what to call him, it'd be easier to forget about him.

He looked so rattled at the coffee shop the other day, so upset that it gave me hope. Hope I shouldn't have or crave. At the same time, my stupid heart wanted to go ask him what was wrong and offer him comfort, all while I was there with Sam. Patient, fun-loving, always-wants-to-be-with-me Sam.

Moving through the crowd, I make my way toward the door. I tell myself I won't talk to Bitsy unless she says something first, but something strikes me as odd.

She's closing up a laptop and shaking hands with the restaurant manager like they're completing a business deal. The manager moves on, and she starts stuffing her laptop into a case.

"Bitsy? How are you doing?"

Her surprise is evident and understandable, considering how we last met. "Oh! Aiden! Hi. How are you?" she asks, glancing behind me as though she's checking to see if I'm here with anyone.

"Good. I just had dinner with my brother."

"Oh, that's nice. I was meeting a client. I love this place. I'm going to help them with their marketing. The owner wants to open a second location in Milwaukee."

That doesn't sound like it involves Johnny and makes me sad. I picture him scrambling around his studio, trying to take pictures and answer phones all by himself.

"Don't you work for Johnny anymore?"

"I do," she says as her phone vibrates on the bar with an incoming message. She glances at it, looking perplexed, but ignores it and looks at the clock above the bar. "I started doing marketing jobs for extra money when Johnny and I moved here, and it sort of took off. The work I do for Johnny, I could do with my eyes closed, so I can handle both."

I'm not doing a stellar job of not thinking about my reluctant dating app partner, but I can't help it. My curiosity gets the better of me as Bitsy starts toward the door.

"Is he…having financial problems?"

"What? Oh! No. Not at all. I've been saving to buy a house and didn't want a big mortgage payment. No. Johnny's way too generous, but he could probably afford to hire two more of me even at my spoiled best friend salary," she says with a laugh. "He…used to be kind of a big deal in the modeling world for such a young photographer. Up and coming, so to speak," she offers hesitantly, as if she isn't sure whether or not to share information about him with me.

Of course, he was. The man is crazy talented with that camera. I still don't understand why he's here, taking family portraits.

"Then he could probably get anybody he wants to work for him," I concede. "Maybe you can market him some more, so you can buy that house sooner."

I hold the door for her as we step outside. Her phone vibrates again, and she frowns at it before looking up at me.

"Um. Johnny doesn't let me market his business too much, and actually, I've managed to save about four times a down payment. I just… can't leave him. He's been so different since his ex. I…well, I worry about him sometimes."

I knew Johnny had an ex, but I didn't know that one person was responsible for his *no dating* rule. I assume she's talking about the guy he said had promised him *everything*, and now it all makes more sense. Still, I'm curious to know what Johnny was like before that relationship went awry.

"Different how?" I ask, my voice sounding nosier now that we're alone in the parking lot.

Bitsy sighs, the corners of her mouth turning down. "He's always been a little dramatic, but that's Johnny, you know?" She smiles, and I can't help but join in. "Ever since Lance, he's moodier, negative, less adventurous. I bought us tickets to Mykonos next month, and he says he's excited to go, but I get the impression he's putting me on." She lets loose a sardonic laugh. "He used to drag me all over the place on day trips back in college. Now I'm lucky if I can get him to go anywhere other than one of his family's restaurants."

Lance? Okay. For starters, that's a stupid name. It sounds like a weapon that pierces hearts.

My lungs seize up at the thought of Johnny still in love with someone else. Maybe he was trying to warn me of that all along, and I just didn't listen.

"He's still that hung up on this guy, huh?"

"No. Not at all. He's just hung up on the war wounds."

Her phone buzzes again, and she glances at it. "I'm sorry. Um, where's your boyfriend tonight?" Kicking at a rock on the parking lot when I blink at her, she peeks out from under her lashes. "Johnny may have mentioned you were seeing someone."

Did he now? Interesting that I was a topic of conversation.

"He's out of town for the weekend, visiting some of his relatives."

"Oh," she coos, her brows arching as though that information is more interesting than it is. He phone vibrates again, and she frowns at it.

"Do you…need to get that?"

She holds up her index finger. "Yeah. Just one second."

Her expression sours as she scrolls through her phone, muttering, "Oh, no. Oh. No."

"Is everything okay?"

Grimacing up at me, she bares her teeth. "I think Johnny's drunk."

"He doesn't drink."

"Well, yeah, but…he's with his family so he doesn't exactly have a choice. I was supposed to be there an hour ago, which in Johnny drunk-years is like raging alcoholic."

The memory of him blathering at the eighties party comes back to me. That was only after half a beer, but he gradually came out of it.

"He had half a beer with me one night," I offer, trying to talk myself out of caring. "He was a little silly for about an hour, but then he was alright."

Bitsy winces, typing back something on her phone. "Ye-ah, but Greeks don't drink much beer. They're more hard liquor and high-potency wine kind of people. We're talking shots after shots, especially at parties. The last time I missed one of his family's parties, it took him three days to recover after he got into a drinking contest with his Uncle Dimitris. He didn't stop slurring for twenty-four hours."

Shit. What's wrong with these people? Don't they know *no* means *no?*

Wait. What the hell am I saying? My own family doesn't know that *no* means *no* half the time.

"Will he be okay?"

"Maybe. If he listens to me, and as long as they let me drag him out of there and get him home. They're just…"

"What?"

Grimacing, she looks at me as though she might be nauseous. "Persuasive? Pushy? Stronger in numbers?"

"You can't say *no* to them, can you?"

Blowing out a breath, her shoulders sag. "No. I try! I really do, but I mean *they're Greek.*"

Don't care, Aiden. Don't care, I tell myself, running my palm down my face.

Picturing Johnny in tiny cycling shorts, throwing up over the side of a guard rail with no one to put him to bed but this pint-sized redhead in front of me gnaws at me though. What about Sam? We've been together for only a month. The first time he's out of town, I'm considering rescuing some guy who loved me and left me?

"I bet he'd listen to you though," Bitsy intones hopefully. "That's half the battle, getting him to agree. He kind of becomes a party-monster once he gets to a certain point, and then his family doesn't help after that, feeding him drinks."

"I'll follow you."

CHAPTER 45

Aiden

Pulling into the parking lot of Oikos behind Bitsy, I curse under my breath. This is Johnny's parents' restaurant, which makes this venture feel like even more of a betrayal to Sam.

Yet, as much as I shouldn't be here, for the life of me, I can't stop myself from getting out of my truck. Johnny's not the kind of person who asks for help. Hell, he's not even the kind of person who would accept help if he were tied to a conveyor belt and headed toward a bandsaw. The fact that I'm here, has nothing to do with the brief history lesson that Bitsy gave me in the parking lot of the bar and grille. Nothing at all.

Adventurous Johnny? Party-monster? No. I am not curious at all to find out what that version of Johnny is like.

Meeting up with Bitsy at the back of my truck, I can hear the beat of music coming from inside the restaurant. The blinds are drawn, so I can't see what's going inside, but from the sound of it, his family doesn't have much concern for noise ordinances.

"I don't think this is a good idea," I tell Bitsy like she's the one who needs convincing. "In my experience, drunk people don't listen to reason, and they especially don't listen to reason if it's someone they don't want to see when they're sober."

"That's not true! The second part, I mean. He does want to see you. I know he does."

My skepticism wars with my stupid, traitorous heart as I glance from her to Oikos. Her hand clutches my arm and starts tugging.

"You know how difficult he is when he's sober. I'm half your size. I don't stand a chance. Can you please just talk to him while your boyfriend isn't around to threaten him?"

"What?" My feet stop moving.

Bitsy's mouth falls open for a beat. She bites her lip, and tugs on my arm again. "Please?"

Sam threatened him? How? When? Why?

We're at the door before I can even consider the answers to those questions. When Bitsy opens it, a blast of pop music with tinny mandolin-sounding instruments affronts us. And is that…it almost sounds like cell phone button noises are mixed in with the melody. Greek pop music is officially genius if a singer can make money off cell phone noises.

"Oh, no," Bitsy murmurs, and something that sounds like, "Not Panos Kiamos."

I can smell rich aromas of exotic spices, grilled meats, cigarette smoke, and liquor…definitely liquor. Whoops, hollers, and clapping flood through the doorway to the entrance hall. There is nothing that could have prepared me for what I see as we step over the threshold.

"Oh, no," Bitsy moans again. "It's so much worse than I thought."

Amidst the crowded room of people, Johnny isn't difficult to miss. He's the only one dancing on top of a table as a ring of whom people, hold hands, bob and kick, circling around him on the floor in time with the music. It's like a modern ritual, worshipping a Greek god. He looks absolutely awe inspiring.

He's dressed to the nines, but in that old Greek style that Dimitris seemed to favor when we were building the patio wall last year. Navy blue slacks, a light blue button-up, completely unbuttoned, revealing a white sleeveless undershirt. His ensemble is complete with brown dress shoes, shined to a polish. And his hair? Well, I guess he was right about its potential. It's curly as fuck tonight, all fluffed out like he's run his fingers through it one too many times and hasn't seen a mirror. He is sexy as hell.

However, I think his hair is the farthest thing from his mind because he's rotating at the hips, deep into his dancing. His arms are outstretched as he accentuates lines from a song I don't understand. Some of the guests are lobbing flower blossoms at him. Either he's too drunk to notice, or it's a custom he's used to, because he pays them no mind as they zing past his head, one even bouncing off his temple. He makes a comically displeased face and mimes pressing buttons on an imaginary cell phone in his hand, then holds it up to his ear and shakes his head as though the caller has the wrong number.

It's clear he's an epic performer by the way the crowd is laughing and cheering at his antics. I don't know if I can pick my jaw up off the floor. The closest I came to meeting Johnny the Party Monster was when he let his freak flag fly for about a minute when we danced at that bar.

When the chorus picks up, both Johnny and the party go wild. He wrestles out of his button up, balling it up in his hand, and whips it into the crowd. Arms out to his sides like a bull fighter, he makes a swooping motion, like an airplane coming in for a landing, and follows it with a series of high-legged kicks and little jumps. I flinch each time he lands, his legs wobbling as the table rocks beneath him.

"Shit. He's going to crack his head open," I mutter.

I'm elbowing past people as fast as I can, but a middle-aged man stops me and plants a kiss on each of my cheeks for reasons unknown. The song ends before I make it to the table. Someone holds up a tray to Johnny with a single shot glass on it. He takes it and raises it high in the air, while everyone shouts, "*Ya mas!*" He throws back the liquid, then tosses the shot glass to someone in the crowd.

Finally, I have his attention or at least half of it. Face scrunched up, he blinks at me, then blinks some more.

"Aiden? *Whuddy-you-doing-khere?*"

A man about my age, who looks like a bigger, buffer Johnny, holds out another shot to him, laughing and encouraging him to take it. What is wrong with these people? Can't they see he's too far gone? Johnny sways and reaches for it, but I catch his wrist and tug him toward me.

"He'll pass," I inform the guy. "Johnny, you need to get down."

"But I'm dancing," he slurs, grabbing onto my shoulder as he starts to topple.

"You can dance on the floor."

I catch him around the hips and drag him down my front like a sack of potatoes. By the way he's hanging on me, I don't dare let him go. His head weaves as he scans the room over my shoulder. When he focuses back on me, his eyes narrow into thin slits behind his askew glasses.

"Where's Sporty McSssalty Stealer of my Brick Layer?"

Wow. Is he…jealous? What kind of guy am I that it makes me a bit giddy?

"Out of town for the weekend."

"Hm. I'm surprised he let you out of his sight that long."

The buffer Johnny appears again at my side, wielding two sticks of skewered meat. "Aiden Brandt, right?"

"Yeah."

Johnny cuts in, practically snarling. "What do you want, Andreas?"

"I'm just saying hi," he tells Johnny, then turns to me. "Welcome, man."

I'm still gripping Johnny's hips. One of his hands is latched onto my shoulder, the other resting on my chest, his fingers slowly stroking it like a cat's paw would. I'm pretty sure his family knows he's gay, but I release one of my hands to create some space between us.

Johnny has none of it though. His arms snake around my waist, and he leans his head on my chest.

"He doesn't want your stupid perfect penis. Go away," Johnny sasses his brother.

Andreas' eyebrows go up along with mine, but he gives me a

sheepish grin and hands me one of the sticks of meat like a peace offering. "Souvlaki?"

I don't even get a reply formed in my head. Johnny's hand smacks the stick of meat, sending chunks flying into the air. One of them bounces off an old woman's back.

"What the fuck, Andreas? Are you trying to kill him? *Malaka!*"

Andreas stares dumbstruck and holds up a hand like he might actually be afraid of Drunk Johnny in spite of their size difference. "I thought he might be hungry."

"It's garlic! Everything is garlic!"

Holding Johnny to me as he writhes, I hold up my palm to his brother. "I've got this. Okay?" I yell over the music.

Andreas frowns. "Well, fuck both of you too," he huffs and storms off.

Johnny starts cackling a high-pitched sound that is half-amusing, half-terrifying.

"What? What did I do?"

"You just told him to fuck off. That was great!" He sighs, using me as a leaning post again. "You see? This is why I thought it would never work. We're too different, and my family would kill you in one day," he grumbles, turning his face up to look at me. His lower lip juts out, and he adds, "But I'd protect you from them. I swear."

His grip on my waist tightens. His curling hair tickles my jaw as he nestles his head under my chin.

I can't believe I willingly came here for this torment. Seeing his sweet protective side when it's too late only opens my wounds.

Bitsy lays a hand on my arm. Crap. How long has she been standing there?

Judging by her apologetic smile, I'm guessing a while. She reaches for Johnny, smoothing his hair.

"Johnny? Why don't we get you home?" she suggests.

Rolling his head to face her, he grumps, "No."

"Honey, you're going to regret this in the morning. Come on. We'll take you home."

"No! I want to dance with Aiden. He's such a good dancer," he slurs and sways, brushing our stomachs together.

Shit. Just kill me now.

An older woman with unnaturally vibrant auburn hair comes up to our other side and places her hand on Johnny's shoulder as she smiles up at me. With her features, that A-line nose and those dark eyes, she has to be his mother.

"Giannis? Who is your friend?"

Shifting my weight to stabilize Johnny, I offer my hand. "Aiden. Aiden Brandt, ma'am."

"Ah! Is this your Greek boyfriend?" she asks Johnny.

"No, Mamá," Johnny practically moans. "He's someone else's Greek boyfriend."

"Um. I'll take him home," I tell his mother.

Johnny's head rattles back and forth, his eyes all squinty again. "I don't wanna go home."

Mrs. Andropolis gives him a pitying look and strokes his hair. Her dark eyes turn on me next. Shit. Is she scowling at me? What did I do?

With the back of her free hand, she gestures authoritatively. "You don't want to dance with my son?"

Christ. I glance at Bitsy to see if this is what she was warning me about. All doe-eyed, she nods as though to say do-what-the-nice-scary-lady-says.

"Uh. One dance," I tell Johnny's intimidating mamá who breaks into a delighted smile and plants a kiss on Johnny's cheek before declaring me a *good boy* and moving on.

Fortunately, the cell phone song has long ended and something slow is playing. Johnny slinks his arms around my neck, resuming his drunk-man yoga pose on my chest as I brace him and sway us to the melody.

I feel myself falling, grappling with my conscience the longer he's in my arms. Our chemistry made him feel like a drug, something my body couldn't keep from wanting. The way I want him now is driven by only one part of my body—Hot Mess Johnny is crawling deeper inside my heart by the second. I feel like I'm home. Why doesn't it feel remotely like this with Sam? I told myself I wanted safe and constant, but maybe I don't know what I need. Maybe I'm only attracted to confusing, crunchy on the outside, mushy on the inside troublemakers.

Resting my cheek against his, I catch a hit of his distinct sweet and salty scent. I wish I could turn this off, this need for him. Underneath the warm sensation fizzing inside me is a current of anger. Why can't he be like this when he's sober or when we're not tearing each other's clothes off?

Is he…singing?

The smooth sound of his voice, wholesome and melodic turns the skin on my arms to gooseflesh as he serenades along with the slow ballad. Johnny speaking in Greek is one thing. Johnny singing softly in Greek makes me want to haul him out of here right now and swallow every note from his mouth with my lips on his. The way his thumb is gently grazing my neck, I wonder if it's a love song.

"That sounds sad."

"It is. It's beautiful." He sighs.

"What's it about?"

"It's about your swiper not being able to let you go even though you do all the opposite swiper-y things. He stays because he knows you need his super swiper strength, and because he loves you, and he's good, and being good makes him happy, so you being a disaster and needing him gives him purpose. But because you can make a swiper happy, it means you might not be a total mess." As my heart splits open, he hiccups. "But it's all bullshit."

A bubble of pained laughter pops in my throat, stroking his back. I'm someone else's boyfriend, and if I saw Johnny on the street tomorrow, he'd probably tell me to run along again. Yet, I'm a glutton for punishment because I want to remember that drunken ramble.

"What's it called?"

"It's called *Eimena Edo*" by Ssstellios Ro—Roko—" He lets loose a painful sound of indigestion. "Fuck! *Rokos!* Ssstellios Rokos. Shit. I'm so drunk," he mutters, leaning even more weight into me.

About ten seconds later, he tilts his head up. His eyes—heavy-lidded, chin resting on my chest.

"Are you going to carry me again?"

"Do I need to?"

"Probably…a good idea."

He starts to slide down my front. Great. There he goes.

Scooping my arm under his legs, I heft him into bridal carry. He doesn't protest this time, resting his head in the crook of my neck as I nod to Bitsy and head for the door.

Alcohol—one.

Johnny—zero.

CHAPTER 46

Aiden

Johnny's sacrifice victim posture is making it difficult to maneuver down the hall to his bedroom without bashing his head or arms against the wall. At least I know he's breathing. Head back, mouth-wide open—that can't be good for his neck.

Damn it. Now to put a hundred and eighty pounds of dead weight on a moving bed. Ten points to Bitsy for holding the swing still while I deposit him on the mattress. Apparently, she's done this a few times. Johnny rouses and rolls over into his pillow with a groan.

Bitsy goes to work on his shoes, while I stand by like a third wheel. I've been in this room before, seen him in less, but the circumstances were different. Part of me feels like I have the right to stay and look after him, but the part that kissed Sam goodbye yesterday afternoon says I'm well past my expiration date to Drunk Johnny Land.

"Thanks so much for helping, Aiden," Bitsy says.

"No problem. Is he going to be alright?"

"Yeah. I've got it under control now. You can go."

"Okay. Well, goodnight." I glance at Johnny again, mumbling into his pillow. Another last goodbye, this one less glamorous than the others. "Goodnight, Johnny," I call a little louder in the hopes it will register.

"Mm. Nooo! Don't go," he whines, grabbing a handful of my blue jeans at the side of my leg.

Bitsy throws me a pitying look before addressing our patient. "Johnny, you're drunk. It's time to pass out now."

"Wasn't talking…to-you," he slurs, his cheek still on the mattress as he tugs at the leg of my pants in little jerks.

I cut off Bitsy's exasperated sigh with a reassuring hand. "It's alright. I can stay until he falls asleep."

"Are you sure?"

"Yeah. It's fine."

It is so not fine, but I need a moment of his unfiltered honesty and a few more minutes of him.

When Bitsy leaves, I sit on the mattress, my knee hitched up against Johnny's side and one foot planted on the floor to keep us from rocking. His hand flails until it finds my knee and squeezes it.

"Uhn," he groans. "Why did you have to find Sporty Mc-Bastard so soon?"

Sporty McBastard? I'd like to know if the nickname is indicative of the level of Johnny's jealousy or something Sam said or did.

"*So soon?*" I query.

"Yeah. You didn't give me enough time. I had to get my head together," he says, eyes still closed.

"Get your head together?"

"Ye-ah. The pieces of it." He turns his head toward me. His eyes making thin slits. "Why aren't we canoodling? I need a canoodle! I'm…ssspinny."

Shit. I'm rocking the bed like I'm lulling a baby to sleep.

"Are you going to be sick?"

"No," he says all breathy and exhausted. "Just spinny. Is the bed swinging?"

"No," I lie, shifting onto my side next to him as he rolls over into a fetal position, giving me his back.

"Fuck," he grumbles, pressing his hand to his eyes under his glasses.

I finagle them off his face and set them on the nightstand next to…a *Your Penis and You* pamphlet? What the hell is that about?

My twisting movement rocks the bed. Johnny groans again, so I turn back and wrap my arm around him.

Placing his hand over top of mine, he sighs. "That's better."

It is better. It shouldn't be, but it is. We might not get words right, but I never feel awkward or unsure in his arms. Resting my chin on his shoulder, I bask in this stolen, forbidden comfort that I promise myself to feel guilty about later.

"Mm. I miss your stubble," he mumbles.

Shifting my head, I brush my jaw lightly against his cheek. The little half-smile on his face is a hard-earned bounty, reminding me of that night in my bed. What did he mean I didn't give him enough time? Did he actually consider giving me a chance or is it just the booze talking?

"Did you go to Greece to get your head together?" I venture.

"No," he mopes like a dejected child. "I got scared and ran…or flew. You can't run to Greece. There's an ocean and a sea."

"But did you?" I ask when I'm sure he's done spewing his drunken travel logic.

"*Go to Greece?* Yeah! I just said that!"

I bite my lip to suppress a chuckle, a comforting warmth seeping into my hurt cracks at the memory of his snarky impatience. "No. Did you get your head together?"

"Yeah," he murmurs, gripping my hand tighter. "My *yiayiá* had a three-way. She's out of her mind, but she still remembers a three-way from like sixty years ago."

And now…I'm at a loss. "O-kay. And that helped you?"

"Yeah. You're my three-way, Aiden. I'll never forget you, even when I'm old and crazy."

The ache in my chest transforms into an emptiness that can only be filled by one thing. I don't stop my arms from tightening around him. I doubt he'll remember it anyway or the blunt honesty I desperately wanted him to share so many times before.

Relief, closure, joy, regret, comfort—they brew an awful concoction inside me. It tastes like a lesson any fool should know without guides. It tastes like the lesson Johnny wore on his sleeve since day one, when he was trying to ward me off to avoid a repeat of the pain his ex caused. Just because you move on, doesn't mean you're over someone.

I'm not over the sexy, infuriating, vulnerable man in my arms— the only person in the world who can use the term *three-way* in a sentence and make it sound romantic. The man who's not and never was my boyfriend.

CHAPTER 47

Johnny

For the love of speedo season, I'm dying. Please, let it end soon.

Oh, Dr. Phil! My head!

Why is there hammering? Was I beaten? Did I pass out on the floor of Oikos last night, my family trampling over my lifeless body?

Everything hurts. Ugh. Everything.

Turning my head should not be this painful or spin-inducing.

Thank fuck. My glasses.

Okay. Now I can see. I'm not blind at least, just dying.

Sweet angel of mercy is that a bottle of water and Aspirin on my nightstand? Yes! The universe has chosen to spare my wretched soul.

Damn it. This stupid bed.

As soon as it stops rocking and I suppress the nauseous urges at the back of my throat, I will hydrate and medicate. Ugh. Why do I have to get hangovers that hit harder and last three-times the length of those of normal human beings?

Rubbing my eyes, I focus on my antidote. Oh, how cute. Bitsy propped my penis pamphlet up against the water bottle. *Hill-arious.*

That note better say she has David Beckham on-call to give me a full-body rub down to help break up these toxins in my body or she can kiss that new desk goodbye. Wait.

That's not… This isn't Bitsy's handwriting.

Oh, God.

Oh, no.

Aiden. Aiden was here. That wasn't a hallucination.

He actually wrote on my penis pamphlet? Did he cross out the '*your guide to circumcision*' line? I stare dumbly at the script below the scratched-out sentence.

Johnny,

Don't you dare!

Fuck me. There's more at the bottom.

Call me when your hang over is gone.
We'll get lunch. That's not a request.

Aiden
555-0712

I can think of only one thing to say about this. "BITSY!"
Son of a bitch! That hurt my head.
The *thud* at the door distracts me from the needles in my eyes that I self-inflicted with my banshee cry. The world's worst caretaker staggers in and slumps against the doorframe. Her pink sleep mask is shoved up on top of her head, her matching mini-robe tied haphazardly about her waist, wild hair rightly bed-headed.
"What?" she croaks.
Holding the two halves of my splitting head together with my hands so I can speak, I channel calm. "What the fuck did I do last night?"
Rubbing her eyes, she groans. "Are you sure you're ready to hear it already? It's only noon. You need to sleep for like two more days."
"Noon? I slept till noon?"
Ouch! Why the fuck am I yelling? My head feels like it's being swirled in a toilet.
"Mm hm. Twelve thirty, actually, and you haven't even started puking yet."
My stomach flips over so violently, I have to cover my mouth. How can I not have any saliva left? Isn't the body supposed to produce that twenty-four-seven?
"Don't say the *v-word*." I gag and flap my hand. "Spill it. What occurred?"
"You…may have danced…on a table?"
"What?"
"There may have been some Panos Kiamos involved."
"Nooo! Not Panos!"
"And a lot of liquor."
"And…Aiden?" I squeak. "I remember seeing Aiden and…and I think we canoodled."
"*Canoodled?*"
"It means *to cuddle!* What the fuck, people? Buy a dictionary! Oh!

Ouch! My head!"

"Oh. Well, then yeah." She nods, crossing her arms. "Pretty sure you canoodled. You begged him to stay and shooed me from the room."

Pieces. Tiny, horrible, beautiful pieces of last night shift into place as my stomach gurgles, pumping a chalky thickness up my throat. Warm arms around me. Stubble scratching my face. Slow-dancing. I made him slow dance.

"Oh, no! I think I told him about Yiayiá's three-way."

Bitsy's eyes come alive. "Yiayiá had a three-way?"

Shit! It's here! Why did she have to say the *v-word*.

I am Johnny the Leap Frog, barreling off my swing bed and face-planting on the floor as I lose control of every muscle in my stomach. Usain Bolt has nothing on me as I regain my footing and dash to the toilet, where I purge the second my knees hit the tiled floor.

Uhn. I'm dying. Definitely dying.

I told Aiden about Yiayiá's three-way, he saw my circumcision pamphlet, and I'm dying.

Is there no dignity left in the world for dear Johnny?

The sound of bare feet slapping against the tile cuts through the noise of my retching. Panting, I brace the toilet seat and use what remains of my strength to see why Bitsy has come to witness my dishonorable demise.

Face contorted, she asks, "Like…a *recent* three-way?"

I drank my liver's weight in alcohol last night—okay, so maybe more like five shots—and she's more worried about Yiayiá's lovelife?

"Bitsy! Priorities!"

CHAPTER 48

Johnny

It is impossible to surmise how this lunch meeting will go or why I have even been summoned. Over the last three days, I've had the misfortune of remembering embarrassing details of Mamá and Papa's anniversary party. Three things became apparent as I wasted away in agony and then subsequently made the effort to restore my poisoned body.

One—my family thinks I'm a roaring good time when I'm inebriated, and therefore, there is a snowball's chance in hell they will ever stop forcing alcohol on me.

Two—as mad as I am at Bitsy for being over two hours late to the party, she is not my babysitter. I need to stop blaming people. The nausea still plaguing me is my own fault.

And three—I made a complete fool of myself in front of Aiden, and very possibly professed both my avid remorse and bitterness.

The plus side? I am now too ashamed to even long for Sporty McBastard's boyfriend in secret. This is the definition of adulting, children. Take note.

Please, tell me Sam will not be at this pity luncheon or whatever it is. The upbeat Mexican music wafting from the speakers outside of La Cantina could not be more grimace-worthy as I tug open the door.

I never should have texted Aiden, but the cryptic penis-pamphlet note wore me down, so I texted him a *thank you* message for seeing me home. The following day, I received a reply, inquiring if I was alive. My response of *barely* earned me another inquiry yesterday that went as follows:

> **AIDEN:** Do you still feel like your bed is swinging?
> **ME:** I am well again. Thank you for carrying me...
> again. Sorry for whatever alcohol-induced things
> I may have said.

AIDEN: Glad to hear it. Meet me at
La Cantina. Noon tomorrow.

So, here I am, because regardless of how scared I am of the stiff talking to that I fear he may give me for my behavior, if Aiden Brandt asked me to jump, I would say, h*ow high, baby? How high?*

There he is. Uhn. All six-foot-plus, broad-shouldered, still makes-my-knees-weak handsome. He's alone, and that's a semblance of a smile on his face. Thank goodness.

"Hello," I greet, reaching his table under a gawdy picture of a donkey in a booth at the back.

His eyes give me a slow once over, making my skin tingle. "You look recovered."

"Heh. Ye-ah. Um. Only two days of stomach purging. I…I didn't vomit on you, did I?"

"No, but maybe you'd have felt better sooner if you had."

The apprehension is clear on his face, but even his attempts at humor are thoughtful. How does he never lose his shit like I do? Because he's perfect like all gorgeous beings that were built to love and be loved.

The impure thought has me checking the dining area and bathroom entryway for obnoxious, sparkling blue-eyed football coaches. *Nada.*

"Where's Sam?" I inquire with an impressive amount of nonchalance.

"At work, I imagine."

Right. It's a school day. He probably has lunch duty. Lunch duty overseeing an army of Bradley Reeves-es. Ha!

Fuck. Being bitter feels awful.

My hand hesitates to pull out the chair opposite him because if Aiden were mine, I would not be jealous or possessive of him being around other men. That shit's not attractive. However, I most certainly would consider deeming him a Sam-free zone. "Um. Will it bother him that you're here with me?"

He studies me for a beat and then shrugs. "We're friends, right? Or… do you think we can be friends?

"No. Right! Yes! We are." Losing Aiden altogether or sitting on the sidelines and seeing him happy even if it's not with me? Fucking adulting. Is there really any debate? "Of course, we can be friends. I'd…like that very much."

That's enough awkwardness for the moment, so I take my seat. What's next? An alcohol intervention? Will he discuss Sam's glorious high school football coaching career? What kind of friends are we to be?

"Your mother seems nice."

"Oh. You met her. Well, of course you did. Yeah. She's… she's a mother."

And I am an idiot who can't form a sentence.

"And your brother, I think," he adds.

"I have an older sister too—Sofia. How's your sister's wedding coming along by the way?"

Did I just ask that? Really? Wonderful. I've become Sam, except Aiden gives me a pleasant smile. Maybe he doesn't care which ice breaker we use.

"Two months to go. They're actually going on a cruise of the Med for their honeymoon. I think one of the stops is in Greece."

"Oh, nice. She'll love it, as long as she doesn't have garlic allergies too."

Aside from the heat in my cheeks for that innocent comment, reminding us both that we know things about each other, the lunch carries on without a hitch. He asks a lot of questions, leaving me to do most of the talking. I comply because it seems to be what he wants. I tell him about the antics of some of my clients, which seems to amuse him. He asks about my days shooting models and why people were throwing flowers at me at the party last night. Apparently, he also thinks highly of Bitsy. Can't disagree with him there.

It is stilted conversation, but it is conversation, nonetheless. The sight of the bill is a melancholy thing. I neither want this to be over, nor divulge more boring factoids about my boring life to a man polite enough to look like he's interested in hearing them.

"We should do this again some time," he says, as we stop at the edge of the parking lot.

I don't know why I thought the whole *friends* declaration was a throwaway comment. Aiden isn't the type to make throwaway comments, but his suggestion takes me by surprise.

"Really?"

"Yeah. Next week sometime?" he asks casually.

"For sure."

We play a silent game of are-you-going-to-say-something as we stare at each other. What does this all mean? What is happening? Am I going to be a pity friend because he knows I'm a disaster? I let out the breath I'm holding when he bids me goodbye and turns toward his truck.

Something is wrong. I can feel it in the pull on my insides as though they want to follow him with each step he takes away from me. I made up for all my curt conversation on our dates by overcompensating in my responses to each of his lunchtime questions, but there's still something that needs to be said.

"Aiden?" I call out, hating the desperate waiver in my voice.

"Yeah?"

Proper apologies should not be made more than five paces away.

That's a rule. Right? I hedge forward a few steps to make up for the distance his long legs have already put between us. I breathe and pinch the hem of my jeans pocket to ground myself in courage.

"I know it's probably not appropriate to bring this up since you're seeing someone. I'm not trying to cut in on anyone's turf, and the last thing I want to do is upset you. I just…I wanted to tell you I'm really sorry about…everything—about the way I've acted the entire time. And…especially the way I bailed out on you…at your house that night. I should have at least said goodbye or given you some sort of explanation."

He looks at me like he's expecting me to give him that explanation now. I am Johnny the Shifty, scraping my feet against the pavement under the weight of my poor decisions.

"I was scared," I blurt. "You—*the idea of you and me*—scared me, and…and I'm sorry."

The crunchy bulge of papers in my back pocket is now saturated with my ass sweat, burning a proverbial hole through my jeans. They were my last resort in case words failed me. Well, words are failing me, so fuck it. He's already seen me in more ridiculous situations than most people. I will manage to survive him knowing the full extent of my shame that made me act like a lunatic for the last two years.

Whipping the folded packet of Lance-letters out of my back pocket, I hand them to him. His confusion is understandable. I will have to speak for this.

"Maybe these can explain what I can't, except my rudeness. That was all on me. I don't know why I ever kept them other than to remind me not to be a fool, but then I was a fool because of them, so…at least maybe you'll understand why. Like I said, it was me. Not you."

His nostrils expand, breathing in my pathetic show of contrition. Slowly, he reaches forward and takes the crumpled pages of my past. My lungs expand at the freedom of having them out of my life.

Say something, Aiden, I silently plead. *Say anything. Please?*

"You hurt me, Johnny. You really hurt me."

"I know! I know I did, and I'm so sorry. I never meant to. I was so caught up in my own bullshit that I kept trying to convince myself you really didn't give a damn about me and wouldn't care if I disappeared. I'm an idiot. I'd really like to make it up to you. Somehow. Anyhow."

His lips press together—those lips that showed me what kisses are supposed to be like. My own agony is compounded by every ounce of his that I can see in those mystical green eyes, that pondering my request for forgiveness.

Turning on his heel, he leaves me with a request that sounds more like a demand. "Then make it up to me."

# CHAPTER 49

Aiden

Lance is fucking a dickhead.

CHAPTER 50

Johnny

"Do I look alright?" I ask, giving the hem of my black cotton polo with three vibrant colored stripes across the chest a tug to smooth out any rumples. "Or is it too Atari meets Pride month?"

Bitsy pops another jellybean into her mouth, swinging her feet from where she sits perched on top of her new desk in the studio. Okay, really, with the scrutinizing up and down eyeballs? That says it all. Fuck. I have nothing to wear.

Shrugging, she finally answers. "Yeah. You look good."

"*Good? Good* isn't good enough."

"You're going to dinner at Olympus Bar and Grille. I've eaten there. It's not fine dining. What's the big deal?"

Sputtering, I gawk at her lack of concern for my dilemma and fashion sense in general. "*Big deal?* Have you forgotten my precarious situation? I am in the friend-zone with Aiden, which is, in short, a miracle considering…"

"That you had sex?"

"No!"

"That he saw you drunk table-dancing?"

"No! That he has a boyfriend and I…I was monstrous to him before *said* douchey boyfriend. Those two reasons alone should refute any ideas of friendship between the two of us. The balance of my fate is at greater risk than a toupee in a windstorm."

I get another careless shrug as she scrolls through her phone. "Aiden doesn't seem to think so if he keeps inviting you out."

"Yeah, but I've seen him three times in two weeks, and each time, it's just been the two of us, reminding me I'm a shameful secret—a friend not worthy of being a friend. First, lunch at La Cantina. Then, early morning coffee at Beans on Banner, the scene of our first kiss, which was unnerving to say the least. I don't know why he even wanted to go there. Then on Wednesday, after he stopped by here to quote *see me in action,* as he puts it, I had to make that stupid offer to photograph his family on their job site."

"That was actually really sweet of you. He looked like he was flattered. You had fun, didn't you?" She smirks.

"*Fun?* His older brother said no more than *hello* to me and yawned the entire time. Graham is the angriest man alive, and Maxie knows things."

"*Knows things?*"

"Yes. She's one of those people who looks at you like they know things. Like a seer or gossip columnist. It's discomfiting. The whole thing was awkward. I don't think they liked me."

"How can you say that? They were smiling in some of the photos." She gestures to the envelope of prints I am to deliver to Aiden tonight.

"Because they were talking to each other in those photos. Not me."

"Well, I think they turned out great. They're going to love them, and I can update their website with them and give their business a whole new image."

Can't this woman ever see reason? I throw up my hands, hoping it will rouse a semblance of my panic in her.

"Yes, but when will this scarlet letter come off? It's Friday night. Friday night is a *date night.* I bet Sam will be there and this whole friendship pact will all go to shit. As soon as Aiden goes to the restroom, he'll probably shiv me underneath the table with his fork."

I didn't even make a dent, judging by the look she levels at me over her phone. "Johnny, you're overreacting."

"I am not overreacting. My survival instincts are just kicking in."

"Just go before you're late."

"I can't," I groan, checking my watch for the twelfth time. "They're picking me up."

"Really? That's considerate."

"Mm. Considerate of the murderer to make it convenient for himself to lure the victim into the getaway vehicle."

Bitsy's hand clamps onto my shoulder, startling my last frazzled nerve. "Johnny, I love you, but you really do know how to kick your own ass. You know that, right?"

***

An hour later

This is me about to kick my own ass. Sliding the prints out of the envelope, I glance at the door again. Aiden said Sam couldn't make it. That's code for *jealous boyfriend will be waiting in the alley to my studio with a crowbar* if I ever heard. Clearly, McSporty is either not happy about our friendship or Aiden has kept his pity meetups with me a secret. I know how I feel about being alive, but I don't know how to feel about being a dirty little secret.

Damn it to hell. I do not do construction worker photography. He's going to hate these.

His calloused fingers spread the prints out over our cleared dining table. I did this as a favor for a *friend* and at the insistence of my soon-to-be ex-roommate. So, why am I more nervous than when I pitched my first model shots to *Body Marvel* straight out of college?

Why does his face look like that? Lips parted. Is it awe? Shock? Repulsion? Is he trying to figure out how to say something nice that's a lie for the first time since I met him?

"Johnny, these are phenomenal," he says with a disbelieving puff of breath. "Just…wow."

Gooey, gooey warmth spreads through me. He's still perusing the images with this baffling look of wonder on his handsome face.

"You actually like them?"

Whatever he sees in my expression makes him laugh. Oh, how I've missed that smile.

"Yes. *Actually*, I love them. You made us look professional and tough, knowledgeable, and…like a reliable family business."

I could survive off that look of pleasure on his face for the rest of my life. "Well, good because that's what I saw when I was taking them."

Pausing to peer into my soul for a moment, he returns to studying the prints some more. I study him. His gaze holds on my favorite one.

It's one of him, hands filthy, arm braced on his wall-in-progress, smoothing mortar with a look of concentration as though no wall has ever been built with more care. The light and shadows were the perfect combination, doing the impossible by making him look even more handsome than he already is. I might have made an extra copy, because one little picture does not equate a shrine of a lovesick stalker.

Shaking his head, he shoots me an appreciative smile. "You have no idea how talented you are. Thank you for taking these."

There are moments in life that leave such an impact, they become forever just a blink away, always on recall in the mind's eye. This moment here with him, right now—the one where I silently hand him all of my heart and accept for better or worse to be a real friend—will be my most painful and most favorite.

A half an hour later, pulling into the back lot of my studio, a looming sense of dread glues me to his truck seat. These past two weeks have given me hope that I may actually be learning how to get over a love interest in a healthy way.

Okay, I know that's debatable, but is there really a healthy way to have your heart crushed? My point is, it feels like we could come out of this as friends. Now I'm worried that what I have left of him, any chance of friendship, will fade away in my absence.

"So, when do you leave again?" he asks.

"Wednesday. For two weeks." Two whole weeks for him to be smothered in Sam with no intermissions of friend-time with Johnny.

"Mykonos," he says, the corner of his mouth ticking up. "Your paradise, right? Should be fun."

"Oh. Um. I may have exaggerated. I'm sure it's just like every other Greek island."

"You don't sound very excited."

"Well, I was just there…in Greece, I mean. But you know that already. Fuck." My hand slaps my brow. "Sorry. I think I'm just tired."

His soft chuff is music to my ears. "Johnny, it's alright. We're good."

Can he really mean it? Come on, idiot. This is Aiden. He means everything he says. "Yeah?" I ask just to be sure.

"Yeah." He nods. "Have a good time. Just stay away from the liquor. Okay?"

"I promise."

I want to touch him so badly, but I know I shouldn't. I want a good-bye hug. I want all the things he offered me once that I threw back at him, but I can't have them. I settle for drinking in the sight of his face, alone and undisturbed, one last time. Then I suck in a breath and bail out of his truck before I fail at adulting and healthy heartbreak. Then…my foot slips off the running board, and I fall flat on my face.

"Shit! Johnny! Are you okay?"

Jack rabbits don't have shit on me. I am on my feet faster than my family cleans out a buffet.

"Fine! I'm fine! All good! Goodnight!"

Slamming the door shut, I hobble like my ass is on fire when in truth it's more so my kneecaps and my palms. I have a feeling this moment will also forever be a blink away.

CHAPTER 51

Aiden

Shifting my carry-on, I sidle down the narrow aisle, counting seat numbers and looking for that face I can't wait to surprise. The woman ahead of me deposits herself in a seat, leaving my view open.

There he is—three rows away—looking agitated as he leans over the window seat. Squinting at the concourse, I hear him mutter, "Where is that woman?"

A flight attendant approaches and stops by Johnny's row to help an old man stow a bag in the overhead compartment. Johnny doesn't even look at me as his head turns in a panic to address her.

"Excuse me, flight attendant? Can you please page the concourse again for my friend, Elizabeth Fitzgerald? She was supposed to meet me here, and I'm worried something happened."

"Everything alright?" I ask, stopping at the back of the row in front of him.

The look on his face is priceless. "Aiden!"

"Hey. What's the problem? You look a little frazzled."

"I…I can't find Bitsy. What…what are you doing here?"

Gesturing to my bag, I shrug. "I needed a vacation."

"To Greece?"

"Why not?" I squeeze in past him to the window.

"That…that's Bitsy's seat."

"Ye-ah," I say with a forlorn sigh. "She said she can't make it and asked if I would use her ticket."

"She what? Is she okay?"

"Yeah. Everything's fine," I reassure. "She said there was a house she wanted to make an offer on."

Frowning, he watches me shove my bag under the seat. "Well, she wasted no time."

From the corner of my eye, I can see him glancing around at the people still boarding. "Are you…um. Is Sam coming?"

Biting my cheek to keep from smirking, I busy myself with the seatbelt. "No."

"Oh. Well…what does he think of you going without him?"

"I don't know. I haven't talked to him in a few weeks."

"A *few weeks?*"

"Yeah." I shrug, keeping a straight face when I look at him. "Not since we broke up."

"You…broke up?" He gapes.

I have to try hard to narrow my eyes and pull off a scrutinizing look. "You're observant, you know that?"

His mouth hangs open a few seconds longer as he blinks at me. Snapping it shut, he faces forward, biting his lip.

Crap. Maybe I read him wrong these last few weeks. Maybe Bitsy read him wrong, and this was a bad idea.

"Why didn't you say anything?" he asks softly, like maybe he'd have done something different if he'd known, making my heart grow wings.

"You only asked where he was, not about us."

That—and I needed some time after the drunken swing bed confession to assess if Johnny was really ready to go all in.

"Where are you staying in Mykonos?"

Tugging the folded-up print outs that Bitsy gave me last week from the seat pocket, I make a show of studying them, my stomach swirling with butterflies. "Bitsy said it's some sort of private villa."

"That's…that's where I'm staying."

"Hm. Good." I elbow him playfully. "Then I'll be there to make sure you don't choke on anything."

Frowning, he folds his arms over his chest and angry-whispers, "You know, not everyone is willing to be adventurous in bed, and after much consideration, I've decided that was a dangerous endeavor. I'm practically a sex dare devil."

I can't hold back my laughter this time. "You sure are."

He settles back in his seat, looking mildly pacified by my comment on the condom debacle, but I can tell he's still agitated by the way he's working his jaw. I'm trying to play it cool, reading the rental info as though it's the first time I'm seeing it, but it's all I can do to keep my heartbeat from hammering out of my chest.

"So, I should warn you," Johnny's voice is cool as he leans toward me without making eye contact. "Mykonos is *the* hotspot of all the Greek islands for gay men."

"Yeah," I say, grabbing a brochure on Greek historical sites Bitsy gave me like it will fill me in on what awaits us. "I kind of gathered that from what you've told me."

"Mm." He hums, looking displeased by my lack of concern as I pretend to read about monuments. "Well, be prepared to be a prime spectacle," he adds, making sure I notice how he eyes me up and down when I glance at him.

"What do you mean?"

"The men there will be on you like spray tans on models."

"Ah. Hm. Maybe I should learn a little Greek then."

Judging by the way his mouth purses, Perplexed Johnny is trying to protect me from being ravaged. That's my green light.

"How do I say, *thank you*?"

With his nostrils flaring, he couldn't make me any happier. I always thought Maxie was an antagonizing pain in the ass, but I'm starting to wonder if I share that trait. Getting Johnny's ire up is quickly becoming my favorite pastime.

"*Euxaristo*," he huffs.

I repeat it back, as though I'm savoring the word for the first time, which I, in truth, practiced repeatedly over the weekend. "Okay. What about, *no, thank you?*"

"*Ohi. Euxaristo.*"

I repeat. He nods, his gaze canvasing everywhere inside the plane but on me.

"And how do I say, *I'd like that very much?*"

He spares me a second of his grumpy face before looking away, squirming in his seat, flapping a hand. "There are a lot of ways to translate that. I'm not a very good teacher. Why don't we pick you up one of those travel phrase pocketbooks when we land in Athens?"

"Yeah. Good idea."

Now I'm scrambling for how to segue into what I want to discuss. Rubbing his hands over the tops of his thighs, he's clearly having silly Johnny ideas. I need to snuff them out before he gets lost in that brain of his.

"Actually, there's a phrase I really think I should learn that probably won't be in one of those travel books."

A muscle in his jaw ticks. Shoving the bridge of his glasses higher up his nose, he eventually lets out a little huff. "Fine. What do you want to know?"

"*I'm with him.*"

CHAPTER 52

Johnny

Nothing beats sitting in a pressurized can of farts when the man of your dreams asks you catch phrases on how to pick up men on *Sex Island*. I am going to lose my shit before he even finds out what a real Greek pita tastes like. No, they're not fucking called *gyros*.

Maybe I can take an island hopper over to see Yiayiá in case she has any other sordid love stories to divulge. I'm sure Bitsy probably had good intentions with this little ploy of matchmaking again, but…wait a damn minute. What did he just ask me to translate?

"I beg your pardon?"

"How do I say, *I'm with him?*"

Ah, I get it. Wonderful. *He's with me,* so he can use me as his fake boyfriend to deflect those on Mykonos he deems creepers. This just gets better and better.

"*Eímai mazí tou.*"

He repeats it. Slowly. Painfully. Battering my heart with each syllable. "Is that it?"

"Yeah. Yup."

"Good. Want to make sure I've got that one down," he says more to himself.

How is the reward for starting to accept the thought of him with Sam having to soon watch him be a fleshy bone thrown to a pack of hungry, horny wolves? I have thirteen hours of flight time to picture it before I witness it for *two whole weeks*. What did I do in a former life to deserve this?

"I also looked a few things up last night," he volunteers.

"Oh?"

"Yeah."

Apparently, he's not going to elaborate. "Mm. Like what?"

I can feel his gaze fixed on my profile. Does he think I need to do lip-reading? Hello. I have two mother tongues. Sighing, I face him.

His voice comes out soft as a cloud. *"Mou leípeis."*

The words yank at the organ in my chest. The way he's looking at me with that tender curve of his mouth, his eyes scan my face, as though he wants more than my reaction on his pronunciation.

"Did I get it right?" he asks, all hopeful-slash-bedroom voice.

Uhn.

My thick windpipe chokes out the translation. *"I miss you."*

"Do you?" He slips his hand over top of mine, squeezing.

I suck in a lung full of stale-plane air and nod like a bobble head doll going over train tracks. "Like polyester misses the seventies!"

"That...sounds like a lot."

"You have no idea." I breathe again, returning a squeeze to that wonderful, warm, scratchy hand.

Some bastard who has no respect for happily-ever-afters comes over the speaker. "Alright passengers. We're about to close the cabin doors. Please take your seats so we can prepare for takeoff."

Aiden smiles at me the entire time, rubbing his thumb over mine, our fingers interlaced. He still wants me. *Bitsy, I love you.* The pilot finally shuts up, but I'm too afraid to ruin this by speaking.

He's leaning in. I can smell his beautiful scent. Stopping in front of my lips, he murmurs, "Can I kiss you while there's still time for you to run away?

"I won't." I shake my head profusely.

"Good."

That mouth I missed, that mouth I dreamt about for weeks—it welcomes me home. It's sweet and dedicated, slow and grateful. No one's ripping buttons or swallowing the other's soul. I cup his jaw with my free hand as his tongue tastes mine, giving him the affection I think I've had stored up in me for years. It was just waiting for the right someone, for him.

Pulling back, he smiles at me like I just gave him the world. A delirious bubble of laughter spills out of my throat.

"How surprised were you?" He grins.

"Yiayia's three-way story surprised."

Laughing, he strokes my jaw. "You're going to have to tell me about that."

"Ew. Fuck no."

"Oh! You've got stipulations already, huh?" he jokes, but a tendril of apprehension curls around my spine.

"Actually, I do." Shit. I don't want to sabotage anything else with this man, but somewhere between Dr. Phil and face-planting in my parking lot Friday night, I realized a few things.

He looks contemplative, trailing his fingers down my arm. "Okay.

Let's hear them."

"So…I'm Greek."

"Glad you cleared that up. I wasn't sure."

"No! I'm serious. I'm Greek, so I'm different. I mean, I'm American too, but I'll always be different. I can't change that."

"Johnny, I don't want you to change."

"You say that now, but what about after five hundred dinners with my family every month?"

"You can only eat dinner about thirty times a month."

"Yeah, but it feels like more. My parents and extended family will ask you to do favors for them. From changing light bulbs to cleaning out garbage disposals, to debugging their computers, shoveling their driveways, and helping them set up baptism parties. All the women will basically try to read your fortune and give you unsolicited advice on sex, children, and cooking. We argue about stupid, trivial things. My mother will force feed you every time she sees you, and probably break into my apartment while we're having sex someday so she can steal my laundry."

I am practically hyperventilating from that speech. Why does he look so calm? Doesn't he understand the shit show I have just laid bare?

"Are you done?" he asks.

"There's more, but that pretty much sums it up. They'll drive you crazy. Hell, they drive me crazy."

"Johnny, that's what families do."

"I know, but…I love them. I can't believe I'm saying this, but I wouldn't have them any other way. They mean everything to me, so…if you don't think you can handle all that I'll understand, but I don't know if I could handle someone who can't."

"Is that the best you've got?" He smirks.

"I beg your pardon?"

"You're trying to get rid of me again."

"No! Never! I just—"

"Johnny, I'm kidding. I can handle anything, as long as it involves you. They make you who you are, so I plan to get to know as much about them as I can."

"Are you unwell?"

Chuckling, he kisses me stupid, deliciously stupid. "No, but I'm a little tired. I was up late last night memorizing Greek and figuring out what to say to you."

My sweet, sweet Aiden. Huh. My Aiden.

"Say no more." I pat him on the chest. "Get some rest. I've got plans for you once we get to Mykonos."

"You better," he rasps, letting me steal another kiss.

Fuck me running! What the hell just slammed into my spine?

Oh, George Michael it cannot be! No! Wait. Okay. It's not. Just an uncanny likeness.

"Excuse me, little boy," I tell our new passenger, who has just deposited himself into the aisle seat. "Mind the elbows, please. Tight quarters here and all."

The freckle-faced, bubble-gum cheeked little human furrows his brow at me. "Why were you kissing him on the mouth?"

Hello. Can you say blunt much? Who is raising these children, America?

Except, I find I'm quite happy to answer the Bradley lookalike's question.

"Because he's…" I glance at Aiden who smiles and squeezes my hand. "Because he's my boyfriend."

Prouder words were never spoken. Is this actually my life? The weirdest thing is, I have faith. It's fizzing through me like soda bubbles. Mm. Aiden. Aiden *and* Mykonos. Somebody pinch me. Nothing could ruin how I feel right now.

Hm. Look at that.

This kid's parents supplied him with a giant bag of *Skittles* before they abandoned him to steerage with strangers. Excellent parenting.

"Um. Do you need some help with that?"

"No," he says, saucier than is required.

"You need to tear it, not pull it apart. They'll fly everywhere. Here. Let me try."

"I can do it!" he growls, a vein popping on his forehead.

Angry much? Just what this little hostile shit needs—sixty-four ounces of sugar to…

"Holy shit! Ouch!"

I don't just taste the rainbow, I feel it, pelting me in *Skittle*-gage buckshot to the face. A direct hit to my temple. Two down my shirt. A dozen in my lap. One just rolled out of my hair.

Breathing in fart-air, I survey my pint-sized companion, searching for signs of remorse. His fingers root inside the torn-open bag. His cool steely eyes staring back at mine with all the compassion of a gun fighter.

"Told you I could do it." Then he proceeds to crunch.

Serenity now. Serenity now.

Opening my eyes, I turn to Aiden. He lifts his sleepy lids as though intuition told him I mean to address him. He always knows.

"Everything alright?" he asks sleepily.

"Fine," I assure him, kissing his knuckles. "Just wanted to let you know I'll be upgrading us to first-class for the flight home."

CHAPTER 53

Aiden

Before Mykonos, I thought I'd never get tired of Johnny's kisses. Kissing Johnny now as *mine*? Yeah. That will definitely never get old. In fact, believe it or not, it's actually gotten better. He sees me and lets me see all of him.

I love how his fingers trail slowly over my skin when we make out like this, gradually mapping and remapping every inch of my body. The ridiculously high thread-count of these hotel sheets against my skin, where we are perched on the bed on our knees, worshipping each other, only adds to the sensory effect.

Holding him during the flight after I woke up halfway through, showering off our travel funk together when we checked in, and rediscovering each other the last four days were only a fraction of the culmination to this moment. We've barely left the room other than for dinner and walks on the beaches. The guy who I had to tease to talk to me never stops now.

The breeze from the sea coming through the patio doors of our villa is cooling my heat-flushed skin from all the dancing we did at the club tonight. Well, from the dancing, Johnny moving like a purring cat against me, and a few rounds of something called *tsiporo* that tasted like gasoline while Johnny stuck to virgin daquiris. It is a cocktail I want to swim in forever.

Damn. Does he know what it does to me when he works my nipples like that?

Tugging his head up, I rasp, "You're killing me. Are you ready?"

"I was born ready, baby!" He grins with that confidence and eagerness on his face that makes my heart smile.

Opening the condom, I pull it out of the packet and strategically place it in my mouth. I can't exactly talk with this thing in, so I wriggle my eyebrows before dipping my head down to his cock, all swelled and ready for me.

He sighs when I clasp him by the root, and he traces those anxious, artful fingertips across the back of my shoulders. "Don't worry," he calls down as I line my mouth up at his tip. "I won't deep throat you."

Freaking Johnny. My snicker makes the latex collapse in my mouth, forcing me to take it out.

"You know, this will work better if you don't make me laugh."

"Hm. That's what you think."

Trying to ignore his playful side that I've been showered with over the last week, I refocus my efforts on the condom. Squeezing his tip, my lips find purchase.

This is more difficult than it looks, but I'm not admitting that to him. The latex is stretching inside my mouth. His gasp is a good indication he's enjoying my antics as I take his length deeper in my mouth, working my tongue to help suit him up. I dared him to let me do a body shot from his waistband at the bar, and this was my offering if he agreed. I have no problem losing a bet if it results in us naked together.

I can feel his entire sheathed length as my lips nudge over the end of the condom, my nose brushing his happy trail. Johnny lets out a little puff of breath.

"Holy *sexcapades*, that's the hottest thing I've ever seen."

I ease off carefully, glancing at my work, and press a kiss to his hip bone. "And that's how it's done."

"Show off." He laughs. "That was just a fluke."

"A fluke?" His skin is warm where I jab between his ribs with my index finger, getting a squeal out of him.

Panting, he holds his side. "Fine. Beginner's luck." His grin melts away into a more tender expression. His arms, circling around my waist for a precious kiss. "We don't have to do this, you know?" he whispers. "I'm fine with the way we've been doing…*things*."

"I know." That look of concern and attentiveness warms me from head to toe. Pressing my lips to his cheek by his ear, I assure him, "I want to. I was always curious about it, but I never wanted to try it until I met you."

His eyes glisten behind his glasses. His nose brushes mine as he rests our brows together. "Are you sure you're real?"

"I don't know. Pinch me."

His gasping bubble of laughter defines the same sensation of disbelief in my chest. I had imagined being with him would bring me this much joy, but living it is still surreal.

"Okay," he whispers, dusting his lips against mine.

"One thing though."

"What?"

I trace my finger, shaking with all the good kind of nerves, above the base of his shaft. "Can you take that off?"

"What?" He glances down at his sheathed cock. "I'm *never* taking this off!" he declares as though my handiwork is a trophy.

Snickering, I run my hand up his side. "That might cause problems."

"You're sure?"

If he only knew how much thought I've given what we're about to do. I've only imagined it about a dozen times since I met him.

"Yeah. If I can't do it, I at least want to remember feeling you."

Looking humbled, he loses the condom and meets me back on the end of the bed. Seeing his anxiousness as he slickens the lube over his shaft both eases my nerves and amps up my arousal, witnessing how special this is to him.

Shifting around, I drop to my elbows. Johnny's smooth hands glide across my lower back, drifting in feathery caresses down the sides of my hips. I can feel his heat radiating into my exposed flesh.

I want to remember every second of this, so I glance over my shoulder. There's this dazed look on his face as he strokes his tip through my seam, sensitized from all the prep we did earlier.

"What's that look for?"

"Heh. I've just never felt so…*toppy* before," he says, running his gaze and hands all over my body. "I mean, look at you."

I'm flattered he likes what he sees, but I have to laugh. "Do you have size issues to go along with all your other hang ups? Because you're kind of bossy. I assumed you'd be *a top* when I met you."

"Really?" he grins, his brows hiking higher. He squeezes my ass with this erotic carnal look. "Ooh, I'm going to top the shit out of you."

"So romantic."

His playful gleam vanishes as we lock eyes, his touch, gentling. "No. Seriously, baby. Tell me if anything hurts or if you don't like it."

We've talked about *everything* over the past four days, cracking ourselves open like cardiac patients. I know he's in a comfortable headspace, that his comment is compassion for me rather than insecurity over how his asshole ex built up his confidence only to destroy it. He still has no idea what a gift it is, seeing him trust me enough to show his affection.

"Get inside me, so I can," I murmur.

"Ooh, power bottom," he purrs and gives my ass cheek a little swat. "I like it!"

Our giggle fit is short-lived as soon as he circles my pucker with his tip. When he holds the head of his cock against it, the sound of our unified exhales hangs in the air, while my heartbeat is in my throat, then he presses carefully, passing through the confines of my aperture.

I moan through the expansion, and he moans with me, stopping once

I've taken his crown. My head is practically spinning, knowing a part of him is now inside me.

Leaning forward, he kisses my shoulder blade, his hands frantically circling my back and hip.

"Are you okay?"

"Yeah," I rasp, breathing deep. I can feel my stretched entrance relaxing around him as his hands massage my body. "I'm good," I assure when his soothing eases the tension inside me.

He nudges back and forth, giving himself to me cautiously. It's a tease, overwhelming me and leaving me aching in anticipation all at once for more of his hard heat.

"Do it, Johnny," I beg, anxious for the wild passion to overtake the remaining discomfort.

He lets loose a choked whimper and thrusts all the way into me until his pelvic bones hit my ass. The bundle of nerves inside me sends a tremor through my body from when his crown slipped over top of it. Any empty caverns of my soul are snuffed out of their loneliness, replaced by the commanding presence of his cock buried deep inside.

I shudder, so overcome by the intrusion and the ravenous need it's igniting inside me. "Oh, God."

"What?"

"Flapper's bigger than I thought," I pant, feeling his heartbeat deep inside my body.

"Hey," he scoffs, easing back slowly. "I thought we weren't…calling it that anymore," he grits through his self-control, kneading my hips. "Do you want me to stop?"

"No." My head rattles at the awful suggestion. I take another deep breath, the tension ebbing after a moment and nod for him to continue. "Okay. I'm ready."

"Okay," he concurs with a pant and slides carefully back home.

His crown passes over the spot inside me again. It magnifies an intense pull of current all the way up my shaft, as though it's tethered to my balls, holding me together and undoing me at the same time.

"Oh, God!" I cry out, unable to bare the sensation in silence. My eyes roll back into my head behind closed lids.

The fronts of Johnny's thighs go rigid against the backs of mine. "Is that a *good* god or a *bad* god? You need to clarify because Greeks have a lot of gods, you know."

"Good!" I moan, writhing against him, lowering my forehead to the mattress.

"Mm," Johnny purrs, circling my back with his palms as he draws back. "Prostate, meet Flapper."

My chuckle comes out between erratic breaths, but it's cut off when he rocks back into me. Each of his tortuously slow thrusts, maddens the pitch inside me. I'm a whimpering mess, rocking back eagerly.

"Yeah, Johnny."

"Oh, shit," he gasps as my body greets him with more force. "Aiden!"

We are a syncopated rhythm now of slapping skin, cries, and moans. When he shifts backward on the bed, I'm desperate to follow. I need more of those electric bursts he's sending through me each time he hits that spot. Wanton for it, I buck back harder this time.

"Fuck, Johnny! Oh!" I cry out at my reward when he nails the target perfectly.

Johnny lets out an awkward cry and pulls all the way out, the mattress bounding under my knees. The breeze wafts my ass as I hear a commotion and ache with loss.

"Johnny?"

A *wham* noise draws my gaze over my shoulder just in time to see Johnny's off-kilter stance as his head reverberates off the dresser.

It all happens so fast, but I see it in slow-motion.

Him yelling, "Ah! Fuck!"

Him wincing, stumbling awkwardly to the floor in a flail of bare arms and legs. Him collapsed on the fuzzy rug on the floor, bracing the back of his head.

"Shit! Johnny, are you okay?"

I scrambled off the bed, kneeling beside him. Face flushed, he glares at me through evident pain.

"No! I'm just a man, not a bull rider!"

Crap. He's pissed.

I bite the inside of my cheek. Only Johnny could get injured during sex. Easing my fingertips into his hair, I search for traces of trauma and feel a knot already forming at the back of his head.

"Ouch!" He winces. "Don't touch it. There's a lump! I can feel a lump!"

"Hey. You could have a concussion," I soothe, rubbing his shoulder and holding my index finger up in front of his face. "Here. Follow my finger."

Waving my finger in front of his field of vision, I focus on his pupils to make sure they'll follow my fingertip. Their diameter is even, but his brown irises don't follow the movement. They're locked tight on mine, eyes narrowed, nostrils flaring. Wow. Correction. He's not pissed—he's super pissed.

"What? What's that look for?"

"Is this going to be a thing?"

"*A thing?*"

"Yeah. Every time I try to charm you, I get injured or humiliated?"

"Is that what you were trying to accomplish with the stop sign?"

Flopping onto his backside on what we've dubbed the llama rug, he lets out a defeated puff of breath. I grab one of our empty shopping bags and toss a scoop of ice in it, then return to the rug. He takes it without meeting my gaze and presses it to the back of his head, a dejected pout on his face.

Caging him in with a hand on either side of his hips, I lean in and press a kiss to his frown. "You are charming," I murmur and pepper little kisses around his mouth.

His hand strokes my side as he sighs and lays back on the rug. "Well, you give a whole new meaning to the term *power bottom*."

CHAPTER 54

Johnny

Aiden curls up next to me on the rug, side-spooning me. I can't believe I fell off the bed. Do I have issues with stationary objects? Aiden certainly gets an A for enthusiasm though. Before I nearly got my skull cracked open, I was delirious from how freaking hot and insatiable my boyfriend can be in the heat of passion.

Whew. Didn't see that coming.

Hm. I guess no one's coming tonight, actually. *Sigh.*

Capturing his hand on my stomach, I thread our fingers together. "I'm sorry," I turn my head and tell him as his lazy finger strokes a lock of my hair.

"For what?"

"Ruining all your firsts—your first time, which was also your first time topping, and now I ruined your first time bottoming."

"You didn't ruin it," he chuffs, silencing my protest with a kiss. Releasing my hand, he sweeps his fingertips across my pelvic juncture. "We can try again some other time."

"Okay, but not on the swing bed."

"Definitely not on the swing bed."

We laugh and share more kisses. He's looking at me again, eyes awash with worry. I don't think even my mother has ever looked at me with such tenderness and concern, and that's saying a lot.

"Is your head okay?"

"Yeah. I think my skull is sufficiently frozen. Thanks for the ice, by the way." I toss the bag at the trash can and miss. Cubes scatter across the floor. Fuck my life. Can't a man ever look like he has moves?

Sighing, I close my eyes, but then the breeze from the bay warms me. Except it's not the breeze. I'm covered with a heavy Aiden-blanket. Mm. That blanket is still hard and is kissing my jugular.

"I want you to enjoy this trip," he whispers just below my ear, his cock slowly grinding against mine, which is recovering from my fall from grace.

"I am," I assure him, *handfulling* his beautiful ass, still in awe I can do that whenever I want. "I love that you got on that plane for me."

He smiles, so I kiss his collarbone. Dusting another touch of my lips to his shoulder, I continue my praises.

"I love that you never gave up on me." I move my mouth to his neck. "I love that you called me out on my shit and can put up with my moods. I love your patience and your sexy dance skills." Stopping at his lips, I can barely get the words out. "I love…"

"What?" He asks, this wonderful man who listens to every silly thing I say with the rapt attention of a number-one fan.

Shaking my head, I swallow against the lump of emotions clogged there. "That's it. Just…*I love*."

As he blinks down at me, my heartbeat stutters, but it's not from a fear of rejection. I'll never have to worry about that with Aiden. My rhythm goes haywire because I know now what real love feels like—the fully reciprocated kind. I see it in his eyes whenever he looks at me. It doesn't matter when or if he ever says it back. It's there—a beacon that connects my heart to his. He straddles my hips and answers me with a kiss that curls my toes and leaves me gasping.

"Johnny," is all he says, sounding pained as he strokes my cock with his seam before diving back in to devour all my air again.

I've lived off the way he always knows me, knows what I want, what I'm thinking. It's a heady feeling to start to know him that well too. Grabbing my shaft, I line myself up, offering what I know he wants and needs.

Eyes glazed, looking drunk, he stares into my soul. His breath, hitting mine as he slides down onto me, watching my face through each centimeter as I memorize his expressions. He lets out an epic, stifled cry that will be etched in my eardrums for all eternity. Then, he leans in and whispers over my lips.

"Love *you*."

Uhn.

We're so fucking cliché, but I don't give a holy damn as he starts to rock on my moan-lever. I don't give a damn about the tear that spills down the side of my face because he's there, wetting his lips with it, giving it back to me, collecting all my broken pieces and keeping me whole.

He sniffles. "Love *you*, Johnny."

"Aiden," I cry in agreement, and because I'm about to lose my mind from the combination of the emotions in my chest and his snug heat around me—hugging and pulling my length, hugging and pulling.

The beautiful confusion on his face as he rises up tells me he's close, his chest rising and falling. I get to do this with this man. I get to be the one who holds him and is held by him—the one who holds his hand walking down the street, the one who kisses him goodbye in the morning and hello at night. Sixty years from now, I'm going to remember this look on his face with perfect clarity as I smile like Yiayiá.

"Baby, yeah," I encourage him, stroking him with my hand.

A flicker of shock flashes across his features, almost like the word *baby* undoes him too. His shoulders hunch forward, his teeth bared.

"Johnny!" he cries out, and I can't hold back anymore at the sight he makes.

He rides my jerky waves as he releases onto me, his hot breath in my neck. Clutching my shoulder to the point it's almost painful, I slobber spent kisses on any inch of skin I can reach, massaging his backside in time with each pulse inside him.

Rubbing the back of his neck, I tap his vertebrae there. "You okay?"

Breathing heavy, he glances up at me. "Yeah. You?"

"Yeah. I might be picking llama hair out of my ass for a week, but it was totally worth it."

Laughing, he kisses my lips and draws off me slowly, curling up at my side. "I meant what I said, you know?"

"Mm. So, did I. There is definitely llama hair up there." I screech when he pinches my nipple. "Ouch! Fuck! Okay. I know what you meant." Kissing him hard, I cut off my laughter. "I've never meant anything more. I'm stupid in love with you."

Tracing my lower lip with his thumb, he gives me the smile of a satisfied man both inside and out. "You think your family will like me?"

"Why not? You're like an eighth Greek, right? Isn't that what you claimed in that app, Mr. *AmericanMade?*"

"Yeah. As long as I don't have to give a DNA test to prove it."

"Mm," I agree, stroking his nipple. "I'll be in charge of the sampling, thank you very much."

Chuckling, he sobers and strokes my jaw. "I don't think I ever said it, but I was glad it was you again at Dimitris' restaurant."

"And again at the speed-dating?" I venture.

"Well, let's not get carried away." He grins.

"Power bottoms, always so cocky."

EPILOGUE

Johnny

Who'd have thought Tapas would become one of my favorite places? I did have a very unforgettable date here once, but Aiden and I have since been busy making happier memories. Maybe my new love for Dimitris' place has something to do with what time of night it is. All the customers have dispersed, so my family and I can be as loud as we damn well please.

Taking another platter from my Aunt Donetta, I reach between Veronique and Maxie to set the samples down on the table. "*Tomatokeftedes*," I tell them. "They're basically fried fritters with tomatoes, onions, feta, and mint."

"Ooh, they smell delicious," Maxie coos. "Go sit down, Johnny. I'm sick of feeling like my brother's molesting me with his eyes."

I don't have to glance at the end of the table to know she's right. I can always feel when Aiden's looking at me—can always feel when I'm loved. He doesn't even have to be in the same building. The proud smile he gives me for Maxie's quip, radiates the warmth of that love inside me.

Fuck, we're so disgusting. It's wonderful.

"If you insist," I ooze. "But I'm sorry again about your caterer's restaurant burning down."

Across the table, Mr. Brandt grunts around a bite of pastitsio, his gaze never leaving his plate as though he's considering cheating on Aiden's mom with his meal. "Wasn't made out of brick. That's why."

Maxie and I exchange our amusement. It's not even strange anymore the kinship we've quickly formed. She is a beacon of roll-with-the-punches that is quickly becoming my new mantra idol.

"What the hell, Graham Cracker?" she blurts as Graham strolls through the door. "Took you long enough. You promised you'd spearhead the catering and you're the last one here."

"I made it. Didn't I?" He huffs, patting me on the shoulder. "Hey, Johnny. Where do you want me?"

In the month that Aiden and I have been dating, I've learned that Graham is not a toucher. To get that shoulder-pat out of him is a huge deal. The man still has some deep-seated hostility toward something he needs to work out, but it has been a relief to know it isn't about me, Aiden, or same-sex relationships as I intially worried. This surly Graham Cracker has been nothing but nice to me. Well, in his own perpetually annoyed and brutish Graham way.

"Um, looks like this is the only one left," I tell him, pulling out the chair in between Dami and Maxie.

His handsome face goes long. His eyes, pinning me. "Seriously?" Sighing, he makes to take his seat, but not before informing me, "You are now dead to me."

I suspect I'll be revived in his graces by the next time I see him. Maxie's too happy tonight to give him too much shit.

Finally, I make my way over to Aiden, who's waiting for me with a patient smile. He snakes an arm around my waist and squeezes.

"You're not planning on serving the food at the wedding, are you?" he teases.

"No. I plan on staring at the best man the entire time."

"*Best* man, huh?" he grins.

"Without a doubt."

"Johnny," Dami interjects. "Do you want me to shift over so you can pull up a chair?"

Crap. There's no more seats. That's what I get for neglecting my man to shower Maxie with my attentiveness.

"Um. Sure, if you think—" The arm around my waist tightens and hauls me onto Aiden's lap. "Oof! Or this works too," I murmur to his pleased face.

"Just in case I have to carry you later. Then we're already halfway there," he says, pressing a kiss to my jugular.

Dami flashes me a grin, the kind that says he's happy for me, and maybe I'm still his hero. It could be he's still pumped about me getting him out from under his parents' roof by offering him Bitsy's old room. I'm not exactly sure why Graham's side-eyeing him like that, but he's going to have to get used to him.

"Are you ready for your first day on the job?" I ask Dami.

"Heck, yeah. I can't wait to get started." Looking to Aiden, he adds, "Thanks again for taking me on. I really appreciate it. I won't let you guys down."

Graham grunts. "You'll regret that soon enough."

"Ignore him," Aiden says. "Graham's going to take you out to work at the old Hodges place with him tomorrow. If he gives you any shit, just remember I have seniority so you can give me a call."

Dami elbow checks Graham in the ribs, and I cringe. *Don't poke the badger*, I want to warn. "What do you say, boss? You going to show me the ropes?"

"*I* need a fucking rope," Graham mutters.

"Was this a terribly awful idea?" I whisper to Aiden.

"No. It'll be good for him. He needs to socialize, and Dami's the most sociable person I know."

"I like Graham. I just don't understand how the two of you are related."

"Well, some of us get the looks and the personality, and some of us just get bodily organs that perform the basest of functions."

Laughing, I dig my fingers into his side, and he yelps. God, I love that sound and that I now know all the spots that can make him do that.

"Oh, my boys! It's so good to see you laughing," Mama says. Clasping each of our jaws in a hand, she presses a kiss to our cheeks, the force bumping our heads together, and then she moves on—no nagging, no nosey inquiries. I don't know if I'll ever get used to that. Smiling at Aiden, I wipe Mama's lipstick stain from his cheek, slowly, taking my time.

"Hey, I found this greenhouse online today that's up in Bartlett. What do you think about taking a ride up there sometime? I can scout out spots for photo shoots and watch you make that dreamy face you do when you look at your plants."

"Are you exploiting my love of plants?"

I've never seen anything as adorable as the way he mumbles encouraging words to his plants under his breath when he's weeding around his house. I don't think he even realizes he does it, and I sure as shit am not going to tell him out of fear he'll stop doing it. So, yeah. I'm exploiting the shit out of that.

"It's supply and demand, sweetheart. I demand you be happy, therefor I'm trying to supply you with sources of happiness."

Snickering, he squeezes my hip. "I will never get sick of how you recycle logic."

Dimitris bumps into my shoulder, a cigarette hanging out of his mouth. "Giannis. Aiden! Eat! Drink!" he orders, setting a plate of souvlaki down in front of Aiden and a bottle of ouzo in front of me.

Aiden's gaze travels to Dimitris' offering, looking wary. We've had a few close calls since returning from Greece a month ago, but so far I've kept him from being poisoned by my family. I've learned to accept that just because people don't understand something, no matter how many times you tell them, it doesn't mean they don't care. Sometimes, you have to help yourself.

Picking up the bottle of ouzo, I exchange a smirk with Aiden. He trades me for the plate of garlic-seasoned meat.

"Actually," I say, glancing down at the plate, "I plan on kissing you a lot later. We need to trade this out full-stop. Andreas!"

"What?"

"Take this. Will you? And pass me that calamari for Aiden?"

"Oh, shit. Yeah. Don't eat that souvlaki, brother," Andreas warns. "Here you go," he amends, switching me plates, but not before telling Aiden, "You should have dated a Mexican. A lot less garlic in their food."

Then Andreas winks at me, so I spare him any incivilities. Brothers will always be brothers, pushing your buttons on purpose just to get a rise out of you, I suppose. I just need to find his weaknesses and exploit them in retaliation. Aiden being mad at him is one of them, so I've got that in my arsenal if Andreas ever pulls a cheap shot.

"No, thanks," Aiden tells my brother. "He's worth getting poisoned for now and then."

"Hm. Smooth talker," I coo.

"You know it."

Leaning back, the vibration of his groan reverberates against my side as he stretches his back. Eyes pinched shut, I hate that tight line of his mouth. Kneading his shoulder, I eventually identify a knot in that solid slab of muscle there.

"Do you need a *Johnny Special* when we get home?"

He blinks up at me, looking surprised. Crap. Did I say that in Greek? That happens sometimes when I'm around my family and especially now that I'm so comfortable around Aiden.

Rubbing my back, he smiles. "*Home*, huh?"

My error floods up my neck in a wave of heat. "Oh. Shit. I just meant, home as in *your home*."

Snaking both arms around me, he rests his tired head under my chin. "A Johnny Special sounds nice."

I breath easier. He always lets me off the hook. One of these days I probably won't even remember what it feels like to be embarrassed anymore.

His lap shifts underneath mine. He squirms again, causing me to tilt to the right.

"Is it your lower back? Let me get up and get a chair. I don't want to hurt you." I make to remove myself from my Aiden-stool, but his grip tightens.

"No," he pleads, putting his lips near my ear. "It's...I tried out some new underwear today."

This should not be breaking news or anything, but when I glance at him, his expression has gone all guilty. "I'm still getting used to them."

Yes, eyebrows. Climb my forehead high. "Oh, really? What kind of new underwear?"

"The kind you can see *after* we…get *home*."

Okay. Now he is teasing me for that slip up. I'm about to suck my lower lip back in and protest this dig at my verbal diarrhea when he presses his index finger to my mouth.

"Johnny, it's home because we're there together. And when we stay at your place—then that's home."

Uhn.

For all my rambling, sometimes I just can't think of a damned thing to say. Actions speak louder than words though, so I grab his hand and passively bite the tip of his finger, then place a kiss there.

"I feel bad," I confess in a low voice so no one overhears. "We have to spend most of our time at your place because of Dami moving into my apartment."

"It's not my fault you're loud," he whispers in my ear.

"Actually…it is," I laugh.

"Shit. Yeah. I guess you're right."

Still fizzing from his *home is you* compliment, I try to suppress a burst of giddiness as I chop up the calamari with one hand. That palm runs up and down my back, making me smile. He always does that when he wants to tell me something sentimental, which is often.

"I guess you should make it up to me," he amends.

Snorting, I hand him a loaded fork. "Oh, yeah? What is my penance for having an excessive vocal range? Do tell?"

He takes the fork, but just holds it, although he told me he was starving not twenty minutes ago. "Haul more of your clothes over so you don't have to go home to swap laundry out all the time."

It's funny how my heart skips a single beat and then settles back into its regular rhythm. There's not that youthful idiotic celebration like I had when Lance asked me to move in together. This feels right like the natural progression we were headed toward, filling me with a sense of completeness. It's where we were destined to end up.

Shit. Listen to me, talking about destiny.

Aiden's throat undulates during my silence. I can see the worry in his eyes. Before I can reassure him, he adds, "Well, at least enough for this weekend. I need your help with something."

"Gladly—to hauling over more clothes, and what do you need help with?"

"I…want to build a gazebo in the backyard and landscape around it."

"Ooh! That'd be a nice touch, and I didn't think your place could get any cuter."

"Yeah?"

"Aiden, you have a great eye. If you ever get sick of schlepping bricks, you should become a landscape architect. No joke.”

Smiling, he sets his fork down on the plate, rubbing my back again. What is up with Mr. Sentimental tonight?

“Um. I thought…maybe you’d like to use it for photo shoots? Like as a backdrop? Don’t people take pictures in those for couples’ photos and stuff?”

Excuse me. Is he for real? He wants to build me something?

Uhn. Kill me now.

Gripping both sides of his face, my heart springs a leak at the concern in his eyes. “Stop it! Just stop!”

“What? I…I’m sorry. Too much too soon?”

“No!” I laugh. “You’re…perfect, but I’m…I’m too little too late. I feel like I have nothing to give you other than backrubs, silly photos, and protection against garlic poisoning.”

“Those are all highly appreciated gifts,” he says, smirking. “So…you like the idea?”

“I love it.” I press and hold my lips to his—my favorite two puzzle pieces. “And I love you. I’m not running away ever again. You know that. Right?”

He studies my face for a moment, stroking my jaw. “You gave me the biggest gift so far, actually.”

“What’s that?”

“*You*. I know that wasn’t easy for you to give.”

Well, fuck me. I thought we were past the speechless phase. My throat constricts, trying to swallow the metric ton of affection he just dropped. This man. I swear.

Damn it. He can still make me happy cry.

I have to clear my throat to keep my shit together.

“Actually, it was difficult not to give that. I wanted to the second I saw you. I just had to get my head out of my ass first. It was…pretty far up there.”

“Well, it was worth the wait,” he whispers, dusting my lips.

When he pulls back, he rewards me again with a smile on his face more satisfied than any other he’s ever given me. That first week in Mykonos, it felt like every one of his smiles healed me a little more. Now, they feed me—make me grow everyday into me again. Even better, I see that same vitality of love in his face when he looks at me like there’s something about me that keeps him grateful too, which is still bananas, but I don’t care as long as he’s happy.

We’re so fucking cliché, but I don’t give a damn. I’m really starting to love cliché.

Drumming my fingertips on top of his shoulder, I purr at his ear, “Now…about these underwear…”

SNEAK PEEK

Graham

My twin sister is a sadist. That's all there is to it.

Maxie never misses an opportunity to torture me over the fact that I've been married twice. That means I had two weddings, which means I had two bouts of choosing caterers. Summary: this is the last freaking thing I want to be doing right now, but she's my sister, and she's happy.

Still, I wish someone could explain to me why she can't pick out her own damn food. It's not like she gives a shit about my opinion…on anything. Ever.

"I still don't understand why I have to be here? How the hell am I supposed to know what you two want to eat at your wedding?"

"It's a family affair, Graham Cracker. I want family input because unlike you, I'm not a grumpy anti-social hermit who only cares about holing up in his cabin, and I'm only getting married once, so I want to make sure everyone enjoys it," she tells me, dropping a dollop of tzatziki onto her plate.

My fists clench on the table, pinning her smug profile as she ignores my reaction like always. "Thank you, Maxine, for reminding me for the thousandth time that I've been married more than once. How could I ever forget it with you around? And giving up my evening no matter how I choose to spend it to watch you stuff your face with the rest of our family doesn't seem very uncaring or anti-social to me."

Why don't I feel better after getting that out?

Maxie's good at reducing me to a petulant child. If she had any clue of the sacrifices I've made for her, I bet she'd wipe that smirk off her face, but I sure as shit am not going to tell her.

Telling everyone about sacrifices defies the purpose of doing the right thing. You don't do the right thing for attention. You just do it because it's right, even if you're paid back with harassment every day of your life by your own flesh and blood.

"So, after I pick out what I want to eat, I'm done with this wedding bullshit?"

Maxie lets out a sigh, her gaze never leaving the Greek salad she's portioning onto her plate. "No, dumbass. I'll give you the list of the menu we decide on. Then it'll be your job to make sure everything is right on the day of the wedding, that all the plates are clean, and the seating arrangements are set. And if the Andropolises run out of something or have a crisis, you'll be in charge of making the decision of what food to replace it with and how to snuff out the fires. Can you handle that?"

"My job is to stop food emergencies? Wow. I feel so important. Am I going to get blamed if anyone gets food poisoning or chokes on a chicken leg?"

Picking up a platter, she drops two filo dough-wrapped fried appetizers on my plate because although she's an obnoxious boil on my ass, she cares about me in her own messed up way. "It's Greek food. They rarely do chicken legs," she informs me. "You're supposed to be the big foodie of the family. Why do you think I asked you to oversee the catering?"

Grabbing a thick slice of bread, her backhanded compliment is appeasing enough for me to drop our squabble. I sit back in my chair when she returns to chattering with Veronique. Except now I can feel Damiano's bicep brushing up against mine again—or *Dami*, whatever the hell playboy-sounding name they call him. It sounds like a pet name like *sweetie* or *baby* not something you call an employee.

At least he has the build for hard labor. He's got an inch on me and probably twenty pounds. Whether or not he's ever done any strenuous physical labor remains to be seen. Lucky me, I'll get to find out tomorrow. For now, my assessment is limited to sound, sight, and touch as we sit sandwiched together at this table. I could really do without the touching part.

The heat of his thigh is seeping through my jeans, making my blood stir. Every time I try to squirm to break the contact for a second, we end up squished back together, making it feel like I'm purposely writhing against him. I already shifted over as far as I could when he checked me in the ribs earlier. I don't know what it is, but something about him agitates me even when we're feet apart.

Maybe it's his stupid cheeky smile, or his bubbly demeanor, or the way I caught him staring at me all the time when we redid the patio wall here at Tapas last summer. He makes me uncomfortable, and I don't get uncomfortable. But what can I say?

I'm sure as shit not going to admit some college kid has my pulse kicking so hard I want to get away from him every time I see him. Maxie and Aiden would both laugh at my ass into the next decade.

Why the hell did Aiden have to hire him of all people to work for us? I know we need help now that Dad's retiring and Skyler will be taking over the office side of things, but I assumed we'd hire somebody who—oh, I don't know—fucking knows something about masonry.

Straight out of college. A city kid. Twenty bucks says he doesn't even own a pair of work boots.

"So, boss!" Dami chirps with that annoying zeal of his. "What time do you want me there tomorrow?"

"Five a.m."

"Five in the morning?"

His widened blue eyes say that early hour is a rarity for him. And so it begins. Give me strength.

"Yeah. There a problem with that?"

"No. That's just when I come home sometimes though," he says with a laugh, his nimble fingers making himself up a pita.

There's not a callous in sight on those pretty hands of his. This kid is in for a rude awakening. No doubt that muscle tone of his was all acquired in a gym rather than from a lick of real work. I am not spending my time on the Hodges job training some newbie or worse, listening to him whine at every turn and not carry his weight.

"You show up drunk or hung over, you're gone. I don't put up with people who aren't fit for work. That's a safety hazard."

"I won't. I'll be on-time," he says, unphased by my stern warning.

That means he's either blowing smoke up my ass, or for some reason my no-nonsense attitude that got me barred from dealing with our crappier suppliers doesn't cow him. Who in their right mind doesn't have a modicum of apprehension for their new boss? I knew there was something wrong with him.

"What should I bring with me?" he asks as though my face says I look like I want to talk.

"Wear old clothes that you can work in. I'm not listening to you cry that you ruined some designer outfit. No tennis shoes. Dress in work boots with a steel toe. If you don't have any, get some by the end of the week. We'll give you gloves, but if you lose them then the next pair is on you. And bring a lunch and plenty of water. There's no plumbing or electricity out there. I'm not driving all the way back into town to take you to lunch every day. We eat on-site and get back to work as soon as we're done."

Good. That seems to have burst his bubble. Except, I can feel those big starry eyes on me—the same curious eyes that were so unnerving they made me smash my thumb last summer when we were building the patio wall.

Freaking Aiden is going to owe me big time for this. And what the hell was with that warning he gave me yesterday when I overheard him and Johnny talking about Dami being gay? I wasn't the one blabbing about people's secrets, and after all these years, does he seriously think I would hold someone's personal preferences against them? If he only knew.

My family has no clue about the things that go on inside my head. To be fair, lately I don't either. Last month, I couldn't stop gawking at the two clean cut businessmen at Olympus Bar and Grille when I went out to dinner with Aiden. My heartrate was hammering so hard, I cut out of there and drove around with my truck windows down for an hour before I went home. What is wrong with me?

The longer I'm away from Jen this time around, the more potent the thoughts get. She needs to figure out whatever she's figuring because I'm only human, not a cactus. And this freaking kid that looks way too old to only be twenty-three needs to stop smelling like concentrated shower gel. I want to ask him if he hung on a clothesline in a mountain glen.

Glancing over, his wary expression tugs at my stupid nurturing heart. I catch Aiden shooting me a questioning look as though to ask if I hurt boy wonder's feelings already.

Fucking-A.

Doesn't anyone have thick skin anymore? All I did was answer his question.

Sighing, I return my attention to Dami, only to find him studying me. His bright smile is gone. His expression is so forlorn my stomach dips. He's a complete stranger. Why am I concerned about whatever look that is on his face?

"What?" I let out more impatiently than I mean to.

He glances at Aiden and then back to me. "He…told you. Didn't he?"

"Told me what?"

He scans the table, his gaze stopping on his parents on the far side of the room. Leaning into me, his breath ghosts my ear, sending a shiver all the way down my spine. "That I'm gay."

The flutter in my chest at his proximity gives me a weird sense of paralysis, locking up my lungs as a rush of shivers run all the way down my arms. What the hell is that about?

I like men. Always have. Like them in the sense that I appreciate looking at them, but that's where it stopped. You don't do more than looking when you spend all your younger years combatting all the crap people talk about your brother and sister behind their backs. And you don't do more than looking when you trade virginities with and then marry your high school sweetheart.

Since Jen left last year though, I've been doing a lot more than looking…I've been feeling…things—things I certainly shouldn't feel if I'm waiting for my ex-wife to change her mind and come back.

It's never made any sense to me. I love Jen. I was married. I'm still supposed to be married. I made my choice about who my person was—made a promise in front of her and God and our families. Done deal. Search over. I'm not supposed to want anyone else. So how in the hell can I get hot and bothered for anyone other than her? And why is it happening more frequently the longer she's gone?

Maybe it means if I hadn't been married, I might have…I don't know. Fuck.

It doesn't matter. I'm thirty years old. What the hell does a thirty-year-old who's only been with one person his entire life know about being bisexual?

Christ, Graham. Get your shit together.

I turn my palms up, not daring to move any other part of my body. "Yeah. He told me. What about it?"

Dami's tongue crests his lips, wetting them. I watch it more intently than I should. I can't help it. It's transfixing and slightly erotic, slipping over that mouth of his. It occurs to me now—that's the issue with my discomfort. There's something highly erotic about everything this kid does, and a guy who's stupidly pining for his ex-wife to come back shouldn't be noticing how erotic some twenty-three-year old's mannerisms are.

Pursing his lips together, it almost looks like he's trying to appear tough for a second, but he just can't quite pull it off. Sure, that jaw of his is square and rugged, but his flawless olive skin doesn't scream intimidating.

"Um. Mr. Brandt, I really want this job. I promise, I'll work hard for you. I want to learn a new trade and be good at, but I have to say, if you're going to hold what you know against me or treat me unfairly because of it, then you don't deserve to have me as an employee."

What the…

A puff of air gusts out of my mouth, watching his jaw set. His throat undulates as he holds my gaze with those chalky blue eyes that now show me a flicker of tenacity in their depths.

The kid's got grit. It's wavering from the look of his fingers fidgeting with the tablecloth, but that took balls, nonetheless. I've never been in a situation where I've seen a man stand up for his sexuality before. Usually, I'm the one standing up for people. Seeing it coming from this unworldly kid who's depending on me for a job is way sexier than it has any right to be.

I can't be fucking friendly with this kid. There's no way, not when he makes my palms sweat and my nuts tingle. But I sure as hell am not going to make him worry that his new boss is some kind of bigot. He can just think what everyone else thinks—that I'm a grumpy asshole.

"Calm down, kid. You asked me a question, so I answered you like

I'd answer anyone. I don't care who or what you do on your own time. I like Johnny, but I don't care how related you are to him. You make your own way. I just wanted you to know there's no special treatment."

He nods, the corner of his mouth ticking up. Nobody should be allowed to look that good. "I don't want special treatment. You can work me over as hard as you want."

Fuuuck.

Looking back at my plate, I pinch my eyes shut and take in a slow breath as the inuendo of his words flit around inside my head. I wouldn't even know what to do with a man if presented the opportunity. How can the mention of working him over hard make my cock swell?

"Wh-whatever. Just…don't be late."

"I won't."

Aaand…he's freaking staring at me again. I can feel it.

What is it with this kid? What's so damn interesting about me? Does he have some power complex obsession? The term boss is practically a joke. I've never been anybody's boss with the exception of overseeing some contractors. If he's trying to kiss my ass, he's going about it all the wrong way.

"So…" he hedges in that thick sultry sounding whisper of his. "We're good then. Right?"

Exhaling, I glance at his parents who are starting to serve another round of selections. Aiden said Dami's folks don't know about his preferences. I'm no one to him and so I shouldn't have as much empathy for his situation as I do, but the part of me that's always wondered what my life might have been like if I'd fallen for a John instead of a Jen in high school does. Be patient, Aiden said the other day.

I can be patient. It doesn't mean I have to be his guidance counselor or BFF.

"Yeah. We're good," I whisper back.

His soft breath of relief brings me more joy than it should, making my heart feel lighter than it has in years. Usually when I try to do something for my family, I end up miserable and berated for it. Why are my effortless sentiments to this kid so appreciated?

Something brushes the fabric of my jeans underneath the table. Fingers rest over the place on my thigh above my knee, and squeeze. A jolt of high-charged static races up my leg and splits off, shooting through every limb in my body.

"Thanks," he says, leaning in so close again I can feel the heat of his breath on my neck. "I really appreciate it."

My heart is flapping faster than hummingbird wings. Its source—that hand on my leg. Even as he withdraws it, the current in my veins is pulsing so much blood to my heart, I can't steady my breathing. What the hell is happening?

I manage to swallow at the dryness is my throat. The tension in my boxer briefs tells me I know exactly what's happening.

Holy hell. It's never hit like this before. What did Dami do to me?

"Hey, boss," he whispers again, rubbing his hand across the back of my shoulder blade. I force slow breaths in and out through my lips, eyes locked on my plate. "Are you okay? You don't look so good."

"Graham?" Aiden's voice breaks through the haze of unbridled lust taking over my body. "Everything alright?"

The lock on my muscles releases, allowing me to move again. Pushing off the floor, I shove my chair back and spring up. At least I have the wherewithal to lean forward like I have a gut ache, clutching the hem of my shirt enough to distract from the outline at the front of my jeans.

"Yeah. Fine! Fine. I just…I ate some bad lunch. I…I've got to go."

The inquiries from my family and Johnny are an incomprehensible buzz around me as I practically scramble to the door. Maybe I'm imagining things, but I swear Dami's gaze is on my retreating back. Just the thought of it sends a shiver down my spine to my nuts.

This is ludicrous. I'm reacting like a horny teenager. The terrifying part is that I don't ever remember being this overwhelmed by arousal from an innocent touch to my leg and a few hot breaths at my ear in my life. It's not possible for a person to elicit that effect in someone. I've just been alone too long.

I need to talk to Jen. And I need to stay as far away from Damiano Andropolis as possible. In the formula for getting my life back in order, he's trouble, nothing but trouble.

Acknowledgements

I am fortunate to have a lot of people to thank for being with me on my continuing writing journey for this story. That means I've been blessed with meeting new friends and growing existing friendships that without this foray into the writing world might never have happened.

Thank you to:

- Bridget—for the Molly-fight idea. Your mind is a fantastic place.
- Colleen—for the support when there are dark days and for always presenting both sides of a situation to keep me thinking.
- Katie and Brey—for believing in my work, taking me on, and introducing new readers to my stories. You guys are a force to be reckoned with and a breath of fresh air for the indie author world.
- Jen & Maxie—for the daily laughs, for *Stop!*, and for unique research only you have the tenacity to endure.
- Angel & Luke—for capturing all my silly ideas for the photography, being all-around wonderful people who went above and beyond, and for trusting me with your work and images.
- K.C. Carmine—for keeping Johnny from being a total twat.
- The Morning Bun Squad—for all the love, laughs, and advice you guys give. You're my book family.
- Alexa—for whipping my story into shape and putting up with the MBS shenanigans.
- Stephanie—for the quick, outstanding artwork that brings my characters to life in a special way for fans to enjoy.
- Larissa—for all the narrator recommendations for this work and future works.
- Bob—for your inspiring words and for telling me a beautiful story about a man named Graham.
- My friends in Syros—for all the Greek lessons, laughter, and your kindness.
- Pearl—for singing along to Mommy's writing playlist with me on our commutes.
- Brian—for letting me do whatever the hell I want.

About the Author

Dianna Roman believes in laughter, happily-ever-afters, coffee, chocolate, talking to yourself, hard work, and above all, love.

She enjoys writing stories about characters who don't have this thing called life quite figured out yet and finding laughter amid the pain. Her favorite writing challenge is tackling the miscommunication trope.

Dianna lives with her husband and daughter in the woods where sunsets and gardening are the reason her house may be a bit messy.

CONTACT

www.diannaroman.com

Instagram @diannaromanbooks

Bookbub @diannaromanbooks

Facebook at Roman's Readers

Tiktok @diannaromanbooks

Goodreads

Works by Dianna Roman

MM ROMANCE

The Shutout

You Again (Men of Olympus Book 1)

MF ROMANCE

A Fair Warning (Grand Valley Book 1)